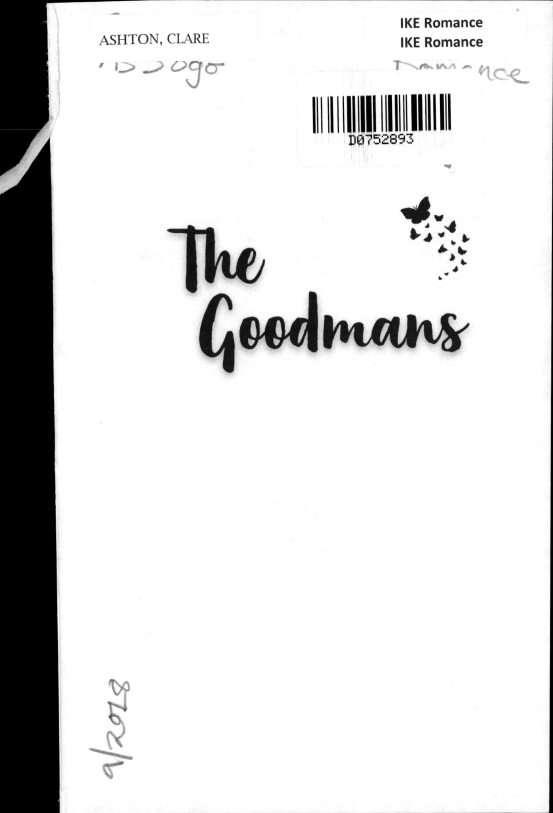

The Goodmans

The Goodmans

Editor: Jayne Fereday
Cover: Fereday Design

Published by:

BREEZY TREE

For Jayne

1

Dr Jude Goodman was certain of many things.

Her beloved home town of Ludbury, in the rolling hills of the Welsh-Shropshire borders, she imagined eternal. It was a quintessential and timeless English town, with medieval sandstone walls encircling Georgian streets and timber-framed houses. At its apex, an ancient church tower rose above the pastel and brick terraces and glowed red in the sun's rays. Change came slowly to this place.

That her parents would live here until their dying days was another unspoken certainty that formed the bedrock of Jude's existence. Her mother, all passion and drama, could test the patience of a Labrador, while her father was the epitome of all things comfortable and predictable. How they'd got together eluded Jude's comprehension, but together they'd been for so long that understanding was no longer required. They simply were.

Her most lasting and closest of friendships with university chum and now resident of Ludbury Dr Abby Hart was another immovable truth.

On this autumn evening, Jude returned from her life with boyfriend Bill and job as an inner-city locum for much needed respite in the bosom of her family and best friend, while Bill worked through the weekend. It was a habit formed over the last five years, so engrained it felt like another universal constant.

But as Jude arrived on the train from across the green Shropshire plains, little did she know that over the coming days all but one of these certainties would remain unchallenged.

For a start, how could she know that when Abby Hart spotted her that her friend's heart soared so high?

"Jude!" Abby shouted. Her vigorous wave hid none of her excitement.

Abby's heart lifted higher still when her friend beamed and waved back from beneath the medieval tiers of the upper street. Jude strode towards her, generous mouth in a wide smile. Wavy sun-kissed hair cascaded and bounced around her shoulders, so thick Abby wanted to bury her hands in its depths while gazing into eyes that shifted in shades between grey and green. Jude towered above the elderly afternoon shoppers and her walk exuded confidence, a demeanour that had made her popular at university and the same friendly authority engendered trust with her patients now.

Abby sighed as Jude came closer, listening to the click of the heels from long leather boots on the pavement and admiring the jersey dress that slipped around Jude's curves in a feminine fashion but left her Amazonian physique undiminished.

You see, Abby couldn't think of Jude highly enough. When Jude made an entrance, it was almost as if angels sang, but it was actually *Waterloo* Abby heard in her head, ever since Jude's grandmother had commented on her "proper woman thighs", which were decidedly Abbaesque.

"Mmmm," Abby said, oblivious to making such a sound.

What a fine place between Jude's thighs must be. Soft and warm, warm and soft, so very soft.

Abby's parietal lobe nagged at her to concentrate on something else.

"Dr Hart. Dr Hart?" Someone tugged on her arm, a small tug like a child's.

2

"Muh?"

Abby looked down to see a grey mop and bespectacled face peering up.

"Mrs Malady. I'm sorry, I was miles away." Or actually a soft place not so far away.

"I missed my appointment Dr Hart. I'm really sorry." The achingly thin woman grasped Abby's sleeve with a trembling hand.

Abby smiled. "No problem, Mrs Malady. We were overbooked in any case. It wouldn't have been an issue."

"I need to see you. I've been waiting over week for my appointment. My Billy was late picking up the kids and I tried to get here as fast as I could, but the receptionist said I was late and you'd already gone."

Abby's shoulders slumped. Even on their quiet days, there were more urgent patients than slots. The non-urgent cases gave up booking until their symptoms worsened and they too became an emergency.

"I'm sorry," Abby said. "Can it wait until Monday when we can sit down and talk properly?"

"She says I'll have to wait a week."

"I'll tell Becky on reception to double book the last appointment, then we can take as long as we like. We'll sort you out."

"Thank you, Dr Hart. You are good to me."

"That's why I'm here."

"Not all's as good as you." The old woman gave her a fragile look of gratitude. "Bless you." And only then did she release Abby's arm.

She tottered down the street with a gait so perilously unsteady Abby winced watching her leave. The woman needed knee surgery but was likely at the bottom of a long waiting list.

"Like many others." Abby sighed and turned her attention to her approaching friend.

At least Mrs Malady's intervention had distracted from Abby's hopeless admiration of Jude. Abby tried not to make a habit of admiring her best friend's thighs. She'd long ago reconciled herself to Jude's unobtainability. Her friend had never shown an inclination towards Abby or any other woman. She had no shortage of male interest and she'd been with her boyfriend for an eternity.

It's just that sometimes Abby slipped. Thankfully not often and it was paramount her friend never knew.

Abby opened her arms out wide as she reached her friend. Oh it was good to see her.

And Jude observed, with not a clue as to why it should be, "You look well. Extremely well." She enveloped Abby in a hug, lifting her from the ground with enthusiasm.

When dropped back to Earth, Abby flicked away her long fringe, and blue feline eyes looked up at Jude. Rosy cheeks and full lips shone in a smile. Although Abby was by no means short she tilted up her head to meet Jude's gaze.

It was easy to see why Abby had been popular with women at university – she'd stood out with her height, especially when accompanied by her statuesque friend, and her open and warm personality was difficult to resist.

Abby was wearing her pale linen jacket and tailored dress for work and Jude narrowed her eyes at her friend.

"It was your day off today, wasn't it? I knew you'd end up at work anyway." Abby was comfortingly predictable.

Abby stroked the back of her short dark hair, a habit when embarrassed and another constant in Jude's life.

"I did try, honestly." Pink bloomed on her cheeks. "The new receptionist didn't check the holiday calendar and went crazy when she spotted my appointments empty."

"I bet she did. Like a little oasis of doctor time."

Abby laughed.

"I knew you'd find a way to sneak in anyway."

Jude was teasing to hide her concern. It was easy to work every waking hour as a GP and she was watchful of her friend becoming overworked. But then Abby had been strong for months, actually years. No panic attacks, no disabling anxiety, no longer crippled by every soul she couldn't save. Not even Jude, who knew Abby's expressions better than her own, better than her boyfriend's, could see the ripples of vulnerability that ached deep inside.

"At least the receptionist rearranged the last appointment so I could get away early."

"Come on." Jude cosied up, arm in arm and bosom to bosom. She didn't have to say where they were headed.

Like every Friday, the pair walked down a narrow timber-framed alleyway, which loomed above them as if trying to peer down at the pedestrians. Abby glanced into the little cheese shop tucked beneath one of the tiers and waved to a woman behind the counter. The petite and pretty blond waved back with a shy smile then pretended to concentrate on the array of cheeses on the counter.

Jude squeezed Abby closer as they walked by. "Has she asked you on a date yet?"

"What?" Abby wrinkled her nose. "No. Why should she?"

"Let me think. Because you are the most eligible lesbian in town."

"That's silly—"

"Because you had them running after you by the dozen at university."

"Not exactly—"

"Because she blushes every time you wave and self-consciously lifts her hand to her face before remembering she's wearing a glove covered with cheese."

"I haven't noticed."

"And I bet she's still looking at you this very moment."

Abby peered over her shoulder, then reddened. "Yes, she is."

"Besides," Jude continued with a smile. "You are the nicest person in the world and she'd be mad not to want you."

Abby was about to protest again when she stopped. "Thank you," she said. "Thank you for saying I'm one of the nicest people you've met."

"It's true. Nicest and most dear to me."

They broke from the shadow of the alleyway into sunshine in the main square. Jude breathed in instinctively. The food market was in full swing beneath white and green striped awnings, trading into the evening to catch hungry workers on their way home. The smell of Mediterranean herb loaves and artisan pizzas drifted from a wood oven. The aroma of warm chocolate wafted from a stall where the holder worked it into flower shapes. The brewery was tempting the susceptible with its spiced ales. A more fragrant and tantalising market Jude couldn't imagine and it was a key feature of this food capital of Shropshire, where the local Indian boasted a Michelin Bib Gourmand.

But they skirted the edge of the market: past the temptations, past the market hall and along the four-storey town houses, which housed more temptation in the Chocolate Gourmet shop.

"Why don't you ask her?" Jude said.

"Hmm?"

"If Cheese Shop Lady hasn't plucked up the courage to ask the eligible doctor on a date, why don't you ask her?"

"You can't call her Cheese Shop Lady." Abby sounded indignant but smiled.

"Ah, is the cheese element an issue?"

"No. It's just Cheese Shop Lady isn't an attractive description. And she is pretty."

"What's wrong with cheese? Love over mouldy Shropshire Blue? Passion with Stinking Bishop? I can see that working."

"Stop it." Abby nudged her in the ribs, the smile still twitching on her face.

Jude could read her so well. When to tease and tickle, when to pull her friend close and when to ease off.

"I'm happy by myself at the moment," Abby said. "That's all. I like things the way they are."

And Jude had no doubt about that from her friend's contentment in her company. Perhaps it was because they were more mature in their early thirties. Not so impatient to accept every date or every suitor on Abby's side, not so precious about Bill to spend every minute with him on Jude's. Perhaps that was it.

"Come on," Jude said. "I think it's my turn to buy."

With no need to specify which café or what they would order, they crossed the square towards their favourite Garden Café and sat outside, ample thigh to Rubenesque bottom, whipped cream and marshmallows topping a hot chocolate each.

Abby gazed at her with big eyes, all rosy-cheeked in the sun and warmed by the hot chocolate, more beautiful than ever. Yes, that must be why the lovely Abby was still single. Another constant. Why would Jude expect it to change?

2

"That floozy's back."

Maggie Goodman's snapped open her eyes. The nasal sneer had emanated from over the garden wall.

"She's up there," the female voice said with disdain. "Darling, are you listening? I saw her with my own eyes. I can't have any respect for that woman anymore."

The weight of the world, at least the weight of Maggie's immediate anxieties, descended with a thump and she groaned as if winded.

She'd been lying on the mossy cushion of grass, enjoying the evening sun that peeped over the garden wall making this usually shady spot a balmy haven. Her body had relaxed into the moss' forgiving hold, a warm kiss to her neck, a soothing squeeze down her spine, a gentle pinch on the bottom through her jeans, all the way to her bare feet.

It was something she indulged in to distract from life falling to pieces and from her body, which was gradually doing the same.

Maggie closed her eyes, attempting to regain tranquillity.

The swollen river at the end of the garden murmured its soothing song and, as Maggie's cares lifted from her body, her mind swirled with the beginnings of sleep. She could have been herself at any age, but always in this blissful state she imagined herself a student again, dozing on the quad lawn on a summer's day, her arms reaching for the exciting touch of another's.

"Carrying on like a scarlet woman," the sneer interjected.

"Oh for..." Maggie sat up.

Barbara Petty. The neighbour. The one thorn in Maggie's idyllic patch. No matter how much pleasure their Georgian garden brought, with its al fresco dining terrace and antique iron furniture, to the colourful acer trees and sweep of lawn to the river, this malevolent cloud would blow in from next door.

"What on earth is Caroline Argent doing with Richard Goodman? If her husband knew, God have mercy on him, she'd be thrown out of town."

Irritation squirmed up Maggie's back and all sensual mossy relaxation was in vain. Her heart rate rocketed, her tension headache pounded and she balled her fists tight.

"Fucking woman," Maggie muttered.

Her pelvis crunched as she shuffled on her bottom and she spared her knees a moment before standing. How she begrudged this procedure. It seemed like yesterday she could leap up from the college lawn without even knowing bodies could have such limitations. She stood up, every joint reminding her thirty years had in fact passed.

Truth be told, she had aged kindly and Maggie was one of those women who although looking her fifty-five years, looked good on it, especially after embracing it the last few years.

It all started when she'd made the mistake of wearing her glasses to check in the mirror. After the shock of a hundred creases in sharp focus, she simplified her makeup routine and returned to soft-focus checks without her cruel lenses. It was a look that suited her much better.

She'd cropped off her much-loved strawberry blonde hair. After years of plucking the grey, her son Eli, who'd inherited her quick wit and sharp tongue, mentioned it odd how she'd only greyed at the back of her head. After an embarrassed

9

hand to cover the neglected area, and an attempt to boot Eli up the backside, she whisked herself off to the hairdressers. Her long locks were removed and she welcomed the ash-grey hair many a younger woman requested at the salon. The resulting short and ruffled style set off her heart-shaped face better than any longer variety ever had.

And, now she'd recovered from standing, it was with a quick fluid step that she retreated towards the house. Her once willowy body, which refused to retain an ounce of fat as a student, had filled out into one which many of her generation would never see again.

"I think it's disgusting." Barbara Petty's vitriol cut through the air and halted Maggie in her stride. "At their age. Carrying on with affairs? What would the children think?"

Children? Children?! Maggie ground her teeth. Christ, Jude was in her thirties and Eli had a mind in the gutter. They wouldn't give a flying fuck about people in their fifties having affairs. Which, she realised, was Richard's argument.

Speaking of the devil, the man himself appeared. Her imperturbable husband leaned against the double-door frame, an amused smile on his face.

"That floozy sneaks in everyday, I'm sure of it," Barbara said from over the wall. "Goes up the new 'fire escape' as they've been calling it. All that noise we've had to put up with, so Caroline Argent can come and go as she pleases. Sordid. That's what it is."

Richard was holding his belly, an attempt to stifle the giggles.

"It's like living next door to a brothel." And a door slammed.

Richard snorted and covered his mouth, and the combination of that and their petty neighbour was enough to ignite fury inside Maggie. It burned her face. That or she was having another hot flush, which made her all the more angry.

Her vexation must have been obvious because Richard's giant form of six feet four pushed off and strode its languid way towards her, greying hair flopping over his forehead and amiable face full of amusement. And if he didn't remind her so much of Jude, their appearance so similar, it was a face she could happily have slapped right now.

"You could stop all this," he said, voice all tempered and reasonable. "Tell everyone we're separated and this goes away."

"Does it? Does it really?"

"Of course. And we have to tell them at some point."

Yes, it was all very obvious, if he must know. "But does it have to be tonight? I haven't seen Eli for months and I don't want to piss on familial happiness as soon as he steps through the door. Welcome home, son. You're just in time for Mummy and Daddy to announce their divorce."

Richard smiled at her, like she was an adorable child. She hated that.

"It's because he's coming home that we should. We can explain to them both we're getting along fine."

Maggie's eyebrows shot up.

"Getting along in our own way," Richard clarified, "which has done us very well over the past thirty years. And we're both staying in the family home should they need us."

Maggie knew he was right. It was the perfect time to acquaint the children with the new arrangement.

"Don't you agree?" Richard asked kindly.

Yes, she did. She nodded, reluctantly and petulantly. Christ, why was he always so fucking reasonable? It drove her insane.

She gazed at her beloved house, their beautiful three-floor Georgian brick terrace. It had been a rough diamond thirty years ago, a rare project in a flourishing town. It had felt like a millstone around her neck at times. They scrimped and saved to renovate the wreck and it never stopped needing their love and attention – the roof under constant repair and the plaster still occasionally falling off the walls. A millstone worth many hundreds of thousands of pounds – all worthless until they died of course. It was when they'd looked to buy a small property each they'd realised how little they could buy with that large sum in Ludbury. Maggie had turned back her fond gaze on the house and appreciated it for what it was – her home, in a town she adored, where her family had grown up. It would just be a little more divided.

"Should we tell them about Caroline?" Richard asked.

"For Christ's sake, can we let them down gently? Can we not tell them about Daddy's lover yet?"

"I thought you said you didn't mind. She can stop visiting."

"I don't mind. It's just…"

She was telling the truth, strangely, even though when they'd agreed he could take a lover she thought it would be bothersome. She'd always thought of Richard as a cerebral, sexless creature, despite being handsome in his sixties, his classic style of chinos and Oxford shirt standing him well, and having competently fathered two children. His passion for archaeology and everything long dead seemed so consuming she was surprised he'd had the time, let alone the inclination, to pick up a living, breathing girlfriend. Perhaps they'd bonded in the countryside, Caroline out walking the dogs and Richard wandering about trying to find another bloody tumulus. Maggie couldn't imagine how else they'd met.

"You've been happy sleeping apart for years," Richard offered.

Yes, she had. Very happy. There was nothing like hot flushes and night sweats as an excuse for kicking a large heater of a man out of bed, especially one who snored like a pneumatic drill.

"And I've been ensconced on the top floor for over a year."

This was true. They met for breakfast often. They dined together at night many times. But she rarely saw him in between and they'd lived separate lives, while sharing this still treasured friendship, for many months without a single argument, by which Maggie meant one where Richard became unreasonable too.

"Yes, I am fine with..." she almost called her Floozy, which annoyed Maggie even more. "I don't have a problem with you seeing someone, Richard. It's just..."

Richard smiled at her in gentle defiance. "It's just...?"

"Did she have to be a bloody Tory?"

Richard laughed loud.

"Seriously?"

"I knew that was bothering you." He was still laughing.

"And a Tory county councillor. Not simply a *Daily Mail* sheep. A bloody fully-paid member of the Conservative Party."

Still, he was laughing.

Maggie thrust her hands onto her hips. "Seriously."

Richard wiped his eyes and sighed, his face red from the giggles. "You see, the funniest thing is that you're quite similar."

"Bollocks."

"No, really."

"Do you mean apart from our fundamentally different world views?"

And her impeccable bleach-blonde hair, perfect makeup and spotless navy suit. It was a blessing Caroline was older, even though she hid her jowls with a floral scarf, and even though it worked very well and Caroline looked fantastic.

"You should talk to her sometime," Richard persisted. "I honestly think you'd get on well."

"I maintain my position: bollocks."

"There's more that unites us than divides us."

"Regretfully, at this point, post-Brexit referendum, I'd have to reiterate: bollocks."

Richard shook his head, a very amused smile still lightening his face. "You know, I never got over how much you swear. You speak like the queen but swear like a navvy."

"Blame mother for the plummy accent and my socialist
father for the cursing – God rest his soul – not that he
believed in one."

Richard thinned his lips. "I wish I'd met him."

"Me too," Maggie shot back. "He would have told you
never bed a capitalist."

"Apart from the fact that he did with your mother."

"That's why he'd know. Because mother's the worst. She
votes Lib Dem."

Richard roared with laughter.

And reluctantly Maggie smiled. They got on better now
they didn't have to. Richard seemed to enjoy arguing with her
more. He used to hide in the attic to recharge in between
facing his whirlwind of a wife. Now he lived there
permanently he seemed more at ease when they met.

Divorce was going to suit him. But what about her?
Where did this leave Maggie? It was much easier to face the
world post-divorce with someone at your side and Maggie
found herself envying his right-wing Floozy. She kicked
herself mentally for persisting with Mrs Petty's slur.

Richard opened his mouth and inhaled the beginning of a
sentence, when the doorbell chimed inside the house.

"That'll be Jude," he said, instead of whatever was on his
mind. "So, are we going to tell them?"

Maggie took a deep breath, "Yes."

"One at a time? Ease them in with hand-holding?"

"Why can't we tell everyone at the party? Get it over and
done with."

Richard raised his eyebrows. Maggie was sure he'd
learned that trick from her. He never did anything so sassy
when she met him thirty years ago – the quiet archaeology
researcher.

"I'm not trying to be dramatic," she said.

His eyebrows went higher. Now that was his own trick.

"Really," Maggie persisted,

"One at a time. It's for the best."

Maggie's heart pounded.

"OK?" Richard peered at her.

"Fine," she growled. "Now, bugger off and open the door."

And Maggie knew it was for the best, although as she watched him go, fear gripped her so tight it made her gasp. She reached for the wall and every limb shook.

3

"Dad!"

Jude greeted Richard with arms out. He dipped beneath the doorway and the hanging red leaves of Virginia Creeper and put his arms around her shoulders.

"Hello sweetheart," he murmured beside her ear. He gave a powerful squeeze that winded her a little, but it was comforting to have him so physically present. Her father's solidity gave Jude confidence in the stability of the world.

He stepped back and smiled at her. He looked well, the best in years. He seemed in higher spirits every time she visited of late. She'd wondered when he'd retired, six months before, if it had been a mistake. For a while he became withdrawn, more reclusive in his attic library, but she held no anxiety for his happiness today.

"Abby with you?" he asked.

"Yes." She gestured to her friend who was pacing along the pavement at the bottom of the garden steps, issuing advice on the phone to a patient.

Richard pursed his lips. "Always on duty."

"Yes, she is." Jude smiled. "You're having some work done?" she said, peering up.

"What's that? Oh, yes." He turned to the building work in the gap between their home and Mrs Petty's. Two men stood at the top of a spiral staircase and chattered in a language Jude couldn't quite catch. A quarrel had erupted with a great

16

deal of gesticulation and, whatever the dialect, definite cursing.

"They've been at it all day," Richard murmured behind a hand. "Silly buggers mis-measured the position of the new external door. It won't open because the stair rail's in the way."

"Oh dear. Is Mum upset?"

"A little. I learned a new medieval curse at least."

Jude laughed. Her mother's background as a history teacher and Middle Ages specialist added colour to their lives.

"She called their boss a yellow-bellied magsman when he tried to charge for the remedial works," Richard said.

"I would have loved to have been there."

"No, you wouldn't. I know that much."

He was right. Although Maggie's escapades amused them both, neither were antagonistic personalities, both tending to well-considered views and responses, and preferring to avoid Maggie's tirades.

Behind Richard, Maggie's silhouette glided down the hallway and warned of her imminent arrival, quick movements betraying her spiky persona. In the shadow of the house, Jude could have sworn a frown pinched Maggie's face, but when her mother burst outside she greeted Jude with a joyful smile and fierce love in her eyes. Jude was about to embrace her when the thud of a sash window opening, high up next door, stopped Maggie in her tracks.

They looked up to see a Union Jack flutter out and hang down the wall. It might have appeared a random event except for the black lettering adorning the material. "British jobs for British workers," was written large and loud.

Mrs Petty's face stared down at them – chin raised, nostrils flared and two beady eyes in disapproving slits. It wasn't her best side and it wasn't her best look.

17

"What the…?" Maggie's face had gone from love to scorn in less than a second. Her changes in mood were legendary and in middle age she was at the peak of capriciousness.

Maggie thrust her arms into the air, her upturned palms shouting her incredulity as much as her voice. "What the hell…?"

"What's up with her then?" the builders shouted down, and Jude recognised their sing-song accent at last.

Maggie shot a disdainful look with the power to curdle sour cream at Mrs Petty. "They are British you meddling sprout."

"Then they should speak English," Mrs Petty hit back. "I don't care where you're born or what your culture is. You should speak the language of our country when you're here."

"They're Welsh you ignorant, racist fathead. You know the country, Wales, the one you can actually see from the church tower?"

The two blokes at the top of the stairs looked pleased, very pleased. They faced Mrs Petty and shouted with fists in the air, "*Cymru am byth!*"

Mrs Petty's face plummeted. It was as if she could taste that curdled soured cream. And before Maggie could ridicule her more she disappeared into the shadows without another protest.

"Unbelievable," Maggie spat.

"Well," Richard said. "I think we can safely say you won that round."

"Pah! That's not the point. It's not about winning, it's about divisive attitudes. I have a good mind to hoist a European Union flag in retaliation."

Richard put his hands on her shoulders. "And would that calm matters? Would it help dispel these divisive attitudes?"

"Probably not, but if the Queen can wear an EU flag to the opening of parliament when she's pissed off, I can bloody well raise one."

18

Richard sighed. "The trouble is that Barbara, for all her xenophobia, may have voted to remain in the EU. Who's going to work on her son's industrial farm if we don't have cheap migrant labour? He'll not want his crops to rot in the ground. And on the other hand, some of your socialist chums voted to leave."

"They voted for proper investment in our healthcare, and 350 million pounds every week was very persuasive. But that pledge was withdrawn, the day – and I mean the day – after the vote. And why that wasn't criminal and didn't invalidate the result I will never understand."

"So, Mum," Jude said. "How about a little tolerance for everyone, including the Brexiters? You know it's a complex issue."

"No, it's not. We're fucked, well and truly fucked. The whole Brexit issue has divided us all and fuelled racism and bigotry."

"There are opportunities." But Jude didn't have the will power, or the answers, it seemed nobody did, and she wasn't there to argue politics all weekend.

"So," she changed the subject. She offered her mother a hug – a brief, emotionally loaded, complex hug, which couldn't be more different than with her father. Whereas her father's embrace instilled in Jude steadfast love and reassurance, her mother's fierce embrace filled her with so many conflicting feelings her stomach swirled with anxiety. Fear of what she might say next. Admiration for the fiery woman who'd defended her builders. Excitement about where she might drive the evening.

Jude took Maggie's arm and persisted with cordial conversation as they wandered through the hallway. "So, why the external stairs? I mean they look great, but they must have cost a fortune."

"Stairs?"

"Yes, the ones outside?" Her mother still looked shocked at the idea. "The ones you've been arguing about?"

"Yes. You're right. We're having stairs put in."

"I know." Jude laughed. Her mother took being difficult to an extreme at times. "I wondered why. I mean even with cheap foreign labour," she smiled naughtily, "it must have cost a fortune."

Maggie tutted and at last focused on the conversation. "Don't joke, Jude Goodman. Yes, they are costing a bloody fortune, but it's a lot less than buying two new…. It's…. It's worth it. Believe me."

Maggie's grip on her arm was firm, her fingers curled over Jude's forearm, tightening with every step.

"So why?" Jude persisted.

Instead of answering, Maggie sought rare approval from Richard. Her parents locked eyes for a moment and communicated wordlessly in the way established couples do.

Maggie took a deep breath, then uttered, "Well, you know how your father snores."

"Maggie," Richard groaned.

"He sleeps beyond earshot in the attic. All the time. Every night. So, I thought we should fit a fire escape for him. Just in case. And, and….if he wants to use it as a front door to his book heaven then all the better."

Maggie nodded defiantly at Richard.

Richard rolled his eyes

"OK." Jude said. "Sounds…a good plan."

"Good," her mother said.

"Good." Jude nodded.

"Yes. A fire escape. That's what it is."

"As you said."

"Indeed." And Maggie released Jude's arm and marched into the main room, her boots pounding the floorboards.

Who knew where Maggie was coming from? What strange lands she inhabited, blowing in from one direction and gusting away again. Richard squeezed Jude's arm and offered an exasperated smile as he passed. What was up with them now?

Jude shook her head and gazed around the room soon to host the party to celebrate her brother's visit – an old dining room and parlour knocked into an open plan area. She could remember the rubble and an incensed Maggie, hair white with dust, when it was renovated in Jude's youth. Grand double-doors led to a modest kitchen behind and as Jude circled the dining table she stroked a finger over its shining mahogany surface that reflected the corniced ceiling. It was a purchase from a house clearance, and now a precious antique, with matching chairs salvaged by the tenacious Maggie over the years.

The room opened into a sitting area with a Chesterfield facing the garden and two chaises longues by its side. Folding glass doors revealed the sunny vista down to the river which could be admired from the comfort of the settees. And although the heritage wallpaper was showing its twenty-five odd years, and the seating was due another reupholstering, the house had a grand decadence which Maggie had achieved on a shoestring, and it was unequivocally the house of Jude's childhood.

But it seemed sparser for some reason, as if something was missing. Her father's map. That was it. A print of a seventh century world chart was gone, leaving a pale clean rectangle on the wallpaper. And his globe. Books. Where were they?

Jude caught her mother's eye for a moment, before Maggie hid behind her glasses and fought with a ball of fairy lights on the sofa.

"Mum?" Jude whispered.

Maggie, she was sure, avoided her gaze. She looked fragile – this frustrating force of nature somehow diminished. Jude's instinct was to run and hold her but what could ail Maggie. It was almost frightening something could weaken her mother. Jude approached cautiously instead.

"So, who's coming tonight?" she said, a tentative start to conversation.

Maggie yanked at the string of lights. "Everyone. Absolutely bloody everybody."

"Who's everyone?"

"You know. Auntie Kate, cousins, the kids."

"Good," Jude said. Maggie adored her two nephews and they'd help ease whatever troubled her.

"Abby said she'd pick up Celia," Maggie continued, her voice agitated. "In fact, is Abby bringing anyone? I told her she could. I always do."

"No, I keep telling her to ask the woman from the cheese shop."

"Oh." And the room chilled noticeably.

Jude felt guilty bringing up the issue. It was a frustrating source of contention with Maggie, one normally so liberal.

"I do wish she'd find someone." Maggie nodded. "But–"

"Not a woman." Jude couldn't help the teenage tut in her voice.

"It's all very easy for you to say – settle down with a woman. But you're not the one who has to live with it."

"What, the shame of knowing a lesbian?"

"Not for me." Maggie's cheeks knotted. "You know that's not what I meant. Abby would have to live with it every day and it wouldn't be easy. And when the hell have I been ashamed of Abby?"

"Then what is it, Mum? What do you have against Abby settling down with a woman?"

"It would be hard." Maggie fixed her with a look over her glasses. "Every day she'll have to watch her back as she walks into town with her partner. Every day people will stare and none too kindly. People will attack their home. People will attack their rights. They will never be as safe as you and Bill and never be able to relax. Abby's life will be harder at every turn. It has a terrible effect on relationships. They break down. And Abby couldn't handle that."

"Not deep-seated homophobia at all?"

22

"It's not homophobic to want a safer life for my…for my Abby."

Jude stopped, her retaliation hanging on her lips.

"She's as dear to me as you are," Maggie snapped. "I want only the best for her, after everything that's happened to the dear girl."

"I want the best for her too, Mum. I always have. I watch out for her more than I do Bill. But it's not up to me what makes her happy. We have to support what she wants."

"Even if it ends in disaster?"

"Yes, actually." Jude didn't hide any of her annoyance. "Because she is not a child, and it's up to Abby what's best."

"Well, let's give her the freedom to find happiness where she thinks best then. People are meant to be fluid these days, aren't they?"

Jude almost, almost, rolled her eyes. How she hated it when her mother provoked her into immaturity. "Maggie, I think Abby has a strong preference and, brace yourself, it's for muff munching."

"Don't use shock tactics on me." Maggie stared at her, eyes wide and penetrating.

She had a point. Her mother had a far filthier delivery than she. It's just for all Jude's composure as a doctor and serenity as a woman, her mother could wind her up in a second. With Maggie's confounding mass of contradictions Jude didn't know where to start, and she seemed particularly antagonistic today.

"I hate it when you use my name," Maggie added.

Jude took a long deep breath, not knowing what to do at the end of it.

"Sorry about that."

Mother and daughter snapped their heads round.

It was Abby, striding toward them and pocketing her phone.

"Mrs Malady needed reassurance," Abby said, her face pink from pacing outside and breathing lightly through her smile.

"Maggie," she cried, as if it had been an age, rather than a couple of days, since she'd seen her. She embraced Jude's mother without a second thought and drew the smaller woman into her bosom. To Jude, it seemed the whole room filled with warmth. There was something about Abby's affection and raw love that was infectious, even though it came from a fragile place.

Jude's spirits lifted watching her friend shower her mother with what Jude realised was much needed tenderness. How grateful she was Abby could give it so freely without the complexity Jude felt.

"Right." Abby clapped her hands together. "How can I help? You must have a ton of things to do."

"Lord, people will be arriving in a matter of minutes." Maggie massaged her temples. She seemed to feel the pressure particularly today.

"How about I relieve you of these lights?"

"Good idea." Jude laughed. "Before she strangles someone with them, probably me."

Jude marched off without looking back, too cowardly to check if her mother had appreciated her joke. "I'll get Celia!" she yelled. And she couldn't have left the room quicker.

4

Jude hadn't reached the bottom of the front steps when a car, careering around the corner, stopped her in her tracks. A Citroen 2CV with ludicrous suspension leaned precariously around the corner at moderate speed. Jude could have guessed at the passenger. She could hear the whine of *Firestarter* played at volume and, sure enough, a slight, grey-haired woman furiously nodded her head in time to the music.

The driver Jude could have guessed too – the bulky figure of Desmond, his grey-tinged black hair touching the roof and his mouth wide in a hearty laugh so deep she could hear it over the music. His black, muscular arms wrenched the steering wheel to park at the side of the road. The engine and music cut out and Jude grinned as the mirth of both occupants reached her ears.

Tears rolled down Celia's cheeks and her mouth formed the word "thanks" as she squeezed Desmond's forearm.

Jude ran down the last couple of steps and gingerly opened the door of Desmond's classic car, wary the old chrome handle might fall off.

"Hoodlums," Jude shouted. "The both of you. Don't you know this is a respectable area?"

The naughty pair howled at her some more.

Celia wiped away a tear and reached for Jude's outstretched hand. "Thank you very much, Desmond. I haven't laughed so much since Abby showed me that stalking cat video."

"Welcome, Celia. Always," Desmond said in his rumbling deep voice which pitched with the intermittent highs of a Brummie accent.

"I was just about to break you out of Sunset," Jude said. "Am I late?"

"Oh no, dear. Desmond had finished his shift and took the opportunity to further my musical repertoire. So." She turned to Desmond. "Are you going to extend my education into the twenty tens next week?"

"Absolutely."

"Goodho."

Celia's cut-glass accent made Jude smile at the contrast with her companion's. "Thanks, Desmond," Jude said, as she put her arm under Celia's shoulders.

"Welcome. Please say hi to Dr Abby."

It was funny how everyone at the home called her friend that. One of Abby's favourite duties was the weekly round at the local care-home. The elderly residents (or inmates as Celia liked to call them) couldn't address her formally as Dr Hart and insisted on using Dr Abby, and the habit had rubbed off on the staff, including care-coordinator Desmond.

Jude took Celia's weight as the old woman rose from the car.

"Thank you, dear." Celia winced as she stood up. "Getting going is the worst."

Jude took the strain as Celia limped up the first step and they waved goodbye to Desmond's distinctive ride as it lurched down the hill.

Celia rubbed her hip.

"Bad today?" Jude asked.

"The same."

"Won't be long," Jude said, hoping more than knowing Celia's hip replacement was booked.

26

"Well," Celia sighed. "It's nice to get out of the institution. If I never see another shade of grey, beige or pastel it won't be too soon."

As one of the younger characters at the care home, Celia brought a lot of colour literally and metaphorically, dressed in maroon with a sequin shawl twinkling around her shoulders.

"Why don't you accept Mum's offer and live here?"

"Yes, well." Celia peered over half-moon glasses with sparking blue eyes that left you in no doubt about the keen intellect behind them. "The poor dear doesn't realise she's the one I'm avoiding. If I can't look after myself I'd rather it be some good soul like Desmond. Family? That's a recipe for disaster."

Jude giggled.

"Avoiding Maggie," Celia said emphatically, "is well worth the price of wall-to-wall pastels and wipe-clean chairs."

"You do love her though."

"Of course, dear. As do you. But Maggie and I are too alike. Thank Christ you take after your father. Can you imagine – three generations of drama queens."

"I don't need to. Eli will be home soon," she said, and they laughed loudly.

"Seriously," Jude continued, "why don't you live with Mum and Dad until the operation? Then perhaps if all goes well, find a flat. I know they'd have you."

"Besides being driven around the bend?" Celia raised her eyebrows. "Oh, that I'd kept my fortune. Gave it all away at the encouragement of my socialist husband. No doubt it improved the lives of many poor souls, but what I would give for my own little dwelling and someone like Desmond full-time." She sighed and Jude wasn't sure if it was independence or Desmond's company which appealed more.

"Hold onto that capitalist boyfriend of yours," Celia muttered. "Nice enough boy and he'll prove useful."

27

"At least talk to them about staying," Jude said.

"It's impossible. They couldn't lug me up and down those stairs every time I need to pee. Besides," Celia hesitated, "they have their own problems."

"Do they? Like what?" Jude said, alarmed.

"Oh you know. Things never stay the same in a family. Children are born, grow up and leave. People die. There are long periods of stability where things seem as if they'd last forever. But they can't. Never can. Then times of upheaval before settling into another state of longevity."

"Why? What's happened?" Jude said, concerned after Maggie's heightened state of irascibility.

"Oh nothing serious I'm sure." Celia squeezed Jude's hand. "My guess would be midlife crisis."

"Who? Maggie?"

"Both, I'd wager." Celia chortled. "Funny things happen to people in middle age. Their hormones go doolally. Poor Maggie. God, I remember those hot flushes."

"Is that all?"

"People worry too. They start to think too much. All this worrying who they are after years of work and children."

"Really?" It was difficult for Jude to conceive of her parents as anything other than their immutable selves. "Then what?"

"They never come to any conclusions – inattention due to hormones makes sure of that. Someone will do something foolish. There'll be red faces all round. Eventually everything subsides and an equilibrium is achieved again. And when they get to my age they'll no longer care. They'll be happy simply to be alive."

"Oh," Jude said, "but they're OK?"

"Insofar as Maggie is ever OK," Celia said, patting her hand. "Mark my words. Changes are afoot."

And Jude entered the house with Celia on her arm, her world beginning to shift.

28

Night was falling and the gathering family filled the house with an excited buzz. Lights were dimmed in the main room and trails of fairy lights and lanterns glowed in the garden. Glasses clinked, bottles popped, children giggled. Jude pinched at her evening dress and steadily sipped at a glass of cool Champagne. It tickled her lips and tongue, but did nothing to quell the building unease inside.

Jude watched as she leant on the doorway to the garden, her father with Celia on his arm beneath the fairy lights and Maggie surrounded by clamouring small children. A four-year-old nephew clung to her dress, while his older brother enthusiastically showed his latest story about killer fart bats. Maggie was engrossed, meaning every word of praise she bestowed on the young boy's tales.

"Hi." Abby's voice murmured close to her ear and her arm slipped around Jude's back.

"Thank you for being here," Jude said and she reached around her friend to return the affection. "For Mum and Celia. And I don't just mean tonight. For everything you do in the week too."

"You don't have to thank me. Look at everything they do for me. Besides I adore them."

Jude pursed her lips. She shared Abby's joy at Celia's company, but her mother was a prickly, complicated character.

"I know she annoys you," Abby said with a sad smile.

"What's that?"

"Maggie. I know she winds you up."

"Oh."

"And I know you don't like to mention it, because," Abby hesitated, "because I might think it ungrateful. But I do know. And I can see why." Abby grinned. "Maggie is not an easy person, especially for family I imagine. But she is wonderful. I mean look at her." Abby turned towards Maggie, love shining in her eyes.

At that moment Maggie was roaring, literally roaring. The neck of her evening dress pulled over her head and fingers twisted into gnarled talons as she stalked after her nephews as they squealed down the garden. She followed them with dramatic, large steps, her arms grasping at the air above her head.

"Isn't she brilliant?" Abby smiled.

Jude chided herself. Maggie had been such an inspirational mother when she and Eli were little. She could throw herself into the role of troll, wicked witch of Ludbury or equally Fairy Godmother. She'd sent Jude and her brother squealing around the garden like her nephews countless times. Jude's guilt twinged inside and twisted with complications. Maggie would love grandchildren. She'd never said, but Jude knew she would. She squirmed in discomfort, partly because she had no plans to have any, partly because of other feelings Jude couldn't describe, all blended in a nugget of anxiety.

"I do know it's more complicated for you as her daughter," Abby said sympathetically, her love for Maggie still warming the sad empathy for her friend.

"Thank you," Jude whispered, and she kissed Abby on the forehead. "Thank you for understanding me so well."

She snuggled closer to Abby, cosy in the warm evening and glow of the lanterns.

"Is it OK to stay the night?" Jude asked quietly.

"Of course. The room's always ready for you."

"Thanks," Jude said, already exhausted by Maggie's company.

"Quiet day tomorrow?" Abby whispered, as if reading her mind.

"Would love to."

"How about a walk in the hills, followed by hot chocolate and a film?"

"Perfect." Jude was filled with comfort at the thought and pulled her dear friend closer.

"Hey," a loud male voice interrupted behind them.

"Bill?" Jude said. She slipped her arm from Abby and turned round. "What are you doing here?"

He was still dressed in his off-the-peg work suit and it seemed his entire pale face and shaved head was filled with a smile. "I wanted to surprise you." He gave Jude an enormous hug, which lifted her from the ground.

"Wow," she said, half laughing, half confused. He was never like this. "You don't have to work?"

"Nope," he said, his grin still ecstatic. "Hi, Abby," he said, his smile fading a little.

"Hi, Bill," Abby replied. "I'm going to help Maggie."

"See you later," Jude said, "I don't know if...," but Abby was already beyond earshot in the clatter of the gathering. "So what's happening?"

Bill insisted on putting his arm around her shoulder, even though he was shorter and had to stretch.

"I," he paused for effect, "have been made partner."

"What?"

"You are looking at the newest partner of Slater Solicitors."

"You're kidding?"

"No. Youngest in the company's history," he said, his face colouring with obvious pride.

"That's amazing. Well done, Bill."

"How about you get me a drink?" he said, nudging her forward.

"You can stay?"

"Yup. That was the deal I made." He punched his hips and widened his stance. "Said I wouldn't keep pulling these weekends and it was time I hired a team to take the strain."

"That's brilliant," Jude said, clutching his hand. "You've worked so hard."

"I have. And it can't go on forever. Otherwise I'd have to leave. Time to enjoy more money and free time."

"You deserve it." She meant it too. He'd worked above and beyond ever since she'd met him. It was an entrenched routine and compromise, seeing Bill in the evening during the week while he played football and worked at the weekend, so Jude could spend time with Abby and family. She was happy for him.

"Where's that drink?" he said, rubbing his hands together. "Then we need to talk."

"OK," she said, put out he was ordering her around. But he was high on his success. She didn't want to detract from that.

Her father approached. "Bill," Richard said, putting out his hand, "did I overhear correctly? You've been made partner?"

"Yes sir, I have." Bill gave a mock salute.

It was as if Bill were drunk on success, saluting her father and calling him sir. Her father was such an approachable gentle man nobody addressed him that way.

"Well congratulations," Richard said. "I hope you're staying for the party and haven't come to take Jude away."

"Happy to celebrate here, sir," Bill said, hands on hips and legs still apart in a power pose. "How about that drink, Jude?"

Admittedly Bill liked his celebrations on the football field and to indulge in a bit of machismo when on the winning side, but Jude didn't usually see this side of him. She was more used to his quiet conscientiousness during the working week, which she much preferred. "Yes I'll get you a glass of fizz," she said, acquiescing to his order.

She could still hear his voice in the kitchen. It boomed over the rest of the party. He waved his arms around, emphasising some victory he related to her father. Richard smiled politely as Bill roared with laughter.

He seemed incongruous. Too loud, and taking up too much space. Bill wasn't meant to be here. Jude couldn't remember the last time he'd visited and she couldn't make him belong in the scene.

"Here you go, darling." The words felt alien in her mouth.

"Cheers," Bill said, looking at the glass for a moment then back to Richard.

Absently, he tugged her to his side, his fingers catching in a pinch beneath her ribs. Jude winced as he drew her in. She folded her arms, more like a doll than a person at his side, uncomfortable in herself and his presence. What was Bill doing here?

5

Maggie wrung her hands as she paced the party, asking after everyone, listening to no-one. There was only Eli left to arrive – her beautiful rascal of a son.

She watched Jude clutched to her boyfriend's side and Abby fetching drinks for guests. What a contrast they were, Jude with her dutiful hug then Abby's overflowing affection whenever she greeted Maggie. The dear girl held tight, as if you were the most precious soul alive, appreciating how ephemeral beings were. And how right she was. Maggie counted her blessings she had Abby in her life, the girl she'd taken in all those years ago and now more integral to her daily routine than her own daughter.

Jude took Maggie for granted. Maggie was always there whenever Jude needed, which she never did anymore. But although Maggie loved the appreciation Abby showed, she wouldn't have wished it on Jude – it was an intensity that came from an ever-present anxiety about death.

Jude put her arm around her beau. How far away she seemed. Maggie could remember, as if a blink of an eye had passed, that Jude would cling around Maggie's neck for her dear young life.

How did the same tiny girl curled on her lap turn into the bright, independent woman who managed people's health? Maggie was proud and devastated at the same time. Richard had maintained his position of respect, always an involved

34

parent although never with the same fierce love as Maggie's – a love that had once nurtured and inspired but one, it seemed, that must be rejected to gain independence.

It never changed for Maggie. How was she meant to let go?

Sometimes, instead of having a single daughter, it felt as if she were grieving the loss of hundreds. The baby that clung to her little finger. The toddler who squealed with delight at her first steps. The small girl who said "I love you" for the first time with no ceremony and without realising it almost broke Maggie's heart with joy. The teenager who broke down when she needed Mum one last time. It was like her daughter disappeared over and over again. All those incredible people who Maggie would never meet again, some of whom were remembered only by her. And she felt colossal loneliness at the realisation.

Maggie gasped. She'd thought she couldn't lose Jude anymore, but the divorce would push her further away. Jude would have an excuse to see Richard alone. No need to put up with her mother to see her father. Maggie trembled. How the hell was she meant to do this?

Eli would be here soon. She breathed out, long and hard. Would he bring someone? Did he have a latest squeeze with the resilience to face Maggie? Although he didn't avoid conversation as zealously as Jude, he wasn't home long enough for Maggie to picture his life. She remembered the great bear of a man he'd brought home last time. It was impossible to know what to expect with Eli – a bear, a beautiful waif, an intellectual, a singer, a soldier – he was omnivorous.

All that worry about little Jude being gay and all the time, behind Maggie's back, she'd had a pansexual boy flourishing. Maggie would receive his girlfriends with elation, then die a little at anyone else, all the while Eli laughing it off and disappearing in a whirlwind. And Maggie decided the best policy was to let Eli blow through them all.

They'd expected Jude to be a boy, Maggie remembered, as she gazed at her gorgeous girl across the room. A mischievous umbilical cord had been masquerading as a penis during the scan. The nursery upstairs had been painted blue with white fluffy clouds and the very healthy and very large boy in the scan turned out to be a strapping baby girl with the physique of her father – a stature which worried Maggie and made Richard proud.

Maggie had fretted. She'd loved the name Jude. Richard told her to keep it, make her a Judith, but Maggie didn't want to burden her with the masculinity.

"She'll be whatever she'll be," Richard had said, with a rare cross word.

All those years worrying about her big, butch daughter and look at her. That hair came through in her teens and Jude rounded with curvaceous hips and thighs and Maggie had finally stopped fretting.

Eli, on the other hand, they'd expected to be a girl, smaller and slight like his mother, and apparently shy about revealing himself on the scan, a reticence he shed early after birth and eschewed for the rest of his life. The beautiful boy was a terror, although easy on the eye and easier on the cervix.

Where was he? Who would he bring to thwart her? All those beautiful boys and exquisite people he'd paraded mischievously in front of her, all the while knowing her opinion, still enchanting and doting on her. And how Maggie's heart ached for them all, terrified for their future.

But her terror didn't run so deep for Eli as it had for Jude, or now for Abby. The man had the resilience of an ox. He'd never be as vulnerable as a woman. And Maggie clutched her belly, feeling sick at the thought.

"Oh God." Maggie trembled.

All these people. She'd have to face them when Eli arrived. Their view of her would change forever with one simple announcement. Her sister would be horrified. Her nephews confused.

I'm no longer a wife she'd say. I'm less than I was. I'm a mother who is no longer needed. A teacher who no longer teaches. A daughter who is avoided. I'm nothing I used to be.

Richard lay his hands on her shoulders. "Are you ready?"

"No, I'm not fucking ready. I'm not doing it. I can't."

Richard squeezed her gently. "That's fine. We'll do it in private, one person at a time. It's by far the best."

"I'm not telling anyone. Let's keep it a secret. You go on seeing Caroline. I really don't care."

"Mags," he said.

She knew that tone. That despairing tone. He communicated the weight of exasperation through his fingers on her shoulder.

"We have to be honest with the kids at least," Richard said.

"Oh bugger the kids. Eli's never home and Jude runs off to Abby's at the first opportunity."

"Maggie–"

"I'm not telling them," she snapped. "Long gone are the days where I felt compelled to be honest for the sake of their moral development. They're as immoral or upstanding as they're going to be. We can happily lie to them for the rest of our lives."

"They will notice at some point. What if they see me with Caroline? How do you think Jude will feel seeing her father apparently unfaithful?"

"I don't care. Jude will get her bloody moral compass around it somehow. The sun shines out of your derriere as far as she's concerned. Let's keep it to ourselves unless we have to. It's for the best. If Eli knows you're on the market, he'll drag you off to God knows where to fulfil your sexual potential. And that will only end in tears or a course of antibiotics. We near enough live together, let's not bother."

"Maggie." It was a firm voice. "It's time."

All the air seemed to disappear from her body and her spirit deflated.

"Like this, or privately," Richard murmured, "but it is time." And he walked away.

The doorbell rang. Maggie inhaled and lifted her chest. She stood waiting while Abby answered the door. A squeal of delight came from down the hall. It must be Eli.

When Abby ran back into the room she had a huge smile on her face. The dear girl, how she wore her emotions for everyone to see. Abby was holding the hand of someone shorter, then they both appeared. They looked so similar at first, Maggie was confused which was her son. Two beautiful beings in tuxedoes with dark slicked-back hair.

"He's here," Abby cried, then stepped back for all to admire the fresh couple.

They stood proud and divine, the centre of attention. Eli to the right, slightly taller and broader, his partner to the left. Maggie noticed the faint shape of breasts beneath the starched shirt. Female partner? It had been a while since Eli had dated a woman but that wasn't what shocked Maggie.

Eli's heart-shaped face, the mirror of Maggie's in her youth, had never smiled like that. And the girl, the exquisite androgynous girl, with cheek bones that could entrance an artist, wore the same expression. She was a beautiful elfin woman with inky eyelashes and hair so dark as to be ebony. The barest sprinkle of freckles touched her skin and eyes as dark as coal scanned the room. Eli turned to her and cupped her face, a soft look of understanding and appreciation on his.

They were in love. Real love.

That had been Maggie once. She'd stood in a couple resembling that picture so closely it hurt. She could remember that fresh, invincible love. The smile on a flushed face, the kind you cannot hide when you hopelessly adore the person beside you. How you cannot help reaching for their touch. Everything had seemed possible. Everything to live for.

Maggie could feel her heart imploding. As her son was revelling in his new life, Maggie must announce the death of hers. Her heart grieved not only for her old life coming to an end, but all life's possibilities.

She stepped forward readying herself for an announcement as Eli did the same.

"This is Selene," he declared, holding his partner's hand proudly. "My fiancée."

6

You couldn't hear a pin drop, but it was awfully quiet. The cessation of chatter, the shuffle of fabric as people snapped round, a nephew asking, "What's a fun say?", the pale shock on Maggie's face, Celia muttering, "What the devil is he talking about?"

Jude laughed, the loudest sound in the room. Oh her little brother had a penchant for the dramatic.

"Congratulations," she said, clapping her hands together.

She had no doubt Eli meant this. The affection and admiration between them was palpable. He hadn't brought her for shock value. The room seemed to relax at Jude's reaction and conversation began to rumble through the room.

She strode toward him arms outstretched and pulled him under her shoulder. "You bugger," she said grinning. "You bloody buggering bugger."

"Ha!" Eli threw back his head. "You are our mother's daughter." And he gestured to the still immobile Maggie.

"Congratulations, Eli," Abby said, shuffling in. "And to you, Selene." She gave Eli's beaming partner a hug.

"Welcome to the Goodmans," Jude said. "You are in for a ride. But having met Eli first, I'm guessing you knew that."

Selene returned Abby's hug and put out a hand to Jude. "It's a pleasure," she said, her voice smooth and gentle with a touch of a European accent. "I've been looking forward to it."

"It will be good to know you more, because Eli hasn't said a single," and she gently slapped the back of Eli's head, "bloody", another slap, "word," and one for luck.

"Do you know, Selene," Eli smirked, "that my dear sister is a respectable doctor and clean-spoken citizen, except with her poor brother who she beats mercilessly and denigrates with foul words. It offends my sensibilities," he said, feigning offence with a hand covering his heart.

"Bollocks, you little shit," Jude replied. And Eli laughed, no doubt proud of what he could elicit in his well-behaved sister.

People were pointing and chatting. But Maggie was still frozen, Celia bothering her with questions she didn't seem to hear. Jude shared a look of concern with Abby and her friend understood, taking Maggie and Celia by the hand, responding to the latter and holding the former. Jude couldn't see her father anywhere.

"Tell me," Jude said, turning a smile on the lovers. "Where did you meet?"

"Well Selene was destitute when I found her in Paris," Eli said solemnly. "A poor country girl come to make her fortune, falling prey to an older man and forced to sell her body to save money for the journey back home."

Jude raised an eyebrow.

Selene's lips curled in the corner. "I found him in the gutter after a night of too much Cognac and doing who knows what."

"I know which version I believe." Jude could now discern with confidence the French accent that mellowed Selene's voice. "What possessed you," Jude continued, "to come to this depraved young man's aid?"

"Poor judgement," Eli interjected. "And you haven't asked what she was doing in the gutter at the time?"

Selene looked at him indulgently. "We met on a post-graduate course of lectures at the Sorbonne while he was writing up his PhD and I was visiting."

41

"Selene's mother was delivering the lectures," Eli said. "And it was a series on the Cathars and I was desperate to catch them. And, no offense to Selene's mother, people say she is one of the most captivating professors in the university, but all I saw was Selene sitting in the front row. I swear I didn't hear a word."

"And," Selene pointed to her chest, "I swear I could feel him staring at me. I turned around to check, quickly in case he tried to look away and pretend he wasn't. But he grinned. Waved. Stood up and gestured for me to come and join him. My mother was furious at him for disturbing the lecture and threw him out."

"Wow," Jude said. "That's almost romantic. And good for your mother quite frankly. But how did you get together?"

"It was a few days later," Eli added, "that she found me in the gutter."

"It's true," Selene said. "He is a disgusting individual."

Dead-pan, Jude addressed Selene, "You still haven't said what you were also doing in the gutter."

Selene laughed. "You are your brother's sister also."

She was right. Although they had very different personalities, when Eli and Jude came together it was like a celebration of the aspects they shared. He brought out her playful side.

Jude hugged Eli to her side. "I've missed you, you little prick."

"Missed you, thunder thighs."

"Eli," their father boomed as he strode toward them. He must have been drinking and he smelled of cigars.

Jude peered around trying to spy Maggie, Celia or Abby but it was Bill she found trailing after her father, apparently caught up on drinks. An end of a cigar smouldered between his fingers.

"Dad?" Jude said, wrinkling her nose. "What have you been doing?"

"Sssh," he said, with his finger to his lips. "Don't tell Maggie."

"I won't have to. It stinks."

"Oh come on, Jude. Just the one. I know as a doctor you think it unhealthy–"

"You should know as a human being with more than one working neuron."

"See," Eli grinned at Selene. "Responsible doctor."

"I would never have guessed you could have such a sibling," Selene quipped.

"When you meet my mother, all will become apparent."

"And Bill, come on," Jude said. "You can't bring that in here."

Bill shrugged, his eyes wandering lazily with the drink, and dropped the stub into his glass of Champagne.

"I'm the responsible father," Richard said to Selene, offering a hand, "and you, it appears, have the misfortune of knowing my male progeny."

"Dad," Jude whispered, although there was no way of it avoiding everyone's ears. "Selene and Eli are engaged."

Richard made a mouth as if to congratulate, but no words issued. It seemed a universal reaction to the engagement. Richard shook his head and proceeded to shake Selene's hand. "Not married then. Good," he said solemnly. "So it's not too late for you."

"Dad!" Eli erupted. "What the…?" Eli looked incredulously at Jude as if questioning where Richard's new-found cheek had come from. Jude had wondered the same.

"Married," Bill blundered in. "You? Eli? You're getting married?"

And not for the first time that evening Jude thought Bill incongruous here. In fact nothing felt right about this evening: Eli getting married; Her father joking and smoking; Maggie in some paroxysm somewhere and Abby, dear Abby, perhaps the only one who was being herself.

"Hey, Bill," Eli said, a little stiff, perhaps embarrassed by Bill's state. "Who'd have thought I'd beat you to settling down."

Bill roared with laughter and slapped Eli on the back, too hard.

"So when's the big day?" Bill asked.

"Next year in the summer we think." At this Eli nodded to Selene for her approval. "We want a woodland wedding with a humanist service."

"Is that some kind of new-age shit or something?" Bill asked.

Jude cringed inside. She didn't like this side of Bill. He wasn't usually so boorish.

"Yes, Bill, some new-age shit, in the summer." Eli exchanged another look with Jude. She could only shake her head.

"Then there's still time," Bill said, seeming proud of himself. "Jude and I could still beat you."

"Are you two..?"

"No," Jude said. "Bill's joking. You haven't missed anything."

"Things are changing though," Bill added. "I'm a partner now. And why not? We should do it."

"Joking," Jude mouthed to Eli.

"We'll have the money to buy a house," Bill blundered on. "I'm going to be home at the weekends. So how about it, Jude? Isn't it about time we got hitched?"

"I..." Jude didn't know what to say with him in this state.

"Just think, we could get a place in a village outside Bristol. A thatched cottage even. I could play Sunday league football in the sticks. You'd get your fix of countryside without having to trek up to Ludbury every week."

Nausea curdled in Jude's stomach.

"It's ridiculous you coming back here every weekend. Let's start a proper life together. Just you and me."

But that sounded desolate. No Ludbury? Unable to see her best friend? Not see her parents, even volatile Maggie? Life with Bill only?

"Perhaps," Jude stuttered, "Bristol might not be the best for us, and this isn't the right time to–"

"This hasn't been very romantic, has it?" Bill slurred. "OK. Give me a bit of space here."

"Please. We should talk about this in private."

"Come on guys," Bill continued, spreading his arms wide.

Eli, Selene and Richard all stepped back, leaving Jude exposed. Bill made a great show of falling to his knee and stretched his arms towards her. A gasp rippled around the room and guests withdrew to the edges to watch the drama unfold.

"Bill, please." Jude wasn't her mother or Eli. She didn't like to be on show for something as personal as a proposal. He knew this. Before several glasses of wine he knew this.

"Jude Goodman," Bill bellowed, an expectant grin on his face, "would you do me the honour of becoming my wife?"

The words cut through Abby with icy brutality. Every part of her being plunged into shock and she was numb from her hands to her cheeks. She clung to Celia, squeezing her arm, in the pretence of aiding the old woman.

"Be my wife, Jude," he boomed across the hushed room.

Bill's command was like another punch. But she mustn't show it. Turn around. Put on a smile. Look at the happy couple. She'd managed it plenty of times before. When Jude had met Bill. When they'd moved into a flat together. Celebrating when Jude had found happiness. All the while dying a little inside.

Abby raised her hands as if to applaud the inevitable acceptance and faced the couple. She stretched a smile across her lips, her cheeks aching with the effort. She swallowed her grief, gulp after gulp.

It was for good this time, she realised. Thirteen years Jude had been there. More than a decade of constant friendship. A message or call every day. Companionship every weekend. Gone.

Her stomach clenched so tight she couldn't breathe and the smile was faltering. Celia's warm hand wrapped around her arm and pulled her close. Abby had forgotten she was there and snapped her gaze down to the old woman.

"This is killing you, isn't it?" Celia said hoarsely. Her eyes were wide and she gripped Abby's arm tighter.

Oh God. Celia had realised. Abby stared at the old woman, stricken and mortified that someone had discovered her pain. She tried to laugh and pull back that celebratory face. She swallowed and swallowed, but the grief wouldn't stay down long enough to dismiss Celia's words.

"Abby," Celia whispered. "Dear, dear Abby. How long?"

Abby stared at the horrible sight of Bill on his knees proposing to the love of her life. Then she was clapping, spurred on by the applause of the crowd, half to drown out Bill's words, half to drown out her rising despair.

Just another minute. If she could get through one more she could take her leave. She slapped her palms together, the force reverberating up her arms and pounding through her head. Just one more minute and it would all be over.

Then Jude caught her eye and Abby faltered. The applause rang on but she was no longer swept up in it. Her friend stared at her, beautiful in the spotlight, and seeming such a long way away. Any resolve drained from Abby's body and a flood of sorrow swept through her. She wilted next to Celia.

"Dear girl," the old woman repeated. "How long have you held this in?"

"What do you say?" Bill shouted above the applause, his bravado unleashed by alcohol and the expectant crowd. "Let's get married, Jude."

46

This wasn't fair, putting her on the spot in public. Jude hated this.

"I'd rather we talked about this privately," she said, trying to pitch her voice for Bill's ears only.

"Come on, Jude. What do you say?"

Everyone stared. Smiling faces ringed the scene, some covering their mouths in happy expectation, some clapping as if knowing the answer already. Except one – Celia. She pulled at Abby's arm, staring up in anguish. Then Jude caught Abby's gaze and any preoccupation with her own embarrassment switched to concern for her friend.

Abby had panic and fear written across her face. What was Celia telling her? Was she trying to calm her?

"Come on, Jude," Bill said. He was less cheerful now. "Say something."

"I…" she looked him in the eye, all the while the same spot in the crowd tugging at her attention. "Sorry. Yes. We can think about it. Of course."

Where was she? Celia stared towards the garden, but Abby had disappeared.

"Jude." His voice pitched higher with irritation.

"Yes, Bill?"

"That's your answer?"

Still she searched the crowd. "Yes, of course we can think about it."

Bill tugged at her hand. He looked stunned and the crowd seemed to fall quieter.

"Like you said," Jude tried to cover up her distraction, "we could think about marriage sometime in the future."

Bill got to his feet. "But …"

"Let's think about it."

"But I asked you now," he snapped.

Jude looked at her partner of five years, the handsome man she'd spied in the cinema roaring with laughter at a romcom. The same man who had a penchant for fine food and whole list of commonalities she'd ticked through the years. At this moment she couldn't feel the warmth of a single one of them. She only wondered at what distressed Abby.

"Something's wrong," she said.

"Yes, there is."

"We need to talk about this later. There's something wrong with Abby."

Bill widened his stance in defence.

"She could be having one of her attacks," Jude implored.

"OK," Richard shouted and Jude was relieved to have her father's arm wrap around her shoulders. People shuffled in the ring and the tension in the crowd eased as Richard stepped forward. "We don't want to overshadow our happy couple."

He lifted his empty glass high in the air. "I'd like to raise a toast to Eli and Selene."

Jude blushed in humiliation, but still grateful for her father's intervention joined in the toast. "To Eli and Selene."

At last the crowd broke into eddies of smaller groups. Her father and Bill stared at her expectantly, but she had no time for either.

"I must find her. Don't try to stop me." And she peeled off into the crowd.

Jude pushed through warm bodies and swept by small children as she searched the room.

"Gran?" she called out, taking Celia's arm. "Where's Abby? What's wrong?"

Something weighed in Celia's expression as she examined Jude. "You don't know," she said. "You really don't know, do you?"

"Is she OK?"

Celia stared at her, searching her face, then answered. "She's fine my dear. She'll be fine."

"What's wrong? She looked distraught."

"A touch of women's troubles perhaps." And she patted her abdomen as if to emphasise the point. "Give her a while. Abby will be OK."

"But she looked devastated."

"Please dear." Celia was firm. "Let her rest."

"She could be having one of her attacks," Jude insisted.

"I will find her," Celia said and she patted her hand. "Let me do it."

Jude watched Celia hobble into the crowd but had no intention of giving up her search. She stepped into the garden and the click of her heels echoed in the emptiness. Everyone must have come inside to witness the commotion.

"Abby?" Jude called out. All she could hear was the hum of conversation from the house and the trickling of water around boulders in the river. The darkness hung cool and heavy around her.

"Abby, are you out here?" She squinted as her eyes adjusted to the lamplight, slowly making her way towards the river as she searched from side to side.

"Please, Abby. If you can talk, let me know where you are?"

Jude studied every dark shape in the garden for what might be her friend curled up in despair. She reached the river and tried one more time, "Please. Are you here, Abby?" before jogging on her toes towards the house.

Eli and Selene hung inside the doorway. Jude opened her mouth to call for them when she heard Selene say, "Is that woman OK? Jude's friend – Abby?"

Eli shrugged. "Crying somewhere over Jude I imagine, after that oaf proposing."

"Really?" Selene responded with more sensitivity. "Abby doesn't like Bill? She thinks Jude shouldn't marry him?"

It wasn't news that Eli didn't respect Bill. They were such different personalities. But it was a surprise Abby wasn't favourable and Jude hesitated in the darkness of the garden.

49

"Oh no, not that," Eli said, a sadness softening his expression. "No. Abby's in love with Jude. Always has been."

It was a moment that affected her like no other – as if the world stopped turning and everything careered out of control, all apart from Jude, stuck frozen to the spot and able only to watch.

Everything was chaos. Nothing was what it had seemed just an hour before.

7

"Well. That had to be the worst party ever," Abby muttered.

She'd have to remember to say that to Celia. It would make her chuckle with its understatement. Abby closed her eyes. Her frivolity evaporated and warm tears seeped beneath her eyelids.

"Shit," she whispered, and she gulped back another sob.

She'd run from the party without a word to Jude. Maybe no-one had noticed in all the celebration. And maybe Celia would let it go. Hopefully Celia would let it go.

Abby sat up in bed, determined not to dwell, yet again, on the night before, because she'd spent the last five hundred minutes doing just that. She'd finally got to sleep around eight o'clock, which was, she squinted at the old mantel clock above the fireplace, about ten minutes ago.

There was a tap at the door downstairs, and she vaguely remembered another which may have woken her. It was likely the postwoman, and although a surprise parcel or an exchange of witty comments would cheer her, Abby really, really needed some sleep.

She lay down, pulled up the duvet and gave her small cosy room a sad smile. Her little cottage, in a terrace of similar colourful abodes on the south side of Ludbury, was her pride and safe haven. She'd always dreamed of a house in a country town, with exposed beams and a wood stove.

One of her favourite memories was of being ten years old: curled up on the sofa with her mother, the view outside of grey sky, punctuated by blocks of flats identical to the one they sat in. Her mother cuddled her as they looked through magazine pictures and dreamed of homes as if money were no object. It was a little place like this they'd wished for – a cosy cottage in a picture-postcard town. Outside, the wooded hills of Shropshire were a stroll down the road, the Welsh hills, golden in the Indian summer, a little further. She lived near to people who cared for her. Abby couldn't think of anywhere she'd rather be. And even on days like today, when she was sobbing with her heart all over the floor, this was the place she would have chosen to do it.

Abby groaned. Her head was swirling and had the clarity of cotton wool. She was nearly too tired to cry. Nearly. Because, a choking pinch of sadness decided, just for fun, to make her hiccup one more time.

"I've got to get some sleep," she moaned. She was crying more from hysterical exhaustion than anything else now.

She turned over, determined to take her own medical advice, when her foot encountered something warm. She wriggled her toes. Something warm and hairy. She wriggled her toes again. Something sizeable, warm and hairy. She lay quite still, eyes wide, wondering why there should be something hairy in her bed. Then the something purred. Her panic subsided a little. Not a great deal, because she didn't have a cat.

Abby flung back the duvet, to reveal a pristine white ball of fur, two disdainful green eyes, and a jewel-encrusted blue collar, all curled up at her feet.

"Maximilian!" Abby cried. "You scared the living… What are you doing here?"

The neighbour's cat purred again and closed his eyes with an expression that suggested he either expected more pleasure-by-foot or intended to kill Abby in her sleep.

Abby sniffed and wondered if more than tears were the cause. Damn that cat. How had he wriggled in this time?

"You know I'm allergic to you."

She could swear he was smiling.

"You know you're not meant to be in my house."

He was definitely smiling.

"Especially not the bedroom."

His teeth stuck over his lip when he purred like that. He was probably mulling over the best way to end her life so he'd have the cottage to himself.

"Come on," she groaned. "Let yourself out the way you came. Don't make me get up." The world seemed determined to kick her out of bed today. Abby looked to the ceiling and, imagining the universe beyond, muttered, "Could you give a heart-broken doctor a break today?"

Maximilian yowled.

"OK. How about tomorrow?" She sat up. "Come on fur ball. Let's get you out."

She cradled him in her arms like a baby and stroked his head.

"Ooo", she cooed. "I'm a terrible lesbian. How can I be allergic to pussy, hmm?"

She sniffed and smiled adoringly at his furry little face, rubbing his jaw line so he drooled and exposed his teeth. Typical the two things she wanted most in life she couldn't have – the woman of her dreams and the cat of her nightmares.

Maximilian suddenly jumped out of her arms, trotted into the bathroom and leapt from the window onto the garden wall.

"Ah, little bugger. That's how you got in." She dipped beneath the door frame and trundled across the uneven floorboards to close the window.

Her heart sank as she spied two beakers on the shelf above the sink: one hers, one for her regular guest. She stared at Jude's pink toothbrush, forlorn. No Jude this sunny Saturday morning. No best friend slumbering in the spare room across the landing. Abby caught her reflection in the mirror behind. Her skin was pale and she could give a panda a good run for its money with those eyes.

She pulled a face, sticking her tongue out and crossing her eyes. It's what her mother did when she caught her in the mirror. Abby used to watch her put on makeup. Her mother never moaned about her looks. Perhaps because she'd been young, twenty-seven when Abby was ten, with no wrinkles to complain of. Abby bit her lip. She could do with her mother right now.

She felt alone staring at her solitary reflection and standing in the bathroom, chilly in the autumn morning, especially because some silly bugger had left the window open.

If she'd been grieving for any other reason, Jude would have been here in a flash, comforting her, distracting her in that playful way at which she was so adept. Or Maggie, blazing in, furious at the cause of Abby's heartache, swearing at the world until everything felt right again. But for this? Who could she turn to? Who do you turn to when you're in love with your best friend, and your entire support network is your best friend's family?

Her phone buzzed distantly from the bedside table and Abby groaned once more. Celia. She'd sent a stream of messages during the night. And after leaving the tenth one unanswered Abby had ignored them altogether. Yes, Celia would have been the other person she'd have talked to.

Abby had never known her grandparents. Whoever her father had been, he'd not hung around long. And with her mother only a teen, her maternal grandparents showed their disapproval by being as absent as the father. So it was with a special fondness that Abby regarded Celia – a grandmother she'd never had. But today she was the last person Abby wanted to see, after her best friend and Maggie, of course.

Abby shivered and tutted at herself again for leaving the bathroom window open. She slung a dressing gown over her pyjamas and padded down the stairs with the intention of lighting the stove. She allowed herself to feel a little pleasure as she stepped onto the luxurious carpet which softened the creaking oak staircase and tickled in between her toes. Today she was going to pamper herself. Without the comfort of her best friend she was going to resort to hot chocolate, a sinful amount of chocolate cake then plain chocolate on top of that. She might even indulge in a glass of a chocolate liqueur if that's what it took to get through the weekend.

It looked like a beautiful autumn day outside, just to rub it in. She peered through the back door window into her snug courtyard garden. The reddening leaves of the vine which grew up the back wall glowed in the sun and bunches of tiny black grapes glistened with dew. Maximilian was curled up on the round iron table, covering it with hair no doubt. She'd sit outside later, maybe, give the self-important little git some fuss and catch a glimpse of the sun's rays before it arced over the house and left the garden in shade, which the abundant ivy on the remaining walls relished.

On a positive note, downstairs was tidy, the flip side being she'd cleaned for Jude. Her shoulders slumped as she realised she would be reminded of her friend's absence possibly until the end of time.

The stove was ready with newspaper, kindling and logs. The world's softest sofa was ready for two occupants to cuddle up for film night. The kitchen beyond was prepped to bake another batch of chocolate muffins. And through the nine square panes of the front door's top half, the sun blazed in the colourful street outside. It shone even on a tuft of grey hair which peeked through a lower pane and fluttered in the breeze.

"Wha...?" Abby screwed up her nose. "Who?" Who was the height of a four-year-old with grey hair? Oh. Had the grey-haired four-year-old been knocking at the door?

Abby skipped through the sitting area and wove past the small kitchen island and opened the door.

"Celia?" she said, surprised.

"Well hello dear," the old woman said, squinting up at her. She was sitting on the stone door step, cradling her knees to her chest.

"What are you doing out here?"

"I've come to visit you."

"How... how did you get here?"

"Desmond," they chorused.

"How long have you been sitting there?" Abby said, concerned about the woman's old bones on the cold step.

"About an hour I think."

"Why didn't you–"

"Phone? Message? Perhaps knock on the door?" Celia's smile hinted at irritation, but mainly amusement.

"Oh," said Abby. "I'm so sorry. Come in. Please come in."

"Thank buggery for that." Celia chuckled. She needed a great deal of aid to stand.

"Let me get you a cup of tea," Abby said, feeling ten tons of guilt.

"That would be lovely," Celia said, leaning on Abby. "But first I need a wee."

Abby sniggered. "Sorry." She escorted Celia towards the small loo tucked beneath the stairs. "I'm really sorry."

8

While Celia weed and the kettle boiled, Abby peeped at her phone on the kitchen top, even though the only person from whom she hid her interest was herself. No messages.

It was probably best Jude hadn't sent anything. It meant she hadn't noticed Abby leaving in tears and was cosied up in pre-wedding bliss with Bill, which of course was the worst thing in the world.

Abby slapped her hands over her face as if to stop the vision of her friend with her beloved, and groaned, a long low rumble. She felt stupid. Of course Jude was getting married. And equally of course it would be to Bill, who'd she'd been shacked up with for five years. Really, what else had she expected?

"Stupid," she muttered. "I can't expect her to be around forever."

"Doesn't mean it doesn't hurt."

Abby uncovered her eyes to find Celia hobbling towards her. Abby blushed and stretched for a couple of mugs from the cupboard.

"Tea?" Abby tried to say lightly, although she overpitched it an octave. "Or coffee?"

"Oh." Celia peered over half-moon glasses. "So we're not talking about it, are we?"

Abby stared at the two white mugs, very much aware Celia was giving her a hard stare.

"Is that a tea?" Abby ventured.

Celia snorted. "That'll be a 'yes, we're avoiding it'." She took a deep breath and let it rasp out her nostrils for what seemed like a good minute. "You're all good at that aren't you. Richard, you and Jude. Quietly carrying on without talking about what's wrong. Then there's Maggie and Eli who won't shut up about it."

Abby continued to stare then offered, "So, tea." And she slid out a pot to warm.

Celia chuckled. "As you wish."

Abby filled the pot, arranged cups and milk on a tray and they shuffled out to the courtyard garden. The sun was still warming the two Victorian iron chairs and table, although Maximillian had abandoned his spot leaving a mat of white hair.

Celia wiped her hand across the table top. "That contemptuous little feline still visiting then?" She examined a wedge of white fluff before chopping it to the ground between her palms.

Abby nodded with a resigned smile.

"Always the way." Celia chuckled. "I'm sure those creatures are bloody-minded. They insist on leaping on the person it seems most likely to vex."

Celia slumped onto a chair with a wince, then relaxed. "Ah. I do love this little spot you have hidden out here. For a start, it means I can do this." She delved into her purse. "Do you mind?" She held up an expertly rolled spliff.

Abby shook her head. "No, I don't." Despite never having being stoned, she'd always enjoyed the smell. "Let me bake some cookies next time though, so you don't have to smoke it."

Celia smiled, "Always the doctor. Always the carer."

"Where did you get it?" Abby asked.

"Scraggs did a drop for me behind Spar."

"You've got a dedicated dealer?"

"Oh yes, dear. It's the best way for a reliable score."

Abby couldn't help giggling at Celia's posh street talk.

"He's very affordable and dependable," Celia replied. "Grows his own particularly mellow variety which doesn't make me too silly. He's carved out a niche as responsible supplier to the over-sixties. An admirable young business man."

Abby giggled again, half in incredulity, half in amusement. "He is still a dealer."

Celia lit the end, circling the flame like a pro until it smouldered at the optimum rate. "You're right of course. But my idea of who the good and bad guys are is very much in flux. He relieves my physical pain and many a disturbed young person's mental state. You find solace and generosity in surprising places these days."

Abby didn't argue. With many falling through the gaps in social security and waiting on endless lists for the NHS, she'd stopped judging the actions of people who fell through the net long ago. Besides, it wasn't in her nature.

"In any case, I might not need it too much longer."

"What?" Abby stared at Celia.

"I know this isn't the best timing." Celia put down her spliff to smoulder over the edge of the table. "I didn't want you to fret so I've avoided telling you." She took Abby's hand. "My operation's come through. This time next week my old hip joint will be a shiny titanium one." She smiled at Abby, not letting her eyes drift for a second.

"Oh good."

Hip operations were safe. Abby knew the statistics by heart. But this was Celia and she squeezed the old woman's hands out of reflex, for her own comfort more than the older woman's.

Celia studied her over her glasses.

"Which day?" Abby struggled to say.

"Monday. First thing in the morning."

"That soon?"

"Richard's going to give me a lift. Maggie offered, but I'd rather make it to hospital in one piece before losing the bit that's faulty,"

"Good, good."

Those statistics, those safe stats, they were just for living through the operation.

"Richard said he would stay all day. That way Maggie can't insist on visiting straight away because she won't have the car."

"Yeah. Plan. Good plan."

And safe meant only so far as a general anaesthetic was safe. And Celia was no spring chicken. Abby's breath stuttered.

"I should be in recovery for a few days before returning home…"

And that was before any post-surgery complications. Blood clots. Deep-vein thrombosis. Infection, that was possible. Chances were small, but Abby always let her patients know it was a possibility. And if recovery wasn't perfect, and the stay was extended, what then? Any long stay in hospital and the stats started to climb. And winter was coming and pneumonia and seasonal viruses were starting to rear their little microbial heads.

"Are you all right, dear?" Celia's voice was distant.

Shit. Abby's throat squeezed tight. She rasped in short, sharp breaths.

"Monday, you say. Richard… Car…."

"Abby?" came Celia's quiet voice.

Celia could die. This time next week, the world could be missing this lovely woman. As well as losing Jude to married bliss, Celia could be gone too. Forever.

"Fine…"

It'll be fine, Abby tried to say, as if to one of her patients. The risks are tiny. It's an operation carried out a hundred times a day. But not on Celia. Not precious Celia. Abby's heart thumped in her chest. Her breathing was ragged. Darkness closed around her.

This time on Monday, Celia could be dead on a trolley.

When Abby tried to speak only a strangled noise came out. The weight of it all. The crushing weight of it. She stumbled from her chair, not knowing where she was going and feeling for the door.

Blood pulsed hot in her ears. Her vision blurred. Knees thudded to the floor and her arms instinctively wrapped around her as everything collapsed in on itself. She closed her eyes and curled into a ball. All she could hear were her desperate breaths and her heart beating so hard it rocked her entire body. She almost welcomed the shutdown into black.

That her mouth was furry was the first conscious thought. Abby opened her eyes and deduced the fuzzy sensation likely a product of her lips splayed on the rug.

"Oh," she groaned. She pulled her legs to her chest and rolled her face from the carpet. She remained in a foetal position, too leaden to move further.

She was no longer distressed. An exhausted calm usually followed the attacks, and she was happy to remain there.

"Bugger it," she heard Celia sigh. "I had an inkling you wouldn't take it too well. Although my dear, I'm sure you can see the irony of shuffling off this mortal coil in a panic attack due to the fear of me dying."

Abby chuckled. She turned her head to see Celia leaning against the back door frame, sunlight blazing through tendrils of smoke from her spliff.

Celia gave her a sad smile. "It's why I put it off for so long, until the worst possible moment it turns out."

"Jude…" was all Abby managed to say, and she let her head fall back onto the rug.

"I know, dear."

Abby felt the warmth of Celia's hand on her back. She closed her eyes and her pulse continued to rock her body in a steady rhythm.

"How long, dear girl?" Celia rubbed her back. "How long has this been going on?"

For how long had she loved Jude? Honestly she didn't know.

"Not right away." Abby curled tighter into a ball. It seemed easier to talk that way. "Although, I found her striking from the start. I'd seen her around university. You couldn't miss her. She was this six foot Amazonian striding around college. She already wore her jersey dresses, leggings and long leather boots but with a biker jacket from her boyfriend, Dan."

"I remember," Celia chuckled.

"I can see her now, walking beneath the arch into the quad, sweeping an armful of hair over her shoulder, sun-streaked locks drifting over her face."

"You sound as if you were already smitten."

"Who knows," Abby said with a sad laugh. "The first time we talked was in the leisure centre changing rooms. I bumped into her, and that's when I was struck by how beautiful she was. All the elements were there: those smoky green eyes, the long straight nose, full lips. And I don't know if you've noticed, when she smiles all her kindness and intelligence shines through. It sparkles in her eyes, in the creases at their corners. I admit, all I could do was stare."

Abby was being honest. That was the first time she'd appreciated the full glory of Jude. She left out that Jude was topless at the time. Honesty had its limits when talking to a relative.

But in love. Deeply in love? Abby knew to the second when she fell all the way down, too far to ever come back.

"When Mum..." Abby trailed off. She breathed quickly, although she didn't feel the sharp pain of the memory as she

62

sometimes did. She was exhausted and numb from the panic attack.

"When the hospital phoned to say Mum had been taken in."

They'd been friends by then. Jude and Abby had formed an easy friendship in the first year at university, both medics in the same lectures, lab sessions and tutorials. They arrived at a party in halls, Abby with her girlfriend of a few months on her arm and Jude with her fifth-year medic boyfriend, when Abby received the phone call. She couldn't hear the nurse at first and sought quiet on the halls of residence lawn. It was night and she stood cloaked in darkness, stunned by the news.

A drunken driver's car had mounted the pavement, hit two pedestrians, one her mother. Her friend had died at the scene and her mother was in ICU. Could she please come to Guys, London?

"It hit me like a train," Abby whispered to Celia. "Except I was still standing and it kept hitting me, over and over."

She didn't know how long she stayed frozen to the spot after the nurse had rung off. She stared into darkness, people passing arm in arm and laughing and carrying bottles to the party.

"Hey, Abby?" Jen, her girlfriend, yelled. "You coming in?" She ran up behind Abby and grabbed her arm. "Jesus, what's up?"

"Mum," Abby croaked. "Mum's been in an accident. I need to see her. I don't know how to get there."

"Whoa, is it bad?" Jen stepped away as if knocked back.

Yes, it was. But she didn't know how to explain.

"You two coming in?" she heard Jude shout. Neither replied. Jude came over, perhaps alarmed at her girlfriend's pale face.

"Hey, what's up?" Jude said gently. She came close, holding Abby's arms and peering into her eyes. It was somehow easier to explain to Jude than her non-medic girlfriend.

"Mum's been knocked down," Abby said, her voice trembling. "Friend's dead. In and out of consciousness. Had surgery, still unstable. I need to see her."

The shocking news had the opposite effect on Jude to Abby's girlfriend. She clutched Abby close in a fierce embrace, pulling her under her chin. Abby held her tight. All her terror was squeezed into that hug as she gripped handfuls of Jude's clothes.

"Dan," Jude shouted over her shoulder. "We've got to get Abby to London. Her mum's been in an accident."

Abby heard him running across the lawn and his shocked face appeared beside her.

"Abby I'm so sorry. But...shit," he stared at Jude, "I downed a triple vodka before we came out." He looked horrified at his timing.

"Lend me your keys. Phone your insurance. I'll pay you back."

"OK, OK." He fumbled in his jeans pocket. "It's probably got enough petrol."

"I'll sort that out," Jude said, energised, calm and effective, just like she'd be through hospital training.

"Are you coming?" Abby couldn't see her girlfriend from Jude's embrace. All she heard was Jen mumble her deliberation.

Jude wasn't rude, although she didn't hesitate either. "OK, we'll let you know how things go." And Jude took Abby's hand and led her into the night.

Abby didn't remember much about the journey, only a single impression of staring at her phone willing it to stay silent. Jude drove like a maniac for once in her life, all the while holding Abby's hand. Beyond that, a sensation of being rigid in panic was all Abby could recall.

64

She stared at her phone while Jude marched her through the streets and into the hospital reception. It rang as they arrived at the ward. Abby and Jude froze.

"No," Jude whispered.

Abby looked up to see the nurse on reception, her mouth open, face pale and phone receiver to her ear. She stared at Abby and replaced the phone and the ringing in Abby's hands stopped.

"Oh, Abby," Jude whispered. It's one of the few times she'd known Jude lose control.

The dead phone in Abby's palms blurred. She heard footsteps, then another hand led her to a seat.

It was quiet for a Friday evening, and they let her sit with her mother. Abby held her hand, the one cleaned only of mud from the verge rather than blood.

"I'm sorry, Mum," she whispered, holding her mother's fingers to her cheek, the tears flowing freely. "I'm sorry I didn't make it in time."

9

"I was wondering if that was when you fell for her," Celia said.

Abby heaved herself up, shuffled her bottom to the wall and snuggled next to Celia.

"I think it was the beginning. But I didn't realise until later."

Celia put her hand on Abby's knee and gave it a squeeze, encouraging her to continue.

"I was a mess afterwards." Abby shook her head. "You didn't see it, but I wanted to give up university and stay in Mum's flat."

She and Jude had returned there after the hospital, Abby sleeping curled up in her mother's bed, T-shirt cradled to her face. Abby slept most of the weekend, Jude bringing her cups of tea and the odd value biscuit her mother kept in a tin.

She remembered Jude looking at the photos on the walls of the one-room lounge and kitchen – a blurred picture of Abby as a baby, first day at school, together on their one foreign trip to Spain, like sisters on the beach. The last was of Abby beneath the halls of residence archway, a snapshot taken on her mum's camera, the first she'd been able to afford.

"I don't want to go back," Abby said. "I want to stay here."

"We can stay all weekend," Jude said quietly. "Dan doesn't need his car until Monday."

"Afterwards I mean. I can't leave." Abby looked around the flat, the walls bare apart from the photos. "This is all I have of her."

Jude held Abby to her chest. "I know," she whispered. "And I've been checking your mum's bills on the fridge and everything's paid until the end of the month. You don't have to decide yet."

Jude held her close for a long time before saying, "I only met your mum a few times, but I don't think I've ever seen any parent prouder than when she took you to university."

Abby smiled despite herself. They'd travel up on the bus together each term, Abby and her mother, carrying two bags containing nearly all Abby's possessions. The last time her mother had taken the picture which hung on the wall. "Look at you, my girl," her mother had said. "My little Abby at university."

"If you want to stay here," Jude continued, "you wouldn't be letting her down. If you want to sleep for the rest of the year, you still wouldn't be letting her down. Because your mum loved you and would have wished you comforted any way possible." And Jude squeezed her tighter. "But I would be letting her down, if I didn't help you."

Abby looked up surprised.

"Come back with me," Jude said, cradling her face. "Come to lectures and tutorials, and do nothing more than sit staring at the wall if that's what it takes. Don't write notes, don't even listen. But I want you to keep going."

"I don't know…I don't know if I can."

"I can't bear to think of you here alone. Stay with Jen. Stay with me. Sleep in your own room at uni. Whatever you need. I'll be there every step of the way."

"I don't want to clear this place."

"You don't have to. Not straight away. Let's come back during the break. See how you feel."

Abby had packed a few of her mother's things to keep at university. A silly Benidorm snow globe – the most inappropriate souvenir ever sold. A little heart-shaped frame with a picture of them when Abby was ten. And a Christmas jumper with a Rudolf nose which lit up when squeezed.

She wandered around lectures after Jude, not even knowing where she was. It was what Abby needed though.

Night time was the worst. Initially, she was so tired from shock that sleeping was no issue. But when Jude said goodnight to spend time with Dan, Abby panicked and broke down. She hugged her friend to say goodbye, but couldn't let go. It felt that if Jude left, she might never come back. Abby knew it was paranoia over losing her mother, but she couldn't let go. That's when the attacks started.

It was the same with her girlfriend. But whereas Jude held Abby tighter, Jen pulled away. At nineteen it was too much for a girlfriend to handle, and Abby didn't blame her.

Others were awkward too. The friends she used to drink and laugh with fell silent when she set foot in the union bar. A well-meaning girl said her mother was in a better place and would be watching over her, but it drove Abby into a rage, a frightening rage she'd never before experienced.

"She's not in a better fucking place," she screamed. "She'd want to be here. With me. This is the best fucking place for her."

Jude took her by the hand and they walked for miles, past the university buildings, along the river, into countryside, marching and marching until Abby's rage was spent. She collapsed on a bench by the river.

"You're allowed to be angry," Jude said, her voice strained, and it was only then Abby realised Jude raged too. She had tears in her eyes. "You're allowed to be fucking angry. You're allowed to swear. You're allowed to throw things and tell people to fuck off. You don't have to speak to me again or anyone else. Because you're right. She should be here. The best place for your mother is right here, right now, with you. And I'm not going to tell you time will heal it. I will never tell you to stop grieving. Because that was your mum. Your lovely mum. And she has left a hole in your life, and you should never have to pretend it's not there." And she grasped Abby to comfort them both.

Abby gazed at Celia sitting beside her now, seeing a little of Jude in her eyes.

"It did get better though," Abby said with a smile. "It did work, plodding to lectures and staring at the wall. Because one day everything came into focus. It was strange. It felt like I was suddenly present, sitting on a hard bench in the lecture theatre, Dr Francis gesticulating wildly about synapses, and Jude next to me writing her thorough notes for me to use later.

"I looked at her, properly, for the first time in a long while, her hair scooped over her head, cascading past her cheek, her eyebrows crinkled in concentration as she scribbled away. She noticed me staring and gave a smile. She reached out and held my hand, then carried on with her notes like she'd done for weeks.

"I noticed what a beautiful human being she was, through and through. She'd been there for me every step of the way, long after my girlfriend had left. In that moment I saw everything there was to admire about her – intelligence, her incredible patience and unending support, the way she'd persevered with her own study all the while carrying me. She was beautiful, she was kind, and she showed more respect for my mother than anyone when she was alive." Abby had to stop for a moment. "That," she said swallowing, "that was the moment I realised I was in love with her."

10

Although Maggie Goodman had dreaded the party aftermath, this Monday morning wasn't quite what she'd envisaged. Her sister was in hospital, her mother wasn't, and Maggie happily termed it all, "a fucking mess quite frankly."

"This is how it works now," she ranted while readying her shopping bags in the hallway. "Everything hits A&E. You never get an appointment at the GP, so people leave it until it's an emergency."

She turned to complain with more force to Richard who leant against the sitting room doorway.

"Kate's been having twinges for months and what was a grumbling gall bladder is now a very angry one. Then, on top of that, someone else's routine surgery is cancelled until they become an emergency too."

She kicked Celia's hospital bag to the wall for good measure.

Richard smiled. He was always damned smiling these days. "I doubt your sister needed the same surgeon and bed as Celia. And I'm sure they'll book Celia in again soon."

"Within her lifetime?" Maggie threw her hands in the air. "Fucking austerity. Why is the entire population paying for the mistakes of the rich? The poorest are paying with their lives. And the elderly? They may as well force Celia to hobble up to her own grave, tell her to dig it then jump in.

Seriously, expect that as a policy for dealing with the ageing population next election."

Richard pursed his lips. He didn't have to say, "Come on, that's getting ridiculous," for Maggie to hear it.

"Anyway," he said heavily. He opened his mouth.

"No," Maggie snapped. "I'm not doing it."

"You don't know what I'm going to say."

"Yes, I do. And now is not the time."

He smiled indulgently. "I know things have not gone to plan"

"To say the least."

The house, this very early morning, was full and Maggie was caring for her nephews. One of the vagaries of having a younger sister, who left having kids until her forties, was the childcare of nephews as young as Maggie could have expected grandchildren. At least being an early retiree she had the same early morning habits as infants, although 5 a.m. had been painful for all, mostly for her sister who clutched her side as the boys leapt from the car at twilight.

Eli and Selene were wrapped up in his old room and wouldn't appear until mid-morning to empty the fridge and cupboards once again, and that was just the beginning of Maggie's woes. Don't get her started on Bill and Jude. What the hell happened there?

"We still need to tell everyone," Richard continued.

"We do not."

"They're going to notice."

"We've essentially been living apart for years."

"But insisting on knocking on each other's front doors while everyone blithely comes and goes through the attic door is starting to look a little odd."

"Well lock the damn thing and make them use the front door."

"With what reason?"

"For the hell of it," Maggie shouted.

Richard was staring at her. She could tell he was about to raise his eyebrows.

"Eli and Selene are getting married," she said before he could twitch those hairy contours. "We have a wedding to plan." Well as soon as the happy couple could get themselves to leave their room. "I do not want to crap all over the happy event with our divorce planning."

Richard opened his mouth.

"You can still see Caroline," Maggie cut him off.

"What if I want to take her to the wedding?"

Maggie gave him a look. A hands-on-hips, hard look.

Richard lifted his eyebrows.

She tilted her head.

He raised his eyebrows higher.

"Oh for the love of God, Richard. Is she that important to you?"

"Getting that way, yes," he said, matter of fact.

"Oh Jesus." Why were people so bloody complicated?

The thought occurred to Maggie that this question was most often asked about her, but she quickly swept it aside. At least she was going to meet Abby later – that was a more consoling prospect. With all the upheaval of Friday night it would be good to see the dear girl, an oasis of calm and affection. Although who knows where she'd got to after the party. Maggie couldn't remember her leaving in all the commotion, much of which Maggie missed by staring at her son's fiancée in a catatonic state.

"Well," she said, to shake away the memory. "We haven't anything in for breakfast so I'm going shopping." She still had a snappy tone. "Would you like to stay for dinner tonight?"

"That would be lovely."

"Do you want a roast?"

"Yes please."

"Will you do the spuds?"

"Yes I will."

72

"Good."

"You're welcome."

"I didn't thank you."

"You did in your own way."

Oh she hated it when he out-jousted her. He never used to. Those thirty years of marriage had been damned training for him. He was now a sharper man who attracted the likes of Caroline Argent. Galling.

"Fine," she said.

"It will be." He smiled.

Again, without a comeback, she swivelled on her heels and walked out the door, then had to retrace her steps.

"Boys!" she shouted. And two small nephews obediently trotted around the corner, encased in identical padded jackets, hoods on and zipped up to their noses.

"Ready, Auntie Maggie," they chimed. Two pairs of hazel eyes stared up at her and Maggie melted.

"Oh, my dear boys," she sighed. She wanted to nibble their snotty noses she loved them so much. "We have a full house today and we need to go shopping. You can choose breakfast pastries and puddings for tonight."

"Yay," they both cried. Four-year-old Mathew leapt forward and hugged her leg. "This is the best day ever." It was heartfelt and heart-warming, and a relief that anxiety over their mother in hospital was no match for the restorative powers of choosing one's own dessert.

She grabbed a small hand in each of hers, tiny fingers curling around her palm. She indulged, for a moment, in a memory of two other small children, before leading them out of the house. It was with doubled joy that she launched onto the pavement, with the echo of the sensation of her own children's hands coupled with the tight grip of love from her nephews.

The sun was peeping above the horizon, the low autumn light transforming the perimeter wall of the church grounds into a rich terra cotta and the trees which thrust above the stone were golden against a cerulean sky. For Maggie, nothing had the restorative powers of a beautiful autumn morning and the company of small children.

She was happy.

It didn't last long.

Barbara Petty, the neighbour, stood a few yards down the road yelling at a young policeman.

"Move him on," she screeched. "He's been slumped against that wall since last night. I can't believe how many times I've had to call the station."

Further down the road, an old man was curled up under a sleeping bag, dozing against the stone wall with steam emanating in snores from his nostrils in the cool morning air.

"Now young fellow," Petty continued. "I know your sergeant. He's a good friend of my husband's. So look sharpish about moving that," she flicked her finger towards the old man, "and we'll say no more."

Maggie stood for a moment with her mouth open in outrage, before launching down the road, two nephews pulled behind like balloons on a string.

"Don't you dare constable," she shouted.

The young bobby stopped dead, his already pale face blanching to an unhealthier hue.

"That man," Maggie said pointedly, "that human being, is going to the church's soup kitchen. It's St Mary's on the rota today. Don't you dare turn him away."

"Move him on constable," Mrs Petty said, eyes glaring in Maggie's direction. "This woman knows nothing about church business."

"It's common knowledge St Mary's is on the homeless rota."

"Not for long," Mrs Petty struck back venomously.

"What?"

"You see. She doesn't know what she's talking about. If she'd attended the Sunday service she would know the church is closing."

"Excuse me?"

"There are plans for this area of town and the church grounds. As I said, if this woman spent any time in God's house she would know that."

Maggie was wrong-footed and indeed knew nothing about this development. She was very much aware, however, of the pleasure this gave Mrs Petty. The woman literally expanded with smug pleasure, inhaling a chest full of righteous air.

"So," Mrs Petty said, expansive with victory, "that has no business in this part of town. Move him on."

"Where the hell to?" Maggie said.

"There are plenty of places he can go. Beyond the train station would be more appropriate. Don't they sleep behind Spar, by the vents?"

"Well that's a nice bit of social cleansing. Officer," Maggie said, her tone sarcastic, "at least give him the luxury of moving him behind Waitrose."

"I don't have to stand here and listen to this," Mrs Petty said. "Constable, move him on."

Mrs Petty retreated up the steps to her abode.

"Well here's an idea," Maggie yelled after her. "How about we save money on police pestering the homeless and spend it on affordable housing instead."

Mrs Petty spun round, her face puce. "That," she jabbed her finger in the direction of the old man and the bobby who was slinking away. "Last night, that was urinating against the wall," she screamed before slamming the front door shut.

"Well where the hell are you meant to piss when you live on the street?"

It was only the twitch of small fingers in hers that reminded Maggie of the presence of delicate ears.

She snapped her eyes down to Mathew, whose hazel irises showed a wide border of white and his little mouth made a perfect "o".

"Shit," Maggie said.

Her nephew's eyebrows shot higher.

Oh buggering fuck.

She peeped down at the older Liam, who she hoped was more worldly wise, but he was equally struck.

"Erm." Maggie gathered her composure and knelt down to Mathew's level. She took her nephew's hands and squeezed them while biting her lip, half in penance, half in amusement. "Sorry boys. Auntie Maggie should have said 'wee'. Where on earth should he wee?"

Mathew giggled. "Were you meant to say 'poo' afterwards as well?"

"Yes, I was. I should have said poo, you clever boy," and she kissed his little pink nose.

And indeed, when they reached the top of the road, the church on the left and the square to the right, there was a For Sale sign high above the church gates.

"What the hell?" Maggie raised her eyes to the heavens and mentally apologised as she always felt compelled to do within the vicinity of the church. She looked down to her nephews but they didn't seem to have noticed.

"Daisies!" Mathew yelled. "Kwee go and make daisy chains?"

Maggie crinkled her nose at the unseasonal spread of white flowers, opening their petals in the dew around the grave stones. "Five minutes then," is all she said. It was like firing a starter's gun. "Don't tread on the graves," she yelled.

Her two nephews started hoovering up the flowers into little fistfuls, leaving dark footprints in the silvery morning grass. They perched on the end of a tomb, one that had seen better centuries with a crack down the side and the carving of a skeleton which had worn away into something of moderate interest rather than the macabre decoration it must have once been.

"Don't sit on the–"

"I wouldn't worry," said a voice. "I don't think The Third Earl of Ludbury will mind after all these years."

"Vicar," Maggie said cheerily.

The cleric was a short, rotund woman, all in black except for the dog collar, pink extremities and a neat bob of blonde hair. She would have looked saintly except for the defiant smile in readiness to engage Maggie but which also held genuine regard.

"Good morning, Mrs Goodman."

"It is a good morning, vicar." Maggie smiled then called out to the boys. "Mathew, Liam!"

"Let them play," the vicar said.

"But the disrespect to the relatives of the Earl?"

"Who are buried beside him?"

"And of course God sees all."

"Indeed. He sees two small children enjoying His creation. I think He'll give them a pass on this beautiful day."

Maggie looked fondly at the young woman who'd moved to Ludbury five years ago. "Your God is much more benevolent than the one who watched me picking my nose at school, and a great deal more besides."

"I do hope so. Perhaps I can tempt you and your nephews into the morning service to learn more about His generosity?"

There were a few stragglers limping into church. The largest part of the congregation was well into old age, with a few middle agers and a couple of earnest, well-dressed, young folk, perhaps twenty in total for this midweek service. It would be a short matter of time before it dwindled to a handful who would rattle around this magnificent church.

"No thank you, vicar. Even your modern God and I don't see eye to eye."

"Really. Are you sure?"

Maggie pursed her lips. "I imagine he was greatly offended when I had sex on the altar as a teenager."

There was a flicker of amusement on the vicar's cheeks, perhaps mortification, then she solemnly replied. "Indeed. As one of His precious creations I imagine Him disappointed by your treatment of your spine. Altars are not made for such activities. But I suppose that's why He invented chiropractors."

Maggie smiled at their game. They'd been swapping unholy banter since the vicar had found Maggie swearing at graffiti on the church wall a couple of years ago.

"I'm going to miss our little chats, Mrs Goodman. You've heard the news?"

"Yes. Is it really for sale?"

"I'm afraid so. Ludbury can't support two congregations and the car park at St Lawrence's is a draw for many."

"What will happen to it? It can't be developed surely."

"I believe the old stables and outbuildings are the major interest."

Maggie peered past the sparkling lawns of the cemetery to the timber-framed courtyard down the hill, and beyond the gardens that ran as far as the river. It was a beautiful spot.

"I've heard," the vicar continued, "the whole block is to be developed into a luxury residence."

"But what about the church?"

"It may be sold off separately as another luxury renovation project."

"Oh for God's sake." Maggie winced inside. There was nothing like avoiding the really offensive profanities in front of the vicar to bring out the blasphemies.

"But this is the heart of the town," Maggie said. "This is where everyone comes at Christmas and Easter. This is where the school play is performed. My son was in the choir, which I must apologise to your deity for."

Maggie had taken Jude and Eli to the Kristingle service every year. It was under the pretence of broadening their knowledge of faiths and traditions, although secretly she enjoyed every minute of it, despite her firm atheist beliefs.

It would be sad indeed for the heart of the town to stop beating, turned into a private home with two Range Rovers

78

outside, rarely inhabited by the owners who would work all hours in the nearest city.

Ludbury had remained vibrant owing to its hippy contingent and tiny streets and houses, too small to renovate into luxury homes, but it lacked the energy it had just twenty years ago. Maggie would hate to see it wither into one of England's silent towns – well preserved and maintained and deserted, the residents either too old to venture outside or absent in city jobs, the young priced out of the town entirely.

"My sentiments exactly." The vicar sighed. "But the maintenance of two churches of this size is beyond the diocese's budget."

It was an uneasy and unfamiliar world Maggie woke to these days. Sometimes she missed the old institutions and beliefs, even if she disapproved of them. It had all been replaced with a confusing matrix of politics and beliefs and an overwhelming sense of greed. She shouldn't have minded the dwindling presence of the Christian faith, but she did at the expense of a distasteful display of money and luxury development where the town's soul should be.

"You know it's funny you find it so troubling." The vicar smiled, and Maggie realised she'd been frowning at the church tower. "It's to be bought by one of the congregation. Strange how you feel its loss more than a person of faith."

Maggie didn't know what to say and unease writhed inside. She offered, "I will never believe in your God, or any other. But I think a strong moral compass at the heart of a community is essential for its health."

The vicar frowned and reached for Maggie's arm, before being interrupted by the piercing cry of "Poooooooooooooooooooooooooooo!"

"Oh Jesus," Maggie said. Oh crap. And she sent an apologetic look towards the vicar.

"Mrs Goodman, you really should indulge your extensive vocabulary in my presence, rather than taking the Lord's name in vain."

Maggie chastised herself again then looked to her nephews who were running at full pelt towards them.

"Pooooooooooooooooooooooo!" Mathew shouted. "I need a poo!"

"I'm sorry. Nature calls," Maggie said.

"No matter." The vicar smiled. "Divinity calls," and she waved over her shoulder. "The café is the nearest. Should be open," she said before turning into the church.

"I need a pooooooooooooooooooooo!" Mathew yelled, his eyes scrunched tight.

And after considering dashing home to let Mathew defecate on Mrs Petty's front door step, Maggie grabbed her nephews and raced towards the square.

11

"Sorry, Auntie Maggie." Mathew smiled sweetly.

A red-faced, sweating, heart-palpitating Maggie led her nephews away from the café. She'd swept the boy into her arms and up the stairs as soon as he'd exclaimed that holding in was no longer possible. And he'd been heavy. She remembered the days where she could carry Jude on her hip and Eli in her arms. But now picking up a four-year-old seemed as ludicrous as attempting to carry an elephant.

It felt as if her thumping heart could burst. And after such a heroic effort the young boy had leapt on the loo only for a whistling noise to emit from his rear. A relieved and happy face had announced proudly, "Just a fart," to Maggie's chagrin.

"They'll be the death of me one day," Maggie muttered. Face burning, she smiled down at her nephew. The little bugger.

She wandered through the square, which clanked with the sound of the assembly of market stalls in the early morning. The two boys drifted and blew around, their hands tied to the wheezing Maggie. She felt no better by the time they'd crossed the square and arrived at a little Co-op supermarket.

"Sorry boys," she said, "I need a quick rest."

She slumped in a seat before the tills and next to foodbank collection boxes. The boys had the easy familiarity of young relatives and without asking piled on. Liam first, crushing

81

enough on Maggie's legs, then Mathew perched on top. The boys leaned back, Mathew with his thumb in his mouth, and Maggie could feel the love, if not her thighs anymore.

"My lovely boys," she wheezed. She didn't have the heart to tell them she couldn't breathe properly.

She stared, recovering, cheeks still blazing, at the newspaper stand. It was a topsy-turvy world when the *Guardian* had a favourable piece about the Royals on the cover. Maggie shook her head. A few years ago she could have predicted the headlines: the *Daily Mail* with a tribute piece to Princess Diana or a Tory puff piece, the worst winter forecast in the *Express* and the end of the world in the *Independent*.

Now, it was the *Daily Mail* eviscerating a banker and Tory MP and the *Guardian* displaying a glowing picture of the Royals. Maggie, even as a devout socialist, had developed a fondness for Prince Harry. Topsy-turvy indeed.

But her heart sank as customer after customer picked up a *Daily Mail*, shaking their heads at the headline, "Muslim Lesbian Drives on Wrong Side of Road". This was the kind of thing Jude never understood about Abby being a lesbian. See, you couldn't even make the mistake of turning down a one-way street without an element of society blaming your sexuality and apparently your religion, if it was the wrong kind.

Maggie groaned. What was the world coming to? Then she groaned again because she'd become the kind of person who said just that.

"Kwee have some of those?" Mathew said, pointing at a packet of Jammy Dodger biscuits in the foodbank collection. Maggie recognised the pile of contributions. It was from her last shop before the weekend. Rice, curry, tinned peas, custard and a packet of Jammy Dodgers. She'd bought the biscuits for Jude then thought better of it. Her daughter would have accused her of infantilising her again, even though they both knew Jammy Dodgers were still Jude's favourite.

Apart from Maggie's donation, the box was empty. Not one person had donated the whole weekend. In this town of culinary excellence, with a Michelin-starred restaurant by the river, an ethical whole-food café on the hill, a well-heeled population of pensioners and ageing hippies, not one had spared a tin of baked beans.

"It's a foodbank." Maggie sighed. "We never used to need them."

"Are they bad things?" asked Liam.

"Yes and no. It's good because we're helping those who are hungry. Bad because in a rich country like the United Kingdom there should be food and shelter for everyone. That's what the government should be doing – making sure it's available fairly."

"Is the government making rich people richer and poor people poorer?"

"Yes, it is. Well remembered, clever boy." Maggie had forgotten her previous chat with Liam about austerity versus thriving corporations. She never shied away from any topic with her nephews. Of course this led to awkward moments, like when they'd asked their grandmother if she had a vulva, but in general Maggie thought it healthy to tackle every subject in a matter of fact way.

"Yes." Maggie continued. "And it's no longer about being richer or poorer. People are dying because of it. Thousands of people have died because of government rules. Thousands of people are told to get a job when they have a matter of weeks or even days to live."

"Will they go to prison?"

"Who?"

"The government."

Maggie stared.

"Because they're killing people?" Liam pressed on.

"No," Maggie said, shocked. "No, they won't."

"Why?"

And for the first time she didn't have an answer, only a very heavy heart. "I don't know," she said weakly.

It was overwhelming, sitting under a warm pile of loving children, despairing at their future and the direction of the world. The disparities seemed Dickensian at times – the homeless man being kicked out of town while others gorged on delicacies in the town square. And no matter how much she ranted, things only got worse. Fewer people listened, fewer people cared. Even Richard dismissed her efforts – "What are you going to do? Give away your worldly goods until you live in a hut with sewage water to drink?"

As she sat, a young man rifled through the food bank, filling a green crate from its sparse contents. It took Maggie a few seconds to look past the fluorescent jacket and food bank badge to recognise the now-broader face.

"Dean?" she said. "Dean Thomson?"

"Hello, Miss," said a voice much deeper than she'd remembered. "I didn't see you there under the pile of boys."

Liam and Mathew giggled.

"Well how are you, Dean?" Maggie asked. He must have left school two years ago and she always remembered him as a kind lad.

"I'm well, Miss."

"What are you up to these days?"

"I'm a builder. I work for my dad." He grinned. "What I always wanted to do."

Yes, she remembered that, although she tried to impress upon him that a sensitivity to history was important for that trade and he should still listen in her lessons.

"Are you enjoying it?" she asked smiling.

"I am. Plenty of work to keep us busy."

"But," she frowned confused. "You work at the food bank too?"

"Volunteer, yes," Dean said, holding the crate in front of him. "I'm getting these before work and taking them to the unit. My dad lets the food bank use his for storage."

"I'm sorry there's not more to collect," Maggie said, looking sadly at the box. "We'll add more meals shortly. In fact we'll put in a week's worth for someone."

"Thank you, Miss. It'll go straight away. The only time it's full is Christmas. People forget folk get hungry all year round. You wouldn't believe how many need it these days."

"Really?"

"Yeah. You remember my mate Gary from school? He has to use it all the time. He works like crazy but he's on one of those zero-hours contracts, isn't he. So when the work dries up he's got nothing coming in. People don't live zero-hours lives, do they."

"No, they don't, Dean. I couldn't have put it better myself."

He grinned, pleased with himself.

"Good for you," Maggie smiled. "Good for you helping out."

"Got to look after everyone, haven't you," he replied. "We've all got to live together and no-one's happy when people are on the streets begging for food or stealing to stay alive."

"Well, yes," Maggie agreed.

"It's like you said, Miss." He squinted skywards trying to recall. "You said, 'The best way to look after yourself is to look after everyone.'"

Maggie laughed. She'd remembered saying it in one of her lessons – a trite remark she'd spouted in rage at the latest figures of thousands dying within days of being declared fit to work by the Department for Work and Pensions.

"Quite right, Dean." And she was tempted to say, "God bless you." That damned enlightened vicar. She could make Christianity sneak into your psyche when you were adamant it shouldn't.

85

Maggie contented herself with, "You have a good heart, Dean." And the young man glowed with pride. She missed that. Being able to help a child shine at school. Being useful. Being needed.

"Better get going, Miss."

"Yes. Don't let me hold you up." And the young man carried the crate out of the shop.

"Well," she said, squeezing her two young nephews. "Perhaps there is hope after all. Come on," she said. "Let's get some breakfast, luxury pudding and a week's worth of food for another. Sitting here feeling useless isn't going to feed anyone," she muttered, more to herself.

And Richard could be damned if he said the luxury pudding cost as much as the week's food. At least she was doing something and, with people like Dean Thomson around, maybe the world had time to right itself yet.

Good God. That run with Mathew had taken it out of her. Maggie's face was still glowing in the chilly morning air and her chest wheezing when they'd finished their shop.

But if that wasn't another good soul over there to cast some cheer on the day. Abby waved from across the square, the tiny Mrs Malady clinging to her arm.

Dear Abby, dealt such a harsh blow with her mother but fate had smiled kindly on Maggie the day it brought Abby into her life. The conversation with Mrs Malady seemed to be over as the frail woman waved to the good doctor and Abby crossed to meet them.

"Maggie! Boys!" Abby shouted.

Mathew and Liam jigged on the spot until Abby had crossed the square then nuzzled into her belly as she hugged them.

"They always love you," Maggie said.

"It's because my clothes smell of cake," Abby replied grinning at the two cheeky faces. "I spent most of the weekend baking chocolate buns."

The two boys seemed happy to cling to Abby's arms and rock back and forth. They must be getting tired.

Abby was another one who looked tired. Her usually rosy face was pale and drawn and anxious.

"Is Mrs Malady OK?" Maggie asked, wondering if she was the cause of concern. The old lady had been the cleaner at school, in between caring for her parents and bringing up her boy Billy, whom Maggie had taught.

"She's overwhelmed with stress, poor thing."

"What's the latest?"

"Losing the roof over her head."

"Isn't she in a council house? She used to share one of those concrete blocks by the station with her parents."

"She was moved out when they bulldozed the site for the new town houses. The council moved her to private accommodation, assuring her that housing benefit would make up the difference, but now that's capped and there's nowhere affordable to live."

"Christ." It was the last straw in this morning's disappointments. "It just doesn't stop, does it? Everything keeps changing, nothing for the better. Not even us."

Abby looked puzzled.

Maggie actually blushed, a rarity in one used to airing her every opinion. She had Richard and her relationship uppermost in her mind. Together for thirty years and, granted, drifting apart but at such a glacial pace it seemed like stability. Then six months ago, out of the blue, Richard had suggested a formal split, then divorce. Maggie, she insisted on telling herself, had been perfectly happy with their slow, cordial disintegration and wasn't sure why it had to change. But seeing Abby's alarm she deflected with, "Look at the children."

"Jude? Eli?"

"Who'd have thought, before Friday, that Eli would be intended for married bliss and Jude would be in crisis?"

Abby looked confused, rather shocked.

"Of course, it's lovely to have her home."

In fact with Eli and Selene, the two boys, her mother not yet in hospital and Jude staying for a few days, it was rather nice to be needed as mother, daughter and aunt again. Yes, what a contrast to Friday. At least dear Abby was a source of constancy.

"Jude's home?" Abby stuttered.

"Well, yes. Didn't you know?"

Abby twitched with the slightest shake of the head.

"She and Bill are taking a break. I've never seen her this distraught. She's been withdrawn the last couple of days. So unlike her. You know how well she copes with everything life throws at her. But this? It's really set her back. Did she not tell you?"

"No." Abby was white. "She's not said a thing."

12

Jude stared from the bedroom window, the sweep of lawn, swirling river, reds, greens and ochres of the wooded hill beyond blurring in her vision.

She shivered and pinched the dressing gown to her neck. She'd stirred all night, a victim to her chaotic and cyclic thoughts. She'd showered at some unearthly hour in the morning, only to wrap her naked body in the comfort of a dressing gown and return to her room.

The knot that wrung tight in her belly hadn't eased for a moment since Friday night. She didn't know how long she'd stood immobile in the garden, reeling from Eli's revelation. Though some part of her cried denial, a chill settled deep inside, dreading it might be true.

"Fucking hell, Jude." Bill's voice had shaken her from her trance. It was loud in the empty garden. "What the hell was that about?"

"Not now, please," she whispered. "I need to find Abby." Abby had to deny it. She couldn't be in love with her.

"That was fucking embarrassing." Bill smoothed absent hair over his scalp. "You made an absolute dick of me in there. Why didn't you say something? Just one word, Jude. That's all you had to say."

"I told you," she said weakly. "I need to find Abby."

"It always fucking Abby," he shouted. "It's always your bloody friend."

Jude was too stunned to respond.

"Abby's always your priority. She has been for years. When is it going to be me? What about us?"

"It will be, but not now, please. I need to find her. Her attacks. She could–"

"We can't put our lives on hold every fucking time Abby's upset."

"It's not like that." Jude shook her head, wishing the swirling chaos would stop. "Don't trivialise it."

"But do you need to be the one on call the whole time?"

"This time," she murmured. "I do."

"Why?"

Because this time, it might be her fault.

"I'm going to find her," Jude said and she stumbled towards the house.

She swam through the crowd, people laughing and congratulating Eli, children running everywhere.

Jude could see her friend in the light of the hallway. Abby's face was pink and swollen and light glistened on a trail of tears. For a moment she seemed to look at Jude, but instead of waiting she sought her coat from the hooks and hurried outside.

Abby was running away, and running away from her. Eli was telling the truth.

By the time Jude emerged from the crowd, Abby was down the front steps and scuttling into the night. Jude watched her in the glow of the streetlight, wiping at her face, then she disappeared beyond the orange halo into the dark.

For the first time in her life, Jude didn't run to Abby. There was nothing she could do, because she was the cause of Abby's pain. She stared into the night, Abby long gone, but her image vivid in Jude's thoughts, until Bill pushed past.

"I'm staying at the hotel," he growled and stormed down the steps.

His great show of leaving was weakened when he turned round, desperation flickering across his face. When Jude said nothing, his expression turned dark.

"That was fucking unbelievable, Jude. We should take a break."

He marched off, drunk and ego bruised, turning back twice to check on Jude still immobile on the door step.

And when the guests had gone, Jude took a sofa in her parents' sitting room and she sat in darkness and turmoil. A weekend later and the same issues still endlessly occupied Jude's thoughts.

When the hell did it start? Why hadn't Abby told her? What would have been the point, she reminded herself. Jude had never been partial to women, and she'd barely been single while she'd known Abby.

How had Abby hidden it for so long? Didn't it hurt to be close to the one you loved but could never have? And Jude had no doubt about the depth of Abby's love. She'd seen it crush her friend when Bill proposed.

Perhaps Jude should walk away. She paced the bedroom at the thought. It wasn't fair to torment Abby and tease her with friendship when Abby wanted more. Maybe this was the kindest cut. And just when Jude decided this was the painful but noble course of action she realised she couldn't walk away. Abby needed her. Her friend still suffered panic attacks.

"What the hell am I going to do?" Jude whispered and she slumped back onto the bed.

A creeping realisation dawned. What if Jude had encouraged her? Had she unintentionally toyed with her friend all these years – their closest of friendships, virtually living with her at the weekends?

"Shit," Jude groaned, head in hands.

But Abby always had a date. There was always someone after her. How was Jude to know? Although lately Abby cancelled dates at the drop of Jude's hat. Jude had taken it as

91

a sign of maturity – neither of them held hostage by teenage hormones or ego. What if it had been because Abby loved Jude more?

Did they flirt with each other? A little. A joke here and there, but nothing out of the ordinary. Abby's girlfriends had been much more risqué.

Had Jude ever found her attractive and let it show? Abby was without question pretty. She had beautiful eyes, cat-like and sparkling through her long fringe which she flicked to the side. Then those lips, full and wide that shone in a generous smile, the one that showed her love right up to her piercing eyes that fixed you with their deep regard. You were left in no doubt of the good soul inside when her friend smiled.

"How long?" Jude murmured.

Jude couldn't remember the first time she saw Abby, only that she was aware of the beautiful lesbian in halls who kindled many a woman's Sapphic fire. She did remember her first words. Abby had run into the changing rooms at the gym when Jude was putting on her sports bra. Abby had screeched to a halt, looked her up and down then coloured, realising what she'd done. Abby had flashed a naughty grin. "Nice tits," she'd said, then flounced out of the room.

Jude laughed despite herself. Typical Abby, bringing a smile to Jude's face even now in a memory. Then Jude realised Bill had nothing like that effect on her. He never had. In fact since he'd walked out throwing the words "We should take a break," at her, he'd barely entered her thoughts.

Oh fucking hell, Abby. Why did she have to fall in love with her? How were they meant to be friends without Jude hurting Abby every single day? Did every touch make Abby long for her? Did every hug trigger a painful craving? They couldn't carry on like that. Then the prospect of losing her dearest friend came crashing down again.

"I don't want to lose you," Jude murmured.

There was a gentle knock at the door.

"It's Abby," came the quiet voice from the other side.

Jude's heart leapt into her mouth, and she couldn't answer for a few moments. She cleared her throat and stood. "Come in."

The door opened slowly with its characteristic creak and Abby shuffled into the room. She wore such a mix of expressions on her face, she was always so open and easy to read. Hurt, for herself and perhaps Jude, with anxiety pinching at her forehead. And Jude could see it now, mixed in with the kind of deep love Jude shared, there was a longing also. Jude was torn between rushing to comfort her friend and sparing her with distance.

Abby remained tense by the door and Jude turned back to her garden view, wringing entwined fingers.

"I'm sorry," Abby murmured. "I've only just heard about Bill."

Jude bowed her head. There was silence.

"I," Abby hesitated. "I would have come sooner."

Jude knew she would. That was part of the problem. Abby came running whenever Jude needed. The silence descended again.

"I can stay if you like," Abby offered, her voice soft. "Or leave if you prefer."

Jude's heart plunged. What must Abby be going through, but still here she was, supporting Jude. At the same time Jude wanted to yell: "Why the fuck did you fall in love with me? You're taking away the best thing in my life, my best friend."

And Jude ached for her. She gulped down the lump in her throat. She wanted to turn back time to Friday evening and everything be the same again.

"I miss you," Jude wanted to say. "I want to hug you, take the piss out of you for not asking out Cheese Shop Lady, put silly braids in your hair and drink too much wine while watching a shitty film and fall asleep on the sofa with your head on my shoulder. I want it all back." How were they meant to do that now?

She heard Abby approach then whisper, "I'm so sorry things aren't good with Bill. I know it must be tearing you apart."

If only it was that.

"But I'm glad you're here today," Abby hesitated. "Because, if you marry Bill, I will miss you." And Abby's warm fingers slid between Jude's.

Whether it was her friend's honesty or the familiar touch she'd been craving, Jude's resistance collapsed and she spun round and clasped Abby to her. She clung on for dear life, pinching the folds of Abby's clothes and squeezing with fierce need as the tears started to fall.

"It's OK", Abby whispered beside her ear. "It's OK"

"I missed you. I missed you. I missed you."

"Me too."

Jude pulled her closer still, chest to chest, and she could feel Abby's heart beat beneath hers.

13

She was back. Her Jude was back. Abby felt the pain of Jude's heartbreak over Bill, but it was an overpowering relief to have her soulmate back.

"God, I missed you too." Abby had been ready to miss Jude for the rest of her life.

Jude's arm wrapped around Abby's waist, another cradled her head. Soft lips pressed against Abby's forehead and fingers stroked her hair.

"I'm sorry," Jude whispered beside her ear.

Abby assumed for not letting her know sooner. She closed her eyes, enjoying Jude close again and the soothing fingers through her hair.

"There's nothing to be sorry for."

As Jude stroked her hair, Abby let her head drop to her friend's shoulder, tired after the weekend of heartache and loneliness. She was dazed in the warmth of Jude's embrace and the scent which rose from her chest.

"I'm so sorry."

Abby pulled them tighter, her breasts snug against Jude's and their legs entwined, thigh slipping between thigh. Jude returned the embrace, urgent like lovers reconciling after an argument, desperate and relieved at the same time. The close warmth was addictive and Abby pulled at Jude, longing for the intimacy she'd craved.

"I missed you."

Jude's robe slipped a little and Abby's cheek touched bare skin. Her friend's tender naked body was another slip away. Abby's nipples tingled with the awareness and she ached where Jude held her. A brush inside her thighs as Jude shifted her weight ignited a glow of arousal inside and her breath deepened, no longer with anguish but a kindling of desire. The warmth of reconciliation intensified the heat.

Yikes. What was she doing? Abby stepped back abruptly.

"So." She cleared her throat and squeezed Jude's arms. "Um."

This was so not appropriate. Really not on. Unseemly arousal when comforting your best friend who's just broken up with her boyfriend, definitely not in the friendship handbook. Abby took a deep breath, slapped hands on hips and resolutely stared at the wardrobe.

"So. Erm. Tea?"

That was good. Very proper. Best way to care for anyone. Tea.

When Jude didn't answer Abby was forced to turn round. Jude had a bemused expression on her face which flickered between melancholy and amusement.

"Shall I get us a cuppa?" Abby offered again, hopeful. "Nice cuppa tea?" She stared, cheeks burning, and elsewhere glowing.

"I would like one very much," Jude said quietly. "I'll get dressed and come down."

"Great," Abby said. So very proper. "Nice cuppa tea."

And she hurtled down the stairs like a truant child.

"Tea. Tea. Where's the shitting tea?"

Abby had made the drink a thousand times in this kitchen, but with the arousal quivering inside she was buggered if she knew where it was now. Abby needed something to distract her, because this was a wildly inappropriate time to be having those feelings between her legs. Frankly, she could do with popping an ice-cube down her knickers before she went near Jude again.

Especially when Jude was naked beneath her dressing gown. Because really, there was nothing Abby liked better than a robe falling away to nudity with a slip of a finger. Especially off Jude. Oh Jude. Oh, a slip of a finger.

"Oh Jesus," Abby cursed out loud. "Get a grip. You're a terrible friend."

But she'd missed her. She was in love with her. And frankly she couldn't think of a more attractive woman on this earth. It was only human to feel liquid warmth when someone that beautiful pulled you close, their naked breasts cushioning your chest, their wondrous thighs slipping in between yours. Abby groaned.

"You are a terrible, terrible friend."

Tea. Tea. Where was the tea? She flung cupboards open and banged them shut. Why couldn't she locate a simple beverage? It didn't happen often that Abby became so overwhelmed. She genuinely felt a platonic love for Jude when cuddled on the sofa. It's just sometimes Abby did slip.

Like that time on holiday in Greece. Jude was resplendent, gazing out to sea from the balcony. The setting sun shone through her diaphanous white dress, her perfect breasts in silhouette and voluptuous thighs a finger width apart. Abby had stared transfixed, agog at Jude's beauty. She was like a Greek goddess of ample bosom and full hip. "It's beautiful, isn't it?" Jude had said glancing back at Abby. "You look in awe." Abby had choked on her ouzo, joined her friend on the balcony and tried not to think of divine thighs and that tempting fingers width between them. She'd failed of course, like she did now as her friend came into the kitchen, soft thighs no doubt stroking beautifully together.

"Have you lost the tea?" Jude smiled.

Abby had lost the entire plot. This was bad. One, Jude was getting over her long-term boyfriend. Two, Abby had rules about this. And they were, another list. She liked lists.

One, no lusting after Jude. Appreciating beauty was one thing, staring at breasts and imagining them next to hers another. And she wished she hadn't thought about that as a wave of appreciation throbbed inside her.

Two, if she failed with One, there was absolutely no imagining Jude during those private moments, you know, she could barely think of the phrase, when she touched herself.

Three, and definitely no imagining Jude doing that either, at any time, ever.

And this was the trouble with listing everything she wasn't allowed to imagine – she, of course, immediately imagined it all. And in this condition that was fatal.

Jude stood close in the snug kitchen. Abby could feel her. The warmth was as good as a caress. If they'd been lovers, they'd be having red-hot make-up sex on the floor.

"Tea." Abby groaned. "I really need to find tea."

"Hello dears." Maggie sauntered into the kitchen with shopping bags.

The last thing Abby needed was another witness to her state. Abby looked at her hands and fiddled with her nails, which were perfectly trimmed and had no reason to be fiddled with whatsoever.

"Um. Um." Abby attempted some vocal variety. "Erm."

"Abby was looking for the tea," Jude said, moving further into the kitchen to make room for Maggie. She leant against the kitchen top snuggled next to Abby, a quizzical look in her eyes. The warmth was intoxicating. Abby was pummelled by her breast and hugged by the side of her bottom. It was heavenly.

"Mmmmmm," Abby moaned. Oh no. "Mmm. Jude's right?"

"Tea?" Maggie said. "Eli drank it all again. If he must drink it by the bucket, he really should stock up again. Here." She passed over a yellow box. "There was some in the shopping."

So, they hadn't had tea. Well that was an evil little trick for the universe to play. No, Abby didn't look aroused to distraction, clattering her way red-faced through the cupboards. Oh no.

"Well," said Maggie. "You both seem better. I thought you were looking a bit peaky earlier, Abby."

"Really?" Abby replied several notes too high.

Dammit. Why did her every feeling have to be apparent. "I can read you like a book," almost everyone had said to her at some point. Well hopefully not this particular book. Not this X-rated chapter at least. Because Jude must never know of Abby's feelings on this particular topic. Ever.

And even more catastrophic would be Maggie knowing. One thing was certain with Maggie. She did not approve of lesbian relationships. Although she'd never shown Abby the slightest ill will – quite the opposite – it was an infuriating constant: Maggie's inability to see lesbian relationships as an option for Abby, let alone anyone else. God knows how she'd judge Abby's penchant for her daughter.

"In fact, you're looking radiant Abby," Maggie said, drawing her head back. "How are you feeling?"

Ashamed had to be the most honest answer, as the mix of arousal, embarrassment and a chill of humiliation did an unholy dance within. Jude shifted closer to let Maggie put down her bags and Abby was overwhelmed by the warm glow.

"Nice," she mumbled. Then inwardly groaned. No-one ever said "nice".

"You two are so good for each other." Maggie clapped her hands together. "You always have been. You can see it in the way you glow."

Oh.

"Really?" Abby said through a tight smile. "Well, look at that," she said turning up a wrist, a bare wrist. She never wore a watch. She always used her phone for the time.

"Look at what dear?" Maggie asked.

"The time," Abby squeaked. "It's probably passing."

"It is," Maggie said, lifting her sleeve to reveal her man's watch. "God, it's only twenty past eight. I feel like I've been up for days."

"Twenty past eight?" Abby said wide-eyed. "I need to go. I'm late."

She shuffled between Maggie and Jude, very careful not to make nipple contact with the latter. "Late. And. Stuff," she said as she stared down at Jude's body, wonderful body, a fraction away from hers.

"I'll see you out," Jude said.

"It's OK. I know the way," Abby squealed.

If she could make it outside without touching Jude, everything would be all right. Just a few more steps. And she was there, over the threshold into cool morning air. Aaaaaaaaaaaaaah. Like a cold shower.

She turned round, a great deal more composed.

"So," she said.

"So," Jude replied. She leaned on the door frame, arms crossed and a sad smile on her face.

"See you later?" Abby offered. "Maybe?"

"Yes, we should," Jude replied.

"Good."

"And Mum's right you know."

"About what?"

"You are beautiful." Jude gave her an appreciative look which made Abby melt inside. "You look stunning today. Just like that time on the balcony in Greece."

Shit.

14

So that's what it was: The coy look, the rosy cheeks, the sudden withdrawal. After all these years it made sense to Jude. Those rare moments when Abby would pull away, when she glowed her most beautiful.

Abby looked stunning in those moments; Jude's heart would race with admiration. She didn't find Abby's reaction embarrassing. Actually, she laughed at her thoughts, she found it adorable.

What the hell was she going to do? She shook her head and resumed her amble up the street. How different everything was from her stroll through the square on Friday evening. And she didn't mean just her personal situation. The church was for sale and her mother on the rampage about that and everything else. Bill was sending a stream of messages, each more savage than the last. Jude stumbled at the recollection. How vicious people turned when rejected, and she pushed the thought of his latest actions from her mind to spare herself.

Peering across the square, Jude detected further rumblings of dissatisfaction. A group of elderly folks gathered around the sweet stall, switching between moaning about the state of the nation and the relative merits of toffees over fudge. One couple was berating a stall holder for selling a shampoo containing glitter while a mother surreptitiously replaced her bottle and sneaked off to Celtic jewellery. Had it always been like this or were the cracks new? The Conservative Club with its hanging baskets of blue flowers seemed to sit less comfortably beside the café proclaiming "The People's Republic of Ludbury's finest coffee".

Jude sat on the end of a bench at the edge of the square and sighed louder than she'd intended so the teenage girl occupant at the other end twitched up from her phone.

The girl gave Jude a shy smile.

"Sorry," Jude said, "I'm in a grumpy mood, like the rest of the square this morning."

The girl grinned and turned back to her phone.

Jude closed her eyes, dug hands deep into the pockets of her woollen coat and dropped her head back to enjoy the sun's rays. Her limbs were leaden and it was satisfying to relax into lethargy.

"Look at that," a disgruntled voice said. "Always got their noses in an iPhone. Shouldn't you be at school anyway?"

Jude opened her eyes as two pairs of legs shuffled past, one in grey, one in beige. The muttering continued as they walked away, not waiting for an answer from her companion on the bench. The teenager blushed crimson and peeped at Jude.

"My mum's getting shopping then taking me to the doctor's."

"It's OK," Jude said. "You don't have to defend yourself. You carry on enjoying whatever's on your phone."

The girl frowned a little and surveyed Jude's face. "You waiting for the doctor too?"

Jude laughed. She must look grave. "No. I'm fine. In fact I am a doctor."

"Oh," the girl said. Actually she sounded impressed. She shuffled a little closer and tipped her phone toward Jude. "It's school work. I've got a mock exam on *Bleak House* and wanted to read some other Dickens for background. I can get them free on my phone."

"I do that, get classics for free on my reader."

"Are you Mrs Goodman's daughter?" the girl said.

Jude sat up, surprised she'd been recognised. "Yes, I am."

"Is she all right?"

"Yes. Well, as much as she ever is."

"It's just, she doesn't teach at school no more."

"Funding cuts I'm afraid," Jude replied. "They asked her to take early retirement."

"Oh. Shame. I liked her."

"Really?"

"Yeah. We all did. Never a boring lesson with Mrs Goodman." The girl's grin widened.

Well that was true. Never a boring moment with her mother. Jude had craved mundanity as a child.

"She used to talk to us," the girl continued. "Not like the other teachers who lecture. She was interested in what we had to say."

Jude smiled mischievously. "I bet she loved it when you argued back."

"She did." The girl's eyes flashed. "She used to encourage it. It was the only lesson where we were allowed to argue with each other. You know, discuss things. All the others were 'shut up, learn your work, pass exams'."

"You found her inspiring?"

"Yes, we did."

That sounded like her mother, and a remembrance of childhood idolatry poignantly mixed with contemporary frustrations stirred inside. Jude could recall in vivid colour her mother putting on plays in the garden, Eli dressed in a tutu and Jude as the prince. She created worlds for them, the garden blurring into a magical woodland, the patio becoming plains of volcanic lava. She'd even incorporated the river into the scenery one summer, when the extended family were invited to watch. It had ended in disaster – a great aunt's dog plunging into the river and spraying the assembled audience. Eli had a tantrum and pushed Jude in the river too. Her mother had almost stopped breathing she'd laughed so hard.

Yes, those were the moments Maggie excelled. Then there were the times of desperation and strife. Jude closed her eyes. What a vexing character her mother was. What drove her constant irritation? She'd rage at the wind some days, telling it not to blow. What fuelled it all?

"My mum's coming now," the girl said. "Will you say hi to yours?"

Jude came to. "Of course. I'll remember you to her. What's your name?"

"Amelia."

"Good luck with your mock exams."

Amelia smiled as she turned to go. "Good luck with whatever you're going through."

Jude laughed. "Thanks. I'll need it."

And like that, her spirits eased. A pleasant interaction with some good soul and the world seemed more hopeful. How precious those characters were.

Jude wandered through the square and towards the supermarket at the top of Broad Street in search of Jammy Dodger biscuits – comfort food to soothe Bill's latest and perhaps final act. She looked down the wide avenue instinctively seeking out Abby's surgery. And there her friend was, another good soul, stepping out into the sunshine.

She watched as Abby skipped from the ex-townhouse surgery and started down the terraced street, giving her fringe a flick from her face. Jude checked her watch. Her friend was running late.

Jude was about to call after her. It was natural to hail Abby, wanting to indulge in her company. But then what? Jude stood at a loss, wordless and feet heavy on the ground. This was impossible.

She turned away with resignation, but felt her friend's presence more. Emptiness gnawed at her stomach and she could sense the pull from Abby on her back. The strength of longing was as powerful as for any lover.

"I can't bear staying away from you," Jude whispered.

She peeped back and watched her friend's silhouette beneath the sun-filled arch of the gate house. Her shape caught her eye and Jude studied her friend's physique, expecting to find it changed. Who was she now? Abby's passion made Jude think of her in a different light. She watched – seeking out differences – only finding the same wonderful woman, the familiar sway of hips, fingers slipping through hair and flicking her fringe away. As Abby strode down the street, Jude was drawn after her, not wanting to lose sight of her friend.

At the bottom of the street, Abby unlocked her cottage door with a swift and practiced movement and disappeared inside. She'd be having lunch at home before, if Jude recalled, spending Monday afternoon at the care home. Walking down the street, Jude caught up, tapped the iron knocker and squinted through the glass panes. A sash window thudded above her and Abby peered down, her long fringe a curtain around her face.

"Hey." Abby grinned. "How you doing?"

Jude smiled at the greeting and her heart filled at her friend's warmth. It was like Abby always was.

"Come in," Abby shouted. "It's…" Her sentence was interrupted by a sharp inhalation. Eyes scrunched tight, mouth and nose elongated then she sneezed loudly. "…open. Excuse me." She sniffed.

Jude sniggered. "Maximilian broken in again?"

"I swear that cat picks the lock with his claws." Abby rolled her eyes. "I can't find a way in this time..." Her mouth stretched into another sneeze.

Jude laughed affectionately. Abby was lovely, even when sneezing, and although Jude was trying to keep a cool distance it tugged at her heart.

"Are you rushing out?" she called up.

"No. Grabbing lunch. Do you want…" Abby waved her hand towards the door as she was gripped by another sneeze.

"I'll come in." Jude said, shaking her head and smiling as she opened the door.

It was darker inside the cottage, the sunlight bright in the street and through the back door, but cosy. It was like the little house hugged you when you stepped inside.

Abby's beloved Roberts radio, a gift from Maggie, was quietly chattering The World at One on the kitchen top and Jude breathed in, relieved to find the sanctuary familiar. It smelled of chocolate cake, fresh oranges and cinnamon. And indeed, as was so often the case, a small mountain of chocolate muffins was stacked on the kitchen top, a glass of juice stood half drunk and bundles of cinnamon sticks hung from hooks on the kitchen cupboards. It smelled like home.

"Put the kettle on," Abby shouted down.

Without needing to search, Jude grabbed the kettle and filled it from the sink by the window. She rummaged in the corner cupboard for two Penguin novel china mugs – *Wuthering Heights* for Abby and a chipped *Room of One's Own* for herself. She'd bought a set of six for Abby when they'd started as house officers at Shrewsbury Royal. Smiling at the fixture in her life, Jude popped a teabag in each and wandered around the room as the kettle began to gurgle.

The stove was ready to be lit and the sofa too inviting to ignore. She slumped down with an easy confidence and cuddled a plush cushion to her belly. Above hung a painting of Marloes Sands in Pembrokeshire. She'd seen it so many times she didn't need to look to see the texture of the brush strokes and ochre and slate colours that made up the distinctive coast. Abby had bought it on holiday with the Goodmans six years ago. In fact Jude knew the origin of almost every item in the cottage.

She'd viewed the cottage with Abby. They'd decorated at the weekends when Abby moved in. Upstairs, she knew every inch of the spare room – Abby called it Jude's room.

Sitting here made her relax. This is where her troubles fell away. Not her parents' house. Not the flat she shared with Bill. This was home.

Abby skipped from the bottom of the stairs.

"Hey." She smiled. "Good to see you out of the house." And she knelt down and held Jude's hands.

Look at that smile. Jude hesitated, not knowing what to say. She stared into Abby's eyes, those deep blue eyes which showed only love. Abby was like a tonic. A cup of warm comfort.

"It's good to see you," Abby said, and she hugged her. It was a platonic, affectionate squeeze with no repeat of the earlier flushes. Jude was relieved, but also strangely disappointed, and she stared at her friend in fascination.

"You want some lunch?" Abby said, getting to her feet. "It's just tomato and mozzarella with a bit of ciabatta."

"Sounds perfect," Jude said and she wandered after her.

Abby slid two loaves into the oven and rifled in the fridge and without a word threw a couple of tomatoes to Jude. Abby sliced the mozzarella, Jude drizzled olive oil, and with a sprinkle of basil leaves from a window ledge plant still flourishing in the autumn sun, they quietly prepared their snack, like they did at weekends.

They peered as one to the back door and seeing the sunlight on the table outside, took their plates into the courtyard garden. A ball of white on the table opened a squint of green eye then reformed the perfect sphere of fluff.

"It's OK Maximilian. We can use our knees." Jude tutted.

Abby bit into her bread dripping with olive oil, and wiped a little from her chin. "Sorry to rush," she said, "It's the care home round this afternoon."

"I know."

Abby turned bashful and stared at her plate, as if remembering their troubles. "Are you staying long? In Ludbury?"

"I've no idea," Jude said honestly.

"Is work OK? Are they letting you take a few days off?"

"Actually they've withdrawn my contract."

"What?"

"I'd come to the end and it was due for renewal but…"

"Bill?" Abby said, her face anxious. "Bill's mate's the manager there."

Jude nodded.

"Well that's," Abby, being a generous soul, stopped herself from saying something she'd regret. "I know they're friends, but that's not fair," she finished.

Jude shrugged with heavy shoulders. "I'm not surprised."

"You'll pick up another position in no time, but how does Bill expect you to take that? You've got to be civil to each other while you sort things out."

Jude swallowed her mouthful of bread and a lump which was forming in her throat. "I think he wants me to disappear as soon as possible."

"But you've got a flat together. It's not going to be easy."

"Apparently it is. He's bagged up my things and left them on the side of the road."

"What?"

Jude looked away. "Dad's gone to pick them up for me. With Celia's surgery cancelled he's free today."

Abby didn't reply and from the corner of her eye Jude knew she didn't move. Eventually she set her plate on the seat and came closer.

"I'm sorry," Abby murmured and she drew Jude's head to her bosom. "I'm so sorry."

Jude was raw again. The comfort and warmth of Abby enveloping her unleashed vulnerabilities and the emotion began to swell. She clung to Abby's arm, clasping it around her.

"You can't control who falls in love with you, or who you fall in love with," Abby murmured. "And people get hurt when they split up. It's rubbish. But that doesn't give him an excuse to treat you like this."

"I haven't been fair to him," Jude stuttered. "I don't blame him for being angry. I wasn't as committed to him as I should have been."

Abby crouched in front of her and held her hands. "Were you honest with him?"

"Yes."

"Were you hurtful?"

"No. Not deliberately."

"Then you can't blame yourself." Abby pulled Jude in again, her arms wrapped around. Jude closed her eyes, safe and warm. Home.

"It's good to spend time with you," Abby whispered after a while, still holding her tight. "Even though it's not under the best circumstances, I always enjoy your company." Abby hesitated and Jude's heart pounded wondering what she'd say next. "You know," Abby continued, "I've taken your friendship for granted at times. Other times, I realise how precious it is."

Jude knew when Abby spoke of, how devastated Abby had been at Bill's proposal and the loss of her friend.

"I always appreciate it," Abby said. "However much time you spend with me, it will always be appreciated."

Jude clasped her fingers desperate around Abby's arm. What could she say? That she knew Abby was in love with her. That Abby's pain distressed Jude more than cutting Bill from her life. That Jude adored her friend and hated she'd suffered all these years. Jude wished more than anything she could make Abby happy, but had no idea how.

"I'd better go. I'm running a little late," Abby said gently when Jude couldn't respond. "Come with me?"

Jude stared into Abby's kind face, holding her arms so firmly she couldn't think how to release her.

"I'd like that."

And after lunch, they walked together, down the street, over the river, through the woods, Jude not letting go of her friend for a second.

15

"Dr Abby!"

It was as if the entire care home had rustled up their best clothes and sat waiting for Abby's entrance. The old-manor day room erupted when Jude and Abby walked in and Jude couldn't help giggle at her friend's reception.

"Dr Abby! I got my new teeth," a woman shouted across the room.

Jude guessed the woman was in her nineties, a frail little thing who hardly took up any of her armchair. She flashed her gnashers in an ecstatic smile and Jude would put good money on there being a large character in that small frame.

"She doesn't want to see your teeth dear," a large woman beside her said. She grasped the smaller lady's hand with a generous arm, which wobbled a great deal. "It's the dentist who does that. Dr Abby wants to hear about my shingles."

And it was a credit to Abby that she greeted them both with enthusiasm. She knelt down before the incongruous pair who looked like they hadn't moved from the chairs in years and took the woman's hand.

"Bev, those teeth are the icing on an already beautiful smile. Of course I want to see them."

"Bless you, sweetheart," Bev replied. "See Dot. Knew she'd be interested. I told her all about having them fitted last time she was here."

"That's not what she's here for. She needs to hear about my shingles and these headaches I keep having."

"I'm here for the whole afternoon," Abby said, "to hear everything from your migraines to your dentures."

"See," Bev said.

"First I must catch up with Ray and Dawn though," Abby said kindly.

"You go ahead love," Dot said. "She's not said a word all week, just groans and rocks to and fro. Poor old Ray."

Abby got up and crossed the room touching Jude on the arm as she passed. "I'll catch you later," she said. "Walk back with you after you've seen Celia?"

Jude grinned. "See how it goes. You're in demand. You might be here all night."

Abby wandered to a corner where an elderly man and, Jude assumed, his wife sat next to an upright piano. The man gripped his partner's hand and gazed into her eyes, but she stared into space. It was the state which frightened Jude most at her clinic, more than cancer or any other ailment – people losing themselves.

She turned away, praying for the hundredth time that the fate not befall her or anyone dear. Then her spirits lifted as she spied Celia by the window, engrossed in a game of chess with Desmond.

"Sorry to disturb you," she said.

Celia looked up with the sharp precision of a woman who could annihilate the opposition in five moves, but not the sharp focus. She peered over the top of her half-moon glasses and relaxed into a smile.

"Oh hello, dear. What a nice surprise," she said, removing her specs. She glanced over the room which still murmured with the excitement of Abby's entrance.

"You're here with Abby?" Celia's expression was suddenly penetrating. Accusing somehow. Then as quickly as the severity had fallen it lifted again and Celia was her welcoming grandmother once more.

111

Another wave of laughter rolled over the room.

"Yes, Abby must be here," Celia chuckled. "They do look forward to her rounds."

"Better keep them in order," Desmond groaned and he heaved himself to his feet. "You mind taking over? She's thrashing me anyway."

"I will gladly hasten defeat," Jude replied.

"Don't worry. I have no pride. If you last another three moves I'll be impressed," Desmond said, as he shuffled off across the room.

Jude sat down and leaned over the board.

"Don't let that amenable Brummie accent deceive you," Celia muttered. "Sharp as a tack that one."

"I don't doubt it."

"Well, my dear. You're looking better for some fresh air." Celia squeezed Jude on the arm. "How are you?"

"Good. I had lunch with Abby, we took a walk through the woods and I thought I'd check up on you."

Celia hesitated, scrutiny again in her eyes, before "Oh, Still here. Same gammy hip. Grateful for Desmond's company."

"Have they rescheduled the operation?" Jude asked, aware she had to speak louder.

"No. It's a matter of waiting all over again I think."

"You should be a priority," Jude said, leaning closer to Celia, but she didn't reply and they both looked towards the source of the increasing noise.

All eyes were turned to the corner where the old man and his absent wife sat.

"Go on, Abby," Ray said. "You know I can't anymore." He lifted his hands, swollen and gnarled with arthritis at the knuckles.

Abby coloured and peeped towards Jude and Celia.

"Go on, Dr Abby," Bev and Dot chorused. "We'll join in too."

Abby stroked the back of her head, always a sign she was nervous. What were they asking of her? Then to Jude's surprise, Abby took her place in front of the piano. She placed her fingers on the keys and although it was too quiet for Jude to hear at first she could catch the rhythm. The one-two-three had the room swaying in time. But she could hear Ray's voice and his smile was clear. He held his wife's hand and rocked to and fro to the first verse.

"Is that…?" Jude frowned. "From Oliver?"

Celia nodded. Still Abby played, too quiet for Jude to hear, but as soon as Ray finished the verse the whole room took a deep breath for the chorus.

And "Oom pah pah" was sung with volume and relish throughout the room. Abby grinned and pounded the chords on the piano to the delight of the residents.

"Again," they chorused and another round of "Oom pah pah" rose through the room as Abby launched back into the keyboard. It had an energy which seemed to lift the residents from their seats. Again a deep breath and "Oom pah pah", this time with fists swinging up into the air.

"My mum loves this one," Desmond said and he offered his hand to a middle-aged colleague and, to the delight of the residents, began a rudimentary waltz around the room.

"Encore, Abby," Bev and Dot shouted, and Abby happily obliged, lifting her hands higher then pounding the chords for another rendition of the chorus.

Jude's mouth gaped open. When on earth had Abby learned to play the piano? It was nowhere near accomplished, but what she lacked in polish she made up for in gusto and it was impossible not to smile while Abby gave it her all and the entire room moved to the song.

"I didn't know she did this." Jude laughed.

Celia gave her an astute look. "I think Abby is one of those people who could surprise you for a lifetime, and always in the best way."

"When did she start?" Abby didn't play brilliantly, but well enough to thrash out a tune and bring a great deal of happiness.

"She plays at your mother's," Celia said, "when she comes for dinner on Wednesdays. She plays by ear and she's been teaching herself sheet music. Mainly she practices tunes for the folks down here."

Jude couldn't believe her eyes, or ears. "Why didn't she tell me?"

"Perhaps it never came up," Celia suggested. "Perhaps she was embarrassed."

"Why?"

"You and Eli are so accomplished," Celia replied. "She possibly didn't want to bother you with her tinkering?"

"Did she say that?"

"Not in as many words."

Jude was strangely delighted by this fresh view of her friend. It was unnerving finding something else she hadn't known, but also thrilling.

Abby peered over her shoulder to survey the room, the words of the chorus on her lips, then she spied Jude. "Sorry," she mouthed in an exaggerated way. "Awful." She nodded to her hands.

Jude couldn't agree. Look what Abby did to the room. Ray and his wife were rocking together and she was gazing at him with faint recognition in her eyes. There was confusion there, perhaps at seeing her husband an old man, but definite recognition and love. Ray swayed and sang his heart out, even though he sniffed between lines.

Jude stood and clapped to the song as she stared at Abby.

"I'm terrible," Abby mouthed, blushing.

"No," Jude murmured. "You're wonderful."

Abby rounded off with a slow and emphatic "Oom pah pah" and the whole room applauded each other and the dancing staff who had twirled around the room.

Jude sat again, not taking her eyes off Abby. People were reaching for her, entreating her to play again as she shook her head, shy and smiling, and pointed to her medical bag. How dazzling Abby was. Jude had always appreciated that Abby was pretty. But right now her sheer generosity of spirit shone through and lifted her to beauty. Jude was transfixed by Abby brightening the place with an almost visible glow. It made Jude warm inside.

"She's come a long way, hasn't she?"

Jude snapped her attention to Celia who studied her with an unwavering gaze.

"She's a special woman, our Abby," Celia continued.

Jude picked a bishop from the chessboard and twirled it between her fingers, more to distract from Celia's scrutiny than any intention to play. "Yes, she is. Very special."

"So different from the broken girl you brought home."

Jude peeked over to Abby. She was in her element here, helping others, but the fragility was still there. "She is," Jude said. "She needs us though."

Celia made a non-committal noise. "Hmm. I wonder."

Jude pinched the chess piece tighter. "What do you mean?"

"I wonder if she'll ever find what she wants."

"I don't follow."

"Sometimes, I think she'd be better off without us."

Jude stopped twirling the piece and stared at it.

"Do we hold her back?" Celia said. "Me and Maggie mothering her. And you..."

Jude twitched.

"...You've been her crutch."

Jude was acutely aware of Celia's eyes fixed upon her. She took a breath and played the bishop, as if unmoved.

"Perhaps that's not what she needs anymore," Celia offered, reaching for a white knight. "It's been a long time since her mother died. And, yes, look at her. See how she helps so many. But what does she need? Isn't it time she had happiness? Real happiness."

Jude swallowed. Celia was frighteningly on point. "Do you mean love?" she asked, her voice faltering.

"Yes."

Celia made her move, her piece tapping onto the board. Jude was rigid.

"If she can't find it here. Isn't it time we let her go?" Celia said.

Jude trembled. "Maybe she could find it here?"

It was Celia's turn to hesitate. "Can she? Is that possible? Is it even wise?"

Jude gulped again. She was shocked at the idea of Abby leaving Ludbury, leaving them all. Actually it was horrifying. "Wouldn't you miss her?" Jude couldn't help that her voice was full of emotion and she moved a piece as a distraction.

"Yes." Celia's look was piercing. "But I can't bear to see her chained. We have nurtured and loved her, and she returns that love many times over. But if we can't give her what she needs, then we should let her go."

Jude inhaled, not knowing what to say. "I let Bill go," she said, so quickly the words ran together. "I couldn't give him what he needed."

"A brave and right thing to do, though I imagine it wasn't pleasant."

"No, it wasn't."

"And what do you need?" Celia said.

Abby. I want Abby. I don't know in what way, or how to do it. But I want Abby.

Before Jude could vocalise her thoughts, Celia said. "Do you ever wonder," still she fixed Jude with her stare, "if you chose Bill so you could see Abby. Because it fitted in with your life here?"

Jude's heart beat hard and cold inside. She was only half aware of the approaching footsteps.

"Well that's me done," Abby said, then paused. "What have you been playing?"

Jude focussed on the board and errant pieces.

"They're all over the place." Abby laughed.

"I don't know," Jude said hesitating. "I don't know."

16

Abby took Jude's arm and held her close as they took the route along the city walls back to the citadel.

"You look tired," Abby said with a sympathetic smile. "Let's get you home."

"I don't want to go back yet," Jude replied. She needed the balm of Abby's company too much.

"You can stay at mine. You're always welcome."

Jude caught the faint blush on Abby's cheeks as she suggested it. And nothing could have been more inviting. Cosying up on the sofa in Abby's warm company was just what Jude needed. But it wasn't fair.

"Thank you," Jude said. "I'd better stay at Mum's."

They turned up the hill and Jude sighed at the prospect of internment at Maggie's and listening to her rant about everything from religion to the price of eggs.

"I wish you could see her through my eyes," Abby said.

"Who?"

"Maggie."

"Oh." Jude blushed, ashamed her dread was so transparent.

"I was assuming that enormous sigh was about her."

"Yes, it was."

"She's a special woman," Abby said.

"That we can agree on." Jude laughed.

"I mean it." Abby tugged on her arm to chastise her. "I can't count the incredible moments with her."

Jude bit back her retort.

"Do you remember the second Christmas I stayed in Ludbury?"

Jude did. It was not long after Abby had spread her mother's ashes on Stepley Hill, a beautiful countryside resting place.

"I dreaded Christmas without Mum. She was all I could think of that time of year. But Christmas morning," Abby hesitated as she focussed on the memory. "It was early, before breakfast and presents. Maggie ordered us to get dressed, put on our hats and marched us out to Stepley Hill. It sparkled with frost in the dawn sunlight." Abby smiled. "We were surrounded by a cloud of steaming breath – you, me, Maggie and Richard, Eli too. She took my hand."

And Jude could remember it as clearly as Abby. They'd huddled in the Welsh hills, in the centre of the stone circle where Brenda, Abby's mum, had been laid to rest.

"Do you want to say something?" Maggie had asked. Abby was too choked to speak. Maggie swept her under an arm and Abby shut her eyes tight with grief.

"Hello Brenda," Maggie said to the lands. "This is Abby's Christmas too and we wanted to start ours by visiting you." She sniffed, perhaps with the cold air. "I wanted to tell you Abby is doing so well at university. She's had a brilliant year. She might be too modest to say. You know her well enough for that to be true." And she squeezed Abby tighter. "I wish I'd met you, Brenda. I know I would have loved you, because how could I not love someone who brought our Abby into the world. Merry Christmas, dear Brenda. We'll take care of Abby, always."

Abby and Jude stopped in the street, baking in the autumn sunshine. "I don't think Maggie realises how much it meant to me, to have Mum as part of the holidays and you all share

119

my grief. It let me enjoy the rest of the day, and I am the luckiest woman in the world to have Maggie in my life."

Jude blinked, affected by Abby's gratitude. Yes, Jude did appreciate how her mother inspired generations, like the girl she'd met in the square, and how fiercely Maggie loved and protected those dear to her.

But that didn't make her any less fucking annoying. And even as Jude thought the words she could hear them in Maggie's voice. Maybe that's why she grated so much on Jude and not on Abby. Because Maggie sometimes surfaced in Jude's personality. Jude was so like her father she guarded against his worst traits, then her mother's reared their heads and took her by surprise. And Maggie was the voice in Jude's head often.

"I think she reminds me of myself," Jude tried to explain.

Abby gave her a sad smile and touched her cheek. "Perhaps that's why I love you both so much."

Jude's mouth dropped open. She could feel the emotion rise up her throat and fill her eyes. She blinked. Abby's love was a gift and Jude felt undeserving of both her friend and Maggie.

"How about," Abby said, her melancholy smile still holding all the warmth of her love, "we get you a loaded hot chocolate."

"That," Jude said, "is the best suggestion I've heard all day."

"Good. Come on, Jude, and don't spare the whipped cream."

"With marshmallows on top."

Jude sat in the Victorian conservatory of the Garden Café on their favourite sofa, the central fountain trickling nearby. It was the blissful, quiet end of the day, the sun setting through silver birch beyond the windows. There were few customers – a mother with two toddlers, both unnaturally quiet and each gumming a biscuit to oblivion, and an old

120

couple opposite, side by side with the same voluminous hot chocolate Abby had ordered.

What was Jude going to do? How could she reconcile wanting Abby, her friend needing her, but love separating them? She'd never desired a woman. Right now Jude wished she could sweep Abby off her feet. It would make life so much simpler. It would also irk Maggie no end and a squirm of pleasurable bloody-mindedness tingled inside at the thought before Jude chastised herself with Abby's voice.

"I wish I was a lesbian," she muttered, then surreptitiously looked around the café. Toddlers continued to gum their biscuits unperturbed, their mother dozed on her arm, and the old couple were giggling among themselves.

"Here we go." Abby passed down a precarious saucer and tall mug of hot chocolate with waves of double cream and clouds of marshmallows.

"Bliss." Jude sighed.

Abby shuffled her bottom beside Jude's without ceremony and lifted her drink to her mouth. It was impossible to tackle without looking like you'd been mauled by a Mr Whippy and Abby sported a moustache of cream. Jude did the same and was similarly afflicted.

"Suits you," Abby grinned, the cream melting and running down the sides of her mouth so she resembled a member of Sgt. Pepper's band.

"Come here," Jude said. "It's going to drip on your suit." Jude scooped up a serviette to catch a drip. She dabbed the blob of cream back on to Abby's cheeks then swept up a curl of milky moustache.

"You look like a very odd Salvador Dali," Jude said.

Abby giggled at the same time as the old lady across the café. The woman was laughing at her husband and a blob of cream stuck to his nose. He raised his hand to wipe it away but the woman cried "Wait!" She leaned close with a serviette raised, her eyes squinting in concentration. Then without warning she licked it off his nose. "That's mine," she said and they both burst out laughing.

Jude smiled at the couple; then it hit her. Their behaviour, ease and comfort mirrored hers and Abby's. That's what they were like – a happy old couple. She instinctively reached out for Abby's hand at the thought. They'd been like it for years. Wasn't that how the best relationships endured – being close friends more than anything else?

Jude sat up, suddenly hopeful for the first time in days. She watched the couple, the woman muttering and searching her handbag. Her husband tutted and eyed her head. She reached up and snatched her glasses perched in her hair and they dissolved into giggles again. Jude's heart ached. It was the kind of happiness everyone searched for. She looked down at Abby's hand in hers. And she already had it here with Abby.

If Abby had been a man, one she'd not been attracted to, she still could have made the common next step – marrying your best friend. They had a far better basis for a lifetime of love than with a handsome face in the crowd. It wasn't crazy to settle down with a friend, especially one she adored and who depended on her, then hope that romantic love would follow.

"Did you ever a kiss a girl and not like it?" Jude asked.

OK. That was a bit random. It would have been nice if her brain had percolated that thought before airing it. Hopefully Abby would gloss right over it.

"Huh?"

"I kissed a girl once," Jude said.

"You did?"

"Yes," she said, alarmed at how quickly this conversation was moving. "It didn't seem anything, I don't know, extraordinary."

Abby stared at her, uncomprehending, over a mountain of cream.

122

"I'd had a drink." Jude said, wishing she hadn't started this. "It was fine. Nothing special."

Still Abby stared.

"Soft though," Jude offered.

"Fine?" Abby queried.

"Yes. It was nice I suppose."

"Fine?!" said Abby again, this time accompanied by an incredulous curl of the lip.

"She was pretty, and soft, but I still didn't feel anything." Jude's stomach was tied up in knots. Where was she going with this?

"How much had you had to drink?" Abby said, wrinkling her nose.

"A couple of pints maybe." Jude's memory was hazy so it may have been more. She'd been a student at the time.

"Were you numb below the neck?"

"I don't think so."

"Numb below the nose?"

"No." Jude couldn't help laughing at Abby's shocked face. "It was fine."

Abby stared a lot more. "You're weird."

"Why?"

"Kissing women is not just 'fine'. It's wonderful. It's beautiful. The earth should move. It's sexy. It's so much more than fine!"

"Well, what about you? Have you kissed a man?"

"Yeah. I'm not doing that again."

Jude laughed at Abby's disdain.

"I'm not even going to say it was 'fine'," Abby added.

"Why?"

"Why what?"

"Why did you ask? About kissing a woman?"

"Oh, no reason."

Abby considered her. "You're being weird. I'll let you off today though." She smiled. "You'd do the same for me."

123

It had been fine, but the girl hadn't been Abby. She didn't have those feline eyes. Her lips didn't have that appealing succulence. Jude hesitated. It was becoming apparent she admired at least some physical aspects of her friend.

Abby stood for a moment and shuffled from her jacket. She sat down and flung the garment over the arm of the sofa and nestled next to Jude.

Were there any other attributes with which Jude could become enamoured? She stared down at Abby, the low cut of her dress now more apparent with her jacket gone. Maybe, and we were talking theoretically here, maybe she could like breasts?

She'd always admired Abby's, coveted them above her own slightly smaller bosom. The curve was pleasing. They'd shared a changing room often enough for her to know. She'd even spied them in the shower as she'd passed Abby's bathroom door in the mornings – Abby's eyes closed, massaging a lather of shampoo into her hair, her breasts moving gently with the motion, those rose red nipples pinched as water sprayed and trickled over them. They really were beautiful breasts. She could see the top of those soft mounds now.

"What do you think?"

"Sorry?" Jude said, alarmed.

"About Eli?"

Shit. What was she saying? Shit. Jude had actually been caught staring at a woman's breasts. And not just with envy. There had been more than a little admiration.

"Yes?" Jude offered. "Yes," she said with more conviction.

"I think so too." Abby carried on.

Jude watched Abby's lips move with gratitude as her friend continued, oblivious to Jude's unsubtle examination. And Abby clearly had attractive lips. Jude had acknowledged that already. Did she find them attractive enough to kiss? Could she kiss Abby? Look at those divine lips moving with luscious tenderness. A lick of Abby's tongue tingled on her own lips. Jude could easily enjoy a quick peck. They did that sometimes anyway. But a kiss? A real kiss? A deep kiss? Jude licked her lips.

"Are you OK?"

Shit. Again.

"What's that?"

"You're very distracted," Abby said with concern.

Is this what life was like as a lesbian? A strange combination of admiration for women which sometimes slipped into something else. Wanting breasts like Abby's full bosom – round, beautiful, with rose nipples – then desiring those same breasts? Jude blushed. It wasn't something she did often. She had Maggie's fortitude when it came to embarrassment, but she was way out of her depth here.

"Let's get you home," Abby said kindly. "You should take it easy after this weekend."

And there she was, Abby taking care of her again.

They drained their mugs – neither were going to let hot chocolate go to waste – and set off. Abby cleared the cups and tray, leaving Jude free to let her mind wander, all over Abby.

And as they ambled home, Jude considered whether she could make Abby happy. Jude was a steady character. Perhaps she could be content herself. She wasn't a fickle soul like her mother or Eli. Exactly how long had he known Selene?

Perhaps they could have a marriage of friends with the possibility of more. And Jude smiled because deep inside there was a flicker of warmth.

"What do you think?" Abby asked.

"Muh?"

This time Jude offered a grin and nod and prayed to the goddess of aspiring lesbians caught out of their depth that she'd got away with it.

17

Before they could unlock the front door, it was flung wide
open. Eli stood across the threshold barring their way, his
arms spread from wall to wall and his eyes wide with
accusation.

"You," he shouted, pointing with great theatricality, "have
been keeping secrets from us." He jabbed his finger at Abby
and his tone was so serious Jude wondered if he was indeed
earnest.

"Sorry?" Abby said.

"A secret with grave consequences," he said ominously.

"I…" Abby peeped at Jude.

"Eli, I don't think this–"

"Silence, sister!" Eli blocked her with his palm. "Abby
must not set foot in this house until she admits the passion
she's hidden for years."

Shit. Abby started to tremble beneath Jude's arm. This
wasn't the time or place to air Abby's love.

"To keep such an inclination secret in this of all families."
Eli tipped back his head and jutted his chin forward.
"Speak!"

"I," Abby stuttered, "I don't know what to say."

"You dare not speak its name?" Eli accused. "Are you
ashamed?"

"Jesus, Eli, what are you doing?" Jude said.

The serene face of Selene appeared beneath Eli's arm. A frown fluttered across her tranquil brow when she spotted Abby's pale face and what must have been horror on Jude's. She smiled up at Eli with love, layered with amusement and exasperation.

"I'm afraid," Selene said, "Maggie let slip Abby's been learning the piano."

"What?" Abby gasped.

"Thank Christ," Jude said.

"Tis true," Eli said. "The matriarch hath confessed."

Abby deflated with relief and Jude could have happily and permanently maimed her little brother.

"Yes," Abby said. "The piano. I've been learning."

Abby peeked up at Jude again. There had been real fear in her eyes.

"Why sister." Eli stayed in character. "Are you not shocked? Hath thee prior knowledge of this transgression?"

"Eli." Jude tutted. "Just let us through the bloody door." Abby felt near to collapse beneath her arm.

"Of course, ladies." He grinned from ear to ear, took a bow and stood aside. "Good to see you, Abby," he said, relaxing into his usual voice, and gave her a kiss on the cheek.

Jude held on to Abby's arm as they entered the hallway, giving Eli a stern look as they passed.

"What?" Eli said, all innocence. "What did you think I was going to say?"

"Nothing," Jude said, then through gritted teeth added, "I could kill you."

"Good to see you back to your old self, but I still don't know why you're all aflutter."

She was definitely going to kill him. Slowly.

Eli bounded after Jude and whisked Abby away to the piano beside the dining table, Selene sending back an apologetic look.

"Hello, love." Richard popped his head in from the kitchen, his thick glasses steamed up.

"Hi, Dad." Jude smiled.

He was draining a pan, dressed in Maggie's floral apron with the crochet trim, a present from an ancient aunt. He seemed quite at ease. In fact he seemed to mind the flowery garment less than Maggie.

"Abby staying for dinner?" he asked over his glasses.

"I don't think she'll have any choice in the matter."

Jude glanced to where Eli had seated her friend at the piano. He was busy shuffling beside her on the bench and leafing through sheet music.

"I've put on extra spuds in case," Richard said. "And as soon as I get these in the oven I'll pop and get Celia."

"Where's Mum?"

"Gone to check on the boys outside. She suggested they have mud pies to keep them going until dinner. I'm not sure they knew she was joking."

Jude peeked through the windows on the far side of the room. She could see two small boys by the river looking decidedly brown.

"Oh," she said. "They are rather literal those two, aren't they?"

Richard chuckled then looked down at his phone buzzing on the counter top.

"Do you need me to take over?" Jude asked. "Is that Celia?"

"Um." Richard peered over his glasses. "No. Someone else."

"OK." Jude waited, expecting him to say more, but he diligently dealt with the potatoes instead. He was steadfast, her father. Always the dependable soul in the family. His thirty-year-long marriage to Maggie was a testament to that.

"Dad?" she said tentatively.

"Hmm?" He held the pan high to get every drop of moisture from the fluffy potatoes.

"Would you say you were more friends with Mum than anything else, when you got married?"

"What's that love?"

"Friends with Mum. Do you think being friends is what's most important for marriage?"

"Oh." He put down the pan. "Well. Do you know," he looked thoughtful, "I think my answer is, it depends."

"Really?" She was genuinely surprised. She'd asked for reassurance, thinking she knew his answer already.

"For many years, I would have said an unequivocal yes. Especially when you and Eli were little. You need a strong team to raise children." And he gave her a kind smile. "I don't know. For some, friendship and respect is everything and enough. But," he shrugged, "others, and other times, if the passion was never there, something will always be lacking." He stared into the garden, his eyes unfocussed.

"But for you?" Jude said, unnerved by the uncertainty of his answer.

"For me, friendship, respect and companionship are everything, coupled with the ability to leave me to my books."

She laughed. That sounded more like her father.

"Of course, being easy on the eye is a bonus."

"Dad!"

"Well you did ask."

"There's a level of propriety when talking to your offspring."

"Indeed."

"What about for others?" she asked, frowning. "Isn't it enough for everyone?"

He stopped and leant against the kitchen top. "Nearly," he said, pursing his lips. "All those elements are essential and they can last you a lifetime. But for some, if there was never burning desire there will always be something missing. Even when old and grey, passion still burns even if it only flickers from time to time. It's death without it. For some."

129

She stared at her father, wondering who he thought of. "Which am I?" she wanted to ask.

"You made the right choice," he said.

"Sorry?"

"With Bill. You did the right thing."

"Oh." Bill couldn't have been further from her thoughts. "I'm glad you think so."

Jude looked at Abby, terrified all her love and respect might not be enough. That was where her mind and heart dwelled.

Eli was exuberantly encouraging Abby through Clair de Lune, turning the sheet music, the elegant Selene resting her arm on the piano top and admiring her beau. Jude had to admit, despite their whirlwind romance and his capriciousness, so familiar in Maggie, Eli had chosen well. Selene was unfazed by his flirtations with every being on the planet and a serene counterbalance to his excesses. They seemed to complement each other, Elis's vivacity and wildness tempered but also nurtured by the unflappable Selene. For some reason she seemed to adore him, and Eli, beyond his boisterous behaviour, was clearly smitten.

While the two lovers exchanged glances, Abby frowned in concentration, her fingers spread across the keyboard with the rigidity of a novice. She looked, and Jude couldn't think of a better word, sweet.

Everything about Abby had an innocence, or lack of guile. "You mean lack of finesse," Abby had laughingly told her once. But Jude hadn't meant that. Abby had an honesty about her. It's what made her a good doctor. People found her approachable and they were forthcoming about their problems because they recognised Abby's very human and broken soul.

Jude's heart ached for her, wanting to protect but also admire. Abby's shapely body was on show as she played. Her fringe obscured her eyes so she tilted her chin to the side and Jude had full view of her beautiful cheekbones and elegant jawline. Her slim neck was bare to the shoulders and the sleeveless dress revealed toned arms, still dusky with a summer tan. The gentle curve of her hour-glass figure was perfectly displayed with Abby's upright posture as she played.

"Carry on," Eli shouted. "Keep going."

Abby was starting to hunch over the keyboard, the notes running away from her and her arms stiffening with the effort of an unfamiliar section.

"You can do it," Eli said, squeezing his hand into a fist.

Then Abby's fingers crashed through a bar and she halted in defeat.

"Again," Eli cried. "You're nearly there."

Jude stepped in. "Move over, Eli. My turn."

Eli leapt up. "Aww, sis. Take pity on this piano bench," he said, patting the velvet cover. "It wasn't made for two such sizeable arses."

"Bugger off you little runt." She swiped at him but he leapt away with ease, possessing Maggie's nimble frame.

"She's doing brilliantly," he said.

"I heard." Jude grinned and rested her hands on Abby's arms. She gave a gentle squeeze and pulled Abby to her. "Fancy some more encouragement?"

Abby peeped up with red cheeks. "This is excruciating. Why did Maggie tell you all?"

Eli crossed his arms and looked to the skies. "To give you something to anguish about and keep her company in rage. Part of her induction to a satanic cult. Or sheer absent-mindedness in a haze of menopausal confusion."

Abby tried to hit him this time. He laughed and grabbed Selene by the hand and escorted her away.

"You're doing very well," Jude said softly. She sat beside Abby, keeping one hand on her shoulder. Jude shuffled into place, their thighs nestling together, and slipped her arm around Abby's body. "Try again."

Abby sighed but lifted her fingers to the keyboard. Immediately they fanned stiff.

"Relax," Jude murmured. She stroked along Abby's arm and spread her fingers above Abby's "Relax. You'll reach them better if you do."

Abby took a moment, her breathing quick at Jude's intervention. She closed her eyes and her cheeks became rosy. Jude squeezed her in encouragement and it was warm between them.

"Try again," Jude whispered.

Abby dropped her shoulders and her arms became supple. "Better," Jude said.

Abby began, her fingers this time stroking the keys with the gentle touch the music craved. Her fingers fluttered across the notes, the tune suddenly more fluid. Her slender hands seemed to caress the keyboard so the music purred.

"Beautiful," Jude murmured.

Jude stretched her legs and closed her eyes to enjoy the piece. The music washed over her and smoothed away any tension. She sighed, enjoying the intimacy of Abby. She could feel her body move beneath hers as she played on. A delicate touch of her breast as Abby reached high along the keys then teasing away again so Jude was left glowing. Her body tingled as if massaged by the music and the closeness of her friend. She became drowsy in her mellow euphoria.

Abby played on, their hips kissing together as she swayed, then parting, leaving Jude craving with delicious anticipation.

"Mmmm. Really beautiful."

Abby slowed into the final bars and became still, the only movement the rise and fall of her chest, the sides gently pressing against Jude's body.

Jude opened her eyelids, heavy with intoxicated pleasure. Her friend stared at the music, eyes dark and lips parted. The rose of her cheeks had spread, brightening the top of her cleavage in a healthy glow, one Jude recognised now. Abby gulped and Jude realised she was preparing to stand.

"Don't," Jude whispered. She shot out a hand to Abby's thigh. "You don't have to go."

Still Abby stared.

"It feels nice," Jude said. "Being close to you is wonderful."

Abby's breathing heightened and a frown fluttered across her face.

"I like it," Jude said.

The warmth beneath Jude's hand seemed to pulse and the air was balmy around them, as if cocooning them in their own intimate space. Jude's chest heaved in synchrony with Abby's, their bodies massaging together then apart, a tantalising touch then a tease.

Jude peered at Abby's lips and listened to the faint gasp of her breath. Abby licked her rose lips for a moment but quickly had to inhale again. They glistened with moisture. How tender they looked. They were lips to enjoy. Lips to kiss. Lips to slip inside and deepen with passion. They were so inviting that Jude wanted to abandon her habits of a lifetime and dip into unknown but enticing waters.

"Wow, Abby," Eli shouted so close behind that Jude and Abby shot in the air.

He slapped a hand on a shoulder each. "That was much better. More fluid. Actually, a very sensuous rendition." He paused for effect. "I wonder what brought that on."

Jude was definitely going to kill him.

18

Well, that was another mess attended to. Maggie brushed her hands together, wiping away the mud that had originated from the mouth of her youngest nephew. The two boys had resumed their play by the river, now with a greater understanding of what constituted a nutritious snack and that their aunt was fond of irony. But not that fond.

Ah, that must be Celia arriving. The sound of the street was audible for a moment as was Richard's gentle baritone encouraging someone inside.

Eli was larking around the piano, twirling his beloved to amuse her. Selene enjoyed his entertainment while elegant all in white today, the contrast sharp between her wardrobe, flawless complexion and raven hair. She looked so beautiful it made Maggie's heart ache. She caught him sometimes, gazing at Selene, mesmerised by the curve of her pale lips and the dark pools of her eyes, the line of inky eyelashes so neat they looked painted.

Maggie prayed to the universe that Selene didn't break her son's heart. Because she could. Maggie had never seen him so besotted. It was alarming, seeing his heart engaged and vulnerable. Maggie could almost feel what it was like to open up to that intensity of love only to have it ripped away. She winced and averted her eyes.

But there was Abby at the piano blushing about something. Always the one to make Maggie's heart light again. That Eli must be plaguing her. The boy was rotten at times, despite the inspiration for his play being their deep fondness for each other. There, the blushes were subsiding. Look how radiant she was. Maggie sighed. If only Abby would meet people. She could have been married several times over by now. Jude was holding her leg bless her, buoying her friend. And Jude looked happier for it. She was listening in earnest to what Abby said, staring at her lips, to make out the words above Eli's din no doubt.

Yes, Celia and Richard were back.

"Hello, Mother."

Celia hobbled in and Maggie greeted her with a kiss on each cheek.

"Hello, dear," Celia replied. She gave a sad smile. "You never did give up that habit did you?"

"What's that?"

"Kissing twice, like the Parisians."

"Oh," it was Maggie's turn if not to blush then to feel anxiety flutter in her chest. "It's because Selene's here," Maggie stuttered. "Slipping into our guest's habits."

Celia eyed her over her glasses. "Must be that."

"Must be that," Maggie echoed. "And Eli of course. He's picked up the habit."

"Indeed," Celia responded. "So like you."

Her mother squeezed Maggie's arm then took a seat at the dining table behind Abby and Jude. The two girls greeted Celia with affection and it warmed Maggie through to see the regard they held for her mother, even if it didn't always extend to her.

Richard shuffled in beside her. He too looked content, his hands slung in his pockets and a smile on his face. The house was filled with Maggie's nearest and dearest, her mother still in one piece, her husband at her side, newly engaged son with the love of his life. It was a pity about Bill, and Jude's heart bleeding all over the floor, but even she seemed remarkably better. She had colour in her face as she turned

135

back to the piano and Abby. What was she peering down at so intently? Something in front of Abby. She must be engrossed in a tricky chord progression.

Maggie clapped her hands together. "This is nice. In fact, this calls for a celebration," she said, looking up at Richard. "I think we have a couple of bottles of Prosecco left from the party. Let's open them."

"Why not?" Richard shrugged.

"Yes, let's celebrate." Maggie swept towards the kitchen, her step lighter and more joyful than it had been in days. It was a good day. It was turning into a very good day.

She was about to enter the kitchen when something caught her eye – a fluttering of white through the hallway window. She ambled closer and squinted up high. Something extensively white with a stripe of red hung from Barbara Petty's window. As recognition dawned on Maggie, volcanic fury rumbled.

"There's a fucking George Cross next door," she growled, clenching her fists by her sides.

"What's that, dear?" Richard's amiable voice reached her ears.

"That bloody woman has put up an English flag in place of the Union Jack."

She could hear Richard's chuckling approach from behind, then he appeared at her side.

"So she has." He was beaming with amusement. "I wonder it took her so long."

"She was probably waiting for it to be delivered from bloody Amazon," Maggie fumed. "Her lovely George Cross, symbol of a great country, made in China and delivered to her door by Hungarians."

"Is this about our Welsh builders?"

"Of course it is."

"I suppose it may be national pride."

"National pride! It's fucking protectionism. We're a rich nation but we're too selfish to feed everyone here, let alone

136

the millions we take advantage of in other countries. You should have seen her ranting at the poor fellow frozen in the lane."

"Ah, well, you know my response to that. Where do you stop? When you've given away everything?"

"That's not an excuse to do nothing," Maggie barked. "For fuck's sake. The George bloody Cross. Her generosity doesn't even extend across the border to Wales." Maggie was livid and had no intention of restraining a drop of it. "We've fucked off Europe. We've fucked the environment. We fuck those we invite here then decades later tell them this isn't their home. This idiotic, superior island mentality when our great nation can't even feed itself from its own farmland, it has its priorities so ludicrously arse end around."

Richard looked at her with familiar resignation.

"Well it's bloody true," Maggie snapped. "We've well and truly fucked the world for our kids. I hope they can save themselves, as well as us." She looked Richard up and down with disdain for his rationalised apathy. "National pride my arse. I've a good mind to hoist a pair of Celia's knickers in response. That would be a much better representation of our great sovereign nation. Underpants. Great frilly knickers."

And as she said the words, her resolve strengthened.

"Maggie," Richard groaned.

She could hear his despair but that would not deter her. She was already rifling through Celia's hospital bag.

"Maggie, how is that going to help the situation?"

"Do you mean relations with our beloved neighbour, or the state of the nation?"

"Either and both."

"Not a jot. But it's going to be immensely satisfying." She glared at him in defiance and thrust an expansive pair of bloomers into the air, complete with lacy trim.

Richard dipped his head in resignation. "This will escalate."

"Good. I'll use your Y-fronts next," Maggie replied, then she turned on her heel and marched out the door.

"National bloody pride," she muttered as she stormed to the external stairs that spiralled up to Richard's attic. "What have we got to be fucking proud of?" she said, stamping out every word with a clang on the iron steps. "George fucking Cross. This will bloody show her."

Maggie looked about for a suitable post for her alternative symbol of national pride and her eyes caught the metal bracket supporting a hanging basket of garish pansies. Perfect. Maggie draped the voluminous knickers over the brackets which unfortunately, oh her heart bled, obscured the dainty flowers. God she hated pansies. The whole arrangement had been a gift to Richard from Caroline, which made the whole underwear exercise that bit more satisfying. Maggie put her hands on her hips and sighed out a white cloud of happiness.

"Better. And two birds with one stone," she chuckled. Or at least one pair of baggy knickers. She couldn't wait for Barbara Petty to feast her eyes on that.

She turned to descend the stairs with pride, stomping her satisfaction on every step. She paused when she spotted a figure in the street.

A woman dressed in a long black coat, whose elegance would have caught the attention of anyone discerning enough to look past youth as the only beauty, was passing the house. She sauntered at a pace which suggested searching for somewhere or something. She glanced at the neighbours then at Maggie's front door and stopped.

The woman stared, her face pale and anxious concern twitching in her cheeks. She fidgeted with her black leather gloves, pulling at the finger tips as if to remove them, then nervously tugging them back down over her sleeve. Her gaze swept across the house frontage, taking in the burning red leaves of creeper, perhaps the size and elegant Georgian style of the house, wondering at the lives of the people within, until she too stopped, her eyes alighting on Maggie.

Her whole demeanour shifted. Gone was any hesitancy. Her anxiety disappeared beneath a wave of attitude which swept up her body. Her cheeks creased into mocking amusement and her pursed lips threw out a challenge before she even said a word.

Maggie stood on the stairs for the longest moment, gaping in unrestrained and very much apparent shock.

"Hello, Maggie," the woman said, the Rive Gauche Parisian evident in those two words. "I wondered if you'd recognise me."

Maggie gripped the rail as she trembled down the stairs. She took uncertain steps to the street, her world no longer the predictable territory it had been moments ago. She stopped a safe metre away from the woman and stared.

It was impossible Maggie would forget that face, that incredible face of her nemesis, Juliette Bonhomme. The slim neck and sculpted jaw. The proud cheekbones and lips, which curled in a smile. The smoky eyes, dark with makeup and sheer attitude. Her look could burn through to the iciest maiden. Her raven hair was swept back and, damn it if it didn't gall Maggie, her face although no longer turgid with youth was svelte. The inevitable changes with time had only accentuated her beauty and lent her features more distinction.

"Not recognise you," Maggie spat. If nothing else that Parisian accent would have given her away in a syllable. She would have had Maggie at "hell". "What the fuck are you doing here?" Maggie said, cold shock now rapidly thawing to fire.

The woman's smile turned more defiant. "I was passing," she offered, the French inflection massaging the phrase into a purr.

Maggie felt the past intrude with a sickening chill, but fury burned at the edges.

"This is a quaint English town you have found. And so welcoming too." Juliette eyed the George Cross fluttering high above and Maggie's offering which sagged opposite.

Of all the times for Juliette Bonhomme to appear. Of all the fucking times. Hanging out her mother's underpants in protest of the neighbour's xenophobia. And here Maggie was prepared to indulge in a little Francophobia of her own. She hated Juliette, with every ounce of her being. The fury that had thawed her shock was well and truly burning now. She was almost tempted to defend Mrs Petty and her sodding George Cross she detested this woman so much.

"It's a wonderful town," Maggie growled. "Not perfect by any means. Show me a place that is."

Juliette tilted her head. The action displayed her beautiful pale neck to more advantage. How the hell had she stayed so beautiful? This Gauloise chain-smoking, Claret-swilling French woman who looked spectacular. The bloody French and their fucking, buggering, sodding she didn't know what. But Maggie would bet good money Juliette did frigging yoga. Hummus-eating frigging yoga, with blueberries on the side.

"Perfection? *Non*," Juliette replied, "but I hope other places would have a warmer welcome."

This was infuriating. Maggie would have ranted in perpetuity about this very fact with anyone other than this woman. She felt as if she would explode at the contradictory urges.

"Well, if you don't like it," Maggie said, her chin rising, "you can move on. Go back to your pretty French villages."

Fuck. Had she told Juliette to go back home? Shit. This woman brought out the worst in her. It wasn't even her own worst. She'd thrown someone else's at her.

"I plan to," Juliette responded, her face flat with hidden emotion. "I'm just passing through out of curiosity. I didn't come to talk to you Maggie."

140

Maggie spun around, suddenly aware she'd been away from the house a while. Juliette Bonhomme was the last person she wanted to introduce to her family. The absolute last. Panic and guilt crept up her back and crawled over her shoulders. No-one peered from the window at least.

"I'm glad you've found a place," Juliette said, the sensual fluidity of her voice now frosty and clipped. "And a life that suits you."

Those flames leapt higher. "Yes, I did. I was extremely lucky. And warm welcome or not, I love this town and many of its inhabitants, from the vicar to the kids at the school to Mrs Malady the old cleaning lady. I picked the best possible place to bring up my children." She threw the words at Juliette along with daggers.

Juliette was disarmed for a moment, then shrugged with dismissal. "So changed. Defiant and radical Margaret, now middle-aged and languishing in middle England. How lovely."

"I haven't changed." Maggie wasn't languishing. She was still radical and defiant.

Juliette nodded towards the top of the steps. "Putting up knickers as a protest. How pathetic."

Shit. She did have a point. Which made Maggie burn more.

"So where do you live?" Maggie challenged. "Which noble town is blessed with the presence of Juliette Bonhomme?"

"Paris," Juliette said, with a glance down before resuming her defiant stare.

"Good," Maggie retorted. Juliette hated Paris. Sterile, barren in its perfection, a grey monstrosity she'd called it. How apt she'd ended up there.

"Actually, I grew to love it again."

Oh fuck off. She wasn't even going to give Maggie that satisfaction.

Maggie again peeked round at the windows. No-one searched for her, but it would only be a matter of time.

"Well," Maggie said. "How pleasant to catch up." She didn't mean a single word and the look Juliette returned suggested she was well aware too.

"I will bid you good day," Maggie said. "I hope your stay in Ludbury is short, for all our sakes."

She turned on her heel, a move she adored, and stamped up the garden steps, her footing more sure in furious exit than her trepidatious approach towards Juliette had been.

"Maggie?"

"What?" Maggie snarled, more annoyed that her dramatic exit had been curtailed than anything else.

"I didn't mean our first meeting to be so antagonistic."

"It comes as no surprise to me that it was."

"I understand," Juliette replied, a little softer, "Perhaps next time, now we've seen each other, will be better."

"I very much doubt it."

"At least, I will try," Juliette said, approaching the steps.

"I owe you no such kindness."

"I know."

"I think we've both said more than enough. I want you to leave."

Juliette paused and bowed her head. "I thought you'd react this way."

"Leave, Juliette," Maggie growled. "Now you know where I live, you can avoid this place forever."

"But I can't."

"Why the hell not?"

Juliette took a deep breath. "I'm Selene's mother."

A thousand thoughts, a thousand images, must have flashed through Maggie's mind in the moment that followed. Memories, poignant and painful. Hopes for a rosy future, burning up in flames. Meadows of flowers that inspired beautiful young women to dance among their blooms, razed to the ground. She turned, her mouth agape, eyes wider than

142

two very English saucers and responded in the only way Maggie could.

"You are fucking kidding me."

19

It all made horrible sense. Those inky eyes of Selene's and their mirror in Juliette. The serene elegance of both. It was sickeningly infuriating, but it did make sense.

"Why didn't someone say? Do they know?" Maggie gasped.

"*Non*. They are not aware of our past."

And the day had been going so well.

Oh God. Maggie felt the whole weight of their situation, then it jumped up and down on her for good measure. Oh shitting God.

Maggie's fury kindled inside again. "So you thought you'd turn up, out of the blue, and announce we're to be related."

Juliette smirked. "Ironic, is it not? But no, I did not intend meeting you today."

"Then what are you doing here?"

"I wanted to know more about your son and where he grew up," she paused, as if to gather herself, "and at some point, talk to you."

"You could have phoned."

"Indeed. That would have been my next step."

"Or written."

"And that subsequently when you slammed down the phone."

"I wouldn't have…" Yes, she would. She'd have slammed down the phone then thrown it across the room.

"So call," Maggie snapped. "And find a way to have as little as possible to do with me."

"*D'accord*," Juliette said icily. "I was prepared to make an effort for the sake of my daughter and your son. But if that's what you want."

"How considerate of you," Maggie snarled. "I think we both know less is best. Beyond the wedding day, we don't need to meet again."

"Perhaps you're right."

The front door creaked open behind Maggie.

"Juliette?"

Oh no. It was Maggie's effusive darling son.

"Juliette!" Eli cried as he bounded down the steps. He threw his arms around Juliette and held her tight. She closed her eyes and smiled, returning his affection. The bitch.

"I didn't know you were going to visit."

Juliette shrugged. "I have a little holiday for travelling and I thought it time to return to England."

Eli faced Maggie, his arm still around Juliette. "This is Selene's mother."

"I gathered." Maggie grinned, rigidly.

"I can't believe she's here."

"Indeed, I was surprised."

"She's the lecturer I was telling you about. You know when I met Selene. Her research topics include the Cathars, that's why I attended the lecture."

They'd never finished that conversation, had they. With all the commotion of Eli's engagement and the aftermath of Bill's untimely proposal, they'd never resumed the polite conversation, getting to know the happy couple's background. Damn it. Maggie was so mad she could spit. Spit on those expensive black heels of Juliette's.

"Isn't it strange that Juliette's speciality and the topic of your PhD should bring us together," Eli continued. "I bet you have a lot in common."

"You'd be surprised," Juliette joined in.

"Perhaps he won't be." Maggie narrowed her eyes.

"Are you free for dinner?" Eli asked.

"*Non, non.* I can't impose on your family." Juliette blushed. A little rose on those lily white cheeks.

"You wouldn't be. Dad was saying to Abby we have plenty to go around."

Damn Richard. "That was very generous of him," Maggie muttered.

"Well," Juliette shrugged. "If you insist."

Really? She was coming in. Why? Like this could be any pleasure for her.

"Brilliant," Eli said. "Isn't this great, Mum? You can get to know each other properly."

"Fabulous." She was as familiar with Juliette as she ever wanted to be. More so in fact. "Just fabulous."

"Would you believe we're having roast beef," Eli said as he made his way up the steps, Juliette beneath his arm. He glanced back to his mother. "We were joking the other day how the English think the French all smoke Gauloises and drink gallons of red wine."

Maggie flushed pink. "Ha. Yes. What a stereotype."

"They still call us Roast Beefs. And here we are having that for dinner."

"How funny," Juliette laughed.

"Hilarious," Maggie muttered, and she followed the joyful pair into her home.

"This is Juliette," Eli boomed as they entered the main room.

Celia, who was sitting at the dining table, almost choked on her glass of Laphroaig.

146

"Dear God," she said. "Have I died in the operating theatre and entered the twilight zone?"

Thanks, Mother. That was subtle. Although the poor dear genuinely looked shocked. But had anyone else noticed her mother's reaction or Juliette's entrance?

Richard was in the kitchen tapping away on his phone, and going by that silly grin on his face was probably sexting Caroline. Maggie shuddered. Her two nephews were asleep on the far sofa. Jude was still transfixed by Abby and the latter was staring at her hands in her lap. It was only Eli and Selene who seemed in the least bit with it.

"*Maman,*" Selene cried. "*Quelle surprise.*"

The girl leapt up and kissed her mother many times. The likeness was obvious now. No wonder Selene's appearance had stirred Maggie's emotions and fears for her son. She shook her head. Who had Juliette found to father a child? Selene had never mentioned anyone. The existence of a child from Juliette was surprise enough, but a father to it incredible. Another galling element to the whole fiasco.

"Let me introduce you all," Eli said. "They're being such a dull lot."

He bounded over to the piano and surprised Jude from her reverie. "This is my sister Jude." Jude stared blank and pink at them all. "Selene's mother has come for dinner."

"Oh," Jude said, apparently still not in the moment.

"You'll have to forgive my sister," Eli continued. "She's distracted and pretending to be heartbroken after leaving her tedious boyfriend of five years."

"Oh Eli!" Maggie shouted. Poor Jude. That was unforgivable.

"Well, it's true," Eli protested. "Bill was a bore. In every respect. A boring boor."

"Time to grieve would be appropriate," Maggie said, but Jude seemed beyond distraction.

"Abby." Eli turned his attention to Jude's alarmed friend. "Dearest Abby is friend to the entire family. Nay. She is family. And she has already fallen foul of my jesting today. You have a reprieve."

Abby relaxed.

"Celia!" Eli leapt across the room to his grandmother. "Celia is a resident at the local care home. She claims she doesn't want to burden the family, but secretly hankers after the company of the delightful Desmond."

"Eli!" Celia snapped. She tried to slap him on his calf but he leapt away again. "You impertinent little shit." Now Eli had managed to make Celia squawk vulgarities. He couldn't have looked more pleased.

"In the kitchen we have Richard, the paterfamilias." His father peered up from his phone blankly. "And as such has absolutely no say in this family."

"Don't be rude about your father," Maggie said.

"Because," and Eli came to a stop before her, a triumphant grin on his face, "we all know who wears the proverbial trousers in this house. My mother, Maggie. Sometimes Mags. Never Margaret."

She wanted to kiss and kill him at the same time.

"*Enchante*," Juliette cried. "I'm so happy to meet you all."

"The pleasure's all ours," Maggie deadpanned.

"Well," Juliette sighed. "This is a pretty home."

She sauntered around the main room as if they all hung on her verdict. Which was closer to the truth than Maggie wanted to admit.

"Interesting to see where you have been living all these years."

The family would assume she meant Eli, but Juliette threw a satisfied and mocking glance at Maggie. Juliette ran her gloved hand over the sheen of the mahogany table, the material sliding without resistance.

"A beautiful piece. I am very envious, Richard."

It needled Maggie that she pronounced his name *Rishar*. She knew the English version well enough. She also knew Maggie well enough to guess the piece was hers.

"Oh that's one of Maggie's finds," Richard said amiably. "Anything you see of taste, Maggie deserves the credit."

"*Vraiment?*"

"Apart from the literature and other books. They tend to be mine."

"Are you not a great reader, Margaret?"

Again. So unnecessary.

"Of course I am." Maggie squirmed. "But Richard is such an unusually voracious reader that books tend to be his, unless it's by a female author."

"*C'est normal. Non?*"

No-one seemed to dare comment.

"This is an unusual item." Juliette stopped. It was sculpture of a nude woman carved from wood. The smooth form reclined, breasts exposed to the sky. The piece had become polished over the years, from fingers enjoying the pleasing surfaces, especially the chest. The children had been fond of pointing out the naked lady's boobies to every guest.

"By Gabriel Bent I believe," Juliette said.

"Well spotted," Richard said. "I would never have guessed. Maggie's again."

She knew that. Juliette already bloody knew that.

"But what about here? There is something missing. *Non?*" Juliette pointed to gaps between the ornaments on the bookcase where Richard had removed items more precious to him than Maggie. "And here?" The clean rectangle of wallpaper and its darkened frame. "There used to be a picture?"

"Ah. That's in the attic," Richard stumbled. "For now. For a change."

"*D'accord*," Juliette said. "I wonder that you don't fill out the gaps again though." And she raised an eyebrow at Maggie.

149

It was as if Juliette knew where to prod. How did she do that? Did she have a sixth sense for needling Maggie where she was most vulnerable? Juliette had been in the house a matter of minutes and she'd sniffed out trouble already.

"Just a question," Juliette said sweetly.

"Can I get you something to drink?" Richard stuttered. "Red wine?"

Maggie tutted, not altogether fairly. "It's not compulsory for the French to drink red wine, Richard."

Juliette smiled. Just a curl at the corner of her mouth. "You are right, Maggie. But actually Richard," again *Rishar*. It made Maggie's teeth ache every time. "You are correct. I love a glass of red wine. I am quite thirsty though. Do you have herbal tea?"

"Herbal tea," Maggie snorted. When the hell did her rampant coffee habit change. Herbal tea.

"*Oui*. I love my tea. Especially a cup of camomile."

Maggie couldn't help the grimace. "Of all the drinks, you choose the one that smells like urine."

Juliette fixed her with narrowed eyes. "Really? I've never found that so. Perhaps you should check yours with a doctor." She offered her arm to Richard to escort her to the kitchen.

And if looks could throw daggers, knives would have flown across the room that moment.

"Well, tuck in everyone," Richard said. He sat at the nominal head of the table by the kitchen. Maggie was grateful he'd taken charge, because her brain was in several other places and times at once.

Next to him was their errant son, mighty pleased with himself, and Selene who was as tranquil as ever. Jude came next around the circular table staring across at Abby. Juliette sat by her side, also unnervingly sedate. Celia sat between the two antagonists, switching her gaze between Maggie and Juliette while swigging a large glass of red. Then Abby sat by

150

Maggie's side, red-cheeked and apparently famished by the way she devoured her meal and remained oblivious to Jude's attention.

Maggie sat rigid, cutlery in her fists brandished more like weapons than culinary instruments.

"So," Richard started. He looked at Maggie, then Celia, then nodded at Juliette. "Yes, um, tuck in everyone."

Things had to be bad for Richard to pick up on any awkwardness.

"So, Abby." The surprise interjection came from Juliette. She put down her fork and dabbed her lips with a napkin. "Eli tells me you're a lesbian."

"What?" Poor Abby choked on a morsel of beef which shot from her mouth in a cough. "Excuse me." Abby hiccupped before dissolving into a fit.

"Here you go, my dear," Maggie said, passing a glass of water. She shot Juliette a venomous look which was received with perfect tranquillity. In fact, a smile began to curve at the corner of Juliette's mouth again.

"Thanks, Eli," Abby coughed. "Thanks for passing that on."

"You're welcome," Eli grinned.

"There's no need to worry," Juliette said. "Because I am one too."

"Jesus." It was Celia's turn to choke on her dinner at Maggie's taboo subject and the usual elephant in the room.

Jude almost dropped her fork and failed to keep her lower jaw in place. A pea may have fallen from her mouth.

Maggie's heart raced and Celia was gripped by another paroxysm. Maggie slapped her mother on her back until the old woman returned to the right hue.

Well thanks, Juliette. Maggie sent another set of daggers flying across the table. Fuck her. She'd managed to keep that quiet for all of two seconds. So she'd come with the gloves metaphorically off then, if not literally.

"Do you have a girlfriend?" Juliette asked. She was unperturbed, nonchalantly placing another neat forkful in her mouth.

"No," Abby spluttered.

"Odd. I imagine you have a lot of, how do you say, interest."

"Yes. I mean 'interest' is the right word. But, no. There's not a lot of interest."

"Really," Eli squawked. "That's not true. I bet there's a dozen interested folk within half a mile, closer even." He turned to Jude. For some reason Jude's face was stormy in response. Abby had resumed dining, the poor thing as red as her glass of wine.

"Abby is a beautiful woman in every way," Maggie interrupted, hoping to ease her embarrassment. "I imagine many men and women would love to date her."

"Mum!" Now Jude aimed her thunderous expression at her.

"Well someday," Maggie said, exasperated at this constant source of friction between them, "Abby might welcome a man's attention. It's not unheard of."

"Abby has never had any interest in men whatsoever. The issue is getting others to accept she likes women. Why do you always hark back to it?"

"Isn't that the vogue now?" Maggie said. "Sexual fluidity." Her two children shuddered as she said the word "sexual". "Well, is it not? After all, whoever thought Eli would find a nice young woman?"

"You don't approve of gay relationships?"

It was Juliette, and she'd said it with an even mix of incredulity and disapproval. She sat stiff, focussed on Maggie, then she suddenly eased. "How very strange. Intriguing indeed. Especially for you." She took a mouthful and left the words hanging there, chewing delicately over her food with a smile.

"Really?" Jude asked. "Why for Mum?"

And Maggie wondered how quickly she could leap across the table and shove her hand in Juliette's mouth.

Celia was squirming by her side. "More wine anyone? I'll get it from the kitchen."

It said a lot about the awkwardness of the situation that the woman needing a hip replacement was virtually running for more alcohol.

"Sit down, Mother," Maggie said sharply, hauling Celia back into her seat. "It's not that I don't approve." She spoke in her firmest classroom delivery. "I am not homophobic."

The effect was somewhat marred by Jude's huffing.

"Well, I'm not," Maggie continued. What was wrong with Jude today? They had their differences on this issue, but Jude was usually more tactful about it. Why was she publicly laying into Maggie now, of all the bloody times?

"I'm not homophobic. I've never disapproved of Abby. You can see I adore her. The rest of the world isn't as accepting though. Lesbians are battered by men with fragile egos. People die because they are gay." And she emphasised the point by staring at Juliette. "Which is why I hope for heterosexual relationships. I want my family to be happy and safe. That is all. Abby especially."

"Abby is gay, Mum," Jude said, exasperation written all over her face. "The only way she'll be happy is with a woman."

For God's sake Jude. Why now?

"I don't want that life for her," Maggie said. "She's had enough hardship already. Let her have a break."

Jude glared with the kind of fire Maggie recognised in few but herself.

"You would deny her love?"

"Of course not," Maggie retorted, with a vehemence inspired by Juliette's presence. "But happiness is more likely through some kinds of love than others."

153

"Isn't that up to Abby to decide?" Again, where had this attitude come from? She hadn't seen this fervour from Jude since she was a teenager.

From the corner of her eye Maggie could see Abby, her head bowed and hands wrung in her lap.

"I'm sorry, Abby," Maggie said, reeling in her anger. "You know my position and reasons. You know I don't disapprove of you."

Abby didn't reply, her gaze fixed on her hands.

"Did you know your mother used to fight for gay rights?"

Juliette. Again. And, as before, she left the words hanging there. At least it silenced Jude. She and Eli had their mouths wide open.

"It is true. Here," Juliette said, with great felicity. "I have a photo."

Shit.

Maggie's heart leapt into her mouth and she readied herself to fly across the table. Juliette reached into her little black bag. Was she deliberately taking her time? She pinched out a phone and examined it with what Maggie could tell was immense satisfaction. "I scanned it when sorting my college memorabilia," Juliette continued.

Maggie sat tense in her chair, limbs coiled tight and grinding her teeth. Juliette flashed the photo in her direction before allowing Eli and Jude to feast their eyes on the evidence. Maggie knew the photo well enough to need no second glance and she stayed her flight, for the moment.

"You knew each other?" Selene said.

"We were at university together," Juliette said with incredible lightness.

"I didn't know that."

"*C'est vrai.*"

"Mum?" Jude looked shocked. "Is this really you?" She turned the screen towards Maggie.

There she was, her hair in a shoulder-length and very unfortunate perm and sporting her favourite pair of dungarees. She had only a vest underneath, no bra, a fact vividly committed to memory when she'd later run for the bus. Her arms were slung around a thin man with pink hair, and woman with none. Behind a great banner demanded research for AIDS. The man was long dead, and the woman lost touch after Eli was born.

"Yes, that's me," Maggie replied solemnly. "London Pride I think."

"One of many marches and protests," Juliette said quietly. "Gay vegans. Lesbians and gays support the miners. Gays against fascism."

Maggie could remember it all vividly. Her arm around the young man, his body bony while hers remained plump with vigour. The love and camaraderie of her friend. And Juliette, smiling proud as she took the photo on her Minolta camera, quickly winding on the film to catch another shot. The smell of London, and the old diesel buses which pumped out black clouds. The rubbish on the street, some left by the march, other debris thrown by intolerant spectators.

"You went to Pride?" Eli said, astonished. It wasn't often she surprised her son. "You used to protest for gays?"

"Then why, Mum? Why are you so adamant about lesbian relationships?" Jude seemed keenly affected as she said it.

"Because what was the point?" Maggie said, and she fought back the lump in her throat. "What was the point of going through all that? Fighting for the right not to be sacked. Being abused for loving the wrong sex. Winning equal marriage rights, all for hate crime to soar again now. The newspapers savage anyone queer, and young lesbians are raped to teach them a lesson. It's hard enough getting through life without the world taking that extra issue with you. It breaks relationships. It tears people apart. Don't underestimate what that pressure does to even the strongest of relationships. And when they fall apart, your whole world dies." Her hands shook.

There was silence. She could feel them all staring at her.

155

"That's why I pray Abby finds a normal life," she murmured.

At those words, Jude threw down her fork and stormed from the table.

Abby shuffled beside her, but Maggie didn't have the strength to look her in the eye.

"I need the bathroom," Abby said and Maggie didn't try to stop her.

The room fell quiet again.

"Happy?" Maggie mouthed to Juliette.

She raised an eyebrow. "It's a start."

Well fine. There were one or two issues Maggie could raise. But before she could open her mouth Richard rose.

"I think we could do with a break. Time for some coffees?"

Maggie looked at him, and was silenced by the expression on his face. A terrible grief lay there for a moment which softened into fond sympathy. Had he realised who was here?

20

Jude stormed out the front door, down the steps and into the road and she was tempted to keep on going. She waited for her eyes to adjust to the dull street lamp and collapsed onto the bottom step with a thump instead, the cold stone on her bottom no match for her fiery temper.

What the hell was wrong with her mother? Maggie had never approved of lesbian relationships, but did she have to air her views so emphatically in front of Abby? That must have hurt and Jude needed to compose herself before comforting her friend. But right now, composure was evading her.

And after Maggie had supported gay rights in her youth. Would she ever stop being contrary? And dear God, what did she have against Selene's mother? Even for Maggie that was a special kind of animosity.

Jude closed her eyes and took a deep breath. She held it in, counting the seconds, slower and slower, until she reached thirty and took the longest time to exhale.

Well that didn't fucking help. She was still livid. And all when Jude was contemplating dipping her toe into sweet Sapphic waters. She took hold of herself. Now, if she was being honest, was that why she'd flared up in such an incendiary way? Well it didn't bloody help. She had the mental discipline to at least credit it but, Jesus Christ, Maggie should never have said that to Abby. Then Jude's heart plunged.

All those years of Abby without a girlfriend, disabled by her love for her best friend and shackled by the disapproval of her surrogate mother. What an unhealthy double act Jude and Maggie had been.

Jude dropped her head into her hands. Perhaps Celia was right. The best thing they could do for Abby was let her go. Jude's mind could entertain the thought, but her heart was heavy and unwilling.

"Shit," she whispered into her palms.

She turned at the sound of the front door and leapt to her feet when Abby emerged. Her friend's face was tense with repressed feeling. Abby's eyes betrayed her though; hurt, even angry, so rare for her.

"I'd better go home," Abby said. "I don't feel comfortable here tonight."

"Oh, Abby." Jude squeezed her arm. "I'm sorry."

"There's nothing for you to apologise for."

But there was. Between Jude and her mother, there was much to regret.

"Let me take you home."

Abby didn't accept or refuse, her cheeks remaining knotted and tense, and they silently set off up the road, arm in arm.

"You're right." Jude said, "Maggie's the one who should be apologising for this evening. I doubt she ever will, but that was unpardonable."

"It was nothing I hadn't heard before," Abby said, and Jude could hear the injured undercurrents in her voice.

"You mustn't let Maggie stand in your way. Don't let it affect you," Jude begged, her own guilt amplifying her entreaty.

"How can it not? She is as important to me as my own mother now. Of course her opinion affects me. And in her own way," Abby peeped at Jude, "she's right."

Jude didn't know what to say.

"You don't know this, but she saw me attacked because I'm a lesbian."

"When?" Jude stopped and clasped Abby's arm. "What happened?"

"Do you remember a few years ago, I went on a couple of dates with a new teacher, Karen?"

"Yes." Jude did vaguely. A young blonde who'd started at the secondary school. A very pretty woman who turned heads in the street.

"It put a few noses out of joint among the men in town," Abby continued. "I was walking home from the square one evening, past the Benson Arms, when a group of blokes tumbled out of the pub. One started jeering at me, calling me lezzer. I recognised him. He'd chatted to Karen at the pub another evening. I tried to walk around them, but he barred my way and his two mates crowded behind me. Even though I'm not small, they could have done anything they wanted. They towered above me."

"Jesus. I had no idea."

Abby shrugged. "Rare in Ludbury, but that kind of behaviour's everywhere."

"What did you do?"

"I tried to avoid eye contact and not engage them. So he started pushing me, trying to get me to react. Then the pushing got rougher. People in the pub could see. I heard them shouting at the men to stop, but none of them did anything. He kept pushing harder, the other two pressing up behind me, and I knew it was going to get very nasty.

"Then I heard an irate scream behind and pounding footsteps from up the street. I turned to see Maggie. She was raging down the road. I mean really raging. She was almost inhuman. The look in her eyes – I've never seen such animalistic fury. She'd come out of the hardware shop and grabbed a fire poker, and none of us doubted she'd use it. She

159

held it high in the air and by the time it came crashing down in sparks on the pavement those blokes had scarpered."

Abby smiled with fearful delight at the memory, her hands trembling.

"She took me under her arm and led me away. Her body was stiff and hot with anger. She kept saying 'no-one does that to my Abby. No-one'. When I burst into tears, she assumed I was upset by the incident. And I was. I'd been in serious trouble. But it was her reaction that made my heart crumble."

Abby stared at Jude, the emotion brimming in her eyes.

"After my mother died, I thought no-one would have that fierce maternal instinct towards me again. But Maggie showed it in spades. I will never forget it and I will never take it for granted."

Jude sighed, exasperated. She'd not known about the incident, but all of it rang true – Maggie's fierce protection of Abby and her deep love.

"Things are getting better though?" Jude said, hopefully. "You should never have had to face that but you can't bury that side of you, surely?"

Abby cradled Jude's arm in hers as they walked on. "Don't get me wrong," she said, "while I agree with Maggie it's not always easy being gay, but I can't change who I am." She frowned at Jude. "I don't doubt Eli is crazy about Selene, the same way it was ludicrously obvious he found hairy Steve irresistible. And I don't doubt people are fluid depending on where they are in their life and who they meet. But this is me. I only like women."

They took a few steps before Abby could finish. "I know who I am," she said. "So one day I will disappoint Maggie. And I dread that day."

They continued walking and Jude pulled Abby close. She could feel the turmoil inside her friend. They traversed the square, devoid of daytime market and empty excepting a few window shoppers. The small crooked alleyway which

160

overhung with twisted medieval houses was silent, the window of the cheese shop dark except for the chilled counter light. Jude twitched her gaze away from the shop and felt Abby tense beneath her arm. She seemed to become roused again as they passed.

"Please don't tell me to ask Cheese Shop Lady out," Abby said firmly.

"Sorry?"

"Don't mock me about my reticence."

"Oh," Jude replied, and she smiled. "No. I won't." She bumped Abby's hip with her own. "I've decided she's not your type."

Indeed. Jude had vehemently changed her mind about the lady in that shop. Not Abby's type. Not her type at all. In fact, the woman should stop staring at her friend every time she passed as if she were trying to undress her and concentrate on her whiffy produce thank you very much. Preferably move her smelly little shop to another town, far, far away. Maybe develop an unattractive rash too, just for good measure. And at this point Jude had to check herself. That was more than a smidgeon of jealousy rearing its head and she settled on, "No, definitely not your type."

They passed beneath the city wall gate and descended Abby's street.

"Good," Abby said. "About time you realised that." And she said it with such vigour it made Jude flinch.

As they reached the cottage, Abby turned and faced Jude.

"Because, no, she's not my type." Abby peered into Jude's eyes, half in sorrow, half in defiance. "She's perfectly nice and anyone would describe her as pretty. But it wouldn't be fair to date her. I'm not interested, because I know what I love."

And Jude was silent under the intensity of Abby's gaze.

"I love the kind of woman who stands by her friends even when it's difficult – a person who loves her family despite all its imperfection and crazy-making habits. I want intelligence

161

and heart and a woman who is at ease with her body. There's nothing more sexy for me than a woman who revels in her assets and doesn't give a fuck about what people call her imperfections – in fact those are the sexiest bits about her, those differences." And Abby's eyes flashed with ardour. "Full lips and hips. Beautiful breasts. A body I could devour and lose myself in. I want to have unfettered hot sex for days and not surface until we ached from love-making." She stared at Jude defiantly. "That's my type. That's my passion. And I would walk to the ends of the earth for a woman like that. So don't tell me to date someone who would pale beside her. It wouldn't help anyone."

Jude stared, dumbstruck by Abby's fervour. Abby wasn't talking nice glowing feelings by the piano here. Abby meant fiery desire. She meant clothes ripped from bodies and she'd said "unfettered hot sex".

"Oh," Jude said, simultaneously aroused by Abby's outburst and intimidated by what that actually meant with another woman.

"Now, I need to get to sleep." Abby said, drawing herself up. "I have an early start tomorrow and a fully booked surgery."

"OK," Jude mumbled.

"And I will see you in the evening for Eli and Selene's engagement bash."

"Uhuh."

"So good night." Abby leant forward, and pressed her soft lips to Jude's cheek. Actually, hot swollen lips.

"Good." Jude gulped. "Night."

And Abby closed the door behind her.

162

21

As soon as Abby became conscious the next morning, she groaned. She rubbed her temples, screwed up her eyes and rolled squirming with embarrassment in her big white duvet.

Her foot encountered something fluffy and warm. She gave the warm thing a stroke with her toes. The warm thing purred. Abby peeked over the mounds of duvet and saw two white triangles twitch and swivel towards her.

"Morning, Maximillian." She sighed and slumped back onto the bed. She sniffed a little but didn't have the energy to turf him out. She was too consumed with humiliation to move.

She'd been full of defiance last night and angry at Maggie. So much for keeping her inclinations towards Jude under control, and so much for being a supportive friend during Jude's heartache. She'd almost combusted with passion the previous day, twice, then virtually declared her love for Jude with the explicit desire for unfettered hot sex.

"Oh God," Abby muttered into the pillow. "I hope she didn't realise I was describing her."

All when Maggie had vividly reminded her of another reason to keep shtum. Everyday this was getting harder. Not helped by Eli in the slightest. She'd always wondered if he'd guessed at her fancy.

"Mmmm." She sighed, transported back to the Goodman's living room and the sensation of Jude against her body as she'd played at the piano. Every cell from her head to her toes had thrummed with forbidden enjoyment. If Jude had been so inclined and seduced her right there on the piano bench, there wouldn't have been a damned thing Abby could have done about it. She really needed to keep her distance today.

No thigh-to-thigh and breast-to-breast piano playing. Absolutely no cuddling when Jude was naked except for a bathrobe. Mmm. Jude. Naked. Nothing but bathrobe.

Crap. No making rules which inspired beautiful images that broke other rules, reference: no fantasising, especially accompanied by touching, and definitely no fantasising about Jude fantasising and touching.

"Oh," Abby moaned. She closed her eyes as a wave of heat inflamed her body. The list had brought to mind the image of Jude naked and in the last throes of self-induced ecstasy. Her long elegant fingers circled between her thighs and her head was thrown back with hair cascading as her body tensed with pleasure. Abby groaned again. If that wasn't the most erotic sight imaginable Abby didn't know what was.

She sat up in bed, acutely aware of the slickness between her own thighs and the heat in her cheeks. Maximillian opened a glimmer of a green eye, a perfect amount to convey complete and utter disapproval.

"Don't start," Abby said. "You're not even meant to be here to witness that."

He turned his head and curled into a sphere. He may as well have hung a sign with "Do not disturb".

"Come on," Abby said to herself. "Snap out of this."

At least appointments would distract her today, and she leapt out of bed, determined to concentrate on whatever in-growing toenail or other oddity she was presented with. Sometimes, as any vestige of passion drained away at the thought of such ailments, her job came in useful. She marched to the bathroom, almost looking forward to being presented with a case of bacterial vaginosis.

The day passed in a blur of mercifully minor afflictions, finishing with an out-of-hours double appointment with Mrs Malady. She accompanied the old woman from the surgery and tottered up the street at an agonising crawl over the cobbled pavements. Ludbury and its hills of pastel cottages was beautiful but a bugger in terms of accessibility.

Abby offered an arm and Mrs Malady gratefully accepted, her bony fingers entwined around Abby's healthy bicep.

"I'm so embarrassed you know," the old lady said.

"Don't be," Abby replied, her voice gentle. "You're not the first I've referred to the food bank and you won't be the last."

"It don't make sense to me. I've worked all my life. How come I can't afford to feed myself?"

Mrs Malady was breathing hard and couldn't finish her thoughts. They pressed on, the older woman limping with her worn knee and wheezing with COPD from a lifetime of bleach fumes and cleaning the facilities of Ludbury. She peeped up apologetically from time to time and Abby made sure she received a kind and patient smile in return.

"Phew." Mrs Malady exhaled when they reached the top of the hill, their destination of the small supermarket and bus stop ahead. Her expression suddenly brightened. "Look. There's Mrs Goodman. Another good soul like you Dr Hart."

Abby flinched and struggled to lift her gaze. Any other day Abby would have been heartened by the compliment. Maggie had stepped out of the supermarket, two bags for life in her hands, warm recognition on her face for Mrs Malady conflicting with sorrowful alarm at Abby. She seemed to bury whatever she was feeling and came to greet them.

"Mrs Malady, how are you?" she said with what Abby recognised as her genuine smile. Maggie dropped her bags and squeezed the old lady, kissing her on the cheek.

"Not bad," Mrs Malady replied. "Well, better because of the likes of Dr Hart here."

"Indeed." Maggie turned her smile to Abby, and although it faltered with anxiety at the edges it still retained its authenticity.

"Hello, Maggie," Abby said and the awkwardness eased a little.

"Although it is humiliating you know," Mrs Malady continued. "Dr Hart has referred me to the food bank. Can't afford anything except the rent these days."

Maggie crossed her arms and gave her a stern but supportive look. "You should feel no such thing, Doris. The people in government should be ashamed, not you." She put her arm around the tiny woman. "I've known you for more than a quarter of a century and seen you raise a family and take care of your parents. You shouldn't have to face this kind of difficulty."

As the two women chatted side by side, it was difficult not to notice the stark contrast between them. Maggie lacked Jude or Abby's stature but she towered above Mrs Malady. Her arm was strong around the frail woman's shoulders and her movements and convictions had the vitality of a well-nourished middle age. Abby realised, with shock, there were only two years separating the women. Anyone would have guessed twenty or more. Maggie was still beautiful and vital. She didn't hide any of her fifty-odd years but none had diminished her, whereas Doris Malady seemed crushed by hers and Abby treated her as if she were in the latter years of her life.

"And your son? Is he well?" Maggie asked Mrs Malady.

"Getting by, he is. He's a good lad. Still calls on his old mum even though he's got kids of his own. Nothing like family is there."

Maggie pursed her lips at this and peeked at Abby. "You're right Doris. Family is so important."

166

"Anyway. I won't keep you two lovely ladies," Mrs Malady said. "Thanks again, Dr Hart," she said with a wave to Abby. "Please say hello to Jude and young Eli."

"Will do," Maggie replied, and they watched Mrs Malady limp to the bus stop.

Maggie tutted. "Surely she's eligible for more support."

"I'm afraid not," Abby replied. "Believe me I've tried."

And Maggie turned to her fully for the first time.

"Of course you have," she said and her expression took on unrestrained concern now that Mrs Malady had gone.

Abby fiddled with her fingers, feeling the awkwardness of yesterday descend.

Maggie peeped at her, not with remorse but definite sorrow, and she began to wear her years more like Mrs Malady than Margaret Goodman. Abby couldn't bear it.

"Come here," Abby said, and she threw her arms around Maggie. She drew her into a warm hug, with no resistance. Maggie squeezed her tight in return. There were no words either could say. They'd never agree on the issue that separated them, but they were more than one issue.

"Abby?" Maggie said, muffled in her shoulder. "No matter what happens, no matter what you do, I will be here for you."

Abby held her tighter. Maggie steadied her, like she had a thousand times over the years, but today Abby felt compelled to say, "Me too, Maggie. I'm here for you."

Abby was surprised by the ferocity of the hug in response, then the older woman let go. She sniffed with a rapid blink of her eyes and tried to hide her tears with a swipe of her hand.

"I need to get back," Maggie said in rapid fire. "Need to feed the children so they have something lining their stomachs before this evening's celebration."

"Aren't you coming too?"

"No. I'd better not. I will call on Celia instead who's missing the party on account of her hip." Maggie looked away at this point. "Besides, Selene's mother is attending and I'm sure Eli won't want his to cramp his style."

"I think Eli would love to have you there. You've only ever enhanced his style. If anything he's naughtier when you're around."

A chuckle escaped Maggie. "You may be right there," she said and she at last made eye contact. "Have a good evening."

"Thank you," Abby replied, and she kissed Maggie on the cheek.

Abby's step was lighter as she walked back to her cottage, and her determination to quell her desires for Jude more resolute. She wanted to support her heart-broken friend not terrify her with desire for unfettered hot sex. And she'd be a fool to think her life complete without Maggie. Now if her mind and body could play along that would be nice.

As she flicked through the wardrobe in her bedroom, her resolution lasted at least five minutes before her mind began to wander.

Should she wear the figure-loving black dress, the one that clung like a second skin? Perhaps she'd get one of those looks from Jude she'd noticed recently – the one that warmed Jude's cheeks and made her lips curl up in appreciation. Because it would be good to cheer up her friend.

Or perhaps the longer number, with a cut so low a belly button check was required before going out. Jude had always admired her bosom had she not? As well as being at ease with her own figure, Jude's compliments slipped off the tongue. It was only considerate to be well-presented and make her friend proud.

What would Jude wear? Perhaps that cream number which fell below the knees? The one that laid bare Jude's beautiful shoulders, athletic with a softness that was Jude all over. The one that exquisitely cupped her breasts, before snuggly circling her belly. That rounded those curving hips and marvellous thighs in a soft stroke of velvety material so that

168

you couldn't admire it without wondering how it felt to follow those curves with your fingertips.

"Oh, for the love of…." Abby slumped onto the bed.

She couldn't even get ready without mentally undressing Jude. What was wrong with her? Ever since they'd held each other, Jude naked beneath her dressing gown, Abby's desire had burned beyond control. More than ten years. More than ten bloody years she'd known Jude and not once had she been like this. Yes, she would have to be dead not to notice Jude was attractive, and yes she was in love with her, but this hormonal mush was new and couldn't have been less timely.

Her phone buzzed and Abby tapped on the message. The care home were asking for a consultation, and although she would work twenty-four hours a day to save the residents of Ludbury, she was doubly keen to help just now. Anything to snap her out of constant infatuation. With any luck, by the time she made it to the party she'd be too exhausted for any passion to stir even if Jude was naked.

"No." Abby shook Jude's undressed image from her head. "Stop it."

She threw her phone into a clutch bag, slipped on a black shirt that was cropped short and slid into a tight pair of black jeans. In the bathroom she slicked back her hair and drew a neat line around her eyes. A routine which took all of a minute.

She caught herself in the mirror. It was as if she was nipping out to knock someone off more than celebrate coming nuptials. Never mind. The assassin look it was. At least she wasn't dwelling on Jude. Now Jude in an assassin look, that would be something.

"For the love of God!"

Abby tore down the stairs, kicked on some boots and stamped her way down the street and into the dusk.

22

"Good lord." Celia greeted Abby at the door to the care home. "Has Maggie put a hit out on me?"

"Oh." Abby said. "I wondered if this outfit gave that impression."

"It's good on you," Celia shrugged. "Gives you an edge." She grinned. "You're too much of a softy oftentimes. What brings you here?"

"Desmond called me in for a consultation."

Celia rolled her eyes. "You're not on call twenty-four hours a day at everyone's whim."

"Yes, I am." Abby gave her a sad smile. "If needed, that's what I'll do."

Celia knew very well what drove Abby. Ever since she'd missed seeing her mother alive one last time, Abby would never refuse a call for help. Anything to save a treasured family member. Anything to make someone's last days more comfortable.

"Desmond's not in the main room anyway," Celia replied.

"I'll try the quiet room," Abby said and waved back to Celia. "I'll catch you before I leave."

The peaceful back room, overlooking the gardens, was empty except for Desmond crouching in front of Mr Argent and his wife. Concern wrinkled his face and Abby padded round and knelt down.

Mr Argent, the old mayor of Ludbury, sat quietly, cradling his elbow. The distinguished gentleman was still a handsome man and young for his advanced stage of Alzheimer's. His wife, Caroline, always flawless, sat beside him gently resting her fingers on his arm, something he usually forbade now he no longer recognised her as his beloved spouse. Abby nodded a greeting. She had a lot of respect for the Tory councillor, despite Maggie's constant sniping at their political differences.

"Sorry to call you in, Abby," Desmond said in a quiet rumble. "Ambulances have been called to a pileup on the motorway and aren't responding to calls."

"That's OK," Abby said gently. "How's he doing?"

"Quiet as a mouse," Desmond replied. "Most unlike him. You know what he's like usually, ordering people around."

Abby smiled as she caught exasperation flicker across Caroline's face.

"It's true," the older woman said.

He'd been cantankerous enough as the mayor when Abby had first moved to Ludbury, but the decline in his mental state had made him quicker to temper. Now he sat unnaturally quiet, like a hurt child.

"What happened?"

"The silly sod tried to climb out of a window. Kept rambling on about a meeting, then clattered to the floor, full weight on his elbow."

"OK," Abby said. "Let's have a look." She shuffled forwards. "Good evening, Mr Argent. I'm Dr Hart and I need to see your elbow." She gingerly rolled up his jumper sleeve. "I'm sorry if it's painful, sir." He winced but didn't complain as she pushed the garment to his upper arm. She heard Desmond inhale as she revealed the dark purple bruising all around the joint.

"Oh God," Caroline gasped.

"It's getting worse," Desmond said. "Wasn't like that a few minutes ago."

Caroline's face crumpled and tears sprang from her eyes. "Is he in lots of pain?" she asked.

"I can give him something for that," Abby said, reaching for Caroline's hand to reassure her. "Desmond, would you?"

Desmond nodded. "I'll get some water," he said as he retreated from the room.

"It will take the edge off while we wait," Abby said. "We do need an ambulance. I'm certain there's a break and you can't take him yourself. He's too unpredictable."

"Why does he do this?" Caroline said, exasperated.

Abby swung round to sit next to Mrs Argent. "It's typical behaviour I'm afraid."

Caroline dropped her hands into her lap in despair. "I don't know what to do. I thought he'd be safer here than at home. I can't watch him every second of the day. He wanders even in his sleep. It's impossible."

"You've done the right thing. There haven't been any accidents since you brought him here six months ago. Remarkable for such a forceful man."

Caroline's mouth twitched with a hint of a smile.

"You mustn't blame yourself. It would be impossible to care for him in a typical house. Far too dangerous. And it would take a heavy toll on you."

"I feel so guilty," Caroline whispered. "It shouldn't be like this. I promised him til death us do part, not to leave him to strangers."

"Unfortunately…" Abby hesitated before telling the brutal truth. "We're all strangers to him now."

Caroline gripped her hand and her cheeks knotted as she fought to control her grief. "You are right. It hurts, but I know you're right."

"I'm sorry," Abby said. "I wish there was more we could do. Keeping him safe at the care home is best. I see you here almost every time I visit Celia. No-one thinks you've abandoned him."

"But I have, you see," Caroline said, broken. "In his eyes, I have."

Abby held on to the grieving woman's hand, unable to console what troubled Caroline inside. "I know you're doing the best you can. Others would have been far less attentive."

Mrs Argent didn't reply, but held on to Abby. Sometimes, like Jude had showed all those years ago, simply being there was the best anyone could do.

The blue lights of the ambulance flashed outside the care home and Abby watched Mr Argent carried away accompanied by Caroline. She stood at the window until the ambulance pulled off then stared at the blackness outside.

"Still here?"

Abby hadn't noticed Celia sidle up with a mischievous air.

"You wouldn't be avoiding Jude, would you?" Celia persisted. "Not avoiding her at the party?"

Abby gave her a look.

"Would you like me to have an angina attack to delay you some more?"

"Stop it." Abby laughed.

"So you are avoiding Jude."

Well yes, and no. Abby wanted to see her friend every minute of the day. But the combination of alcohol, Jude dressed to the nines and Abby's current hormonal imbalance were cause for alarm.

"Worried you might give yourself away?" Celia grinned. "Blushing all pink when she comes near?"

Abby spun round, eyes and mouth circular.

"During a little sexy piano playing perhaps?" Celia chuckled.

Abby actually and audibly gasped. "You noticed?"

"Anybody with eyes would have noticed."

Well, this was a fresh hell of humiliation.

"And Maggie did note how well you looked after your visit to Jude's bedroom."

Oh Christ.

"Does Maggie know? Did she really notice?"

"No, my dear." Celia smiled and squeezed her arm. "Far too much insanity of her own going on. But I've been wondering…." Celia considered. "Do you think perhaps Jude has?"

Abby's heart skipped a beat and fear tickled her tummy.

"I hope not."

Celia tugged at her with affection.

"Have you ever wondered what she might do if she knew?"

"Nope." Abby trembled even at the thought.

"It must be a huge weight to carry around with you. I've been wondering, why not tell her?"

"Because nothing good would come of it."

"Why not?"

"She's never been remotely interested in women. The other day, she told me she once kissed a woman and felt nothing." Abby stared at Celia with disbelief. "Nothing."

"Hmm. People change, in all kinds of ways. God knows Maggie did," Celia grumbled before quickly moving on. "I still think it worth unburdening yourself. Jude is a bright girl, very tolerant and able to appreciate people's different inclinations. She grew up with Eli for goodness sake."

"But there's a difference between accepting Eli's pansexuality and me lusting after her and almost combusting every time we touch." Then Abby blushed. "I mean loving her."

Celia snorted. "I might break it to her more gently than that."

"Oh." Another wave of humiliation flooded through Abby. "So telling her I wanted unfettered hot sex might not be a good way to broach the subject."

"Well no, indeed."

"Oh."

Celia peered over her glasses and eyed Abby with new understanding. "Good lord. You didn't?"

"I did."

"Did she say yes?"

"No. Well. I didn't say it in such a straightforward way."

"When was this?"

"Last night. When we said goodbye."

"Gosh. That was moving fast. Perhaps you should have asked her in for tea first."

"Celia. It wasn't like that. She's always pressuring me to ask Cheese Shop Lady out, and I wanted to set a few things straight. I was hypothetically describing what I wanted in a relationship – the physical type of woman, who may have sounded similar to Jude, and the type of personality, who may also have sounded a lot like her, and perhaps what level of, um, passion I'd, um, like." Abby stroked the short hair above her neck.

Celia stared at her, eyes narrowed with study and amusement. "And you say she doesn't suspect?"

"I hope not," Abby groaned.

Because the way Jude looked when Abby had told her of her ideal woman was not encouraging. In fact, she'd never seen Jude so shocked.

23

So now Jude knew.

"Unfettered hot sex," she murmured as she walked beneath the street light towards the square. That's what it would take. If she was going to make this work – this old married couple – she needed to give Abby screamingly good sex.

What did that even look like between two women?

She immediately recalled a bondage video of an ex-boyfriend's at university. Two women in scant leather suits, with strategic zips and rather unnecessary fish-net stockings, tying each other up. One even had a whip. Oh God, was it all cuffs and dildos?

Then she remembered Abby laughing when she'd told her and explaining lesbians were just as boring, just as kinky and just as varied as everyone else. So what the hell did they do?

Jude, her mind buzzing, walked around the edge of the square and dipped her head down a narrow passageway between the old Assembly Rooms and Tudor shops. Her heels clicked and slipped on the cobbles and she slowed her pace in the dim light. Halfway along the passage, out of sight of the square, she pushed on the warped oak door of the Chequers Tavern. It wasn't much lighter inside, the medieval pub panelled with dark wood, and snug corners perfect for hiding lovers or smugglers. It was Jude and Eli's favourite pub from their teens, and many an hour of their youth had been spent, disreputably on Eli's part, in this establishment.

"Evening, Jude," the portly landlord called from behind the bar. "You lot are set up downstairs, although you're one of the first. Eli's not here yet."

"Thanks, Bob." And she rolled her eyes. Typical of her brother to be tardy in attending his own party.

She tip-toed down the spiral brick steps into the old cellars, her head just clearing the ceiling where it curved down from the supporting pillars. She bought a glass of Sauvignon Blanc from the bar and looked around the low-lit room.

The middle was clear, no doubt at Eli's request, for dancing later in the evening, and any guests were sat at the artfully battered tables around the edges. She recognised the odd classmate of Eli's from school and nodded with recognition, then her eyes alighted on Selene's mother. She sat at the far end of the room, alone, a glass of liqueur raised elegantly in her hand as if a cigarette were more her habit. Whether it was the dim light, or Jude's scrutiny returned, it appeared as if Juliette studied her.

Jude hesitated, wondering if she should merely nod an acknowledgement after the bizarre ructions between Maggie and Juliette the night before, but she imagined the fault of those more likely her mother's. And a little effort with Eli's future mother-in-law would be appropriate, especially since Eli and Selene adored her.

"Good evening," Jude said, approaching. "We weren't properly introduced." She smiled, remembering Eli's brutal description of them all the previous night. "I'm Eli's sister, Jude."

Juliette stood and offered her hand, pulling Jude fluidly towards her for two kisses. "*Enchantee*. Please," she said, sweeping her arm wide, "join me. I think we are both early."

"A habit of mine. My brother has the opposite."

177

"I've noticed." Juliette smiled. "I already tell him an hour earlier than I plan to meet."

"A very good idea. It's taken me a lifetime to come to the same conclusion." Jude sat down, reminded of how sharp and formidable Juliette was.

Selene's mother clearly had a keen intellect, something that never intimidated Jude and she freely admired it. In fact, there was much to admire about this woman. Juliette's posture was impeccable – straight back and open shoulders, slim legs crossed, all draped in a black dress that was inimitably elegant. She possessed a poise which Jude with her curvy Amazonian physique and cream dress could never even pretend.

"You are very different to Eli I think," Juliette said with a curl of a smile.

Jude laughed. It was as if Juliette had been studying her at the same time.

"Eli's very much my mother's son," Jude replied. "I take after my father."

"Hmm," Juliette responded with a hint of amusement. "I think Eli has some of your father's amiability though and you a little of your mother's fire."

Jude was about to disagree, but Juliette had witnessed her outburst at her mother's homophobia. "Yes," Jude said. "Apparently so. Although until recently I would have disagreed. Something about being back home brings it out." Jude wondered, "Do you know my parents well?"

"Richard, *non*."

Jude loved the way Juliette said her father's name. *Rishar*. It made her down-to-earth father sound comically exotic.

"But Maggie?" Jude pressed.

"Yes, I know your mother better." Juliette took another sip of liqueur as if to signal an end to the subject.

But Jude couldn't help but stare at her expectantly. The combination of Juliette's intriguing character and the friction between her and Maggie made curiosity inevitable.

178

Juliette raised a single eyebrow. "We were rivals for many years."

"How so?" Jude leaned closer.

"I was a PhD student at King's when I met her. She was a very bright woman." Admiration shone in Juliette's expression as she recalled. "I tutored a group of students including Maggie and none had her spark. She was the only one who challenged my opinions. The others," Juliette shrugged dismissively. "They wanted hints about exam papers. But Maggie, she was incisive, and even when her opinions were not as rigorously supported by the literature as mine she would tie me up in knots with her linguistic abilities."

Jude was about to reassure Juliette about the admirable fluency of her English.

"I'm more confident now." Juliette dismissed any concern with a wave of her hand. "Many years practice lecturing in America. But back then as a new PhD student." Juliette smiled, her eyes distant. "Maggie was challenging. I adored and loathed her for it."

Jude's interest in her mother was piqued. She knew very little about Maggie before she'd met Jude's father. Maggie had Jude so young it seemed impossible she did anything of note before. Jude had seen pictures of her mother at school – farcical shots of the young, rebellious and scowling Maggie, forced into a pinafore and tights – then nothing until wedding photos.

"Do you have any more pictures of my mother?"

"Ah," Juliette said with an expression which flickered between amusement and embarrassment. "That was naughty of me to show you all that photograph. It seems Maggie still brings out the worst in me and I wanted to ruffle her feathers."

"You do have more?" Jude pressed.

"One or two, yes." Juliette hesitated. "When I realised who Eli's mother was, I searched through my old college photos and scanned a few. I was a keen photographer at university." She looked at Jude with indulgence. "I suppose Maggie wouldn't mind these."

She retrieved her mobile from a black clutch bag, flicked across the screen then handed the device to Jude. The black and white shot showed Maggie studying in a library, her brow furrowed in concentration in exactly the way it did now.

"Maggie was brilliant," Juliette said. "She could have done anything. But she wanted a family and sacrificed everything for that. She could have been much more than a school teacher. "

Jude smiled. It was a criticism she'd heard frequently applied to Maggie and she knew her mother's response off pat.

"Teaching children is one of the most important careers," Jude said. "Little is more vital beyond being a farmer and providing food."

Juliette tilted her head. "Is that your mother's answer?"

"Yes, I've paraphrased. Maggie says it with much more finesse."

"She was always capable of beautiful eloquence," Juliette said. "But also of nauseating vulgarity."

Jude laughed. "You know her well."

"Yes," Juliette said, and again her words implied so much. "Here's another." And she swiped her finger across the screen.

"Oh," Jude said, sitting back.

It was an intimate picture of Maggie's face, a little blurred and overexposed. She was smiling, like a satisfied cat rolling in front of a blazing fire. Jude had never seen Maggie as carefree. Not a hint of ire wrinkled her features, no concern furrowed her brow, no scathing comment about to issue from her lips. Simple bliss. It was difficult to reconcile the young woman with her mother. What happened to Maggie to make her so irascible?

Jude stroked the image, then felt foolish. She'd expected the texture of a matt photo but her fingertips encountered the impersonal perfection of the screen.

"Would you?" Jude said, almost shy. "Would you send me a copy?"

"Of course."

They swapped numbers and moments later Jude possessed a secret glimpse of her mother's life.

"Thank you," Jude said, embarrassed at coveting such an artefact.

The room was beginning to fill, the crowd at the bar two people thick, and music played in the background. Jude peered over the heads of the throng but couldn't spot Eli or, more importantly, Abby.

"Are you looking for your friend?" Juliette said, her head tilted to the side and her eyes observing with piercing clarity.

"Yes, I was."

The older woman placed her liqueur on the table and clasped her hands elegantly in her lap, her attention focussed solely on Jude. "You like her, don't you?" she said, her study unwavering.

Jude's heart fluttered at the exposure. She deflected. "We've been friends for years. Since the first year at university."

"I didn't mean that way," Juliette replied, and the way she meant was abundantly clear.

Jude hadn't talked to a single soul about her growing feelings towards Abby and the changing way she viewed her friend. The weight of her secret seemed suddenly unbearable.

"Actually," Jude said, "yes I do."

Was that a smirk on the other woman's face?

"It was very plain to see," Juliette said. Then she no longer hid her amusement, breaking out into a broad grin. "Although I must admit, Eli briefed me about Abby before."

Bloody Eli.

"He briefed me on you all."

"Thanks, Eli." Jude tutted.

"And so far, I agree with his colourful assessments." Juliette eyed her and sipped through smiling lips.

"I imagine he described me as an embarrassing dullard of a sister with thunderous thighs."

"*Non*," Juliette said with satisfaction, "although you are right; he wasn't gracious about your thighs."

Jude burst out laughing at Eli's impertinence and Juliette's.

"He admires you very much," Juliette added. "He described you as very intelligent, secure, supportive and central to the family – qualities he abhors in himself of course, but recognises as essential in others."

Jude had to laugh again. Juliette, it seemed, was spot on about Eli.

"I think he was right too. You are an admirable woman."

"Thank you," Jude said, still amused by Juliette's observation of her brother.

"I think he's right about your friend also. She adores you." And Juliette's expression softened.

"Yes," Jude conceded. "I think she might."

"So." Juliette threw up her hands. "Why are you two not together?"

"It's complicated."

"Love always is, but then it's so simple too. Your heart sees to that. It must have what it wants even when your brain tells you a thousand reasons why not."

"There's a lot to lose." Jude said, tensing up. "We've been friends for years and Abby relies on me and my family. If it went wrong…."

"But if it went right," Juliette said breathlessly, opening her slim arms out wide and embracing the potential. "It could be beautiful."

Jude's heart thumped in her chest. "And, I'm not… I'm not a… I've never had a relationship with a woman before," her words rushed out.

"Ah," Juliette exclaimed and she dropped her hands, her face effused with warm envy. "Then you have so much to look forward to."

Jude gulped. "I don't know what I'm doing. I don't know how to do this."

"It will become apparent." Juliette tilted her head. "If you choose that path, you won't have time to think. It's always a rollercoaster."

"But it must be so different."

"Hmm." Juliette shrugged. "Do you always fall for the same type of man? *Non.* I bet all your lovers were different and your relationships too."

"True," Jude conceded. But Christ, none of them had breasts and a vagina.

Eli once told her he fell in love with a person from the eyes down. If he saw a spark of intelligence, wit and a kind soul in their eyes, he'd listen to their voice. If he found their tone beguiling and their words inspiring, he'd fall in love with whatever body they came with. By that time it was unimportant to him and everyone was physically attractive in some way. The biceps of hairy Steve. The curving hips of Arabella. The sheer fragile beauty of Jack. How Jude envied her brother now.

"It has to be different with a woman," Jude gasped.

"For me, yes." Juliette smiled. "Love and sex with a man is like listening to a soloist. Pleasant, sometimes beautiful and moving. But with a woman." She was wistful. "It is a symphony of sound and colour. You cannot help be swept up in it. So much to look forward to," Juliette exclaimed again with not a little pleasure. "Oh I envy you. That first rush with a woman. There's nothing like it. Once you start down that path, you won't be able to stop, and you won't want to. Not with a woman you gaze at with those eyes."

If anything Juliette's reassurance frightened Jude more. What if Abby felt that rollercoaster ride but not her?

Jude shook her head. "My mother wouldn't approve."

183

"That is unfortunate. I'm sorry she's like that." Juliette hesitated, then with a flash of defiance urged, "Don't ever let that stop you." She reached forward and squeezed her hand. "Never."

Jude was about to respond when Juliette stood. "They're here."

Jude turned and spotted Eli and Selene skipping down the steps with matching tuxedoes and Converse shoes. But it was the woman behind who dominated Jude's attention.

Abby entered the room almost a different person. Her hair was slicked back from her face and the bright jewels of her eyes, so often hidden behind her fringe, shone bright. Her lips pulsed red and she was dressed in head-to-toe black with an elegant androgyny that was potent. She looked devastating. Gone was Abby's soft caring local doctor and in her place was a woman ready to kill, or at the very least ready for unfettered hot sex.

Jude was halfway across the room before she realised she'd taken a step.

24

The cream dress. It was the cream dress. Abby was done for.

Jude's sun-kissed waves cascaded over bare shoulders. Her breasts were cupped to perfection. The material slipped around Jude's magnificent thighs as she sauntered fluidly towards Abby. She looked divine.

Jude stopped an inch away, her half-naked bosom radiating heat. "Hi," she whispered.

Her beautiful friend's eyes were dark in the shadows and lips parted a fraction so that Abby stared at them waiting for words to issue. Those were the most delicious lips in existence, with the prominent curve which perpetually seemed to smile and commanded attention. And soft. Abby melted inside just gazing at them. How could you not want to kiss those lips?

"You look stunning," Jude murmured.

Jude's fingers curled sensually around Abby's hips as she drew her into a hug. The touch was overpowering and the sensation radiated through Abby's body and warmth shot to her core. It tingled up her spine and its deliciousness was surpassed only when she was drawn into Jude's sumptuous body.

As they embraced, every inch of Abby, from her toes to the hair which stood on the back of her neck, appreciated that hug. She flung her arms around Jude's shoulders and succumbed to the desire to pull her closer, breasts embracing her friend's supple bosom, thighs slipping between the wonders that were Jude's, Abby's body reacting as if they were naked.

The urge to run her fingers through Jude's silky curls, grab great handfuls and kiss those swollen lips was insane. She wanted nothing more than to strip Jude of her dress and have her prodigious thighs roll between her own.

"Oh," she moaned.

Was there any point trying to disguise it?

"Hello, sis."

Abby twitched at Eli's unmistakable voice behind her. He'd drawn out his greeting achingly slowly so that innuendo and sarcasm dripped from every syllable. She sprung from Jude's embrace, eyes wide in alarm.

His grinning white teeth shone like a spotlight. "How about a hug like that for your brother?" he said to them both, arms out wide.

Abby's desire curdled and she couldn't help the feeling scrunching her face.

"No?" Eli said teasing her. "But it looked so nice."

"Eli, you bugger." Jude stepped between them. "Now, congratulations on your engagement. Let me buy you a drink."

"Aw, sis. You're too kind. Better get Abby a drink too. She looks hot."

Abby thought she heard a slap and a yelp, but couldn't swear to it. She shuffled behind Jude as they headed to the bar, with only Jude's voluptuous bottom for view. That was torture enough but when Jude turned she was more beautiful than ever. The heat of the crowd must have elicited a glow – her cheeks rose, lips swollen, even her bare chest which peeped from her dress was flushed. If Abby hadn't known better she would have said Jude glowed with desire and the idea alone was intoxicating.

Jude leant down close to Abby's ear and the warmth which rose from her chest was dizzying.

"What would you like?" Jude murmured. "To drink."

"I don't care," Abby gasped.

"Perhaps some wine?" she whispered and her breath tickled Abby's bare neck and teased down her cleavage in a sweet caress. Then Jude leaned a little closer so her lips tickled against Abby's ear.

"Or a finger width of whisky?"

A quiet groan escaped Abby. It may have contained words. Equally it may not. Abby suspected the latter when Jude added, "I'll choose," and mercifully turned to order at the bar.

"A bottle of Prosecco," Abby heard her shout, now the music was louder. Jude brandished the bottle and four glasses above the crowd and stood them on the ledge around one of the square pillar bases.

"Here you go," she said passing a large glass to Abby, another for Eli and a smaller one at Selene's insistence.

"Congratulations," Jude cried to her brother and fiancée before slipping an arm around Abby.

Such a simple touch, and frequent throughout their friendship, but enough to make Abby tremble now. Enough to want to turn round and pin Jude up against a wall. The compulsion was so strong it felt as inevitable as jumping off a tall building when peering over the edge.

"Drink up, Abby," Eli said. "You could be in for a long night."

Abby had been half way down her glass and little shot up her nose as she coughed. Oh for a long night with Jude.

Eli smirked over his glass. "How are you enjoying the evening so far?"

"Great," Abby said, bubbles popping up her nostrils. Apart from the small problem of being reduced to lower brain function and losing any sense of control or inhibition. Oh this was dangerous. She took a long swig in a desperate attempt to cool her urges.

"You know what would make it better?" Eli said. "What would really heat up the action?"

Abby couldn't help her eyebrows shooting skywards. "What?"

"Dancing. I love it when you two make music together."

"No," Abby groaned, beyond alarmed. "Dancing?"

"Dancing." Eli grinned.

Abby was about to plead with Jude, but she was mouthing something at Eli. I will kill you? But it can't have been that because Eli continued.

"Come on beloved," he said, offering his arm to Selene. "Let's see these two get up close and personal."

And before Abby's brain could fail again to produce anything coherent she found herself guided to the floor by Jude's arm circling her body.

So dancing. They were going dancing. She could do this. She'd danced with Jude thousands of times. She danced with friends often. And the track was perfect as she followed Jude into the throng. Some grating harsh rock to erase her desire. Not in the least bit sexy. Absolutely perfect.

Then it wasn't.

The guitars crashed to an end, followed by silence, then the unmistakable clap and Spanish guitar intro to *When We're High* reverberated around the room. Abby knew what was coming next – a pulsing rhythm and slinky beat made to inspire swaying hips. A song that spoke of smoky bars and sultry love-making. It had this effect when Abby was alone, dancing in an ironic sexy way around her kitchen. Now here was Jude, all pheromones on legs, her voluptuous body inches away and beginning to move to the music.

Before Abby could take her leave, Jude took her hands and slipped her fingers in between hers. Oh God, they were sinfully soft.

Jude held their hands, palm to palm, hips undulating to the beat of the song. Warmth flowed through their hands and bodies, and Jude didn't take her eyes off Abby's for a moment. It was if they plunged into her very soul.

"We're only dancing," Abby told herself. "Relax. Everyone's doing the same."

The tension dissipated from her shoulders and unlocked the fluidity of her body. She began to move her hips in time with Jude. Their bodies slipped closer and Abby closed her eyes to the music, dizzy with the warmth from Jude and headiness of the wine.

This was fine. It was dancing. They could have been anywhere at any time over the last ten years. Then her nipples stroked Jude's. It was just the lightest of touches but the thrill shot to her core and the fire ignited again. Jude pulled her closer, hands dropping to Abby's hips, thighs slipping together and the inferno consumed Abby. She was beyond control as Jude swayed and rolled with the sensual rhythm and Abby's head swirled intoxicated by the intimacy of Jude's dance. She couldn't have stopped if she'd tried.

Jude's hands trailed Abby's body, her fingers exploring up tantalisingly close to her chest so that Abby's breasts tingled with anticipation. She craved Jude's touch and willed her to stroke higher. If only Jude would rub her thumbs across her nipples. Pinch them. Squeeze them.

But with a smooth movement Jude spun her round so she spooned Abby from behind. Not missing a beat Abby found herself back between Jude's thighs, her friend's fingers exploring more freely and cupping tantalisingly beneath her bosom. Her breasts cried out for attention and Abby pleaded silently, "Touch me".

Without thinking, Abby reached back to Jude's warm thigh, letting her hands move in time. With every note she ran her fingers higher up the sultry material. Closer and closer she caressed to where she hadn't even dared imagine before.

189

Abby snapped open her eyes. This wasn't dancing. Who was she kidding? She wanted to plunge her fingers into Jude's slick depths.

Shit. There was no doubting Abby's desire or intentions. She'd lost herself completely in the rhythm. She panicked. The dim cellar lights were forgiving and the room so crowded no-one would have noticed. All except Jude, who must be in no doubt about where Abby's hand was wandering.

"I'm sorry," Abby gasped, and she stepped forward. She stood with her chest heaving. "I'm sorry. Please forget I did that."

Hearing no reply, she peeked over her shoulder. She couldn't see Jude's face clearly but her friend didn't move at all.

"I'm sorry," Abby said. "Forgive me. I'll see you tomorrow," and she dived through the crowd towards the door, humiliation burning on her cheeks.

25

She'd let Abby leave, after that incredible dance. Why hadn't she turned Abby round and kissed her? Because Abby had been way ahead of Jude. There was no second guessing what her friend had desired, hands wandering closer to where Jude had longed for her to touch. But what were Jude's hands meant to do?

She tried to imagine touching Abby, but she couldn't. There was a block too strong, through stigma or, worse, real aversion on Jude's part. What if she recoiled in disgust when she caressed Abby? That would devastate her friend.

But the throbbing waves of arousal which ached inside Jude were real and begging for Abby. Jude could still feel the sensation of Abby's body stroking between her thighs as they danced. And if they hadn't been somewhere public Jude's hands would have been all over Abby's breasts. Then what?

Jude shook her head and skipped up the steps, hoping to catch up. Her dress and heels hampered the chase and Abby was beyond the passageway by the time Jude surfaced. She clipped down the alley after her.

What was she going to do? What the hell was she going to say?

"Abby, I want you. I very clearly want you. But I don't know if I can do this. I don't know what to do."

Abby was fast. She was already beyond sight of the square when Jude emerged from the passageway. Home. She must have gone home.

Abby burst through the cottage door, switched on the lights and collapsed against the kitchen island. She closed her eyes and groaned. The march home had done nothing to quell her desire.

So she wasn't always the best at keeping her passion for her friend under control, but Jude wasn't exactly helping. That dance. That exquisite dance. Jude's hands all over her, sliding down her sides, brushing against her breasts so they tingled with expectation. The way her hands explored around her thighs so that Abby wanted to grab them and guide them to where she ached.

"Nyaah," Abby gurgled and she buried her head in her hands. She couldn't keep the images from engulfing her mind and sensations fraying her body.

"Radio," she gasped. "Music."

Anything to distract her from the onslaught of provocative memories. She fumbled with her Roberts radio on the kitchen top, twizzling the knob until a loud dance song throbbed from the set. The thumping bass blasted any thought, red hot or otherwise, from her mind.

"Better," she said, with relief.

The monotonous number thudded in her mind, so all she imagined was a white room pulsing with music. She began to breathe more easily. The vision was soothing.

Then clapping started to overlay the back beat.

No. That was very familiar clapping. Very familiar indeed. Then a Spanish guitar limbered up. No, no, no. It couldn't be. And a slinky bass line which made swaying hips inevitable. Someone had remixed the song from the cellars. That wasn't fair. So not fair.

Images of their dance flooded her mind. She could feel the warmth of Jude's body behind her, hands exploring the curve of her breast and achingly close to her centre.

Abby groaned and closed her eyes. The rhythm of the music transported her back to that delicious moment. If Jude had only stroked a little further. If she'd cupped her breasts and teased her nipples with a pinch, again and again. The imagined caress sent very real pulses of excitement through Abby's body. She pictured Jude's fingers tightening around her nipple and a lightning strike of arousal shot from her breasts to her core. At the same time, she willed Jude's free hand around her thighs. If only she'd slid her fingers further, slowly, purposely, and slipped between her legs.

Abby moaned into her hands. "Oooooh."

Then, "Nooooooooo."

The rules. She had rules. This was definitely against those rules. This was breaking every single one.

But that seductive beat, its slow rhythm, perfect for aching, tantalising sex. It was so evocative it was as if Jude's hands were on her again.

"Nooooo," Abby groaned as she pulsed between her legs. "Remember the rules."

She pressed her fingers to her jeans, but the warmth intensified and she staggered along the kitchen island. She must not fantasise about Jude. Absolutely no fantasising. The rules. Remember the rules. She must not imagine Jude's soft fingers stroking her clitoris.

"Oh," she gasped. The sensation was almost real. The tips of Jude's fingers, which Abby knew so well, virtually touched her core, tenderly circling where she throbbed.

"The rules," she groaned. "Oh fuck the rules."

Abby ran from the room, up the stairs, her body thrumming with arousal so strongly it beat in her ears. She stripped her shirt, tugged it from her arms, unclipped her bra in a millisecond and flung it across the room. She stamped and tripped out of her trousers and tugged her knickers off almost mid-air while she dived into bed.

Abby slipped a finger between her legs into hot, soaking desire. She moaned with the intensity. She clutched her own breast imagining Jude holding her pushing up behind her.

"Fuck."

Her orgasm was already building, its tingling grip spreading through her body. Its warmth flooded her. It was huge. It was as if Jude squeezed and embraced every part of her body with electrifying pleasure.

"Oh," Abby moaned out loud.

"Abby, Abby, Abby," Jude murmured as she clicked down the street. She hadn't fathomed what to say. "I have so many feelings. I'm without doubt attracted to you."

The memories of Abby's buttocks stroking between her thighs was vivid and heavenly in too many places, she knew she wasn't lying. And Jude was definitely coming round to breasts. But what would touching Abby's clit feel like? This wasn't something Jude could mess up. This was Abby who depended on her like no other.

The lights were on in Abby's cottage, shining onto the pavement, and music blared from inside. Jude peeked through the door windows, moving from one small square to the next, peering around.

"Abby," she called.

Her friend didn't hear and Abby stumbled from the kitchen further into the house.

"Abby!" Jude shouted.

Still she didn't turn and she disappeared up the stairs.

Jude stepped back into the street and peered up, expecting the bedroom light to come on, but it remained dark.

"Abby, come on," Jude whispered.

She rapped her knuckles on the door. They sounded weak below the music that thudded inside the house. Jude stared at the lock and tentatively tried the handle. It was open, and she went inside and pushed the door to.

"Abby?" she called. "I'm sorry. I need to talk to you."

There was the sound of footsteps muffled upstairs then they ceased.

"Abby?"

She wouldn't be able to hear Jude above the music. Jude started up the steps, the stairwell and upper floor in darkness.

"It's Jude," she said hesitantly. "I wanted to talk to you."

There was a moan. A long, drawn-out, satisfied moan.

"Are you there?" Jude ventured.

The bedroom door was half closed, obscuring her view. Jude padded up the carpet and peered through the gap. She was about to call out again when she stopped. Dead. Completely still.

The sight effected an impressive number of things. Shock froze Jude to the spot and innumerable other feelings assaulted her body. The room was lit by streetlight through a gap in the curtains and it shone its soft light onto the naked form of her friend lying on the bed. Abby looked beautiful, the curve of her breasts and the tantalising line from her chest down her belly, straight to the triangle between her hips.

Abby was completely naked. Jude wanted to admire every inch for hours. But what transfixed her was the sight of Abby's hand vigorously squeezing her own breast and the other between her slick loins, circling ever faster around her centre.

The blood simultaneously drained from Jude's cheeks and filled elsewhere in her body. That look on Abby's face. The mixture of painful ecstasy and uncontrollable satisfaction was terrifying, arousing, shocking. Jude gasped and sunk to her knees.

She thought she knew everything about Abby, every reaction and expression. But this anguished ecstasy was new. It was exciting, embarrassing, incredibly arousing. Abby was completely exposed. It was just so rude.

195

Abby circled her clitoris, moaning, face frowning in gratification. She stroked faster, her body tensing and arching from the bed and Jude felt her own insides tighten in empathy. Her breathing quickened as Abby's did and the warmth intensified between her legs. Then Abby climaxed, rigid and taut except for the anguished groan which escaped her lips.

Jude shuddered with the release, chest heaving and trembling with hormones that flooded her body. It had been the most debilitating and erotic sight she'd ever seen.

"Oh God," Abby gasped. "Oh fucking God."

Abby collapsed onto the bed in what must have been a potent post-coital daze, so relaxed she seemed fluid. She rolled over and buried her head in a big fluffy pillow.

"The rules," came a muffled groan. "So many broken rules."

Jude watched as her own breathing eased back to normal. She heard Abby's breath become slow and minutes later acquire the heaviness of slumber.

Jude walked in a daze downstairs, turned off the music and flicked the door off the latch. As she wandered home she stared at the ground, her mind incapacitated by the images she'd witnessed, and the sounds, even the scent. Her body had focussed all its resources on the sensations between her thighs and it was a primeval part of her psyche that returned her home safely to her room. And there, she removed her gown and her underwear and slipped between the sheets.

Apparently, Jude had no qualms, no rules at all, about picturing Abby and reliving that scene while her hand comforted between her legs. And now she had no doubt how she'd react if she ever touched Abby.

26

Maggie had been awake for hours. She gazed from the acres of space in the marital bed, watching the sun sparkle through the beech trees on the horizon and over the church grounds.

The rest of the house was silent. Her nephews were home with their father and sore mother. Eli and Selene she imagined sleeping off all kinds of excesses from the engagement party and Jude had returned with the wordless determination of a teenager and gone straight to her room.

Maggie had been left alone for too long. She did believe those souls who insisted they enjoyed their own company, but frankly she pissed herself off after a few hours and craved someone to bother. Especially when her own company and past were tormenting her.

Maggie sighed, letting the air whistle from her lips for as long as possible. She lay her head back on the mountain of pillows, which had once supported a family of four when the children had nightmares, then two, and were now hers alone, and closed her eyes.

The autumn sun danced through her eyelids and the light seemed to warm her body and spirit, one of her favourite experiences. Her mind drifted, remembering other mornings, lazily making love and lying in bed all day and the memory of Juliette's naked breasts on her own was suddenly vivid, so much so the sensation felt real.

"Shit." Maggie snapped open her eyes. "Fucking, buggering, shit."

The memory had been a secret indulgence over the years. They'd luxuriated like that often in their flat overlooking the university parks. The one thing they'd found uncontentious was their love of holding the world at bay until the morning was old, banishing it entirely from their routine at the weekend. They'd nuzzled in bed for hours, dozing, love-making, talking, never letting go of each other. The forbidden memory was always followed by a wave of melancholy. Except today. Given the woman's proximity and reality, it was fury which cantered in.

"Bollocks," Maggie huffed.

What pissing curve ball of fate had sent Juliette? How perverse Maggie should encourage Eli in his study of the era which would lead him straight to Juliette's lectures and her beautiful daughter. The universe had a wicked sense of humour.

Finding her right outside the door. Not there to cause trouble. Only passing by. Then showing them all that sodding picture. At least it wasn't a nude of Maggie. She rolled her eyes at her young self. All those artful photos she'd posed for, thinking they'd be together forever. She hated to think where those intimate shots now lay.

And Tiff, with her shaved head. Maggie hadn't thought about her in years, sloping off after the birth of Eli, finally bored with her Maggie supposed. Tiff had always been more enamoured with Juliette and Maggie was surprised she'd lasted that long. And Mike. Poor Mike. One of the losses in the terrifying wave which engulfed their scene in the eighties. And Juliette of course. Not pictured, although always present in the memory.

Maggie growled and swung her legs out of bed. She'd mellowed toward mornings over the years – the children had necessitated that – but she wasn't going to greet this one with any benevolence. She cleaned vigorously in the shower, crashed around the kitchen as she made coffee and thumped onto the sofa. Every part of her home would feel her chagrin this morning.

There was a knock at the door.

"Who the fuck's there?" she shouted.

Whoever it was mustn't have heard because another polite knock ensued.

Maggie tutted and leapt off the sofa and marched into the hall. She opened the door, without bothering with a conciliatory face, to meet the amiable expression on Richard's.

"For the love of God, come through the attic door," Maggie snapped.

"Good morning, dear." Always amused. He was always so damned happy these days.

"Just use the bloody internal door."

"No. We've agreed our boundaries. I believe they work well."

"I'm overrun with all sorts at the moment, you may as well have the run of the place too." With the chaos, no-one seemed to have noticed the changes in their living arrangements. The children were so wrapped up in their domestic bliss or blight they'd not ventured to the attic or noticed when Richard slept away. At least Jude was looking better, in fact refreshingly so.

"I will respect the rules under your roof." He smiled. "I'm back from Caroline's and just checking in."

"Kind of you, dear. I'm alive and, once I warm up, will be kicking."

"Do you fancy some company for breakfast?"

She did. "No thank you."

"I'll cook it."

That would have been lovely. "No need."

"I come with ingredients for French toast," he said, lifting his shopping bag.

Maggie raised her eyebrow. Toast which had to be, of all things, French? Did he do that on purpose?

"Sorry," he added. "Funny how the brain works."

"Hilarious," she deadpanned.

"It occurred to me when I was at the corner shop that I hadn't cooked it for you in an age. Not in the slightest bit intentional."

"I still don't want it."

"You're avoiding me."

"Yes, I am."

"I know who she is."

"I assumed you did."

"Maggie," he said, as exasperated as a parent, which was, of course, galling.

"You of all people should understand the impact of that woman."

"Yes, I do," he said gently. "Which is why I thought you might appreciate some company and moral support before you see her again."

Maggie was silent. She stared at the hessian shopping bag in Richard's hands, trying not to think of the irresistible French toast he'd make or the wretched woman he talked of.

He looked at her with doleful eyes. "You have to find a way to get on with her."

"Do I? Really?"

"It's been a long time."

"It doesn't fucking feel like it." And a strike of pain burned through her.

"Oh, Maggie." Now Richard seemed on the verge of tears. "Will it never fade?"

That really wouldn't do. She couldn't bear to see this good man cry. "Go on," she said. "Be gone with you. Go and cuddle Caroline or read a book."

"Maggie." The petulant look was back. There, she had her excuse.

"Good day, Richard," she said, shutting the door in his face, albeit very softly.

She ambled back to her coffee and sofa, a little of her vexation relieved by Richard's company. The poor sod. She would always be grateful for his presence. There never existed a more patient and supportive man.

There was another knock at the door.

"Oh for God's sake, Richard," she yelled.

She wrenched the door open ready to chastise, but the words died on her lips because there stood Juliette.

The woman seemed taken aback by the ferocity with which Maggie opened the door. Then she smiled. "Hello, Maggie."

Like their last meeting, all Maggie could do was stare. That smile, a pinch of the lips in the corner of her luscious mouth. The intensity of her hazel irises. The delicacy of her jawline. The proud shape of her cheekbones. Her eyes smouldered with smoky makeup and with her raven hair swept back and long black coat she looked like a Gothic queen.

"Muh," Maggie said. She hadn't the slightest idea what she'd intended, but that is what issued. She drew herself up. "So." Her face twitched with more customary disdain. "Still trying to pull off the dark, sultry look?"

Juliette raised an eyebrow and the taunting pinch of her smile became keener. "Yes." And by that she didn't mean simply yes. It conveyed so much more. Yes, I am. Yes, it works. Particularly on you.

"Hmmph," said Maggie. Not knowing what she'd meant by that either.

"I come in peace, Maggie."

Maggie was tempted to say, "Well you can peace off," but Richard could hear them from the attic. "Well... Well," she said instead.

"I was meeting Selene and Eli this morning for a tour of the town. I'm calling early to see if we can clear the air a little."

Maggie stared. She clenched her teeth. If she had to put a name to what she was doing she would have called it being bloody stubborn.

"Would you like to overcome our differences, or should we air our dirty laundry out here?" Juliette suggested, her head tilted provocatively.

"Very well," Maggie said, her nose in the air. "Come in, if you must."

"Thank you. Very gracious of you."

And Maggie didn't know if Juliette said it with irony or genuine understanding, or, it was entirely possible, that she'd delivered it so perfectly to be exactly equivocating, which annoyed Maggie more.

Juliette smiled again. "I'm not trying to tease you, Maggie."

And that she'd read Maggie's mind was even more aggravating.

Maggie marched into the house leaving Juliette to shut the door and hang her own coat. She took refuge in the kitchen and the noise of water filling the kettle.

"Coffee or tea?" Maggie yelled.

"*Café, s'il vous plait,*" came the velvety voice from the doorway, much closer than Maggie had anticipated.

Juliette leaned against the frame, her arms crossed beneath her bosom. Her charcoal cashmere jumper looked as soft as the cleavage it left bare. It was a garment and shade that suited Juliette to perfection, enhancing the glow of her skin and plunging her eyes into mesmerising pools of seduction. And that was before Maggie inadvertently checked out her bum. Juliette carried off jeans with a sophistication unattainable for an Anglo-Saxon and had maintained her trim figure.

"Do you still do yoga?" Maggie said, attempting conversation and distraction.

"You think I've kept in shape?"

Shit.

"Just trying to be polite."

"How unusual."

Damn it, this was worse than talking to Richard.

"I'm sorry, Maggie. I didn't come to spar with you."

Juliette laughed and Maggie couldn't help turning round. That sound. It had been so long since she'd heard that joyful sound. It had a more mature timbre but the same sense of fun.

Juliette had always had a kind laugh, her face rejoicing in humour with warmth for others. When some people laughed, it seemed unnatural, as if their face was unused to the emotion and on the verge of cracking. Not Juliette. It was what Maggie had first fallen in love with. Incredible, intelligent Juliette was intimidating in tutorials, but Maggie had commented something humorous and unusually self-deprecating one day and elicited that mirth. Juliette had looked at her with a softness in her eyes and a laugh that betrayed a good heart and warm soul, and Maggie had melted.

Of course, it had all soured.

"Please," Maggie said gently. "Have a seat. I'll bring you a coffee. Do you still take it black?"

"Yes. Thank you," Juliette replied in kind and she quietly left.

They sat on opposite sofas, both nursing mugs and staring down the garden.

"So," Maggie inhaled. "You are a mother."

"Clearly." The knowing smile was back.

Maggie wished she'd not started the conversation that way or with that topic, but being Maggie she didn't stop now. It had nagged at her since Juliette's arrival and the revelation that Selene was her daughter. "I would never have predicted it."

"That isn't fair," Juliette said, and her eyes betrayed vulnerability. "I always wanted children, but not at any cost. I wanted a family of my own and my partner's, not to defer to a man about them, not to worry that my children could be taken from me by their father in name only."

Maggie sipped her coffee, feeling a small, it was very small, pinch of guilt.

"So," Maggie tried again. "Who did you find? Were you impregnated by a miraculous lesbian and have the perfect marriage and family?" Maggie knew she was being unreasonable as the words tumbled out.

"No. I didn't."

"So, a partner who wasn't afraid of being left out of biology plus a donor."

Juliette flinched and the little nugget of guilt inside Maggie grew.

"I will tell you, because Eli is marrying Selene and you need to know her family." Juliette stared at Maggie with a sad defiance. "I had Selene with a good friend. His name is Martin and he is a lecturer at the Sorbonne. We raised her together, sharing a flat when she was a baby."

"Really?" Maggie's tone was unmistakably insinuating.

"We shared a flat, not a bed. He is gay. I am gay. It was never a possibility. Unlike some."

Maggie's guilt disappeared in a puff of smoke as furious flames kindled inside.

"Don't you dare," Maggie growled.

She breathed out noisily as she calmed herself. "I just find it odd." Maggie tilted her head in defiance. "After all our issues, you turn up decades later blithely saying you are a mother. You were so adamant to make a baby with the one you loved."

"I do love Martin," Juliette replied, her face stony. "He is a much cherished friend and someone I trust more than any lover."

"And what do they think? Do you expect your lovers to accept your cosy family, to play mum to a child who isn't theirs, as you were so loathed to do?"

"No, I do not." Juliette's face coloured. "Some had close relationships with Selene and still do, although I have been single for many years and it has not been an issue."

Maggie clenched her teeth and stared hard at the buddleia growing in the garden wall. This had been so contentious for them. Yes, they'd bickered about almost everything under the sun, but this? This issue had torn them apart.

"Just," Maggie shook her head. "After all our problems I can't believe you, of all people, have a child with someone virtually random."

"And I can't believe you, of all people, ended up with a man. *C'est la vie.*"

Ouch and, Maggie had to admit, *touché.*

"Maggie, please."

Juliette looked affected and the wall around Maggie's heart wasn't impenetrable.

"I'm sorry," Maggie said. "This was bound to come up. Everything considered."

Juliette nodded. "I know. Believe me, I didn't come here to make trouble."

"You could have fooled me yesterday, brandishing that bloody photo."

"I was surprised at your views. But I won't mention your history to your children again." Juliette stared into her coffee and Maggie recognised contrition when she saw it.

Maggie sipped at her drink and furiously searched her brain for a less contentious subject.

"The photo," Juliette started. "You heard about Mike all those years ago?"

Maggie twitched. "Yes. I went to his funeral."

"Good," Juliette said quietly.

"And Tiff," Maggie asked, "did you keep in touch with her?"

Juliette slowly lifted her gaze and met Maggie's eyes. She hesitated for a moment, then without looking away said, "For a while, yes I did."

"I always assumed you'd shack up with her or your ex. Tiff was always trying to get into your knickers," Maggie snorted. It hurt even though she said it with derision.

Juliette hesitated again. "Yes she was."

"Ha!" Now that was a change. "You always denied it. You said I was being paranoid." And Maggie had never doubted she was right. There were no shortage of women who wanted Juliette. It had all contributed to their strife.

Juliette nodded a touch. "You were right, Maggie."

Maggie's sarcasm fell from her face. "What did she do?"

"She waited a few weeks after we'd split up. Granted she was patient, you may say calculated. Only then did she show her interest."

Maggie tried to recall. Tiff, supportive when they'd split up, had been strangely absent afterwards. Then she'd surfaced weeks later, tail between her legs. "You turned her down?"

"Yes." Juliette said, her eyes fixed on Maggie's. "I may have been wrong about Tiff's intentions, but I wasn't about mine. I had no interest in anyone except you, Maggie."

It was a good job Tiff had disappeared a long time ago. A very good job. Maggie had very unkind thoughts at that moment.

"Maggie?" Juliette voice was quiet. "Do you know where I went when I left?"

"Yes." Maggie gulped. "Your fucking ex's." Another woman so intent on bedding Juliette. They probably fucked the same night Juliette walked out. Maggie couldn't breathe. She felt as raw as the day Juliette left.

"Did Tiff tell you?"

Maggie nodded, unable to speak.

"I wondered," Juliette said. "How long did you wait before loving another?"

Maggie flushed with indignation. "Do you mean after you left?"

"Yes."

"None of your fucking business."

"I know it sounds impertinent, but please tell me. How long did you wait before you moved on with Richard?"

Maggie glared with fury.

"Was it hours?"

"How fucking dare you," Maggie spat. "You left me. After that, it's no fucking concern of yours what I did."

"Days?"

"I'm not doing this."

"Weeks, months–"

"A year," Maggie shouted. "A year is what it took. I married Richard a year later."

"And to fall in love?"

"Fuck you." Maggie stood up ready to leave.

"Please." Juliette's plea wasn't one of cruelty, Maggie could see that. She was ashen, not a scorned women twisting the knife.

Maggie relented, wishing an end to the subject. "I kissed Richard for the first time when we exchanged our vows. There was nothing before that."

"Thank you," Juliette whispered and she dropped her gaze. "Thank you for indulging what must seem a very cruel question."

The pain was evident in Juliette's voice. If Maggie had hoped her answer would mollify, it had no such effect. Her adversary looked devastated, and it was the first time Maggie let herself acknowledge their breakup had crushed Juliette too. A breakup still hurts the one who leaves.

But Juliette had still fucking left. At the most vulnerable moment of Maggie's life, she'd left. So Maggie did too, out into the garden.

27

"Beloved mater!" Eli shouted from the patio.

Maggie wiped a tear and blinked away the rest that threatened. She turned from the river and waved to him with an energy that overcompensated for her mood.

"You're up," she hailed and she marched up the lawn with excessive enthusiasm.

"We're going on a tour of the town with Selene's mother. You must come too."

"Oh." Her brave face waned. "No. You carry on without me. I'm sure Juliette would appreciate time alone with you."

"Nonsense. She needs to get to know my formidable mother better while she's here."

"I think we can spare her that," Maggie said, unable to keep the regret from her voice.

Juliette appeared at the doorway, her face pale and eyes swollen. It could have been mistaken for morning puffiness, but Maggie knew better. She could read the sorrow in the way Juliette approached them, her steps more tentative. She gazed at Maggie with a harrowed expression, reflecting the same feelings which had flooded Maggie while she'd stared at the river. Maggie's fury had burnt itself out, and she was left exhausted in the smouldering ashes.

Juliette's lips twitched in a brave smile. "Please come, Maggie. I would welcome your company."

It was debilitating seeing Juliette bruised and vulnerable. Maggie had always found it so. Juliette was such a strong, principled and intelligent woman, it would undo Maggie when she was exposed. Maggie's whole being wanted to reach out and soothe her even after all these years.

The same feeling persisted as they all walked out together, up the hill alongside the pale ochre walls of the church lands. Maggie walked arm in arm with Eli while Selene and Juliette lingered a little way behind. Maggie kept turning back, the wounded Juliette a constant draw on her being. It was strange looking at her, many years older but essentially unchanged.

Good God. Juliette was the mother of a grown woman. It seemed impossible. At the same time she was a lecturer, a heart-breaking siren and an in-law to be. Her persona changed from one moment to the next. Maggie could look at her with almost impartiality and see Selene's mother – someone to organise the wedding and dote on the bride. Yet, when Juliette caught her eye, she transformed into the sensual woman Maggie had loved with passion. It was impossible to reconcile all the people that were Juliette. Another blink and she was a mother again.

There was an enviable tenderness between Juliette and Selene, mother and child caring for each other. It was a bond Maggie and Jude had never managed to nurture, and the pain of that realisation began to fester inside Maggie.

She tutted at herself. She had Eli, her boy, on her arm. She smiled at him – her one and only, and thank God it was just the one, Eli.

"They're incredible aren't they?" he said, smiling back.

"By that, do you mean defy belief?" It was a catty thing to say, and her heart was no longer in it.

Eli laughed all the same. "Why do you hate Selene's mother? Did she shit in your soup at university?"

"I don't hate her. And don't be vulgar."

"I'm the product of nature and nurture." He smirked. "Either way it's your fault."

"Impertinent little shit."

He beamed, highly satisfied.

"No, I don't hate her," Maggie said, looking away. And it was with a coolness inside that she realised she didn't detest Juliette any longer. It was frightening. She'd been surviving for so long on feelings of injustice, that she wasn't quite sure what to do. It was difficult to rage against someone who was so obviously affected.

"No," she said. "Not anymore." And they walked on.

At the churchyard, Eli took Selene's hand with the glee of a child and hurried away to show the skeleton carvings on the tomb.

Juliette ambled beside Maggie, past the church and over the land that cascaded down towards the river. The grass was still deep green with vigorous growth and the orchard golden with leaves and ruby jewels of fruit nestled within. The landscape was beginning to warm in the mid-morning sun, and the full palette of autumn colours was vibrant on the hillside beyond.

"This is a beautiful spot." Juliette sighed with pleasure at the sun. It seemed to warm her through and a gentle smile suffused her face.

"I'm glad you like it," Maggie said, although she didn't know why. "I think it the best in Ludbury."

They wandered down the hill, through the long grass which divided the ancient orchard in two and towards the courtyard.

"And this." Juliette beamed. "This is incredible."

They'd stopped beneath the archway into the brick courtyard.

"Georgian I'd guess?"

Maggie nodded.

"My favourite architectural style," Juliette continued. "There's something so pleasing about the dimensions and simplicity while at the same time it's never too plain."

211

"You must be in heaven in Ludbury," Maggie replied.

"Very much so. I have been walking aimlessly around your town gawping at the Tudor buildings and Georgian town-houses. I've missed English architecture, you know."

Maggie didn't know what to say at the allusion to the past. Juliette's enjoyment of the present seemed too fragile to indulge in a memory.

"Do you remember our little flat?"

There, Juliette had said it.

"I was thinking the same thing," Maggie replied.

"I loved our Gothic building by the park. The bathroom up in the tower. The creaking stairs to our room. It should have housed a princess."

Maggie smiled. It was an innocent and naïve reflection, almost childlike and utterly compelling because of it.

"Or perhaps," Juliette continued, "the ghost of an insane woman wronged by her husband."

Maggie laughed. "That's more what I imagined."

"Of course you did." Juliette grinned.

Juliette gazed around the courtyard. "This is empty? Unused?"

"Not for long," Maggie said, annoyance fraying her mood. "The whole site is up for sale."

"*Non*," Juliette said with the full vigour of an incensed French woman.

"Don't get me started."

"Surely this site can't be developed. It must be protected?"

"Grade two listed no doubt, but the likely buyer plans to convert it into a luxury house and perhaps the same with the church."

"*Dommage*," Juliette said, shaking her head.

They wandered back towards the church and followed Selene and Eli inside, the sound reverberating around the aisles as the door shut behind them. Maggie never failed to look up when she entered the building, impossible when the nave was so high, surpassed only by the tower midway which brought visitors to a standstill as they admired the stained glass windows.

Eli's footsteps echoed as he ran along the empty nave. He peeked over his shoulder with a cheeky grin then skipped up the steps to the pulpit that perched beneath the towering pipes of the organ above.

Maggie rolled her eyes expecting Eli to announce something vulgar and blasphemous. He took a deep breath and with the gentlest rising voice sounded out a perfect note.

She stopped and gazed in awe, her hand clutched to her heart. How did such a naughty boy still have the voice of an angel? His alto resonated with seductive melancholy in the empty church, and Maggie closed her eyes, moved by the ancient chant in this oldest of churches.

She sat down on the pew and looked to the heavens as Eli's ethereal psalm floated through the nave, the echoes lending the rendition a depth and a haunting quality. And she hung on every word right through to the last note which seemed to fade imperceptibly into every nook of the church.

A single burst of applause broke the reverie.

"Well. It's the Goodmans." A smiling vicar emerged from the chapel. The short woman walked down the nave, her gown billowing behind. "Good morning, Mrs Goodman. And what use will you make of my church today?"

Maggie twitched, regretting telling the vicar about her teenage proclivities on altars.

"Good morning, vicar," she replied hastily. "We're here only to admire and show Eli's fiancée and her mother the highlights of the town."

The vicar greeted Juliette and Selene with a warm handshake for both, and Eli crept down from the pulpit with an air of contrition. He giggled as he took Selene's hand and swept her away, no doubt to show her something rude.

"Appreciate it while you may." The vicar sighed. "Preparations are underway for the sale and the townsfolk will no longer have access."

The nugget of vexation which always burned in the pit of Maggie's stomach started to smoulder.

"The luxury development?"

"The very same."

"It's such a beautiful building," Maggie said, shaking her head, "built in the heart of the town by the people of the town." She looked to the vicar, "You know I follow no religion, but I respect many principles of those with faith. If the heart of the town is no longer to be filled by principle, must it be replaced by a monument to money?"

"My feelings exactly."

"And the same for the courtyard?"

"Another development for a couple."

"Jesus Christ," Maggie snapped, and her blasphemy echoed around the church. "That building could house ten, twenty, more, and when you see people living on the street and struggling to pay rent in some crappy single room because of unscrupulous developers and landlords, it's fucking immoral that the heart of the town be snatched away from the many for the few."

"I couldn't have said it better myself, although I would have omitted the expletive."

Maggie heard Juliette snigger. "Is this what you do Maggie?" she said coming closer. "Is this what you've become? An angry middle-aged woman raging at the world and raising frilly knickers up the flagpole in protest."

How dare she? Maggie rounded on her. "At least I vote for people who aren't cruel. I religiously donate to the food bank even though I find it obscene and archaic that they exist." Then she stopped. It had been a long time since she'd done much else. What did she do? Despair when others didn't vote the way she wanted. Rage at inequality. But what else? Fuck Juliette. She had a point.

"You used to be so active." Juliette's eyes narrowed with challenge. "You were insatiable with your demands for rights and equality. What happened, Maggie?"

214

She got tired. That's what happened. Tired and lost faith in people. She didn't want to admit any of that to Juliette though. Damn her. Maggie wanted to prove she was still as vital as ever. But what could she do?

"This site must cost a fortune," Maggie said.

"So?" Juliette shrugged. It couldn't have been more Gallic.

"There'll only be a handful of interested parties in a site like this."

"It's true," the vicar chipped in. "Development is restricted to the two existing buildings. It's not an attractive proposition for most developers."

"Then who?" Juliette pushed. "Who should live here?"

"Everyone," Maggie said exasperated. "Kids I taught who still want to live in their home town. The Mrs Maladys of the world who need affordable rooves over their heads, not a crippling walk to the amenities. The care home staff who look after Celia, who can only afford the city and use all their income on transport to work. Everyone."

"Then perhaps they should buy it."

Maggie was about to dismiss Juliette's suggestion as ridiculous, when the penny dropped. "A co-operative?"

"Why not."

Maggie laughed. She was reminded of her university days and dreams of a commune when the eighties boom pushed everything beyond their reach.

"If the space is needed by the people, then perhaps the people should take it back," Maggie muttered. "But these are some of the poorest in town. They can't afford to pool any kind of finance."

"Others can," Juliette replied.

"It's true."

Maggie swivelled round. It was Eli who'd spoken.

"You wouldn't believe how many are searching for somewhere to live," he continued. "At the engagement party,

215

I spoke to several mates all desperate to stay here. They've saved deposits, but housing in Ludbury is too expensive."

"And would they be interested in this kind of development?" Maggie asked, not sure whether to give the idea credit.

"Absolutely. So it's not a house, but everyone needs a roof over their head."

Maggie looked to the heavens as if for inspiration. "It could be a brilliant site." She smiled at her vision. "The courtyard could house several families with plenty of room for affordable housing for people like Mrs Malady." She laughed. "They could even feed themselves by resurrecting the kitchen gardens and orchard. Does that sound fanciful?"

She turned expecting them to baulk with incredulity, but not one did. Eli sloped away to join Selene and the vicar stepped forward.

"Those sound like achievable aims for the courtyard," the vicar said. "But I wish something could be done with this building too. You know," she came closer, "we've all lost our way recently, the country divided in more ways than ever. We've forgotten we're all human living on the same patch of Earth. This church could be converted into a community space. Perhaps even, you will laugh at this, a multi-faith centre to encourage debate and exchange of ideas. Some in the church would disapprove, but I would invite humanists too. I'm a strong believer in following a good life more than a doctrine, and I support anyone pursuing that goal."

"Actually, vicar," Maggie said. "I approve."

Juliette looked amused.

"Well," Maggie snapped, "great things can come of different religions talking to each other, as well you know."

"Indeed," Juliette countered, the amusement still fresh on her face. "The Cathars for instance."

"Exactly," Maggie said, and she turned to the vicar. "We can thank the medieval Roman Catholics engaging the

Cathars for the foundations of science. They wanted to persuade them to rejoin the Catholic Church and had to decipher the ancient Greek texts to argue against the logic of the Cathar religion."

"That's true to an extent," Juliette chipped in. It was her subject after all.

"The Catholics just killed them all in the end," Maggie acknowledged. "But still."

Juliette grinned, and there was a spark in her eyes. Maggie felt a warmth in her belly – the excitement of student days when they sparred in tutorials. Maggie turned away and cleared her throat. "So, yes, vicar."

The vicar was staring at her, to Juliette, and back again.

"What?" Maggie asked.

"That is between you and God." The vicar smiled. "But I have a suggestion. You know who would be good to talk to, if you wanted to pursue the idea."

"Yes?"

"If you wanted to go ahead, she'd be very useful because of her town planning experience."

"Who?"

"Caroline Argent."

Maggie's face dropped. Well of course it would be frigging Caroline. Just to make Maggie's life that bit more vexing. Just to add to the pissing humiliation.

"I'm not sure the Tory council woman would have time for me."

"Really? I find her most approachable," the vicar replied.

"You're a politically neutral party, but we come in very different colours."

The vicar tilted her head. "Remember though, great things can come from the meeting of different faiths."

Oh the gall. Throwing her words back at her.

The vicar chuckled. "Excuse me, Mrs Goodman. I have a sermon to prepare. Keep me appraised of your 'fanciful idea'."

Maggie watched the clergywoman retreat to the chapel and when she turned back Juliette's face was full of concern.

"Oh, Maggie." Juliette sighed.

Maggie crossed her arms.

"What's wrong with talking to a Tory?"

Well apart from the fact Caroline was fucking her husband. But that seemed to have lost its potency recently.

"It's a miracle you talk to anyone," Juliette said exasperated. "Wrong opinions. Wrong political party. And these days the wrong sexuality too for poor Abby."

"You know damn well why that is." The rage filled Maggie in an instant, so powerfully it almost knocked her back. "I can see now that you were hurt too, but that only adds to my conviction. That kind of life cripples people. I will never wish it upon Abby."

And they were back to arguing.

"It doesn't have to be like that," Juliette replied, fiery colour in her cheeks.

"It's hard enough for young people these days, left behind by society and unable to afford a home, without the added pressure of bigotry from this fucking country."

"You cannot deny people love. They will fight for it, every step of the way."

"Really?" Maggie's hands knuckled into her hips. "Is that what you did?"

"Did you?"

And they stared at each other with anger.

"*Zut alors*, Maggie. Can't you get along with me for a few minutes? Our children are getting married."

"It will be over soon enough. They will live somewhere far, far away. Then we will never have to see each other again."

"Good," Juliette snapped.

"At least that's something we can agree on."

Maggie would be relieved indeed when the wedding was over and they no longer needed to even attempt cordiality.

She turned her back on Juliette, her final word on the matter, and found Eli and Selene approaching, hand in hand, rather meekly.

"Mum?" Eli said.

For a moment Maggie feared they'd heard their argument and her history of passion with Juliette had been revealed, but it was much worse.

"Selene and I," he gazed at his fiancée with a silly look of affection. "We want to move to Ludbury." He was grinning. Constantly. Perhaps he was expecting some reaction, but Maggie was catatonic with surprise.

"We like your idea. The co-operative? We could move here and see each other all the time. The whole family."

Shit. There was nothing like timing.

"What do you think?" Eli asked.

Maggie spread her lips with an attempt to smile. "Great," she said though her teeth.

"*Formidable*," Juliette said.

Just fucking fantastic.

28

"So much for keeping control," Abby muttered.

She woke with the sun peeping over the terrace opposite and beaming through the gap in the curtains. It was late Saturday morning. She'd slept well. Very well.

She rolled her eyes and groaned. "I wonder why."

Indeed, so much for keeping her desires contained. They'd burst out in a fanfare and fireworks last night. Abby slapped her forehead, then realised her hand was still scented from her own fumbling.

If Jude hadn't suspected her inclination before the tavern then Abby really needed to confess now. She couldn't go on like this. She was surprised Eli hadn't announced his suspicions last night after enjoying his little allusions. She cringed at how blatant her reactions to Jude had been and scrunched herself and duvet into a tight ball.

She'd half expected a feline scolding, but there was none. Perhaps she'd finally remembered to close the bathroom window. She peeped from beneath the knot of duvet. The mattress was free of that blasted furball, but a ring of white was curled upon her fireside chair. Two green apertures shot open in the fur and Maximillian squinted disdain from the distant chair, eyeing his customary place on her bed with disgust. How long had he been there? She hoped there hadn't been any spectators to her solo act last night, not even of the feline kind.

Maximillian's stare was unrelenting.

"Wow. Way to make a girl feel guilty, Max."

The disdain turned to venom.

"Sorry, Maximillian."

And she did feel guilty. So, so, so many broken rules she didn't want to count them, and thinking them through was always a bad idea.

She swung her legs from the bed and headed for the shower, hoping its soothing waters would wash away her embarrassment. When she returned to dress, she found a message on her phone.

Can I see you? I'll come round late morning. Jxxx

That soon. Abby slumped on the bed. She'd have to tell Jude today and her whole body felt leaden at the prospect. Why couldn't she control this ardour?

There would be no more dancing with her friend. No more carefree embraces lest Abby burn with want. It would change everything. Would Jude back away with abhorrence? Abby hoped she knew her friend well enough to predict that wouldn't happen, but there would be a distance, and that was unbearable.

She let out a long, dawn-out groan and Maximillian twitched his ears.

"Well I'm pissing heartbroken here, so you're just going to have to lump it."

His ears snapped to the front.

"OK. I'm sorry. Go back to sleep. You can let yourself out today."

She sloped down the stairs, wondering when she'd switched off the radio and finding the door locked to her relief – it was miracle given her distraction last night. And like every time of stress and when in need of comfort, she did the one thing certain to alleviate it. She baked a cake.

Abby sat on the bar stool by the kitchen island, chocolate cake decorated with swirls of butter icing, and waited in the sunlight that shone in nine beams through the door. She'd dressed in her most comfortable jeans and a T shirt which hung loose around her shoulders, revealing her collar bone and a little cleavage. Now that she'd decided to confess, a sense of calm washed over her. This was her, at home, being her most genuine, with nothing to hide. She hoped Jude would find a friend she could still love there.

It wasn't long before the shadow of Jude's long locks passed over the door and her face appeared.

"It's open," Abby said, and her friend entered.

Jude looked more beautiful than ever. The waves of sun-kissed hair flowed around her cheeks, softening her face and aquiline looks and lending her dusky green eyes a velvety bewitchment. Her complexion was heightened with a hint of rose and her lips rude with health. Abby doubted she'd looked more alluring.

Jude cradled a small bunch of tiny white flowers to her breast, tied in a maroon ribbon, a delicate cloud of blooms. She approached and wordlessly made her offering.

"Hi," Jude whispered, her eyes so intent Abby thought she might melt under their spell.

"Hi," Abby murmured.

"I brought you flowers," Jude said, a coy smile lifting her cheeks.

"I made you a cake." And a melancholy warmth stirred inside Abby at their quiet intimacy and mutual offerings. They stared at each other a few moments, the shy regard between them palpable.

"Am I disturbing you?" Jude said. "Did you have plans?"

Abby shook her head and smiled sadly. "No. I was going to pay my respects to Mum. That's all."

"May I come with you?" Jude asked.

"I'd like that. But," she lowered her gaze, "I need to tell you something."

Jude came closer and placed her flowers on the top and held Abby's hand. The touch was exquisite. It almost made Abby cry.

"Tell me on the way," Jude said. "I need to talk too, and sometimes it's easier while we walk."

Abby nodded, grateful for the reprieve but also aware it prolonged the agony.

Abby threw on a long woollen coat and they walked down the street towards the wooded hillside beyond the river. Jude took her arm, and Abby expected her to loop it over hers, the way they customarily did, but today Jude held her hand and stayed snug beside. Abby looked to her face, trying to ascertain the reason. All she saw was Jude's warm familiarity and regard, not a hint of reserve.

Over the stone bridge they wandered, beyond the swirling river and island trees, along the pale ochre cliffs which had built the city walls of Ludbury. Up the hill and through the ancient beech trees, Abby's feet swishing through the golden carpet of leaves, onto the moorland which glistened with dew in the morning light.

All the while Jude held her hand and stayed close. Abby couldn't remember such a beautiful day and her heart sat heavy at the prospect of ruining it.

"I've been thinking," Jude said, smiling down at her, "of moving back to Ludbury."

"Really?" Abby was filled with joyful hope, until she remembered.

"I've been living here at weekends since you bought the cottage, and I wondered if this was where I belonged." She looked to Abby, perhaps for encouragement. "Do you," she seemed almost shy, "do you think that a good idea?"

Abby could have cried. "I'd love it." She couldn't look Jude in the eye, too painfully aware she was about to endanger this happy event.

"I was wondering." Again Jude was hesitant. "Would you like to see me more often?"

"Always," Abby murmured. She hoped the tears wouldn't brim. "I treasure every moment with you. Truly I do. When I thought you were going to marry Bill… I…" Abby's throat choked and she had to stop.

Jude squeezed her hand, a reassurance Abby knew, and they ambled on. The stone circle crowned the first peak of moorland ahead. Abby had another reprieve as they laboured up the slope. They broke out at the top, their cheeks pink and clouds of breath billowing around them. They stood at the summit, the ancient druid ring and golden moors of Wales on one side, the soulful Ludbury on the other.

Jude held both Abby's hands and faced her. "I love it here, more the older I get. I've been wondering why that is and what I want out of life." Jude looked away a moment, perhaps gathering her thoughts, perhaps afraid how Abby might take her words. "It hasn't changed so much, it's more that I've realised what's important to me."

This was unbearable. Abby was about to have everything she wanted. Her friend home for good. To see her every day. Just when Abby had to ruin it all and admit her passion.

"I've never asked," Jude said suddenly. "But do you want to leave Ludbury?"

Abby took a second or two to answer, surprised by the change in tack.

"No," she said honestly. "Everything I love is here, from Celia to Maggie and Mum's resting place. This is home for me. It holds me deep, deep down. And you," Abby said, lowering her gaze, "There's always you." She was breathing so hard she couldn't speak.

"I'd hoped you'd say that," Jude said. "If you ever want to leave, say the word and I'll follow."

Abby could tell Jude was trying to catch her eye.

"But what if we weren't friends anymore," Abby stuttered. "What if you moved here and we fell out."

"Why would we?"

"But would that affect your decision?"

Jude pulled her closer and the warmth of her body made Abby dizzy.

"I can't think of a single reason we wouldn't be friends," Jude said gently. "You're the first person I think of when I wake, and the last I dream of. You're the one I message "I love you" before I turn in. It's been that way for years and I never want it to change."

Abby couldn't lift her face. "It's the same for me. It always has been."

It was as if her chest were about to implode with grief. She couldn't wait any longer. "Jude, I need to tell you something."

"And I need to tell you so many things."

Jude's soft fingers cupped her cheeks and tilted up her chin. Abby closed her eyes, the tears forming freely and pooling hot beneath her eyelids.

"Please look at me," Jude whispered.

Abby shook her head.

"Please look at me, beautiful Abby."

Abby's heart cantered in her chest. She couldn't bear to see the effect of her confessions. She reluctantly opened her eyes and found not a friend, but a woman who regarded her with deep longing.

Jude's lips parted and she pulled Abby achingly close.

"What are you doing?" Abby murmured, her head swirling with anguish and confusion.

"Falling for the one I already love most of all."

And she kissed her with a touch as delicate as the flowers she'd brought.

29

Abby stared at Jude, captivated by the deep regard in her friend's eyes and disbelieving even though the tender kiss still tingled on her lips.

"How long?" Abby whispered. "When did you start to feel this way?"

"Not long. But with every passing day this feels more right."

Abby's spirits sank. "Are you on the rebound?"

"No." Jude smiled indulgently. "I love you and I need you and I definitely want you."

If Abby was in any doubt, the look of hunger as Jude pulled her closer dispelled it.

"But," Abby's mind went blank, overcome with the narcotic effect of Jude's intimate embrace. "I've loved you so long. Do you know that?"

"I didn't until recently. But I do now."

Jude dipped her head and Abby closed her eyes, unable to resist the sweet kiss. Her body was ready for it this time, and she slipped her lips around Jude's with longing. She threw her arms around Jude's shoulders, clasping her hair in great handfuls as her whole body cried out for this union, and their kiss deepened with Abby's desperate lips hot over Jude's mouth.

When they parted, they were both breathing hard.

"I can't resist you," Abby said, dazed. "You're everything I've longed for. So I need you to think for me. Is this a good idea?"

"I have. Over and over. It's what you've wanted and everything I long for now."

"What about Maggie?"

A sharp determination stole across Jude's face. "She will get used to it." Jude said it with such conviction Abby feared for Maggie. "I want this," Jude said and any misgivings Abby may have had evaporated as she pulled her close again.

Jude kissed her harder and Abby welcomed the firmer touch. She pulled at Jude's locks and pressed her body tight. Jude released her hand, and for a moment Abby wondered if she was moving too fast, but Jude's fingers urgently stroked higher to her breast.

A moan stole from Abby's lips. She was melting, every kiss and caress turning her insides velvet and when Jude firmed her touch around her nipple she openly groaned.

"Let me take you home," Jude murmured.

Abby quickened. She knew what Jude meant. "We can take things slow," she said. But when she leaned away, Jude's dark eyes showed no reservation.

They walked home, burning in the chilled air, stealing a kiss every few paces and stoking the flames once more. As soon as they stepped through the door, Jude tore Abby's coat from her shoulders.

Abby took Jude's hands. "We can go slowly, you know. I've waited this long, I can be patient."

"I don't want to wait," Jude said. "I've been thinking about you every second."

Heat burst onto Abby's cheeks. "Me too," she admitted.

Jude trailed her finger along Abby's shoulder where it lay bare from the loose T shirt and gently along her collarbone, then teased down her chest where the material draped over her bosom.

"You're so sexy in this," Jude said.

Abby smiled. "I wasn't trying to be."

"But you always are." And Jude's voice was desperate with longing. "Please come upstairs."

Abby felt clumsy as they took the steps, tingling with anticipation and the hormonal rush. "The bed's a mess," she said embarrassed.

"I don't care," Jude replied as she slipped her hands beneath Abby's shirt. "Lift your arms," she begged.

Abby couldn't believe this was happening. Her friend had been unobtainable and disinterested for so long, it seemed incredible. But the craving in Jude's eyes was real. Abby stretched high and the shirt was gently lifted from her body and shaking fingers unhooked her bra. The sensation heightened all over her body as Jude slipped away the straps, then her jeans then underwear leaving Abby naked.

Abby couldn't help stare as Jude undressed. Her body, which Abby had admired so often but never let herself linger on, was revealed in all its beauty. What was once forbidden now stood achingly close, heaving with the same passion that filled her own.

Abby tentatively reached out, disbelieving that she was about to touch her, and it was almost a shock when her fingertips encountered the smooth curve of Jude's breast. Abby closed her eyes, basking in the delicate pleasure of Jude cupped in her palm. She slowly and deliberately stroked her thumb across Jude's tender nipple, and her whole hand, arm and body became charged with the sensation.

Abby opened her eyes. "You are gorgeous," she said, her voice shaking.

Jude's pupils were wide, her breath rasping through open lips. "Lie down," she pleaded.

Abby gulped and complied, wanting Jude to set the pace but also completely surrendered to her. She lay naked on the white sheets, her whole being exposed and thrilled with expectation as Jude lay beside her, hair flowing around her shoulders and eyes fixed on Abby's.

"You're the one who's beautiful," Jude whispered and she dipped down to her neck.

Jude's breath tickled the nook of her neck, then her succulent lips teased Abby's sensitive skin. Abby closed her eyes to enjoy the sensation and moaned as she felt Jude's body pass above hers and kneel between her legs.

"You have the most wonderful breasts," Jude murmured, and Abby smiled as fingers cupped their shape. "I love the line of your cleavage." Jude trailed down her chest so that arousal shot through to Abby's core, then she tensed tighter as the trail was replaced by hungry kisses.

"I had no idea your skin would taste so good."

Abby wanted to joke she owed that to baking but she couldn't speak. She was enthralled to the sensation of Jude touching her, bathing her with hair, kissing every heightened inch of her body.

Jude lifted her head away and Abby imagined her admiring her bosom with the same hungry eyes that had stolen across her body as they'd undressed. Keen hands engulfed her breasts, and Abby groaned as the caress became firm.

"Oh God, I love that," Abby gasped, and she panted in time to Jude squeezing her harder and flicking her thumb across her nipples.

She could have laid like that for days, paralysed in rapture by the rhythmic tantalisation of her breasts, her body glowing hotter with every stroke. But Jude had other ideas and Abby almost complained when she took a hand away.

A finger snaked down her belly, slipping from side to side. There was no doubt about its destination and Abby thrust her hips up, desperate for Jude's touch to reach her centre. She could feel herself aching and wet between her legs, and warm anticipation surged through her body.

229

Jude stroked her finger down the triangle between Abby's hips agonisingly slowly, then almost as it made its target, she circled wide, round and round so that Abby thrust up with frustrated ecstasy.

"Oh, you look good," Jude breathed.

The way Jude had said it was shocking. Her voice was overcome with desire, the words choking in her throat, and the idea Jude would find her beautiful there was beyond erotic.

Abby grasped the bed sheets as her body shuddered at the thought of Jude's finger making its mark, as if she were already coming.

"Please touch me," she begged.

She felt Jude move and Abby held her breath, waiting for the delicious contact, then her mind exploded as her friend's lips closed around her centre.

"Oh God."

She wasn't expecting that. Not in a decade had she expected that.

"You don't have to...." And the words were strangled in her throat by wave after wave of glorious sensations elicited by Jude's tongue.

Delicate at first, Jude soon became greedy, kissing, licking, savouring. She devoured Abby's clitoris and every nerve in Abby's body seemed to fire. Down her legs, up her back, to the tips of her fingers.

Abby opened her eyes and stole a look down, but it was too much. The sight of her naked friend, the warmth of Jude's soft locks trailing over her thighs and lips around her centre were too much. She began to cry out as the vision took her over the edge and again when Jude held her in her mouth.

Abby wasn't sure if she'd momentarily passed out. Her eyelids were heavy as she roused and she blinked with surprise at daylight. Jude stared down at her, eyes wide in shock and arousal.

"Hi," Abby whispered.

"Hi." Jude panted her reply. "Was that OK?"

Abby grinned. Jude was absolutely dying with aroused anticipation. She could read it in her face. She could see it in her trembling arms.

"So much more than OK. Lie down," Abby said, and Jude obediently rolled beside her.

Abby could see Jude was overwhelmed by the experience.

"I love seeing you come," Jude said and she gulped, as if even the memory triggered tides of pleasure within her.

Even if she hadn't admitted it, Jude's flushed cheeks and slick thighs would have betrayed her. Abby could see Jude was well beyond light seduction. Her whole body shook, aching for relentless attention and Abby didn't make her wait.

She slid between her thighs and slipped a hand under her body, holding her tight. Abby gently thrust her hips and watched Jude close her eyes and roll back her head. Abby caressed her shoulders, trailed her fingers down Jude's beautiful breasts and squeezed her side in a satisfying handful as she rocked harder. Then sensing Jude needing more, she ran her fingers lower and gradually, a little at time, slipped her fingers inside.

Abby groaned at the sensation of Jude warm and tender around her fingers. Jude threw her arms around her shoulders and they thrust together, enthralled by the intimacy. And as Abby felt the urgency of Jude's thrusts tighten, she slipped her thumb over Jude's clitoris.

"Oh fuck," Jude gasped.

She was close. Abby could feel her swell and she circled slow and firm in tune to the rise of Jude's climax.

"I'm going to come."

It was Abby's turn to gasp, unspeakably aroused by her friend's admission. They were words she'd thought she'd never witness and their eroticism was powerful.

Jude's body gripped inside and she arched her back, starting to climb the bed. Abby held her tight, uncontrollably devouring her chest, all the while keeping to the entrancing rhythm.

Jude started to speak once more, but the words merged into a single loud moan as her orgasm took her. Jude shuddered in great waves as she came and Abby groaned with incoherent euphoria.

30

Abby dreamed she drifted on fluffy clouds, her face buried in softness she'd never imagined. Her palms rested on divine cushions and she swayed on her heavenly bed with a soothing rhythm. The clouds drifted back and forth, in and out.

Her head swirled with soporific joy and she voiced her appreciation with a long "Mmmmmmmmmmm."

"Hey, sleepyhead," someone murmured.

"Mmm?"

She opened her eyes, blinking several times, and came face to boob with Jude's glorious bosom. For a moment, so used to hiding her inclination, she twitched away.

"Sorry. Oh God. Sorry." Then a rush of images caught up in her brain. "Oh," she said. She peered up and found Jude regarding her with affection and not a small amount of amusement. Abby lifted her face, or at least slid it away.

"Oh no."

She'd dribbled, clearly, while she'd slept in Jude's cleavage. Of all the places.

"Really sorry," she mumbled and she tried, as surreptitiously as one might in this situation, to wipe drool from her cheek and Jude's breast. She was jiggled on Jude's bosom as her friend sniggered.

"Don't worry," Jude said. "I noticed a while ago, but didn't want to wake you. Are you always this sleepy after sex?"

"Isn't everyone? And isn't that the best part? Falling asleep in a blissful daze, naked with the one you love."

"You're right." Jude's face was warmed with deep affection. "So there's no need to look confused. Although," and she stroked her fingers across Abby's frown, "I love it when you do. You twitch your nose when something's not right. It's a dead giveaway."

"I didn't know that."

"It's lovely," Jude said, and she leant down and kissed Abby's forehead.

The touch instantly dispelled every tension, from the frown that had rippled across Abby's forehead to the knots in her neck. The sensation flowed down her spine and flooded her legs until the sweetness of Jude's kiss seemed to diffuse through her whole body. It was heavenly, being in this embrace and loved by her friend.

Abby's heart suddenly felt heavy remembering her anxiety about confessing to Jude. She'd been so swept away in passion it still hadn't registered that here she lay, with the person she'd loved for more than a decade and who she'd feared she might disgust.

"I thought I was going to lose you," Abby whispered. "When you arrived this morning I was going to admit I loved you."

Jude lowered herself down the bed so she looked Abby in the eye. "You will never lose me," she said gently. "Although for a while I didn't know what to do."

"After the party when Bill...?"

"Yes," Jude nodded. "But I do now. Oh I do now." And a smile, a rather a lascivious one, lifted her face.

Abby giggled. "I love that you're a screamer."

Jude blushed. Actually blushed. "Up until now I didn't know I was."

"And kissing a woman?" Abby put on a poker face and raised an eyebrow. "You still feel nothing?"

"I just needed the right woman and to kiss her in the right place." Jude stroked her finger all the way down Abby's cleavage and didn't stop until she made her point.

Abby's poker face dissolved in a flare of arousal when Jude touched between her thighs. "Oh," Abby gasped. "I see."

Jude looked sublime nesting beside her in the white duvet, her features softened by their love-making and the affection with which Jude regarded her.

"I don't know how," Abby said, "but you seem more beautiful today. And believe me, I have admired you often."

The full curving lips of Jude's mouth broke into a bright smile. She reached out and stroked Abby's cheek. "It has to be said, Dr Hart, the post-coital glow suits you too. Very much."

They stared at each other, at sea in each other's loving gaze, snug beneath the duvet and with the afterglow of their passion. Abby could have spent hours doing only this but suddenly frowned.

"Are you hungry?"

"Bloody starving, and I really need a wee."

Abby laughed.

"I didn't want to move though," Jude said. "I want to stay here all day."

"Me too," Abby said. Then "Cake! We've got cake. Nip to the loo and I'll bring some cake up."

"Deal."

Jude leapt out of bed, but Abby lingered for a moment. Whether it was intentional or she was stricken by the sight of her friend's naked body was moot, but sit and admire she did. Amber waves of hair flowed over athletic shoulders, reaching down to curving pale breasts and an exquisite bottom worthy of a Botticelli painting.

"Nyumm," Abby murmured.

Jude glanced back. "Get that cake."

"M'on it." Abby said, clearing her throat and leaping out of bed. "Honestly."

Abby looked around for her dressing gown but couldn't see it anywhere. Then a tinkling noise came from the bathroom. It was funny. Never had the sound of someone having a wee inspired such an ecstatic smile. Abby listened, with a silly grin on her face. Jude was here again. In her home. Naked on the loo with bathroom door wide open. It was lovely.

"Cake!" Jude shouted. Abby could hear the laughter in her voice.

"Yup. S'coming."

She tip-toed from the room and down the stairs, nervous energy in her legs. She heard Jude return to the bedroom and hesitated at the bottom of the stairs. She listened to the crinkle of the duvet pulled back and the sigh of mattress as Jude settled back into their bed. Abby's smile broadened.

"Jude is in my be-ed," she half chanted, half sang in her head. Then out loud, "Jude is in my be-ed," and she tip-toed a jig into the lounge in time with her song.

She stopped, dead, in the centre. Come on. Play it cool. Be calm. Then her delight rose up her chest again and she couldn't keep down her joy.

"Jude is in my be-ed. We had great se-ex." And she rolled her shoulders and jigged to the kitchen.

"We had incredible se-ex."

Crap. The windows. Daylight was flooding through the door and windows either side, enough for a street-wide, full-frontal. She whisked the curtains shut and pulled down the blind on the door, and locked it. In fact, double locked it. Wouldn't want people walking in on a screaming orgasm would she. She would just die.

"There," she brushed her hands together.

Then, "We had incredible se-ex. And we're having coffee." She sashayed over to the kettle. "And we're having cay-ake. It is chocolate cay-ake."

And as the kettle began to sing, she realised she might be, a little bit, ecstatically and overwhelmingly happy.

Jude was in her bedroom. And that had been some sex. Abby groaned and her insides caved at the memory of their caresses. Jude had even kissed her. It made her weak at the knees all over again.

She'd longed for Jude over the years, but never had she dared hope they'd be together or have anything like that in bed. She closed her eyes. That was wonderful, mind-blowing, clit-lickingly good sex. And Jude. A rush of heat filled Abby. Dear God, she hadn't expected Jude to be so enthusiastic. That was one of the best surprises of her life.

"Oh," she moaned, then she smiled. "And we're having cay-ake."

Life really didn't get much better.

She swayed more gently on her return, plates of sliced cake in one hand, two mugs of coffee in the other, very aware of her naked and vulnerable nipples and thighs and all the bits in between.

When she stepped into the bedroom she hesitated. Jude lay supine on the sheets, hand behind her head with hair flowing across the pillows. She was like a classic reclining Venus with her pale breasts and arm draped over her virtue.

Abby may have gasped. She definitely blushed. And automatically she looked away.

"Come here," Jude said. "Put those down and come here."

Abby obediently arranged the refreshments on the bedside table and sat next to Jude. Her friend took her by the hand and seemed to will Abby to look at her.

"I think after that," Jude smiled, "after I've kissed your clit and you've touched me inside," she was starting to giggle, "that you're allowed to look at me when I'm naked."

Abby blushed deeper, but couldn't help snigger. It was going to take a little getting used to, being free to appreciate Jude whenever she liked, but she would manage.

She shuffled next to Jude and they sat together, propped on the pillows, soft bottom next to ample cheek, naked arms and breasts brushing together. Abby passed a small plate with a large piece of cake and peered down at their naked bodies. She couldn't stop grinning.

"You're in my bed," she said, her grin getting wider.

"And we have chocolate cake."

"It's bloody perfect."

Jude laughed. "Have you been drinking downstairs?"

"No," Abby said, indignant, but she still grinned. "I'm just incredibly happy." She was tipsy on nerves and euphoria, and there was no point denying it.

Jude looked at her, an indulgent expression softening her face. "I love you, Abby. In every single way. I don't think I've been this happy or so exquisitely fucked in my life."

Abby smiled, then her heart sank. Jude reminded Abby a little of Maggie then, with her humorous vulgarity.

"We have to tell people, don't we? We'll need to tell Maggie."

"No, we don't," Jude whispered and she touched her chin so she'd look her in the eye. "I won't deny it if anyone asks. I'll never hide how I feel for you. But let's enjoy each other a while before we let the world in."

31

"No," Maggie growled. "No. No. No."

She wasn't having that. It was a sight to make her soul sicken and temper burn. She marched towards the church gate, her fiery breath clouding in the early morning air.

"Un-fucking-believable!" She glowered at the courtyard. A small group of people surveyed the building, one dressed in a suit and high-visibility vest, the other two a rotund middle-aged mother and her wealthy son.

So that's who it was. That's who wanted to develop the church. Mrs bloody Petty and her son. It was unbearable. Yes, there was the social injustice of it all, but Maggie was buggered if she was going to let her sodding, bigoted neighbour grab the heart of Ludbury.

Maggie clenched her fists and blew an enormous cloud of disapprobation into the air. She'd dismissed her own plans for the church as delusional when she'd discussed them with Richard and Eli, even though both had been enthusiastic, but there was nothing like a personal grudge to fuel the fires of determination.

Maggie turned on her heel. No, this was unsupportable. People homeless in Ludbury. People having to beg to use the food bank while others lorded over the town. Maggie marched through the square, past the Georgian terraces sweeping down the side of the citadel. Past the grand station and luxury flats built on the foundations of council houses

239

and the welfare state. Further still, beyond the old town boundary where planning was more lax and houses built more cheaply, and the pastels of the old town gave way to the grey of the new.

She glanced up towards her destination on the hill opposite, the 1960s school block where she'd worked since her late twenties and where today she had been called in as a supply teacher.

Christ, her legs ached and breath laboured. She seemed to have lost her fitness without her daily walk to school and she sat on a garden wall to rest awhile.

"Bollocking hell," she rasped.

How had she become so unfit? She made a mental note to buy an annual ticket to the swimming pool, then she mentally scribbled the note out. Who was she kidding? She loathed swimming. She'd have to think of something else. But it definitely wasn't frigging yoga.

She was late. The streets were empty of teenagers excepting the usual stragglers, the ones people called lazy, the ones which did a paper round before school because their parents couldn't afford pocket money. She recognised a group of youths who'd left school the year before with few academic qualifications although not lacking ability in other areas. They kicked a can around the pavement and sat in a huddle with their hoodies up. She imagined there was little for them to do and nowhere to go.

As she sat catching her breath, she watched an old homeless man, looking wet and dirty from a night outside. He lurched his way past the youths in painful steps.

"Fucking hell, he stinks," one of the youths cursed.

"Shut up, man," another said, and he elbowed his friend in the ribs. "Here you go, mate," the youth said, and he stood up and handed the old man a can of soda from his pocket.

Maggie didn't know whether to be heartened or to despair. It was a different world beyond the historic walls of Ludbury. How quickly she'd forgotten. But at least the youth had achieved one act of kindness this morning and had done more than Maggie to alleviate the old man's condition.

She stamped to her feet irritated by the whole world, mainly by her perpetual inaction.

"Good morning!" she announced as she strode into the classroom. She dropped her bag on the wooden desk at the front and surveyed the room of fifteen-years-olds that she'd taught the year before. She expected a murmur of discontent this early in the morning from the nocturnal teens.

"Mrs Goodman!" a girl cried out.

The class shuffled to attention.

"Miss. You're back," a greeting boomed from a rotund boy not used to his man's voice.

"Are you back for good?" another called.

Maggie smiled and leaned back against the desk, arms crossed in satisfaction. "What a lovely welcome," she said peering over her glasses. "Regrettably, it's only for the day, while Miss Detrain is absent."

"Shame. We've missed ya'," the booming voice said.

"Thank you." She nodded in his direction. "That's cheering to hear."

She noticed an empty seat at the back and after scanning the rows of faces asked, "Where's Tyler?"

"He's off again," Dan replied from the front.

Dan was a confident boy, a man already in stature and voice, his broad shoulders and physique ludicrous in the modest school seat.

"He's in hospital with his asthma."

Maggie's shoulders sank. Tyler, the poor kid, was in and out of A&E with attacks, not helped by the pervasive mould that grew in his home. The boy even had rickets. The contrast between his malnourished frame and the alpha boy Dan in the front row was absurd and sickening in modern-day Britain.

Maggie shook her head and growled beneath her voice.

"What's up, miss?" Dan asked.

She spun back to the class, ready to fob them off and ask where they should pick up, but she hesitated. She looked over the faces of nearly adults, soon to be released into the world, and people who would inhabit it for longer than she.

"Right," she said. "Before we start, I'd like your opinions." She looked around the class. She had their attention. "What do you think about living in a town with Michelin-starred restaurants in one street, and in the next people malnourished with diseases we associate with Victorian poverty? Do you think that's fair?"

The class shuffled, some frowning at the unusual start to the lesson, others seeming more than happy to delay the teaching, others again deep in thought.

"Well, it's not right is it, miss," a girl from the front said.

A boy from the back crossed his arms and leant back in his chair before claiming, "My dad says people should get off their arses and work harder and stop buying shit."

Maggie nodded to indicate she'd heard. "Do you think everyone who can't afford food is lazy?"

"People can always work harder," the boy said.

"No, they can't," said the girl at the front. "My aunt's a nurse and works every shift she can, and she still has to come to ours for a decent dinner."

"Precisely," Maggie said. "The inequalities in our society have become so extreme that even if you have a full-time job, pay can be minimal, your landlord takes the lion's share and you're left with nothing to feed your family."

"It's been the government's fault, hasn't it," the girl said.

"Well, I think you all know which way I lean politically, but even if there's change it will be slow. So what can we do now?"

"Do?" the girl said.

Maggie shrugged. "I want your ideas on how to help."

You could hear a pin drop. Nobody moved. One or two rolled their eyes and looked as if they'd rather be anywhere else, but they were mainly shocked that anyone had asked them for a solution.

"My mum puts things in the food bank basket," the boy with the booming voice offered.

"Yeah, mine too," the girl at the front said. "Especially at Christmas."

Maggie smiled. "I do the same, but they rarely get the right food, in the right quantities and at the right time. People need food year round and unfortunately people's generosity can be quite seasonal."

"My mum says you should give food banks money instead," the girl piped up, "so they can get what's needed."

"Yes, and she's right. But people don't like giving money. They're more likely to donate food."

Dan, the alpha boy who'd been listening intently sat up in his chair. "They should tell people what they need then. Give them reminders when they shop and let them know what's running out."

Maggie thought for a moment. "Yes, that's a good idea, but resource intensive. These places are run by volunteers and collection points are spread throughout the town. It's quite an overhead to keep so many sites up-to-date."

"What about using technology, miss?" Dan said.

Maggie suppressed a roll of the eyes, then mentally kicked herself for being a technophobe. She drew herself up straight. "How can technology help?" she said with a more open mind.

"You could let people know on their phones, couldn't you?" Dan replied.

"True." Maggie nodded.

"You could get people to sign up, then the food bank could send out a reminder every week with a list of things they need most."

"Why not?" Maggie smiled. "Do you think people would sign up?"

"Might if you give them an app," came a voice from the back of the class.

Maggie peered over the heads to see the familiar face of Anisha Patel, a bright girl who held no shame in her intelligence, a product of her able and confident mother who managed the surgery in town where Abby worked.

"An app?" Maggie said.

"People love a colourful app," Anisha replied. "Put a poster in the shops to ask people to download it. They can get rid of it any time and can't be spammed like when they give away their email address."

Maggie mulled it over. "Actually, I think you're right. It might even be popular with old farts like me."

The class sniggered.

"But that's going to cost….God knows how much," Maggie said.

"I could write one," Anisha replied. "I could develop an app."

"Really?"

"Yeah. It'd take me a couple of days to do a prototype. More for the real thing, but not long."

Maggie surveyed the room for signs of dissent, but found none. They were all looking to her, waiting on the edge of their seats for her pronouncement.

"She's good, miss," came a confident voice. It was Dan at the front, the alpha boy. "Trust her. Let her put something together for you."

Murmurs of approval rippled around the class.

What struck Maggie then, between the handsome boy at the front enabled by his popularity, and his approval of the intelligent girl, was that it was he who blushed at the situation. Anisha looked at Maggie, patiently waiting and assured in her own abilities, pleased at the boy's support but not needing it for her resolve. Dan peeped back, gave the girl a smile and flushed a little deeper. He was clearly smitten.

Maggie sat down, removed her glasses and looked over the expectant young faces, all waiting to see if she approved of their proposal. And in the first time in an age, along with her burden of responsibility, she felt hope.

"Well, why not." She laughed, and the class rumbled with excitement. "Let me talk to Dean at the food bank, and see if they're interested. Then," she shrugged, "let's do it."

32

Maggie walked back to the citadel at the end of the school day with greater alacrity, her mood and energy buoyed by the teens.

The market was in full swing as she passed though the square, stalls busy with after-work trade. She wandered between rows, eyeing the morsels of Mediterranean antipasti on one side, inhaling the spicy vapours of Middle Eastern offerings on the other, her senses overwhelmed. What a contrast indeed.

The clientele were well-heeled locals and tourists alike, including Caroline Argent who lingered at the Mediterranean stall. She looked as austere and impeccable as ever – blue blazer, floral scarf, blonde hair swept to perfection. Maggie stared ahead, pretending not to have noticed, but as the church came into view she hesitated.

She gathered herself and walked back to the stall.

"Caroline?"

The woman was handing notes to the stall holder and didn't hear initially.

"Caroline? Could I have a word?"

She heard then and the change in her demeanour was notable to say the least. "Maggie." The Tory council woman stepped back and put her hand to her heart. "You gave me a surprise."

"Sorry. I wondered, do you have time for a chat?"

Caroline stared, clearly disturbed by Maggie's approach, but she straightened herself, twitching the blazer with her shoulders, and held a shopping bag defensively in front of her.

"If it's not convenient," Maggie started.

"No, I have time. Richard," she hesitated glancing around, "isn't visiting this evening and I'm eating alone, so I'm in no hurry."

It was strange to hear her husband's name uttered with familiarity by another woman, but nothing worse than that, and for once Maggie was heartened by her own balanced response.

"How about I buy you a coffee?" Maggie suggested.

Caroline stood stiffly, chin too prominent for ease. "If you like. Thank you."

"Let's go to the Garden Café," Maggie suggested, wondering at how awkward Caroline seemed.

The woman's agitation didn't lessen while Maggie bought the drinks. As Maggie waited at the counter, Caroline sat down in the middle of the conservatory, on the edge of her seat, back straight and shoulders square as if preparing to face a firing squad with dignity.

Maggie passed a black coffee down to Caroline, the woman's anxiety not alleviated for a moment, and Maggie took a seat and sipped at her indulgent Mocha.

"I need a favour," Maggie ventured, realising with shame, given her attitude and behaviour over many months, how little this woman owed her that.

"I'm listening," Caroline said, chin aloft.

"I need advice on planning permission."

Caroline's mouth dropped open.

"It's for a conversion of an historical site," Maggie continued. "I may as well tell you; it's the church and courtyard that I'm referring to."

Caroline seemed set in stone, her mouth still open.

"The vicar suggested you might be useful."

There was no change in the other woman's response. Now even Maggie was unnerved by Caroline's reaction. Was it really that much to ask? Did she despise Maggie that much?

"Is it too much of an imposition?" Maggie said, cautiously.

"What did you say?" Caroline gasped.

"I know it's cheeky of me, all things considered." Maggie had hardly been helpful, refusing to make the divorce public and forcing Richard and Caroline into secrecy. And God knows everyone knew of Maggie's political polemics against the woman. "But I need planning advice and I'd value your expertise."

"Oh." Caroline covered her mouth. If Maggie was in any doubt about the expression Caroline hid, then the woman's eyes gave her away. They brimmed with tears and her entire face twitched with emotion.

"I thought," Caroline stuttered. "I thought you were going to tell me to stay away from Richard."

"No. No, I've no intention of talking about him."

"Oh, thank God." Caroline sniffed back tears in a fashion most unlike her. "Thank God."

Maggie had never seen Caroline anything but contained and composed. It was unnerving.

"I'm sorry." Caroline gulped. "You have every right to tell me to keep away."

"I have no plans to. He hasn't been a husband for a long time, and he's happier than I've ever seen him."

This was too much for Caroline. Her face crumpled with grief and her body shook, overwhelmed. "I'm so sorry," she kept saying.

"It's fine," Maggie reassured her. "I'm…." She didn't know what she was.

Caroline reached into her bag for a white handkerchief, either new or perfectly ironed. She quietly blew her nose and dabbed her eyes, checking for smudges of makeup.

"I'm sorry," she said. "I've barely been holding it together." She rushed out her words before swallowing in between sentences. "I've been close to breaking point, putting Malcom in the home and his constant struggles there. I don't know what I'd do without Richard."

Caroline's forehead crinkled again and she breathed heavily trying to control herself. It was a feeling that if anyone could sympathise with, it was Maggie. Empathy flooded through her. She put down her drink and reached out, pulling Caroline close.

"You've nothing to worry about," Maggie said, her voice shaking and all her own woes amplifying her response. "I'm not going to take him away."

Caroline clasped Maggie tight. It was the fierce grip of a woman overwhelmed and fighting to keep everything inside while at the same time desperate to reach out for consolation.

"He's there for you, Caroline," Maggie whispered. "I don't doubt that."

Caroline held on, her body shuddering with release, and only after her breathing became regular did Maggie let go. Caroline sat back stiffly and dabbed her eyes, while Maggie did the same. And after they'd sniffed, blown their noses, shuffled, rearranged their coats, skirts or trousers, they stared at each other – two middle-aged women beleaguered by family and life, their mascara streaming and faces blotchy with tears. They burst out laughing. For all their differences, Caroline was very much a woman like Maggie.

Caroline took a sip of her coffee and smiled. "How can I help?"

Maggie opened her mouth to explain then hesitated. "I don't know if this is going to sound like the foolish fancy of desperate left-wing mother."

Caroline raised an eyebrow. "Try me."

"The church and courtyard that's for sale, I believe has some interest," Maggie tried not to look as if she was drinking curdled milk, "from a luxury developer."

"I've heard the same. I'm no longer on the planning committee, but I've heard rumours."

"Well, I want to offer the church a different proposal." Maggie's confidence was waning.

"Go on. I'm not a fan of the current plans, so please go on."

Maggie searched Caroline's face. She seemed only good humoured and receptive.

"OK," Maggie sighed. "Is it viable to turn the courtyard into a multiple occupancy development? I'm thinking family flats, small studios, perhaps micro dwellings – a mix of housing for a range of families with a high percentage of affordable housing. It's something that's severely lacking in Ludbury and I think it's obscene to invest in luxury developments when housing is so scarce."

Caroline frowned a little, as if slipping into work mode. "As long as the conversion is a sympathetic design, I don't see a problem. The luxury single dwelling would face the same issues. But the planning board will consider the increase in population on the site and concomitant increase in traffic. I doubt they'd approve any extension to parking."

"Actually I wouldn't plan any. The idea comes from wanting to save the historic site and keep it open to residents and the public. The old gardens could be managed as an allotment. The orchard could be maintained as communal gardens to the courtyard. Parking would be restricted as it is now and a number of pool cars and bikes may be a possible option for residents."

Caroline nodded. "That will go down well in general. Anything environmentally sensitive will be popular with the council. It is Tory run and environmental concerns are rising up our agenda but the Greens have a significant representation."

"We're investigating ground-source heating and solar energy."

"The latter might be troublesome with the aesthetics of the building, although the board are generally more amenable than they were."

"OK," said Maggie. "Good to know."

"And the church building itself and graveyard?"

"I'm not sure yet. That's more difficult. The maintenance overhead for that kind of building is significant. And the easiest option is a single dwelling, but that's what troubles me." Maggie frowned. "A building which has been central to town life for centuries doesn't belong in private hands."

"I agree," Caroline said.

And not for the first time, Maggie was surprised by how in tune they were.

Caroline smiled as if reading her thoughts. "We may not have the same political allegiances, but I suspect we're similar in many ways."

"You might not agree when I tell you how it will be financed."

"Really?"

"A co-op," Maggie challenged, "of young people and other residents."

Caroline frowned. "I have no issue with that. Everyone needs a home and responsible groups of young people should be encouraged. We can't deny there's a housing crisis, even though we may disagree on some of the causes." Then she smiled. "I am not a radical politician, Maggie. So much of our news and politics is dominated by extremes – the media sensationalising everything as outrageous for sales and views – and we forget most people have moderate beliefs."

Maggie considered and found herself nodding in agreement. "Yes, it is easy to forget these days."

"I think we've forgotten how to talk to each other as human beings." Caroline spread her arms wide. "Look what can be achieved when people talk face-to-face rather than shouting at a preconception. Please forgive me, but I had a very different expectation of you today."

"Me too," Maggie sighed.

"But when do people meet? And where?" Caroline said with a shrug of despair. "No-one goes to church anymore."

"No-one even goes to the bloody pub," Maggie added, and they both laughed. "They've closed down the youth centre."

"And the library." Caroline raised a hand. "Yes, austerity," she acknowledged. "I won't deny there've been painful cuts and there are consequences."

"So where do people go? Where caters to everyone young and old?"

Caroline looked around where they sat. "I think the café is as close as we get."

They both caught sight of the vicar striding towards them, a towering glass of hot chocolate and marshmallows in her hand.

"Good evening ladies," she hailed.

"Are you in need of your spirits reviving?" Maggie said, eyeing the indulgent drink, then kicked herself for slipping into spiritual puns.

"I am indeed." The vicar smiled. She seemed tired. "The good Lord is always there, but there's no harm in that extra lift that cocoa can achieve."

"Will you join us?" Maggie invited.

"I would love to. In fact I have a proposition for you, Mrs Goodman."

"You're propositioning me?" Maggie said with a grin. And again. Why did she have to be smutty whenever she encountered the vicar? Would she ever outgrow her school-girl temptation to be naughty under the gaze of the god-fearing?

Thankfully the vicar sat down with a smile, and for a woman devoted to God she didn't half have a wicked one.

"I've been talking with the bishop as it happens," the vicar started, "and he's also concerned about the church site after it's sold, particularly access to the graveyard and the community services. Of course, some services will be transferred to St Laurence, but not all. Do you have anything in your latest plans to support community use of the church building itself?"

Maggie shook her head. "Not yet. We've been focussing on the courtyard."

"Actually, we were just talking about the lack of central meeting places," Caroline added. "I'd hate to see the church go."

"You see," the vicar started, "because of our conversation, the bishop wants to hear the concerns of locals and alternative proposals for the site, before the finance department go further with the sale. I think he'd be particularly receptive to your plans if they included continued use of the church."

Maggie sat back. The mix of hope and despair was excruciating. The project, even at this preliminary stage, was overwhelming and there was no way current funds would extend to a public building and maintenance.

"You need investment, Maggie," Caroline said.

Maggie eyed her suspiciously. "Are you suggesting a company?"

"In the short term."

"So Ludbury Church, sponsored by McDonalds?"

Caroline smiled. "Not exactly. I do have some ideas though. We need to make the church maintenance sustainable by providing services that pay for it. But the purchase needs to be funded somehow."

Maggie ground her teeth at the prospect of corporate ownership of the public and spiritual site.

"Not all companies are evil," Caroline said. "Let me look into it? I'm keen to help with this."

"I'm prepared to listen," Maggie conceded at last.

"Good," said the vicar with a beaming smile. "I will arrange a date with the bishop. I hope you will both help publicise the meeting?"

"Of course," Maggie and Caroline chorused, and they laughed at their identical response.

Maggie looked around their small table, at a woman whose religion she'd never follow and another who belonged to a party she'd thought diametrically opposed to hers. Maggie Goodman was making plans with a woman of the cloth and a Tory. Hell must have truly frozen over.

Maggie walked home, turning over the possibilities in her head and chuckling. She even caught herself humming. Maybe there was something to be said about reaching out and she returned home more receptive to establishing an entente cordiale with whoever might be interested, even Juliette.

As she put her key in the front door, a voice shrieked from the neighbouring garden.

"He's back in the marital home then. But not with his wife. I suppose she avoids him when his women are round. Look at them flirting in the garden."

Maggie almost shouted out, "Who's she? The cat's mother?" then groaned. It was one of those tiny things which made her feel one hundred and five. Then she growled. Trust Mrs Petty to piss on her fire. And who the hell was her blasted neighbour talking about? She'd only just left Caroline at the Garden Café. It wouldn't be her.

Maggie kicked at the bottom of the door and went inside. She was welcomed by the sight of her mahogany table covered with courtyard plans and blueprints, studied intently by Eli, Selene and Dean.

"Evening, Mrs Goodman," Dean said with his jovial smile. "You've got quite a project here."

"Good evening," she replied with genuine pleasure. "How are things looking?"

"It's an exciting project. Always tricky with a listed building, but we've plenty of experience of that in Ludbury. We're meeting with a surveyor tomorrow to discuss some of the options."

"Good," Maggie said.

"We can do this, Mum," Eli said, and she couldn't help be charmed by her son's enthusiasm. He looked to Selene for approbation, gently slipping his arm around her waist. He was very protective of her, Maggie noticed, always physically reassuring her. It was a mature quality she'd not seen in him before.

"It's very exciting, Maggie," Selene said. "My mother thinks so too."

"Ah," Maggie said, always a little defensive at the mention of Juliette. "Good. Yes. Good."

Maggie sauntered through the sitting area and dropped her bag on a sofa, smiling at Celia dozing on another.

Richard was indeed in the garden. He'd taken out two deckchairs and was facing the river with a companion. He was wearing his Panama hat, of which he was inordinately proud, and was brandishing a cut-glass tumbler of whiskey. Maggie ambled outside trying to ascertain his company and the reason for Richard's good spirits. He was rattling away about something with much enthusiasm. Then his companion laughed and Maggie stopped.

It was unmistakably Juliette. Her former lover pushed herself up so that Maggie could see her raven hair above the back the chair. Maggie edged closer, transfixed by the bizarre sight of her husband happily in the company of the love and heart-break of her life. Maggie couldn't make out their conversation, but the way they laughed and threw comments back and forth, Richard's warm deep voice then Juliette's tumble of words like a vivacious stream were unmistakably cordial.

"I told you it wasn't the floozy."

Maggie's whole body knotted with tension as Mrs Petty's shrill voice cut through the moment.

"It's despicable. Who's he with now?"

Richard and Juliette twitched round in the direction of next door, their profiles in view. Juliette put her hand to her mouth as if to amplify her voice. "It's none of your fucking business," she shouted. And that it was delivered in an elegant French accent made it even more perfect.

Richard guffawed loudly. He laughed so much he almost fell from his chair. He raised his glass and Juliette smiled, chinking her tumbler against his.

"Here's to a beautiful friendship," Richard said, and Maggie could see the warmth in their faces.

The moment made Maggie's heart full with so many feelings she couldn't name or separate them. It was a glimpse of a perfect life – Maggie's family around her, the future daughter-in-law eager to move nearby, her son maturing while still as playful and doting as ever. Richard, her greatest friend, and Juliette, her most ardent lover, were content in her circle. She clutched her heart as it lurched with realisation.

This is what she craved. It was what she'd always craved. It seemed frustratingly within reach yet forever unattainable, a surreal vision of what might have been.

"Maggie?" Juliette was peering back at her with concern, the mirth of her conversation with Ricard fading from her face. "Are you all right?"

Juliette rose from the deckchair with a fluid grace and walked towards Maggie. Her feet were bare in the grass, so reminiscent of their lazy days in the park long ago, and it was impossible for Maggie not to respond to her.

"What's wrong?" Juliette whispered. She reached for Maggie's cheek, the tips of her fingers stroking her skin. Maggie closed her eyes and Juliette's faint touch stirred deep inside, exciting memories and sensations decades old but as vigorous as youth. The sensation consumed her body and overpowered her mind with sweet rapture.

She opened her eyes and pulled away, so entranced by Juliette's presence that no riposte occurred to her. She walked away, back into the house, and couldn't look back.

33

"Fuck it," were Maggie's first words the next morning.

A persistent unease had robbed her of sleep, the kind which tightens its grip in the small hours when nagging concerns take on preternatural potency. It seemed to Maggie that she stood on a precipice, one which could lead to happiness but still necessitated a fall.

She snapped her legs out of bed and marched to the bathroom, showering and dressing at a pace to distract herself from anxiety. But it was still there. It tickled inside her tummy when she checked herself in the mirror – a striking middle-aged woman, with styled grey hair, lightening blue eyes and a look that could wither a Viking. She pulled at the cuffs of her honey-coloured trench coat and patted the inside pocket for her favourite maroon reading glasses.

Apprehension still gnawed as Maggie made her way through the square and it bit a little sharper when she peered up at the Coaching Inn, its tiered Jacobian façade looming above. It didn't release its grip when she enquired after Juliette Bonhomme at reception and it stayed her knock when she lifted her hand to the Stokesay Suite.

The door opened before she had a chance to fight anxiety's grip and Juliette stood before her.

"I heard you approach." Juliette smiled. "That's the trouble with this gorgeous old hotel. Every footstep on the floorboards makes her groan."

Maggie stared. She'd expected Juliette to be her immaculate self when she'd invited Maggie up on the reception phone, with her dusky makeup and a crisp shirt. But her face was bare and she wore only a short white dressing gown.

"I'm sorry," Maggie stumbled, awkward in Juliette's undressed state. "I don't have your number. I would have called ahead."

"No matter. Come in." Juliette gestured into the soft light of the boutique bedroom.

They stood facing each other beside the oak bedframe, the sheets still unmade. It was inappropriate to be here.

"I thought you'd be up," Maggie said. "I'd forgotten...not forgotten, overlooked that you weren't an early riser."

"Actually I prefer mornings now, but I indulged in a lie-in this time."

"OK." Maggie said, not knowing where to look. "Eli and Selene had an appointment and went to see a friend. I realised you might be alone all day."

"I am," Juliette said, not releasing her gaze or moving back from her intimate proximity.

"I'm giving out leaflets," Maggie stuttered. "I wondered if you'd like to come and post them. I mean, would you like some company? A stroll around town. With me. Would you like to spend some time with me?"

"Am I making you uncomfortable?" Juliette smirked, her semi-naked presence impossible to ignore.

Maggie stared at the floor, and perhaps Juliette's slim legs and bare feet on the plush woollen rug.

"Do I remind you of forbidden things? Is it too much to recall you were once with a woman?"

Maggie looked her in the eye. "No, I've never been ashamed. It's not that."

"Then what?"

"I shouldn't see you like this."

"You have seen me naked a thousand times. You can cope with a bathrobe. If we were at the beach, I could grace you with my stretch marks also."

"Just because we were...." And Maggie did stumble over this. A lifetime of burying the pain had led to a degree of denial. "Just because we were once lovers does not give me a lifetime pass to see your body."

"True. I don't mind though. I'm not so prudish as you English."

Maggie's shyness evaporated. "When the fuck did you ever find me prudish?" and not a small number of images flashed through Maggie's mind to illustrate her point. She was on the verge of recounting them when she stopped herself. If seeing your ex half-naked in their hotel room was inappropriate then indulging in past tales of lust and delicious perversion certainly was.

Juliette tilted her head to the side. "You have a point. And I have many memories to back it up." She slowly lifted an eyebrow, so lasciviously it would have undressed Maggie in her youth. Then Juliette laughed. "I'm sorry. I'm baiting you. It's just strange to see the biggest lesbian on campus as this respectable wife."

Juliette turned and rattled through the large oak wardrobe. "I will get dressed and make myself into a respectable middle-aged mother also." She peeked over her shoulder. "You are welcome to watch."

Maggie gave her a look, one that would have crushed anyone but Juliette, who laughed a bubbling laugh that tickled Maggie inside.

Still shy at the sight of Juliette's unprepared state, Maggie sought the lead-panelled bay window and sat on the bench. She took a sideways position as if to admire the view outside but couldn't help peeking in Juliette's direction. She was stood by the bed readying her clothes, all the while watching Maggie.

259

"Very well, I am warning you that I'm about to remove my robe."

Maggie looked away but was met by Juliette's reflection undressing in every small panel of the window. She couldn't have focussed her gaze outside if she'd tried. A miniature naked Juliette was reflected a hundred times, and Maggie's jaw dropped as a glimpse of her breasts was revealed over and over again. It was too much to resist turning round as Juliette shimmied into a slip.

Juliette had a raw beauty when she wasn't styled and manicured, her face appearing naked without its makeup. It was an intimate and more familiar face, the one Maggie woke to. It had changed with the passage of time. The doe hazel eyes and full lips of Juliette's youth had matured. Her eyes had a dark intelligence and her still full lips an accentuated shape that curved with even more allure. Her slimmer face revealed the glory of her cheekbones and that elegant jaw line was beyond compare.

Her body had been slim like Maggie's in their youth, and both had benefitted from the curves life brings; it was impossible to ignore Juliette's healthy bosom half hidden by her slip.

"Am I so changed to you?" Juliette said, the bravado of a moment ago gone and a sad smile replacing it on her lips. "Is it strange to see me old?"

Maggie blinked, caught in her study and still stunned by the intimate sight of her former lover.

"I was wondering," Maggie said, "how is it possible that you are more beautiful? I luxuriated for hours admiring you when we were young. But it's as if your body and face have found their perfect age. Youth suits some better, others reveal their finery later, and your beauty is striking now."

Juliette's sad smile slipped from her face. She looked away and smoothed her shirt on the bed. "That's so like you, Maggie," she said. "So impossibly like you."

"How?"

Juliette shook her head, then fixed Maggie with an unwavering gaze. "You can destroy someone with a single word. I've seen you wreck fellow students in a tirade of brutal honesty from which they'd never recover. And just when I consign you to my furthest memories and abandon all hope in us ever being friends, you come here and deliver one of your rare compliments. Do you know how much your compliments hurt, Maggie?"

Maggie didn't move.

"They're like your criticisms, they are brutal. They cut through to your essence with their passion and you remember them for a lifetime."

They stared at each other, the air heavy with regret, old desires, memories so painful Maggie never wanted to indulge them, and cutting through it all an urge to remain in each other's company.

"I need to dress," Juliette said. "You can turn away if you want. It still seems silly to be prudish in front of you of all people."

"Sorry," Maggie said, and she did turn away.

"You can admire the courtyard garden through the window."

"Or watch you in the reflections," Maggie replied, amused. She saw Juliette's pale image put her hands on her hips then throw something towards the window. A moment later Maggie found a pair of knickers around her head.

They wandered down Broad Street, the largest and most grandiose of Ludbury's avenues – two well-dressed, handsome women with pamphlets urging the residents to an emergency meeting at the church.

One posted a leaflet through a town-house door, the other the next. Maggie occasionally nodded to a passer-by she recognised then they reconvened to amble further.

261

"I like Richard very much by the way," Juliette said. "I had a chat with him yesterday. It's the first time I've really spoken to him."

"He is a lovely man. One of the finest." Maggie nearly added: "If only you'd met him earlier." But she was too bothered by their current marital status. "We're…" But then Maggie stopped, unable to articulate the truth.

"I know you're no longer together," Juliette said quietly.

"How?"

"Richard slipped up while we were chatting in the garden. He mentioned Caroline."

Maggie's cheeks flamed. "Damn it, Richard. The absent-minded old fool." But when the waves of heat receded it felt more like relief. "Good," Maggie muttered. "Well. Good."

"I'd guessed already so it didn't come as a surprise. Richard said that Eli suspects too but Jude doesn't know. You've not told anyone yet?"

"We were going to," Maggie grumbled. "But events have overtaken it somewhat."

And bloody Eli. Of course the nosy little bugger suspected. They strolled a little further, Maggie still chuntering to herself.

"Maggie?" Juliette murmured, and she gently took her arm. "Are you OK?"

When she looked up, she found genuine concern in Juliette's face and Maggie tutted a laugh. "Yes, I am." Splitting up with Richard was now the least of her concerns. "We've been more friends than anything else for…" Always. Always for Maggie. But she was torn between respect for Richard and honesty with Juliette. Maggie felt as if she owed her former lover that. "He's been my support and closest friend, and he's someone I will always love very dearly."

"You needn't say any more. I have enough respect now for Richard not to pry."

Maggie nodded, grateful for the reprieve, but also that Juliette didn't release her arm. She held on, the comfort of it warming Maggie through as they wandered further.

"You know," Juliette said lightly. "This," she waved the handful of leaflets in the air, "reminds me of college."

"I should be standing on the corner yelling '*Socialist Worker*'. It's quite a change from 'Coal Not Dole'."

"And the anti-nuclear leaflets," Juliette replied.

"Women's equality."

"Vegetarianism?"

"I think we gave that one a miss," Maggie said. Juliette's persistent and delicious cuisine had tempted Maggie off that wagon.

Juliette tugged at her arm. "Even I eat less meat than I used to."

"The marches were always my favourite," Maggie carried on. "Good excuse to shout at people."

"At least you admit that it's one of your greatest pleasures."

"You knew them all," Maggie quipped then blushed at the indecent allusion.

Juliette gave a smile, the one that pinched naughtily in the corner of her mouth. "Do you remember our first Pride march in London?"

"Vaguely," Maggie grimaced. "Those were the days I drank too much Newkie Brown."

"I could never understand your obsession with beer. What on earth is the problem with a glass of wine for goodness sake?"

"You were such a snob about alcohol, especially wine."

Juliette shrugged. "I still am." And they both laughed. "Do you remember?" Juliette said conspiratorially, "when we ran away into Soho and lost the others?"

Yes, Maggie did.

263

"We were so tipsy." The way Juliette said tipsy in her French accent made it sound so youthful and pleasurable. "That was the first time I set foot in a sex shop."

Maggie definitely remembered. And it wasn't the last time they visited.

"Do you remember the size of the dildos? *Zut alors*," Juliette said with mock mortification. "How my young head spun. We stuffed our rucksack with merchandise," she said gleefully. "Bondage ropes. Blindfolds. Fishnet stockings. That suit with the zips and openings everywhere. Do you not remember?"

How could Maggie forget? They'd made serious use of those ropes and the memory of Juliette in that suit made Maggie weak at the knees. There was something about just a glimpse of a delicate area that fatally appealed to her.

"Maggie," Juliette whispered. She stopped and frowned. "I hope you're not going all British and coy with me. You can't deny we had sex. I hope you've not wiped that from your version of our history."

"Of course I bloody haven't. We fucked like rabbits."

"Hi, Mrs Goodman," a teenage girl said, walking up the road.

"Oh." Shit. "Hi, Penny." Shit.

Maggie waved awkwardly to the former pupil then straightened her coat unnecessarily.

Juliette was watching her, that damned smile in the corner of her mouth and her eyes shining.

"Good," Juliette said at last. "I'm glad you've remembered your kinky ways. Now, let's deliver these leaflets about saving the church."

Maggie could have kicked her. But in the end she decided to snigger.

They climbed the hill past the old assembly rooms on the last street of their tour. Maggie handed the remaining leaflets to the shopkeepers in the square, and stuck the final poster in the bookshop window. She called out her gratitude to the owner, who heartily replied, before joining Juliette outside. She was watching her, head tilted.

"What?" Maggie tutted. "What now?"

This only made Juliette's smile broader. "Look at you," she said. "How did such a ferocious activist become the darling of a middle England town?"

"Oh believe me, I'm far from popular in many quarters. You won't find me in the souvenir shop. Mr Huff, with his wall to wall Union Jacks, will turn venomous the moment he sets eyes on me."

"Then maybe not all quarters. But, Maggie," Juliette looked at her more seriously although amusement still played on her lips, "you are respected."

"Puh," Maggie said, actually in a way more akin to Juliette than herself. How quickly she fell into her old mannerisms and emulated those of her former lover.

"It's funny, you know," Juliette said. "Seeing you as a teacher, mother, respected resident of Ludbury."

"Really, the respected part is nonsense."

"I see it everywhere though. From people in the street, the shopkeepers, the vicar. Your son adores you and even the man whom you're divorcing thinks the world of you."

Maggie sighed. There was a notable omission. "Not Jude though."

Juliette observed her, a sad smile of sympathy on her face. She took Maggie's arm and they wandered from the square, past the church and down the road towards home.

"I've only talked to her a little," Juliette said. "But I like her very much."

"She's a wonderful human being," Maggie said. "My God I'm proud of her." Her words caught in her throat, a mix of choking pride in her child and heartache at their detachment. "She was the brightest girl, but never arrogant. And her resilience? She had the confidence of a much older person.

Always a leader and always looking out for others. You see it in her friendship with Abby."

"Hmm," Juliette said and she fell quiet as they continued. "Everyone needs someone though. I hope she realises she can reach out for help too."

"I suppose so. I hardly believe she'll ever need it. She's rebounded from breaking up with a long-term boyfriend in the blink of an eye, and is god knows where happy as the cat that got the cream."

"Hmm," Juliette said again. Maggie knew that "hmm", but Juliette carried on before Maggie could cajole her.

"Eli described her as a female version of Richard – the paragon of responsibility. But actually," Juliette smiled at her, "I see a lot of you in her."

"Ha! You mustn't let her hear that. And I can't see it, unless," she narrowed her eyes, "you mean when we're bad-tempered."

"Yes," Juliette replied, without a hint of remorse.

This time Maggie did give Juliette the gentlest boot.

"But it's true." Juliette laughed. "There is fire there, you can't deny it."

"God help her. It's never done me any favours."

Juliette fell quiet and they walked on, Maggie sensing a change in mood in her companion.

"I thought about you over the years," Juliette said at last. "Mike told me Jude had been born, a great healthy girl, and I wondered what she looked like."

Maggie slowed her walk, her heart heavy at Juliette's words. Every time she sensed Juliette's mood flag she would feel it keenly. It had been a strength and a weakness, this mirroring of emotions. Juliette wounded would sober Maggie even from the foulest temper, mollifying her in a second so that all she wanted was to soothe her lover. But when they'd argued, fire burned hotter with fire.

Maggie stopped and peered at Juliette's harrowed face. "Would you like to see some photos? Do you want to see what she was like? And of course Eli too. Your future son in law." Maggie smiled at the prospect.

"Yes," Juliette said. "I would like that very much."

And as they wandered home, arm in arm, Maggie's heart beat with a myriad of emotions.

34

Maggie prised two large albums from the bookcase and carried them to Juliette on the sofa.

"These are from the early years," Maggie said, sitting next to her companion. She slipped on her reading glasses and smiled when Juliette leaned down to her bag to retrieve her own.

"Comes to us all," Juliette said with an elegant shrug that showed how little she cared about signs of maturity. It was Juliette all over, unruffled by life's petty strife. She carried off wearing spectacles with poise and confidence. It's what had made her so attractive to Maggie when they'd met.

"Here," Maggie said, opening the book at the front. "Here she is. Just born and a few weeks afterwards."

Juliette adjusted her glasses and peered at the photo of newborn Jude swaddled in white and another of her cradled in Maggie's arms. The note below said six weeks.

"Oh," Juliette exclaimed. "She's beautiful. Look at those eyes." And she placed her fingertips on the page as if to stroke the child. "How I miss having a baby, don't you?"

Maggie gazed at Juliette's face and soppy expression. She could have melted.

"I adore Selene and the person she's become," Juliette continued, "and there's something magical about every age. But I wish I could hold her in my arms once more, feel her skin as soft as a butterfly's wing and inhale her milky breath." She stroked the page again and melancholy blanked her features. Did she regret never knowing Jude?

"She's beautiful. And big." Juliette looked at Maggie with alarm. "*Merde*. Six weeks? She was that size at six weeks?" She put a condoling hand on Maggie's knee.

"Jude was bloody enormous. Eleven pounds at birth. Little Eli shot out like a pip after that."

Juliette howled with laughter. "Well my lady parts have just done a little squeeze in sympathy," she added.

And Maggie tried very hard not to think of Juliette's lady parts.

Maggie turned the pages, through the toddler years until Jude's first day at school. Maggie felt a teary smile blossom on her face. Jude looked so proud, standing to attention by the door, her little school rucksack sat neatly on her shoulders.

Jude had been excited about starting. It hadn't lasted. By day three she questioned the need to attend school so often and by week two she begged to stay home. She missed Maggie, wanted to play bears and ogres in the garden and tickle baby Eli. Maggie clutched at her heart. It was a desire she took for granted when they were little, their constant need for her affection. Maggie would never get over losing it.

She sniffed and turned the pages. "High school," she said.

There was photo after photo of Jude excelling – playing netball, performing in the school play – but in Maggie's favourite she scowled. Jude's arms were crossed and her jaw jutted. She was ready for the school disco and didn't want Mum taking yet another photo while her friends waited. It was her thirteenth year and the beginning of distance. And while the photo broke Maggie's heart, it was the one of which she was most proud. There was more than a little familiar attitude in that face.

And for a while there were fewer photos, until Jude left for university. Then the smile was back, a more mature expression on a person who would pose for photos but say no to too many, and the grown woman had arrived.

Maggie closed the album and stroked the leather cover. She was about to suggest another with more of Eli when she noticed Juliette's pallor.

"I'm sorry," Maggie whispered. "Perhaps that wasn't a good idea after all."

Juliette shook her head and sat back. Her pursed lips trembled slightly. "Thank you," she said. "Thank you for showing me."

Maggie quietly returned the albums to the shelf and took her seat again next to Juliette. She looked drained.

"What about Selene?" Maggie offered. "Do you have any photos with you?"

"Actually, yes," Juliette said, dispelling her languor. "I've been scanning my old prints." She fished out a phone from her bag and swiped across the screen. "Some are accessible here, although in no order." She smiled at Maggie as she offered the snapshot. "She was around nine in this picture."

A leggy Selene in shorts, knees wider than her thighs, stood in the sea with a beach ball beneath her arm.

"They're like baby deer at that age, aren't they; all limbs and bones."

Maggie nodded. "Eli was. Jude was always more substantial."

"I hope you never said the word substantial to her."

"Of course not. I was called skinny rake at school and was thoroughly sick of it. Eli wasn't quite so sensitive."

Juliette chuckled. "I was going to say that tact wasn't his strong suit, but he has no compulsion to sensitivity at all. He revels in tactlessness. Much like you do."

"I do not!" Maggie was indignant. "I wouldn't say diplomacy was my greatest gift."

Juliette snorted.

"I don't wind people up on purpose," Maggie said

Juliette raised an eyebrow.

"But when I'm being honest with people," Maggie clarified, "it's a bonus if I do."

They both laughed.

"Here's Selene's graduation photo," Juliette said, swiping her finger across the screen.

It could have been a photo of Juliette, the similarity at that age was so strong. Slight differences occurred to Maggie. Selene was shorter than her mother who stood proud at her side in the photo, and her face more easy and relaxed. Her appearance was true to her spirit, Selene a gentler woman than her incisive mother. It made Maggie maternal suddenly, and protective of her future daughter-in-law.

"Oh, we are much earlier now," Juliette said. "Three months old."

Maggie was transfixed by the sight of Juliette, long raven hair around bare shoulders, cradling her baby to her bosom. The baby grinned in the gummy, dribbly way Maggie adored but it was Juliette's face that made her heart heave. She was little changed from when Maggie had known her, they must have split a few years before, but her face was softened from recent pregnancy and glowed with maternal love. The tenderness between them was so apparent Maggie could almost feel their embrace upon her own cheek and she imagined herself in the picture, the silky Juliette on one side and baby on the other.

It had been everything she'd craved when they'd been together, her beautiful lover and a baby nuzzling between them. Everything she longed for.

Maggie tried to speak. She had to say something, but no words would come. She shuddered as she tried to fill her lungs, and hot tears ran down her cheek.

"I'm sorry," she managed and she got to her feet. She wiped at her tears as she stumbled from the house, but they flowed easily and trickled warm over her fingers with every stride down the garden.

Her feet thudded down the lawn, uncoordinated and clumsy with her blurred vision, and jarring her whole body. Maggie collapsed on the riverside bench, buried her head and curled her body tight. She wished herself as small as possible so she could crush the aching emptiness inside.

She imagined Juliette would be startled and remain politely in the living room, so when arms wrapped around her Maggie cried out in overwhelmed surprise. Juliette enveloped her and held her tight. Surrounded by the warmth of her once lover, Maggie released every ounce of sorrow and regret.

When Maggie came to, the last of her sobs exhausted from her body, she felt foolish. She sniffed and wiped her face, not wanting Juliette to see. She stayed her head on Juliette's lap, ashamed to face her.

"I adored you," Maggie murmured. She meant it as an apology for her unseemly grief.

"I know," Juliette said. "I know because I felt the same way."

Maggie sat up and found Juliette's face a similar mess of feelings. Juliette touched her cheek. "You were everything to me."

The admission took Maggie's breath away with the weight of the world that had been Juliette, as if Maggie were twenty again. For years, she'd indoctrinated herself, reiterating Juliette could never have loved her, and to hear her say otherwise made it more unbearable.

"I loved you," Maggie whispered, and the three words had never sounded so inadequate for the magnitude of feeling.

They both twitched at the sound of company inside. Richard's deep voice rumbled into the garden and a blur of energy in the living room suggested Eli was back. A more leisurely shape suggested Selene was too.

Maggie rubbed at her face preparing for company.

"Let me," Juliette said, gently touching Maggie. "Stay here while I distract them a while." And she left, dabbing her cheeks and walking slowly up the lawn.

Maggie closed her eyes when she heard Juliette inside and the eruption from Eli and Selene. She was exhausted. The day's emotions had taken their toll and she hadn't an ounce of energy or vexation left in her soul. The sun warmed her face, and her skin tightened as her tears dried.

Maggie sighed and got up, wandering only far enough to find a spot to lie down. She rolled onto the thick cushion of moss and spread her arms wide, open to anything the world had left to throw at her.

"Well now she's crying in the garden about that rude foreign woman." Mrs Petty's voice drifted over the wall, as welcome as a shit-covered fly on a French Fancy. Maggie realised she didn't even have the energy to yell back obscenities. A shadow fell across her eyes and Juliette's amused face peered down.

"Don't get up," Juliette said. She lay down beside Maggie and gazed at her with beautiful hazel eyes, her lashes still dark with tears. "I had a nice day," she murmured.

"Me too," Maggie replied, her heart heavy with the poignancy of that truth.

"Pity about your obnoxious neighbour."

Maggie shrugged, too tired to care.

"Perhaps we should give her something to really complain about." Juliette's eyes flashed. Maggie recognised that look. Naughty, playful, insinuating.

"Fancy a roll around in the grass, Mrs Goodman?"

Good God, yes. Maggie laughed. Oh good God, yes.

But she contented herself with the offer of friendship which Juliette extended when she held her hand and lay snug beside her.

35

Jude basked in the morning sun, luxuriating in Abby spooned in front and touching breast to toe. Abby's chest rose and fell with the easy rhythm of sleep and Jude was content to admire her.

Even though they'd breakfasted and made love that Saturday morning, Jude ached for her, Abby's naked body against hers irresistible.

She stroked the nape of Abby's neck, revelling in the soft hair that swept together into a short downy line. She nuzzled, inhaling Abby's scent, and closed her eyes to the warm lure. Jude kissed her, taking a nibble every time. She couldn't remember wanting to taste someone so much. She could have kissed and caressed Abby all day.

She reached round to hold Abby close and smiled as her lover stirred. Abby groaned with sleepy appreciation but as Jude cupped her breasts she quickened. That hitch in breath, the short sharp inhalation, was an instant aphrodisiac. Jude couldn't resist the sound of Abby's arousal and she nuzzled closer, taking more hungry mouthfuls and rolling her tenderness in her mouth.

"Mmm", Abby moaned. Her body writhed as Jude stroked a trail of seductive intention down to her thighs. She leaned back, parting her legs in anticipation, breath heightening with every tantalising touch. These moments where Abby desired her were overwhelming and Jude had to fight to control the wave of arousal that almost overcame her.

She hesitated a moment to enjoy Abby's trembling craving, to tease a little longer, then they both gasped as Jude slid her fingers into Abby's slick heat.

Abby didn't wait. She reached her hand back, eager to feel her lover's desire and Jude groaned when she so expertly found her centre.

They moved together, their breathing matching the rhythm of their caresses. Quicker they writhed, and quicker they gasped, each sending the other higher with every moan. When Abby began to tense, Jude was with her and she pulled Abby so tight into her body that when fluid darkness swept over her, the boundary where she ended and Abby began seemed to blur.

They surfaced as one, sated by their exquisite coming together, and Abby rolled into Jude's chest.

"Morning." She giggled. "Again."

"Good morning." Jude grinned.

"Should we do that again to check if you're attracted to women?"

"Well I don't know," Jude feigned. "It might be a one off. I mean the one on Tuesday morning before you went to work, the one when you came home, then again in the night. Then the ones on Wednesday, Thursday, Friday…"

"I see." Abby sighed mock disappointment. "We should keep checking then. Every single day." Abby couldn't hide her smile: a great, big, delighted one.

Jude ran her finger down Abby's chest. "I'm still finding these attractive you know. Although I should explore them to make sure," and she swirled her fingertip around Abby's nipple.

"Stop," Abby gasped. "I can't again."

"I bet you could," Jude murmured.

"You're probably right." Abby trembled as Jude indulged her caress. "But I might die. Seriously, I'm beginning to think it's possible to die from too much sex."

Jude relented and kissed Abby delicately on the forehead. "Let's leave it another hour then."

Abby laughed. "Then we need food. We've run out and neither of us do hungry well."

"True," Jude conceded, "but for this I'm prepared to go without."

"High praise indeed."

Jude looked at her more seriously. "I can't keep my hands off you. You're all I think about."

It was true. Jude's mind was consumed by Abby – this woman she thought she'd known as well as herself. How in tune they were. Everything they'd been as friends but now more, as if Abby had another level that Jude had discovered. Jude's heart flooded just thinking about it. She'd never imagined how complete a relationship could be. It all seemed effortless, while that ease took away none of its magic. Everything fitted like no other relationship had, and how quickly it fell into place. It was enthralling.

Abby gazed at her, with a happy face.

"I can't stop touching you," Jude whispered, and already her body craved Abby once more.

Abby closed her eyes in the doziest, most content smile Jude had seen. "Good," she murmured. "Let's go out for food, and when we come back you can fail to resist me all over again."

-

"This is so exciting," Maggie said as she walked away with Juliette from the supermarket and down Broad Street. Together with Dean and the class, Maggie had quickly launched an initial test phase of the Food Bank mobile app and she felt light with energy.

"Anisha's prototype has everyone intrigued," Maggie blustered as they walked beneath the Jacobian arcade. "And it's raising awareness too. I don't think many in Ludbury realised poverty is only a few metres from their doorstep. And Dean," she said beaming, "he and his father are developing another property with the council for affordable housing. And I had a message from the bishop assuring me they would expand the shelter to cover the loss of the church's accommodation."

Juliette smiled. It was an expression part empathetic joy but also amusement.

"What?" Maggie huffed.

"You should think about running for the council," Juliette said.

"There's no need to mock."

"I'm not. I think you should. And afterwards, maybe more."

"Politics?"

"Why not?"

Well why not. Maggie had the time through enforced semi-retirement. She'd always had the inclination, and now it seemed she had the motivation too. She smirked at Juliette. "You know, maybe." They continued on.

"I hope, next time I visit, you'll have given it some thought," Juliette said.

Maggie nodded, as her heart sank. She absent-mindedly took Juliette's arm as if to cling to her presence before she left the next day.

"Are we becoming friends?" Juliette said, amusement still sparkling in her eye.

"We're going to be bloody related soon."

"Seriously though. Are we finally managing to become friends?"

Maggie grinned. "I'll think about it."

It had been a good day and Juliette's pronouncement that they were now friends made it even better. But there would always be a part of Maggie that craved more, and that part ached. It was the vestige of the heart that had pined for Juliette to come back, and had kept her awake all night waiting for her return. And in the years that followed something inside would never be satisfied with the remainder life offered. A flame was very much alive for Juliette, even though Maggie's being would rage against such a union, and any union between women.

Juliette placed her hand on Maggie's and it was only then she realised how hard she gripped Juliette's arm.

"Sorry," Maggie said. She would have taken her hand away had Juliette not gently held it in place.

"Maggie." Juliette stopped and they faced each other. "I'm sorry for everything that happened between us." And she looked at Maggie with deep sorrow. "I know if we'd stayed together, I would never have had Selene and you Eli, and neither of us would change that. But I never stopped thinking about you, and after the initial pain I always regretted what happened to us. I would be very grateful to be your friend."

Juliette's words affected Maggie acutely, capturing, as happened so often recently, Maggie's own feelings. It always surprised her. She'd assumed Juliette the least injured party because she left, and the lingering effect of their breakup on her former lover was a constant source of surprise during Juliette's stay.

"We need to find a way to get on with each other," Maggie said, "For Eli and Selene's sakes. But I want it for us too. I've enjoyed your company very much."

She meant it. It had been years since she'd spent so much time with someone and not wanted to throttle them. Far from it in fact. Juliette's company had soothed and revitalised Maggie and she'd found herself smiling for no apparent reason while doing things as mundane as the washing up, and more than once.

Then Maggie spied another who gave her cause for joy. "Is that Abby?" She peered over the heads of the crowd. "It is. I haven't seen her in days. Abby!" She waved. "Is she with someone?"

36

"Shit," Jude said. She dropped Abby's hand.

"What's the matter?"

"I don't think I'm ready for this. I can't do it."

"We don't have to hold hands if you're uncomfortable." Abby withdrew and the look on her face made Jude's heart ache.

"It's not that." Jude smiled to reassure her. "Not that at all. In fact it's hardly any different to how we used to walk together, except I want to drag you back to bed."

"Oh," Abby said with relief. "Then what's the matter?"

"Maggie," Jude said. "Maggie's up the street and I'm not ready to tell her."

Abby's reaction was immediate. It was as if she became small, wanting to shrink away from the world. "I'm not sure I'm ready either," she said.

"We don't have to say anything, not yet."

Abby nodded, her face pale.

"So not now," Jude said. "And not here. We need to prepare and tell her privately at home."

"OK," Abby replied. "But soon, please. I won't lie to her." She peered at Jude mournfully. "I'll be lying by omission if nothing else, and I can't do that to Maggie. We need to talk to her as soon as we can."

Jude's heart sat heavy in her chest. She didn't want this blissful carefree existence to end – sunny days wrapped in each other's arms, away from the eyes of the world.

Jude squeezed Abby's hand. "It'll be OK. I'm here."

They both looked up as a loud "Girls!" was hollered down the street. Maggie strode towards them, arms out and a beaming smile on her face.

"Oh my goodness," she said, throwing her arms around Jude and tugging her down for a kiss. "I haven't seen you girls in days. Where have you been hiding yourselves?"

Abby blanched at the question but managed to return Maggie's embrace.

Jude was about to politely enquire how Maggie had been spending those days as a distraction, when Juliette sauntered down the road and stopped at Maggie's side.

"Good morning both," she said, clearly already in Maggie's company.

"Err, hi," Jude managed. The manner between her mother and adversary was markedly changed since Jude had last seen them.

"Are you walking anywhere in particular or simply enjoying a promenade this fine morning?" Juliette asked, her charming French accent lending the whole suggestion an indulgence. It seemed to work its magic even on her mother, who stood at Juliette's side with a pleasant smile on her face.

"We were, erm," Jude shook her head. "We're out for food together."

"Ah." Juliette raised an eyebrow in a clear question towards Jude whose cheeks heated under the scrutiny. Juliette nodded and Jude had the feeling she'd answered whatever the other woman had posed.

"Perhaps you would like to join us?" Juliette offered. Maggie was still strangely quiet and content at her side. "I'm treating Maggie to coffee and some of those exquisite petit fours at the hotel restaurant? I would love to treat you both."

Abby looked more than a little alarmed, but Jude couldn't see a way to refuse.

"I leave tomorrow, so I would be grateful for the opportunity," Juliette pressed.

"That would be lovely," Abby accepted.

And it was with a nervous tension, which could rival a piglet snuggling with a boa, that Jude and Abby followed the bizarre sight of Maggie and Juliette arm in arm. Which made the amused expression on Abby's face all the more strange.

"What's tickled you?" Jude asked.

"Oh nothing."

"Come on. Out with it."

"It's just," Abby had to break off to snigger, "don't you think they make striking couple?"

"Who?"

"I mean in theory."

"Mum and Juliette?"

"Yes." Abby's face flickered between confusion and mirth. "They look great together."

"What on earth? What's got into you?"

"I don't know, but maybe in a parallel universe they'd make a phenomenal couple."

"Mum?"

"Yes," Abby looked at Jude with amused incredulity. "You do realise she's attractive don't you?"

Jude shrugged. "She's always looked good, and Juliette is obviously beautiful, but that's about as likely as Mum talking to a Tory."

"Funny though. I can't help thinking how great they are together."

"We need to get you to the café stat. You must have dangerously low blood sugar."

"Lead the way doctor," Abby said, giving her an affectionate tug, and Jude smiled, warm inside at having Abby near.

They took the box window overlooking the sunlit gardens at the rear of the hotel. Maggie sat on the window seat, plans rolled out in front discussing them in detail with Abby while Jude and Juliette sat cross-legged in their chairs opposite. Maggie spoke nineteen to the dozen about the upcoming meeting. She always talked more to Abby these days, and Jude felt a twinge of jealousy akin to sibling rivalry. She supposed they shared concerns about the town and its people and Abby somehow understood her mother more than Jude ever had. Of course Abby's infinite well of patience was an advantage when it came to the vexed Maggie Goodman.

But there was something different in her mother's manner today, and not just the apparent ease in Juliette's company. She was almost, Jude stumbled over the word in her head, but it was the right word and it was: relaxed. Jude could have added content, even happy. Maggie was leaning over the plans and scribbling notes, listening to Abby's suggestions. There was enthusiasm there. Hope. Jude hadn't seen her mother like this in a very long time.

Jude turned at a light touch on her arm.

"Let me show you something," Juliette said quietly. "The gardens are only open to residents so I would love to show them to you. Would you care to look?"

"Yes." Jude was surprised by the invitation. "Why not."

They ducked through the warped doorframe and into a small formal space outside – a knot garden of trimmed box hedges and abundant herbs between the leafy threads, surrounded by the black and white wings of the hotel.

"Here," Juliette said, patting a bench at the edge of the garden. "Now tell me everything." Her conspiratorial smile told Jude much more than her words.

"What do you mean?"

"You know very well. I can guess the cause of Abby's rosy cheeks. And yours by the way. Well?" She raised an eyebrow.

Jude tried to speak but she couldn't stop grinning.

Juliette tilted her head. "So did you take your seat on that rollercoaster?"

"Oh yes. Oh good God, yes."

Juliette clapped her hands together. "I'm so glad. I am happy for you. Abby adores you, and you make a terrific couple. Eli thinks the world of you both."

"Thank you," Jude said, her cheeks aching with the ferocity of her happiness. She couldn't help it. "But..."

Juliette nodded to encourage her.

"Is this normal?" Jude gasped. "I'm overwhelmed by her. She's all I think about, since we got together."

Juliette nodded indulgently.

"I'm this mad, crazed woman who wants to jump into bed with her constantly. Really, is this normal?"

Juliette clasped her hands together. "Perfectly. Isn't it wonderful?"

"But it's insane," Jude said wide-eyed. "I don't know what I expected, but I literally want to eat her up sometimes. I don't know how to describe it."

"Devour her? Surround her as if she is a part of you? Be consumed so you are part of her? Crave every taste and inch of her skin?"

"Yes," Jude gasped.

"All fantastically normal."

Jude's belly tingled with butterflies – part hunger, part elation.

"Isn't it remarkable," Juliette said, "how something so universal and common can be so incredible? The peak of feeling, the pinnacle of existence, all just ordinary."

"Perhaps it's because I love her so much," Jude wondered out loud, "because I already loved her as a friend before this. I don't think I've been so close to anyone else."

Suddenly the weight of Jude's regard for Abby sat heavy in her chest. "I love her with such depth and intensity I think I could break. I'm incapacitated by this." Jude clutched the edge of the bench. "I would do anything for her." And the

284

love that ached in her chest flooded through her entire body making her light and heavy at the same time.

"The rollercoaster." Juliette smiled. "Wonderful, but terrifying also."

Jude looked to Juliette tentatively. Baring this rawness of experience was unusual for her. She thought that kind of vulnerability consigned to her teenage years.

"Thank you for listening," Jude said. "Thank you for being here."

"My pleasure. Really, I'm very grateful for the opportunity. I'm here if ever you need me. I leave tomorrow, but come to the hotel and see me again if you want. And I will be back for another visit soon."

"I can't talk to anyone else."

Juliette shrugged. "Everyone needs someone to tell of their new love."

"Usually that would be my best friend." Jude stared at Juliette, still incredulous at the turn of events and the adventures of her heart. "But, it turns out she is my greatest love."

"I'm so happy for you." Juliette squeezed her hand.

"I can't tell Eli. He would be unbearable."

Juliette laughed.

"Dad and Celia would say 'very nice dear'. They wouldn't understand the enormity of this. And Mum's the last person I want to confide in."

Juliette hesitated a moment, still holding Jude's hand. "Do you plan to tell her soon?"

"I don't know. I want to wait, but Abby," she looked towards the hotel. "Abby can't stand to lie to her."

"I see."

"I keep telling her it will be fine, that Maggie will come round. But, truthfully, I'm dreading it."

"I can understand that."

"Just why?" Exasperation flooded through Jude. "Why is she so adamant? What the hell does she have against lesbians? It's not even that. She loves Abby without reservation, but the minute she mentions a partner… It doesn't make sense to me."

"Maggie," Juliette took a few moments to respond fully, "Maggie is complicated."

"She's impossible."

Juliette shook her head sadly. "Not impossible. Not in many ways."

"I don't understand her. I never have," Jude said, the frustration of years bubbling up. "How can she support gay rights when she was young, then despise lesbian relationships now? She's so extreme. You know," she looked to Juliette, "when I was growing up, she was a vivacious inspiring mother one moment, open to the world and experience, the most loving person you could imagine. Then, when I was a teenager, she withdrew. As soon as I didn't need her every minute she seemed to fade."

An image filled Jude's head, the most vivid of her teenage years – Maggie sitting by the river and staring past the swirling waters, her long cardigan wrapped around her body as if to protect her from the cold wind when there was none. It was the overriding memory of her mother during that time. And sometimes she remembered her father, gazing forlorn from the living room window, watching her too.

"I don't know who she is," Jude said. "I don't understand her at all."

"I am beginning to," Juliette said, quietly. "I don't agree with her always, especially when it comes to relationships between women, but I'm beginning to understand why she thinks as she does."

"Really?"

"Unfortunately yes. It's partly her nature," Juliette said, "but also we are our own histories and Maggie is very much a product of hers."

Jude held onto Juliette's hands, an anchor in her storm. "I don't know what to do." It was the first time since she was a child that she felt at sea.

"Please," Juliette said. "Will you give me a little time before you tell Maggie? I need to clear something between us. I hope it will help."

"Of course."

"Thank you." Juliette stood and smoothed her dress, seeming to gather herself. She pulled at her sleeves then straightened her back to stand tall. "We should get back to our companions," she said.

But when they returned, Maggie was already rolling up her plans to leave. Her cheeks were knotted as if trying to bite her tongue, and the rose colour of her cheeks wasn't from any kind of pleasure.

"What's wrong?" Jude asked. Abby's face was white.

Maggie cleared her throat. "Abby was catching me up with her news. Tell me the rest another time, dear," she said cutting off Abby's plea. She stiffly leaned over to kiss Abby's cheeks, the usual warmth and ease gone. The peck on Jude's cheek was similarly cool.

Maggie turned to bid good bye to Juliette but Jude didn't hear what they said. She could see Abby was shaking.

"Take me home," Abby whispered and Jude didn't hesitate to take her arm. As soon as they stepped into the cool outdoors Jude held her close and stroked her hair.

"Did you tell her?" Jude began.

"No." When Abby looked up, tears flooded her eyes. "I didn't even get that far. I admitted that I was seeing someone, then she froze."

37

"Come with me please, Maggie," Juliette said.

"I'm going home," she snapped.

"I need to talk to you."

Juliette stood across her path with such calm inevitability that Maggie relented and allowed Juliette to lead her to the room. When Juliette closed the suite door behind them and asked her to sit, Maggie obeyed out of reflex, her mind dwelling on Abby's confession. The bed dipped as Juliette sat beside her.

"What did Abby tell you?" Juliette peered at her intently.

"She's seeing someone and she didn't need to tell me that it was a woman. The guilt was written all over her face."

Juliette nodded, shifting her weight on the bed, as if preparing for an ordeal. "She is not you, Maggie," Juliette said quietly, "and her partner isn't me."

"You're right," Maggie shot back. "She's not me. She's fragile inside. She lost everything when her mother died and it has taken years for her to recover. I can't bear to see it all go up in flames. Because it will. It always does. Gay relationships do not last and nothing shatters the soul like the broken love of two women. And when the rest of the world's hurling stones, forgive me for not rejoicing that Abby is throwing herself into the fire."

"It doesn't have to be that way. It doesn't always end in breakup."

"But usually it does, and it will crush her."

Juliette shook her head.

"She's not strong." Maggie tutted. "For Christ sake, look at me." Maggie's eyes burned as she stared at Juliette. "It's been thirty fucking years since we split, and it still hurts." She held her fist to her heart that pounded with a savage ache. "I never got over you. Life went on and I lived a very different one to that I'd craved, but your absence was always raw. You only had to walk in again thirty years later for me to fall apart."

Juliette stared at her hands. "We shouldn't have ended. It could have worked."

"That's what I wanted."

"I should have listened to you and trusted that you loved me enough to have a family."

"Yes, you should have." Maggie's voice wavered, overpowered with emotion. "I wanted you as my wife and the mother of my children. And thirty years later there's still a bit of me, there's still a bloody part of me that wants that."

"I was scared." Juliette looked at Maggie with inconsolable eyes. "I thought you would change. I feared that when you gave birth, you would bond so closely with the child and father I would be left out. I was terrified I'd love the child as fiercely as my own blood, with no rights as a parent. The thought of losing you was unbearable. The possibility of losing more, completely overwhelming."

Maggie, at last, understood that fear.

"I did try," Juliette said. "I'm sorry it made us argue. But I did want to try."

Maggie turned away. This she couldn't stomach. "So instead you left and high-tailed it to your fucking ex's."

"But that's the thing; I didn't."

Maggie glared at Juliette in furious disbelief. "You walked out."

"Yes, I did," Juliette said, distraught. "That was nothing new. Sometimes you needed to blow off steam. You would get so irate there was nothing else I could do and, yes, I would leave the flat for a while."

"You knew what staying at your ex's meant. There was no doubt about what she would do."

"I slept at the department. I still had a key to my old office."

Maggie stared at her.

"I slept on the floor, then went to work the next day in London."

"But...Tiff...?"

"Tiff told you I stayed at Alex's."

"Yes," Maggie said emphatically.

"Many months later," Juliette started, "I wondered if that's what she'd done. Did Tiff invite you to stay with her?"

"She did. I was distraught and frightened." Maggie clutched at her belly, feeling all the vulnerability there. "I thought it kind of her, considering she was more your friend than mine. I felt guilty, in fact, for all the times I'd accused her of trying to steal you."

Juliette's eyebrows raised in despair. "And did she invite Richard to see you?"

"Yes... How...?"

Juliette hesitated. "I came back."

Maggie laughed a nasty laugh. "I know. One day you were there, another you left, the next all your belongings were gone."

"I came home, you weren't there and I was worried. I asked Tiff if she knew where you were. Of course, she invited me round," a shadow fell across Juliette's face, "just in time to see Richard."

"You were there?"

"Tiff opened the front door and looked furtive, but I could see through the house to you in the garden."

Maggie chilled inside as she remembered. She'd stayed for a week at Tiff's, inviting Richard round every day for support.

"It was everything I feared," Juliette said, barely a whisper. "You and him together. It was everything we fought about, everything that terrified me."

Maggie wracked her brain. "But we were nothing back then. He was kind and concerned, but we were not together."

"You were sitting on a blanket in the garden, side by side. He was smiling at you, his face full of awe and love. You didn't look well and how my heart grieved. But then he asked you something. You nodded and he gently and lovingly laid his hand on your tummy." Juliette stopped. "It killed me seeing that."

"But didn't Tiff say? Didn't she explain?"

"No. She looked apologetic then let my fears eat away."

Maggie got up and walked to the window trembling. "You realised the other day, didn't you? When I told you that I'd only kissed Richard a year later when we married."

Juliette nodded, as devastated as when they'd argued at the house. "Until a few days ago, I still hated you. Less over the years of course, but until that moment I was hurt like you. When you admitted you didn't immediately fall for Richard, I realised Tiff had lied to you, and it all disappeared. All of it. Thirty years of hurting and hating you. Gone. If nothing else comes of this, I'm grateful to be relieved of that hate, because it's not something I ever wanted of you."

Maggie stood stunned. What an impact three little words had. "She's at Alex's." That's all Tiff had said to Maggie. Her friend with the shaved head, appearing so distraught. "I think she's at her ex's." And it rode on the back of so many of Maggie's insecurities, she believed it with little question. And when Juliette's belongings disappeared, she knew for sure.

"Oh God."

Maggie sank onto the window seat, head in hands. Images of their past swirled inside – the arguments, Juliette's old lovers, their circle of friends, Maggie's insane hormones and vulnerability – a heady cocktail of passion and friction.

"They all wanted you didn't they," Maggie gasped. The beautiful French post-graduate then researcher, the one who turned heads when she walked in the room. Elegant and beautiful even in her cheap student chic, everyone desired Juliette. When they walked into a bar, hungry eyes would feast on her, no matter how obvious a girlfriend Maggie made.

"You never believed me," Maggie said. "I told you to stay away from them, but you dismissed me every time. You told me I had nothing to worry about."

She felt Juliette take her hand. "Because there was nothing," Juliette said. "I wanted only you. I wanted my Maggie. My beautiful Maggie."

She held down a sob as Juliette stroked her cheek and Maggie lifted her gaze to see a tear-streaked Juliette kneeling before her.

"Don't you see how poisonous that atmosphere was?" Maggie whispered. "No matter how good your intentions, that constant threat took its toll. And then," Maggie could hardly breathe, "it broke us."

Juliette closed her eyes and her lips twitched with grief. The sight hit Maggie square in the chest and she clutched at her heart. It was unbearable. If ever she had reason to warn Abby from love then here it was – two of the strongest women, reduced to tears and heartache for a lifetime.

She struggled to her feet and walked away from the sight of Juliette, as fractured as Maggie had been all those years ago.

"Maggie, wait," Juliette pleaded. "This isn't why I told you."

She didn't listen. Maggie stumbled from the room, feeling for the walls as she lurched along the uneven floor. She clattered down the stairs and stumbled into daylight.

It was shocking to find the world in glorious sunshine – smiles on people's faces, baskets of flowers hanging from every shop. It was obscene that existence was coated in bright civility.

Maggie blinked in the bright light and staggered down the road, her breath laboured and chest heavy. She stopped for a moment to recover and stared down the street. The coloured town houses and city gate blurred rainbow in her tears and she swiped at them to clear her vision. Shapes of cars became distinct and people recognisable as men, women and children. Then, in the distance, two became more recognisable still.

Maggie's heart seemed to stop when she saw Jude and Abby. Jude held her friend's hand, begging her, consoling her. Abby shook her head and Jude lifted her chin to look her in the eye. Nothing was unusual about that sight, but the brief kiss they shared was new, and when it deepened into passion it removed any doubt from Maggie's mind.

38

The fan of playing cards shook in Abby's hands, again.

She drove her elbows into the top of the kitchen island in a desperate attempt to steady her nerves. She couldn't rid herself of the sight of Maggie's distraught face. They had been too far away to hear, but it was obvious Maggie cried "no" over and over.

"Oh fuck," Abby said, as her hands fluttered again.

Celia's fingers curled over the top of the cards. "Come on, dear. We can do this. Don't make me come round there and cuddle you again."

Abby smiled. Her surrogate grandmother sat opposite, perched on a stool, a feat that had required the aid of both Jude and Abby.

"Right," Jude said, striding into the kitchen. She flicked her hair from beneath the collar of her woollen coat. "It's time."

Abby's shoulders sagged. "I feel awful. We should have gone to her."

"No. I was not having a scene in the middle of town with Maggie."

Abby noticed Jude was calling her mother Maggie again. She always did when there was distance, and this rift was the worst they'd suffered, and then some.

"I've called Dad and she's home alone. I want to talk to her in a civilised way, not have her yelling for all of Ludbury to hear. She and Eli may thrive on public dramatics, but I don't."

Abby nodded sadly and Jude seemed to hesitate.

"Go on, dear," Celia said. "It needs to be done. And good luck."

"Are you sure you don't want to talk to her first?" Jude asked.

"No. It's Maggie who needs to do a lot of talking. Besides, this is between you and your mother. I'm not getting in the middle of that. I value what short life I have left."

Jude put her arm round Abby and she buried her face in Jude's chest.

"Are you going to be OK?" Jude asked.

Abby mumbled something into Jude's jumper. She couldn't even hear it herself and only succeeded in making the jumper warm and moist around her face. She wished she could go to sleep. It was cosy in Jude's bosom.

"Can I stay here?" Abby mumbled.

"I wish you could," Jude replied, stroking the back of her head before pulling away. "OK. I'm going this time." And she walked towards the door. She peered back one last time towards Celia. "Look after her," she said, then disappeared into the dusk.

Abby breathed in, then out for a long, long time.

Celia's eyes flicked above her cards. "Enviable lung capacity, Dr Hart. Now play your card."

Abby wasn't even sure what they were playing. Honeymoon Bridge? That's what Celia had called it. The game seemed unfeasibly complicated in Abby's state, but she suspected Celia hadn't kept it simple for that reason – to make her concentrate on anything other than the sight of Maggie up the street, with a look of pain that tore into Abby's soul while simultaneously scaring the crap out of her.

The cards started flapping again.

"Are you sure it's worth this?" Celia said, a sparkle in her eyes betraying she knew the answer very well.

Abby put her hand down and grinned, unable to hide the gooey feelings inside. "Every day Jude makes me smile. Every day I fall in love a little more, even though I think that impossible because I've adored her for so many years. This is better than anything I let myself dream." Abby sniffed and hot tears brimmed. Her hands started to shake. Her mouth dropped. The trembling extended down her arms and Maggie's face appeared once again in her head.

The attack was stifled by a sharp needle-like jab to her scalp, short but acute enough to make the eyes water.

"Ow!" she moaned. When the tears cleared and she could focus again, she found Celia frowning over her glasses with a brown hair thrust forward, pinched between finger and thumb.

"What the…?" Abby said, rubbing her head where the hair had happily been. "What did you do that for?"

"You're not having one of your panic attacks," Celia snapped. "Now concentrate."

"Couldn't you think of a better way?"

"Better? How?"

"Gentler. Avoiding pain entirely if possible."

"Maybe," Celia shrugged. "I didn't have time to think." She smiled, naughtily. "Now play a bloody card."

"OK," Abby said through gritted teeth. Shit. She had no idea what was going on. "What are trumps?"

"Spades."

"Oh." She looked at the tricks already won. "Hang on. No they're not. It's hearts."

"Good girl," Celia said. "Now, mind on the game."

Abby scanned her hand and the additional card turned up on the island. She was not in the mood for cards. Not in the slightest. How was she meant to focus on strategy when her family was tearing itself apart? Her heart began to thud. Would Jude be there already? She hoped, despite everything, that Jude would go easy on Maggie. It was normally

Maggie's ferocity that burned brightest, but Jude was showing a resilience that surpassed even that.

Shit. Her hands were shaking again.

"Ow!" she yelled. That was worse than the first time. Celia sat grinning, three hairs pinched between her fingers.

"For the love of God, think of a better way."

"Lack of time again," Celia shrugged.

"Well take a moment," Abby whined in consternation. "Have a good think about that gentler approach."

"All right." Celia gazed to the heavens. "It's pulling hair, strip poker or getting stoned. Those are your options."

Abby stared at Celia. "You've never...? Do you play strip poker with Desmond?"

"Now there's an idea." Celia looked over her glasses with the most salacious grin Abby had seen. "I wipe the floor with him at cards. I'd have him in his undies in no time."

"Good to know. Let's leave the strip poker."

"Which leaves you with hair removal or drugs."

Abby slumped. "OK. OK. I'm concentrating."

Which, of course, she failed to do, and she would lose several more hairs before the night was through.

-

Richard came to the door of the Goodman residence, his drooping jowls betraying his knowledge of Jude and Maggie's brouhaha.

"Hi, Dad," Jude said sadly.

"Hello, love." He drew her into his chest. "I'll be upstairs if you need me. Your mother's in the living room. I'm afraid she won't listen to me, but I think you and Abby make a terrific couple." He squeezed her tight. "I have my worries, every parent does, but you will only have support from me."

"Thank you," Jude said, filling with relief before having to baton it down in preparation for seeing her mother.

Richard retreated up the fire escape to the attic and looked down one last time before disappearing inside.

Jude stole herself and entered the house. She hung her coat on the hooks in the hallway, like she'd done thousands of times, all the way back to childhood, but this time it felt like an intrusion in a stranger's home and she felt impertinent for hanging it there without invitation.

She took hesitant steps into the dim room, lit only by the failing light outside. Maggie sat on a sofa beyond, staring into the garden, her back straight, posture impeccable, hands on her lap. It irritated Jude. She recognised her mother's stance: self-righteous, unbending, impossible.

Jude persevered and slowly approached. She sat on the sofa alongside, close enough to converse but the distance telling. Her mother didn't react. She stared into the garden and they sat in silence, the heavy tock of the grandmother clock marking the awkward passage of time.

"Mum, please," Jude whispered.

Maggie at last turned towards her. Her face was in shadow, barely visible in the dying light.

"So you've decided you're a lesbian."

The virulence of it was like a physical blow and Jude had to compose herself. "You can throw that at me if you like, but I will not take offense."

"Get used to it. People will fling it night and day."

"Come on, Maggie. I've had a lesbian best friend and pansexual brother. Do you think I'm going to be offended by that?"

Maggie's look was defiant. "What do you think you're doing? Why are you interested in women now? Of all the times."

"Because of Abby."

"Really? It's not sheer bloody mindedness?"

Jude laughed, not altogether pleasantly. "No." She wanted to add. "Bloody mindedness would only occur to you."

"Then what is it? Was Bill's desire for you to settle down so traumatic it's suddenly turned you into a lesbian? Has he put you off men for life?"

"Come on," Jude said. "No, I haven't suddenly turned into a lesbian."

"Then what are you? Really?"

"Someone who wants Abby. She's in love with me, has been for many years, and now I love her."

Maggie's gaze was withering. "All of a sudden?"

"Perhaps, I was more attracted to her, to women, than I realised," Jude replied, finding Maggie's questions bruising but in no mood to take the punches.

"And not men after all?"

"This doesn't negate every relationship I've had with a man. Neither does having loved men take away from my love for Abby. I don't know what that makes me. Ask Eli," Jude said, throwing her hands up in exasperation. "But I do love Abby."

Maggie glared at her. "Regardless of what you are, you are still the last person Abby should be with."

Every word was deliberate. Every syllable dripped with venom, and the verbal strike made Jude twitch.

"How could you?" Maggie rasped. "When you leave, you will destroy her."

"What makes you think I'll leave?"

"When have you ever stayed?" Maggie fired back. "You're in your thirties and haven't shown a serious attachment to anyone."

"That's not fair. I was mad about Dan and I lived with Bill for Christ sake."

"You bunked there during the week. And as soon as he proposes, you take flight and in the blink of an eye you've moved on."

"There were issues," Jude offered, her confidence faltering. "I admit, I wasn't fair to him. But it's nothing like that with Abby."

"Then what is it like?"

This was brutal. With every question Jude flinched. She was laid bare and vulnerable to her mother's expert attacks.

"I'm in love with her," Jude said. "Deeply in love with her. Perhaps I always was. It's difficult to tell where friendship ended and passion began, but I love her more than anyone in the world and it feels right."

"Like life would end without her?" Maggie fired.

"Yes."

"Like she's the heart that makes your body thrive? Does she fill your head every waking hour? Do you dream a whole life ahead relishing even old age together."

"Actually, yes."

"So imagine she feels the same. And now imagine crushing her when you take all that away."

Jude winced, imagining it so vividly she was swayed for a moment by her mother's potent argument.

"Abby needs you like no-one else," Maggie growled. "Which is why you shouldn't do this. When you break up, she will have nothing."

"I will never leave her," Jude struggled to say. "I have always taken care of her."

"Is that it? Some kind of chivalrous duty? Noble Jude to the rescue?"

"No," Jude hesitated. "I did feel some obligation when I realised she loved me. I didn't know what to do. But now? I've never been more certain of anything."

"You've no idea. You haven't a clue what it's like." Maggie fixed Jude with a burning stare. "That life. Always having to watch your back. Not able to hold hands without checking who's watching? Will someone shout obscenities? Will they hurl a brick at Abby's head, just because she loves a woman? I held a friend as she bled to death on the road because her existence affronted a fragile male ego. And then," Maggie's laugh was a hideous blend of despair and hate, "others you call your friends will stab you in the back in the name of love too. Are you really ready for all that?"

Jude felt like she was being beaten back by Maggie's attack.

"For all the apparent progress of rights and marriage equality," Maggie continued, relentless, "the large and dark underbelly of the world will not rejoice in your relationship. It will make it harder every step of the way and you could lose your lives because of it."

"Enough!" Jude leaped to her feet. "I cannot change this. I'm in love with Abby and she's in love me."

The disdain on Maggie's face was clear.

"I don't care if this is harder," Jude said. "I don't care if I have to watch my back. I do believe things are getting better, but even if they don't I couldn't choose another way."

Maggie was intransigent.

"Abby has been a part of my life since I was eighteen," Jude said more softly. "I thought I knew everything about her and loved it all. But every day, I find something new to adore and," Jude stopped, the love for Abby building inside so that tears threatened, "there is no-one else for me. There never could be. That I've had such a friend, I'm eternally grateful for, but that she should be the love of my life," Jude had to swallow to keep her voice even, "I'm the luckiest person alive."

"You're being naïve."

"Don't patronise me."

"Have you even thought about children? What will a third person do to your relationship? You have no idea of the pressure that brings."

Jude cried out in frustration, "We might not even have children."

"Don't be contrary," Maggie spat.

"Don't be so close minded," Jude fired back as quick.

The silence descended again and the clock echoed around the room, beating out the painful time.

"I will not give her up," Maggie said, defiance in her eyes. "If you split, I will not abandon her."

"I wouldn't expect you to."

"It won't be like Bill. You can't grab your things and leave without a trace. I will always be there for her."

The vehemence with which Maggie said it made Jude step back, her foot hitting the sofa.

"And me?" she wondered out loud. "Are you there for me too, or is it just Abby you worry about?"

"You need me less," Maggie said simply.

If the sofa hadn't been there, Jude would have reeled back further. She couldn't deny what Maggie said. Abby did need her more, but it still felt like rejection.

"My dear," Maggie said, her voice softened with regret. "If ever you needed me, I would be there. I couldn't help myself." She looked at Jude. "But you never have. Not since you were thirteen."

Jude suddenly felt sorry for Maggie. Guilty too. There was a wide streak of that pulling hard inside. It pricked her bubble of fury as she stared at her mother, looking smaller suddenly in her empty house, children grown up long ago and no longer heeding her advice let alone compulsion.

"Abby has been in love with me for years," Jude said quietly. "What do you expect me to do?"

Maggie was silent.

Jude waited and the clock counted the minutes as the sun was snuffed out and only the faint glow from the town's streetlights formed the edges of the room.

"I'm taking my things to Abby's," Jude said finally, and she walked to the stairs. She stopped with her foot on the first step, her hand resting dejected on the bannister.

"You know," she called out, "you're not saving Abby from women. You're trying to save her from love." Jude listened for but didn't expect a response. "And I can see why, Maggie. I really can. But it's impossible."

The house was silent.

Maggie sat in darkness, the garden faded into silhouettes and the moon glistening on the river. She heard Jude pack, the rumble of Richard's voice upstairs and the front door click shut when Jude left.

She didn't turn when Richard padded into the room, his presence looming.

"I've never blamed you," he said at last. "All the things you felt, everything you said and did, I understood. Truly I did. That was until now." His disapproval hung heavy in the room. This mild man's disapproval was worst of all.

Maggie twitched and peered round. He was barely visible in the room.

"I can't understand this," he said, shaking his head. "I will never understand this." And he left the room.

Night became darker and the house colder. Maggie stared on through the window. She remembered Jude when she was three years old, still small enough for Maggie to carry. When Jude was tired she'd throw her arms around Maggie's shoulders and nuzzle into her neck, her breath warm and humid on her skin. Jude would hum *Twinkle, Twinkle, Little Star* to soothe herself, and Maggie too.

Only Maggie remembered. For a while she kept the memory alive in Jude with her reminiscing, until Jude grew tired of the repeated story; then it was Maggie's once more.

It was the most tender of memories, little Jude's fingers clutched behind her neck, and Maggie would walk the long way home, just to hold her that bit longer. It could have been yesterday.

39

Maggie knocked on the door with a trembling hand.

"Who is it?" Juliette's voice came from within.

"It's Maggie. Please let me in."

The door opened without hesitation and Juliette's anxious face appeared.

"What's wrong?"

Maggie opened her mouth to respond but noticed the soft light of the hotel room and Juliette wearing only a large white shirt. Her feet and legs were bare and the shirt loosely buttoned. "Sorry, had you gone to bed?"

"I retired early to read," Juliette replied. "It's no matter. You must come in. You are upset."

Juliette led her inside and Maggie sat despondent at the foot of the bed.

"What's happened?" Juliette knelt before Maggie and gently took her hands.

"It's Jude. We argued horribly and I don't know what to do. She and Abby are together and I can't think of anything worse."

Juliette smiled with sadness in her eyes. "And I can't think of anything better."

"Really?" Maggie said. "After everything we went through? Even now, the past can reach in and tear open my heart. And with Jude of all people. If there was anyone who could crush Abby beyond recovery it's her. She's never had a romantic interest in women and Abby will be left with nothing when she leaves."

"Maggie," Juliette sighed.

"And even if they stay together, how long until some bastard crushes their skulls in rage?"

Juliette's spirits visibly flagged. She couldn't refute that. She'd been there at the death of Maggie's friend too.

"Christ, it's bad enough fearing for Abby's safety, now it's Jude as well."

"Have some hope," Juliette pleaded. "As for everything else, I've rarely seen a more responsible young woman than Jude. You couldn't ask for a better partner for Abby. And in any case, you are too late."

Maggie frowned in response.

"They are in love." Juliette beamed and she pulled Maggie's hands into her chest. "They are madly in love. You can see it blooming in their faces. They won't be able to help themselves for months, hopefully years. And right now their greatest threat is you."

Maggie felt that, as a sharp twinge inside her chest.

"Don't you remember how my mother's disapproval weighed on me?" Juliette begged. "Please don't do that to Abby, because you are a mother to her now. And Jude," Juliette laughed quietly, "she is a mature woman, but a mother has the power to make or break a child no matter their age."

Maggie suddenly couldn't look her in the eye.

"I know this, Maggie, so please listen. A mother can provide a bedrock even when their child has flown the nest. But your disapproval will fester like a disease. If you let it spread untended, Jude will have no choice but to cut it out for her own sanity."

Juliette knelt closer, her belly touching Maggie's knees. "You will lose her. You will lose them both. I beg you, don't let that happen. I can't bear to see our past ruin everyone's future."

Everything Juliette said rang true. Maggie remembered how a phone call from Juliette's mother would drain her. Maggie's confident, intelligent lover would sit on their flat window ledge staring outside as the mother rattled on inside the hand piece, and Maggie would watch Juliette wither, clutching knees to chest and shoulders sagging with the weight of incessant disapproval. That Maggie could do this to Jude or Abby made her reel with nausea.

"They are in love," Juliette said. "It cannot be stopped. You can support and nurture it, or blight it with your disapproval. It will not simply disappear. It cannot be taken back."

Juliette smiled and knelt up to cradle Maggie's face, her own just a few centimetres away.

"They have so much to look forward to." She gazed at Maggie. "Don't you remember? Don't you recall what it was like to be in love? Fresh, young love when your world is filled by the light of another person?" Juliette stroked round Maggie's cheek, her fingertips gentle and urgent. "I envy them. What I would give to feel that again."

She kissed Maggie on the forehead, a light consoling touch. "You mustn't stop them. Don't stop their young love." She kissed Maggie's eyebrows and Maggie closed her eyes, succumbing to Juliette's appeal. "Don't stop this," Juliette murmured, as her delicate kisses fluttered on Maggie's eyelids.

Juliette cradled Maggie's head with the determination of someone consumed. "I can't bear to see you in pain anymore. You must remember what it's like."

And Maggie did. As Juliette covered her face with urgent consolation, the familiar caresses awakened her body. Her face tingled, head swirled, stomach fluttered inside.

"Remember," Juliette whispered as she traced across Maggie's cheek with kisses of entreaty. "Don't tell me you can't."

Juliette pulled her close, hands desperately clasping at her sides, higher and higher, and when she stopped shy of Maggie's breasts, warmth flooded though Maggie and her body caved with an audible breath.

Juliette froze, her mouth nuzzled on Maggie's cheek. Her breathing was fast, matched by the rapid rise and fall of Maggie's chest. Juliette pulled back to gaze at Maggie, wide eyes betraying utterly her longing. They stared at each other, desire burning in their faces. They wanted each other and with another touch there'd be no turning back.

Juliette inched her hands higher, ever so slowly, the tantalising expectation building inside Maggie as her breasts cried out for her lover's touch. The two women gasped in time, deeper and deeper with anticipation. When Juliette stroked her thumbs over Maggie's nipples her reserve was spent and she groaned. Maggie caved forward and was met by Juliette's ardent kiss.

She remembered. Maggie remembered with vivid, fluid heat. As Juliette swept her tongue inside her mouth Maggie responded with impassioned kisses. Pleasure burst inside her with Juliette's every stroke of her breasts.

Yes, she remembered. Juliette could have seduced her like this for hours, incapacitated by this deliciously incessant touch. Every shot of arousal coursed from her breasts to her centre and stunned her in tingling ecstasy so that she couldn't think or move. All she could do was kiss Juliette deeper and deeper like all those years ago.

She couldn't help her desperate moan when Juliette slipped a hand away for a moment. Maggie gulped as their lips parted, ready to beg for Juliette again. But her eyes were drawn irresistibly to Juliette's chest. Her lover slipped her own shirt buttons apart, letting the garment tease open a little at a time. When Juliette reached the last, her shirt fell open to reveal her breasts in shadow.

Maggie groaned. Juliette too, it seemed, remembered. Nothing aroused Maggie so much as a glimpse of what she craved. She couldn't help but reach out, her fingers encountering the tender softness of Juliette's belly. Neither could she resist exploring higher, until the exquisite curve of Juliette's breast filled her palm, her nipple warm and pert at its centre.

"Oh," Maggie moaned, and Juliette took her again. They kissed more fervently than before, Juliette pressed between her legs. Maggie could feel the warmth of Juliette's naked belly while the taste of her lover's lips made her mouth water. Like the sweet tang of fruit on a summer's day, Maggie was overcome with the intense gratification of Juliette's intimacy. For years, nothing had matched its compelling piquancy and Maggie's body flooded with forgotten sensation.

"Come to bed," Juliette urged. "Please come to bed." The plea from Juliette had Maggie unravelled and they stood, struggling to keep their hands from one another.

Juliette drew back the duvet and slipped inside, her beautiful body reclined on the bed. It was the perfect sight for Maggie – her lover's skin darker against the bright white of her open shirt, her shapely breasts in full view. Juliette raised her knee so her thighs fell apart, and Maggie's gaze swept down. Juliette's underwear was wet and the temptation to slip her fingers around the edges was building inside Maggie so strongly she feared she might lose control.

"Undress for me," Juliette said.

While glimpses of Juliette's body had always driven Maggie insane, Juliette had craved nudity, and Maggie teased her buttons apart with no reservation. Even though they hadn't seen each other for years, she held no embarrassment. The way Juliette's eyes devoured her as the clothes slipped away urged her on. It had always been like this. To undress in front of the impeccable Juliette and see her undone with need had always captivated Maggie, as it did now.

She lay beside Juliette, her lover's body thrilling with anticipation. Maggie reached out and trailed her fingers down Juliette's belly.

"You are divine," she whispered. "Your body has been seared into my mind as perfection."

Juliette quivered with the attention, her mouth clenched against a cry as Maggie explored further. Maggie leant down and took Juliette's nipple in her mouth, pinching it gently between her tongue and teeth. The reaction was as beautiful as it was predictable, and Maggie purred as Juliette clenched her fingers hard into Maggie's back. Again she squeezed and deep pleasure thrummed through her body as Juliette kneaded her back in desperation.

Maggie's fingers explored lower, teasing and dipping into the waist of Juliette's underwear, but she had no intention of removing it. She lingered to enjoy the smoothness of Juliette's buttocks and around her thighs so that Juliette thrust into Maggie's hand trying to catch her touch. Maggie stroked at the material between her lover's legs, becoming dizzy at the warmth there, then teased some more, circling through the material where she knew Juliette craved.

She circled and circled, her head spinning with the pulsing rhythm of want that sent Juliette thrusting into her. And at last she could resist no more. She slipped her fingers around the edge of material, gaining a tantalising glimpse of Juliette beneath. Maggie doubled over at the sight but it was nothing to the surge of excitement when finally she slipped her fingers inside.

They clung tight to each other. It was so familiar. It felt the same yet agonisingly arousing, like Maggie had craved this for years.

They matched, moving together, and without thinking found the position where they fit. Maggie lost awareness of where she lay and how she made love. All she knew was she was bound with Juliette again and they loved with the same flow and rhythm they always had. Juliette caressed her and they embraced each other as they built together. They didn't speak, only clasped each other cheek to hot cheek, listening to each other's gasp become tighter and feeling the tension build exquisitely through them both.

When a groan built at the back of Juliette's throat it was all Maggie could take. The familiar sound of her lover coming had her undone. The soft grip took her inside and started to squeeze as every nerve in her body turned hot. Harder and harder it took her so that she grasped her lover with the same ferocity that Juliette held her.

They thrust together as their orgasms peaked and rode out the wave in a passionate knot pulled so tight Maggie didn't think it feasible to undo. And when their breathing became slower and regular it was almost a shock to find they were two separate women.

40

Maggie was drawn into Juliette's dark eyes and her soft expression as they lay together, the duvet snug around them.

"Don't go," Juliette whispered, reaching out to stroke Maggie's cheek.

"I don't want to. Although," her heart sank with all the repercussions, "that was probably a bad idea."

"A terrible idea." Juliette chuckled. "But I wouldn't change it." Her eyes devoured Maggie again. There was no doubt about the depth of Juliette's hunger. Maggie felt it herself and she couldn't let go of her lover.

"Stay," Juliette said. "Please. I'm only here tonight and it will be weeks until I return."

Maggie nodded. "I…" She could hardly say the words.

"I've missed you too. So very much," Juliette said, taking pity on her and she kissed her with a tender touch that spoke volumes about her regard.

"What are we going to do?" Maggie said.

"I don't know."

"I promise, wherever this is going, I won't let it interfere with our families."

Juliette smiled, with a sparkle in her eye and pinch of naughtiness in the corner of her mouth. "They are used to us tearing each other apart one moment, then laughing the next. I shouldn't worry unduly. I doubt we could be any more perplexing."

Maggie had an urge to kick her, but settled on a kiss instead.

"I love you," Juliette murmured.

Even now the words caught at Maggie's heart. She gulped, trying to return the declaration. "Never stopped," she whispered.

"And with Jude and Abby?"

"I will try. Of course I want to support them, despite my reservations, but please," she gazed fearful into Juliette's eyes. "Don't even hint about us." The prospect of explaining this relationship to Jude made her icy cold, and a sharp pain twinged in her chest.

"Hey," Juliette said gently, and it was only when Juliette placed her hand on Maggie's chest that she realised how fast she breathed.

"We'd have to handle it very carefully," Juliette said. "I'm sorry I was brash and careless when I first arrived. I won't be again."

Maggie inhaled deeply, her stomach swirling with fear. What a confession this would make to her daughter. Another sharp pain seared across Maggie's chest and she winced this time.

"If something happens between us," Maggie said, frowning through the discomfort, "we'll tell everyone. We mustn't rush though – whatever this is, or telling Jude about it."

Then Juliette kissed her, delicious lips slipping over Maggie's so divinely that she had to moan in appreciation and her fears and pain were, for a moment, wiped away.

Juliette pulled back to smile at her. "This is not what I expected when I walked past your house that first time."

"You're not kidding."

"Although," Juliette's eyes narrowed. "I could have sworn you admired my plunging neckline."

"You have a nerve," Maggie muttered.

"Well did you? Did Mrs Goodman perhaps sneak a glimpse of my chest?"

"Shut up."

Juliette laughed that beautiful mirth so that Maggie had to kiss her. She traced a finger around Juliette's chest.

"You do have the most appealing breasts. I always thought them the perfect size and shape. And your gravity-defying bosom is still wonderful today."

Juliette laughed again, this time a good hearty one.

"You haven't done badly yourself, Mrs Goodman." Her expression softened, "Still my beautiful Maggie. So severe and intimidating one moment, so loving the next." She caressed her forehead where Maggie realised there must be creases of time. "You have become more formidable with age, and it's very sexy."

"Really?" Maggie said, her tone heavy with disbelief.

"Really," Juliette shot back. "It speaks of experience and maturity. And for some things experience, shall we say, makes things interesting." Maggie knew what she insinuated. "Of course, vigour and gusto can get you a long way," Juliette insinuated some more, "but apparently you still have those too." Her grin was ecstatic.

Maggie grumbled.

"Do you remember," Juliette's smile faded from her face, "the last time we did this?"

She stroked down Maggie's cleavage then circled her tummy, tracing the thin pale lines remaining from her stretch marks.

"I know we should expect the odd senior moment these days." Maggie tutted. "But dear God woman, it was only half an hour ago. Of course I remember the last time we did it."

"Maggie," Juliette growled. "You know what I mean."

Yes, she did, and they both watched Juliette's finger trail around Maggie's flat tummy. Juliette lay her head on Maggie's stomach for a moment. "I'm sorry," she murmured and she kissed her. "You looked so beautiful."

313

Maggie lifted Juliette's face to her, hating to see her melancholy. "This may amuse you," Maggie said wanting to cheer her. "Eli, the cheeky bastard, when he was fifteen, asked me if women could have sex when they were pregnant."

"It doesn't surprise me. He loves to shock almost as much as you do."

Maggie indulged in a look, but otherwise ignored the comment. "I thought I'd reward his impertinence with an unnecessary level of detail. So I told him: women could, were more likely to want to and when they did it was so gripping your belly went hard right up to your tits. In fact it was the most incapacitating orgasm possible."

Juliette stared at her, mouth hanging open. "You told him that?" Then, "Of course you told him that. Was he appalled?"

"Very satisfyingly so. Shut the little bugger up for a while."

Juliette giggled.

"Of course, he told the whole school the next day."

And Juliette burst out laughing. "Eli is more than your match." And she stroked around Maggie's tummy. Suddenly she looked tired.

"Are you OK?" Maggie asked.

Juliette nodded slightly. "You?"

"I feel exhausted."

"This visit has proved more of a journey than I anticipated. Perhaps more so for you, with Jude and Abby to come to terms with. "

"I will talk to her and support them, and apologise too," Maggie replied, having to breathe in sharply to calm her nerves. "Maybe Abby first. More often I seem to be able to reach her than Jude."

"Jude will come round. She is a reasonable woman and won't reject an olive branch when she sees one. Not dispassionate by any means, but ultimately reasonable, unlike her hot-headed mother."

314

This time Maggie did give Juliette a firm nudge beneath the bed clothes.

"Hmm," Juliette purred. "Be careful where you touch, Mrs Goodman. We may have to start all over again."

"Oh don't," Maggie said. "I'm tired."

She did feel exhausted, the current familial predicament now weighing heavily on her.

"Hold me," she said, and Juliette drew her close, Maggie resting her cheek on Juliette's chest.

"It will be all right," Juliette soothed. "Jude knows your value to Abby. She will listen, no matter how much you tell them, whether an apology and support for their relationship or everything about us."

Maggie's heart twinged again. It felt like she'd carried a stone in her chest this last day.

"Jude hates me," she said.

"No she doesn't. She's frustrated by you and who can blame her? She doesn't understand you. How could she, not knowing you?"

Maggie averted her eyes, afraid she would cry if she caught Juliette's gaze.

"And look at Eli," Juliette continued. "He dotes on you. Even though you freak him out with stories of orgasmic pregnancies. And Abby has an affection for you that fills my heart whenever I see it."

Maggie held Juliette tighter, grateful for her presence and wondering how it might have been over the years to have had her understanding lover closer.

"Get some sleep." Juliette squeezed her. "I will hold you all night."

Maggie closed her eyes, anxieties and fatigue flooding her head in swirls of colour and darkness.

"I love you," she whispered at last, then drifted off in dreams.

Maggie woke warm beneath the duvet and to the mellow sound of Debussy. The bed dipped next to her as Juliette sat down. She was already showered and immaculate in a cream dress.

"Do you need to leave?"

"No, not yet," Juliette said, smiling. "We have a little while. Here," she said, offering a steaming mug. "Fresh coffee."

Maggie shuffled up in bed and gratefully accepted her drink, arranging the duvet over her breasts.

"I've ordered some croissants and other pastries. They should be here in a moment."

Maggie smiled at the indulgence and at Juliette's impeccable beauty beside her in bed.

"I like this," Maggie said. "Seeing you in the morning."

"Me too. I hate to leave today." Juliette reached out and cupped Maggie's cheek. "Promise you will look after yourself. You've been under a lot of strain."

"I will. Except for facing my estranged daughter, divorcing a husband, arranging a wedding, battling my neighbour and the council about housing and trying to get Ludbury to feed itself, all while trying to generate enough income to crawl towards retirement."

"Good," Juliette said, with a smile. "As long as it's only that."

A knock came at the door.

"That was quick," Juliette said. "One moment please," she called out.

Maggie put down the coffee and slid out of bed. She quickly dressed in her underwear, shirt and jeans and sat on the window seat as a respectable guest. She crossed her legs and put on a neutral expression before Juliette opened the door.

"Thank you," Juliette started, but Maggie could see it wasn't room service. The door opened to the expectant faces of Jude and Abby.

41

"Hi, we wanted to catch you before…"

The words died on Jude's lips.

For a few moments, no-one moved – Juliette, her arm still holding the door open, Abby behind Jude's shoulder, and Jude staring at Maggie's bare feet, her bed hair, her makeup softened by the night.

Abby was the first to recover. "Sorry." She reached for Jude's arm. "We can call back later. We're sorry to intrude."

"What the hell?" Jude stepped into the room. "What's going on, Mum?" Her voice was quiet. Injured.

Maggie's hands shook as she clasped them in her lap. "Hi, Jude. Hello, Abby." She didn't want to explain. She didn't want to tell them this.

Jude walked slowly past Juliette, her movements wary. "Why are you here? What are you doing in Juliette's room?"

Maggie closed her eyes, not wanting to see the disappointment and confusion in her daughter. Her heart pounded and cheeks blazed. And Abby? Even though Maggie squeezed her eyelids tight she could still see Abby's expression – embarrassed, humiliated, let down. She looked like she wanted to hide.

"I'm sorry," Maggie whispered.

"What is this, Mum?" Jude said, louder now. "What the fuck is this?"

Maggie flinched. She heard shuffling, Juliette's entreaty to come in and the click of the door shutting. She opened her eyes to find Jude, her face darkened, and Maggie had never felt more ashamed.

"It's not what you think," Maggie tried. "I'm not being unfaithful to your father," she offered. She could at least start there.

Jude's quiet laugh of incredulity made Maggie wither.

"Oh, I know you and Dad are separated. I'm not stupid," she snapped. "I suspected something after your reticence about the fire escape and apparently Eli twigged your arrangement a while ago. You can't have expected him to keep quiet." She laughed again and Maggie died a little every time. "We were waiting for you to tell us, if you ever were. But this," Jude said, opening her arms to indicate Juliette and Maggie. "This is new."

The sardonic realisation in Jude's face was horrible. "You are so many things, Maggie. So many infuriating things. But I never thought you a hypocrite."

That hurt. It all hurt.

"How can you tell me to leave Abby one minute then jump into bed with Juliette the next?"

"This is, perhaps, not as it appears," Juliette said softly.

She walked past Jude, and Maggie was incredibly grateful when she stood beside her and took her hand. Juliette gazed down with love and affection and squeezed to reassure her.

"This isn't new," Juliette continued. "We have known each other a long time. We were lovers before your mother met your father. More than lovers. We lived together for several years at university and afterwards."

Jude stared at them both as if trying to take it all in. "Is this true?"

Maggie clung to Juliette. "Yes," she said. "Juliette was the love of my life. I thought we'd be together forever."

"Then why?" Jude pleaded. "Why are you so homophobic, Maggie? I don't understand. What made you so bitter?"

318

Maggie winced. It was like being dragged hard through the mud. She didn't want to be here. Her chest ached and her heart was leaden. She wanted to blink and it all go away.

"Many things," Juliette said, her voice heavy with regret. "We made so many mistakes. We were young and didn't take care of our relationship, and of course others didn't make it easy."

"Is this why?" Jude said, her face contorted with grief. "Is this why you've always disapproved of Abby?"

"I wanted to protect her. I didn't want her damaged like I was." Maggie looked toward the door and Abby standing there, but the young woman stared at the ground, uncomfortable and upset.

"That's all it ever was," Maggie murmured.

"This is incredible." Jude blew out a lungful of air. "You've excelled yourself this time, Maggie."

Maggie again. She hated it when Jude used her name.

"It was a different time and different place," Juliette said. "There were more strains on our relationship than I appreciated at the time." Juliette hesitated, perhaps wondering how much to say. "We had no rights as a couple, no employment protection, and we had friends who were killed because they were gay. My mother was horrific to Maggie and poisonous with me. Although we loved each other very much, there were incredible strains on our relationship."

"I know," Jude snapped. "I've heard how difficult lesbian relationships can be all my life from my mother. This is no excuse."

"We wanted a family," Maggie blurted out. Her heart thundered in her chest. Her breath rasped. "I wanted a family."

Juliette sagged at her side.

"We argued about it constantly," Maggie said, barely able to look at Jude. "It tore us apart."

"That doesn't mean Abby and I will want children."

Maggie didn't know if she had the strength to carry on. "You may not. But what about Abby?" She checked towards Abby and a slight flush on her cheek told Maggie she was right.

"So what if we do," Jude cried out. "Plenty of women manage. What the hell's the problem?"

"You don't know how much losing it all hurts. Juliette was everything to me. She was the wife I cherished and the perfect mother for my children. She was my world."

"So why didn't you just do it Maggie? Christ, you're the bravest person I know. Why didn't you try?"

"I did," Maggie yelled.

"And what?" Jude said, almost petulant.

"She left me," Maggie gasped. "She left me when I was fucking pregnant."

Jude had frozen, but Maggie couldn't stop now.

"She left me when I was eight months pregnant and it wrecked me. I had no job, no partner and I was terrified. When I started bleeding, I thought I was going to lose the baby. I fell apart when I thought the baby would die and it completely destroyed me."

Maggie rocked in her seat she breathed so hard. Hot tears burned in her eyes. She clutched at her stomach, remembering her terror as she woke alone in the flat with the sheets bloody. Her lover gone, Maggie still raw at her departure and the flat cavernous in Juliette's absence. The world was a more forbidding place without her at Maggie's side, when she needed Juliette most of all.

Maggie had lay rigid in terror, cradling her swollen belly. The baby shuffled and a little foot nudged out a bulge in her side. She stroked it tenderly with trembling fingers, her whole being filled with despair thinking this could be the last time she felt her baby alive.

Maggie had cried out in an attempt to stand, the weight of the baby straining her back. She needed the phone on the other side of the room and what might have been a few easy strides months ago seemed impossible while the baby pressed down on nerves and her legs collapsed from beneath her. The fall jarred her knees, tore at her back and hit her baby so hard it made Maggie nauseous with fear. She wept in the dark and silent flat, her cherished child in trouble and her heart torn apart, feeling like the last person in the world.

Maggie barely heard Jude's response.

"What baby?"

Maggie's heart pounded inside her imploding chest and her head fogged.

"Maggie," Jude shouted. "What baby?"

"It was you," Maggie whispered. "You were our baby."

"But," Jude seemed far away, "but Dad?"

"He was the donor. That's all he was meant to be. You and Juliette were my family and I thought I'd lost everything."

Maggie's mind went black for a moment. Then when the light came back it swirled around in her head. Her aching chest. It wouldn't ease. She clenched her teeth when the pain shot to her jaw. She felt the old grief all over again, now razor sharp with Jude's disapproval.

Maggie didn't hear Jude's response, but she was aware her daughter had left the room and Juliette no longer held her hand. Was she alone again?

That loneliness. It seemed to crush her chest with great force. The emptiness of that night when Juliette abandoned her had forever left its mark. Even though she didn't stop pining for Juliette for months afterwards, ever hopeful that she'd somehow come back, she never did.

Her lover gone, good friends dead, then others quietly staying away after the baby was born, suspicious of Richard's presence. Maggie found her world entirely changed through no choice of her own. All she had was a young baby and a kind man, and devastated she turned her back on her old life, with wounds that never healed.

"Maggie?" It was a soft voice. Abby's. "Talk to me, Maggie."

She felt an arm encouraging her to lean back. Maggie reached out wanting to hold dear Abby. "I'm sorry," she tried to say.

"That's it. Keep talking, Maggie."

"I wanted to protect you. I didn't want you to go through this." Maggie broke off as pain stabbed her chest. "It hurts."

Abby's fingertips circled her wrist. "Keep breathing, Maggie. Please keep breathing."

"It hurts so much," Maggie gasped. "I can't stand it."

"Stay with me, Maggie. Keep talking. Keep calm."

"I'm so sorry. This unbearable agony. I didn't think you would get over it."

"I know." And for the first time she noticed Abby's voice trembled. "Tell me more. Just a little longer."

Maggie clutched at Abby's arm. "Don't go," she gasped. "Please."

"I won't let you go, Maggie. You're going to be OK. I'm not going to lose you."

And everything went black.

42

Jude sat breathing into the cavern of her hands, intent on listening to the air rush through her fingers to calm her panic. She closed her eyes to the glare of the hospital corridor and steadfastly ignored the rising dread inside.

"Dr Goodman."

She opened her eyes to the senior registrar she knew by sight from her house officer days. She was flattered the woman remembered her name.

"Your mother's out of surgery and is recovering on the ward. Would you like to come through?"

"Yes, of course." Jude leapt to her feet and joined the registrar, her legs light with nerves.

"The surgeon's very happy with how the angioplasty was performed and we've inserted a stent."

Jude nodded, spending every ounce of energy on listening to the clinical information rather than panicking about the state of her mother.

"And thanks to Dr Hart's quick intervention and persistence on arrival at A&E, your mother has escaped quite lightly."

Jude had to suppress a sob at the mention of Abby's name and her care of Maggie. "Good," she whispered.

"Of course," the registrar continued, "we'll keep her in for a few days since it was an emergency operation, but the prognosis is very good."

They'd reached halfway down the long ward and the doctor stopped at a single-occupancy room.

"Luckily, your mother can have some peace in here for recovery. We're quiet this evening."

Jude smiled. "Enjoy it while you can."

The doctor opened the door and even though Jude had walked in on severely ill patients in recovery countless times, it was impossible not to be affected by Maggie. She was pale and unconscious in a hospital gown, her face drawn thin in her state. It was surreal for Jude, seeing her own mother rather than another transitory body in care.

"The procedure was undertaken using local anaesthetic but she's been asleep since arriving in theatre. I imagine she will be for a while."

"Thank you," Jude replied, and the doctor left.

She approached the bed slowly, as if Maggie were aware, and sat next to her. Jude couldn't take her eyes from Maggie's face. It was so different to how her vibrant mother usually appeared. Maggie's eyes, which sparkled with every emotion from deep love to fury, were hidden by sleep. Her brow was smooth, without a care rankling her thoughts. And Jude realised, with a little amusement, that it was rare to see Maggie's mouth motionless, with not a pronouncement or cutting comment issuing from her lips.

"Oh, Maggie." Jude reached out for her mother's hand. It felt familiar yet strange in hers, Maggie's skin now darker and lined with age since the days Jude grasped it as a child, and a wave of guilt flooded through Jude as she realised the distance she'd kept.

"I'm sorry," she said. "But how was I meant to know?"

It was with a certain clarity she saw Maggie, but at the same time her mother was more unfathomable than ever. The image of Maggie sitting distraught in the hotel room with Juliette at her side was vivid. It was strange to see her mother with someone other than Jude's father, but at the same time it had looked right, as if it had always been that way.

324

"I don't know who you are," Jude whispered, and she squeezed Maggie's hand, the sensation both comforting and foreign.

A noise from outside pulled Jude from her thoughts and she glanced up to see her brother through the door.

"Eli, come in," she called.

He pushed the door gingerly, his eyes wide as he stared at their mother. He let the door swing to and stood motionless inside the room. He was like a little boy, all the impishness absent from his demeanour, terrified at seeing his mother stricken. He seemed small, with that slight stature of Maggie's. They were two large characters who could fill a room with the force of their personalities, then so fragile when reduced only to their physical presence.

"Ju Ju," he said, quietly. He hadn't called her that in years. "She's going to be all right, isn't she?" And he looked at her with terror in his eyes.

Jude rushed over and drew him under her arms. "Course she is," she murmured into his hair.

"She's scaring me, sis."

"Me too," she said, anxiety pulling at her chest. "Me too." She rocked him from side to side, waiting for the alarm to recede. "But do you think this'll keep her down for more than a few minutes?" she said, forcing optimism.

"Nah," he said, muffled by her chest. "She'll be up in no time."

"You know what she's like. She'll not let the small matter of a heart attack slow her down. Imagine how fucked off she'll be when she wakes up."

He sniffled with a laugh.

Jude squeezed her little brother tighter. "They said it went well. So I mean it, you might not want to be here when she rouses."

"Let's leave it to Dad then," Eli said, cheekiness returning to his tone.

Jude took in a lungful of air. "Where is Dad?" And she breathed out the whole lot at the thought of facing her father. "Did Abby find him?"

"Yes, he was at Caroline Argent's. They're on their way over."

"Good," Jude said, for the sake of saying something. "Good."

"Hell of a way to avoid announcing the divorce."

"What?"

"Having a heart attack."

Jude laughed. "Well, you know Maggie. Never does anything by half."

They both turned as the door opened and their father stood large in the doorway, his towering frame stooped and his face haggard.

"They've finished the procedure, Dad," Jude said hastily. "It's looking good. I imagine she's out with sheer exhaustion."

Richard nodded and moved into the room. He and Eli took opposite sides of the bed and held a hand of Maggie's each.

Seeing her mother in good care, Jude relaxed for what she realised was the first time in hours, letting the knots in her neck loosen and her shoulders ease.

"I need to get a drink," she said. She was falling asleep on her feet, most likely from the draining worry since arriving at the hospital. "I'll be back in few minutes."

"I'll come with you, love," Richard said, and he peered at her with heavy eyes. "Let's get a coffee."

They sat at a table in the hospital foyer café, neither even nursing their coffees.

"Abby should be with Celia by now," Jude said. "She'll bring her over if she can."

"Good, good," Richard said absently. "I'll ring Maggie's sister in a moment."

"Abby said she'd do that too."

"Oh right. Please remind me to thank her."

Jude pursed her lips, aware they had a great deal to thank Abby for.

"What happened?" he asked.

"They think it was a panic attack preceding the heart event. They tested immediately so there was no delay in care. Abby said they couldn't have treated her any quicker.

"Abby?" Richard asked confused.

"Abby called the ambulance. She took Mum in. I," and the words were crushing, "I wasn't there."

Jude was always going to regret walking out. A moment of pique and self-righteous outrage, and she'd turned her back on her mother at the wrong moment. Even when Juliette had run after her, begging for understanding for Maggie's sake, Jude had carried on walking, filled with fury and indignation, until a phone call from Abby at the hospital had poured icy water on that fire.

"Thank Christ for Abby," her father sighed, and he absently took a sip of coffee.

"Dad?"

"Yes, love."

"She was with Juliette."

"Who? Abby?"

"Mum. She was with Juliette."

"Oh," he said, and his tone conveyed full understanding. "I see." And again he looked away. "I imagine you have some questions," he said at last.

"Yes, I do. It can wait though."

Richard reached out for her hand. "Now might be as good a time as any. Tell me, what did Maggie say?"

"She said you were just a donor." Jude swallowed, unexpectedly affected by the admission, as if she were losing her father and his role was demoted to biology. "Mum said she loved Juliette and she'd wanted a family with her."

327

"All true," he sighed. "She's right." He took another sip of coffee while he collected his thoughts. He smiled at last and looked at Jude.

"I was introduced to Maggie by a mutual friend, someone who turned out rather poisonous and manipulative, unfortunately." He shook his head.

"Go on," Jude said. "Please."

"Well, her name was Tiff and she worked at my department. We'd been friends for years. We often argued about all sorts, from things as mundane and esoteric as the rules of rugby to obscure philosophy. One thing she found fascinating about your dusty conservative father was how little gay folk bothered me. She was incredulous I found gay parents neither scandalous nor outrageous, so much so that I said I'd have no qualms about donating to a lesbian family. And it was true. A child needs a loving parent and both need a supportive network. Who or what gender that parent or network I think hardly matters. And one day, I think as a mischievous challenge, she introduced a vivacious, outgoing, fiercely intelligent post-graduate. And that gorgeous woman was Maggie."

Jude listened fascinated. This wasn't their pat answer of meeting at university. Richard's explanation was vivid with the colour of real people rather than stale parents.

"I never met Juliette. I knew her by sight from around the university and Maggie told me much about her. She adored her. I don't think I've seen anyone so in love. They had issues over having a family, but those seemed surmountable to me, and I agreed to be a donor and available should any child want to meet me later in life."

He frowned and had to gather his emotions for a moment. "But they split rather painfully. I remember being surprised at how vicious it was at the time. Maggie was devastated and her health became poor and I worried for the child. I supported Maggie through the birth then," he looked up and smiled at Jude, "Well I was swept away after that. There's

328

nothing quite like a newborn to soften your soul. As soon as I saw your face and touched your tiny fingers, so fresh and new that your nails had a tinge of purple." He had tears brimming. "I invited Maggie to stay while you were young, to share the broken nights." He grinned. "You were adorable, but good lord babies are maddening. I've never been so tired in my life."

Jude laughed. She could see the love in his eyes.

"And, I couldn't bear to see either of you leave. Maggie very quickly suggested I take a greater part in your life, but I didn't want to miss a single moment. I was crazy about you both. So, I asked Maggie to marry me, being ultimately an old-fashioned sort, and to my great surprise she said yes."

He sniffed and took a moment. "It was after Eli was born that I realised I'd been naïve. Tiff came to the christening, and she was a little worse for wear with alcohol when she smugly declared she'd engineered it all. 'I gave her to you,' she said. And I will always remember the chill that ran through me. It was sickening – her conceit and the mendacious way Maggie and I had come together. She'd forced Maggie and Juliette apart, you see. Oh they had problems, but I have no doubt they would have stayed together otherwise."

"What did you do?"

"There was nothing to be done." He shrugged. "We were a family now. Years had passed, and you knew me as your father. We had another child together. I debated for months whether I should tell Maggie, and to this day I don't know whether I should have." He seemed drained simply at the remembrance. "And so I remained silent, and we stayed together."

"But." Jude felt overwhelming sorrow for her father. "Didn't it feel like a sham? Don't you feel cheated by Maggie? By her friend?"

"Yes and no," Richard replied. "There was real love there. No question. For Maggie too."

329

"But you could have fallen for someone who wanted you."

"Ah, you forget," he smiled. "Your father was a dusty researcher, a consummate bachelor at thirty-five. I hadn't had a serious girlfriend in all my life. And in walked this beautiful, terrifying woman carrying my child. When her world fell apart, I stepped in to help. And I was rewarded with thirty years of love, laughter and experiences I thought reserved only for others. Maggie gave me the best years of my life."

Jude found it difficult to reconcile this history with the parents she remembered as a child. "Doesn't it bother you that she carried a flame for Juliette? I know she did now. And I've realised you knew too."

He dipped his gaze for a moment. "Yes, there were difficult times."

"Mum used to sit at the bottom of the garden, and we would watch her. I wondered where she went to in her thoughts, but you knew didn't you?"

He nodded sadly. "We all carry a flame for someone. Granted Maggie's burned that bit brighter. But look at you. Look at Eli. I have two beautiful children. I have a best friend in Maggie that was worth it alone. And," he blushed and scratched his head, "I seem to have got myself, at the ripe old age of sixty-six, a girlfriend."

Jude laughed at the ridiculousness. "Caroline?"

"Yes," he said, incredulous.

That had been a surprise when Eli had told her. What a polar opposite in outlook Caroline must be compared with Maggie. Jude sniggered. "Hasn't that driven Mum nuts? You going out with a Tory?"

"Yes, it has," he admitted. "It's been rather satisfying." And they both chuckled.

Jude considered him. "I love you, Dad. Mum was lucky and Eli and I more so."

Richard pursed his lips, awkward as always with accepting compliments. "Balderdash dear first born. It was me who was the lucky one," and he ruffled her hair.

Jude laughed out loud.

Their drinks had cooled as they'd talked, and they gulped down their coffees before standing to return to Maggie.

"Dad?" Jude suddenly thought. "When did you know?" She stared at him shocked. "When did you realise Mum and Juliette would meet again?"

"Ah," he grumbled, and he slumped back into his seat. "Well, that I didn't take so well."

Jude slowly sat down again, staring at her father, concerned.

"I don't know if you remember, but I popped out to Paris six months ago to see Eli. I wanted to visit a museum while I was there, and he'd not long been dating a woman. I'd never seen him so besotted. You know what he's like usually. As joyful but blasé about a new love as a new shirt. But he was different about this woman. I took him for dinner and all he could talk of was this Selene. He showed me a photo on his phone." Richard paused. "She was a beautiful girl, but it was the woman in her embrace that almost stopped my heart. I'd forgotten she even existed. But there she was, Maggie's eternal love, the mother of Eli's."

"Did you tell him?"

"No," Richard shook his head. "I feigned feeling unwell. Actually, I felt sick as a dog. And when I returned home–"

"You stepped back."

"Yes."

"That's when you moved to the attic."

"Oh you noticed?"

"Of course we bloody noticed."

"Ha. You sounded like Maggie then."

"Keep on topic, old man."

"You're only proving my point. But yes, I stepped back."

331

"Why?" Jude cried. "Mum loved you. Didn't you still love her?"

"Very much. But it was a mature, respectful love. And while that contentment is everything I crave, it's not what sustains your mother." He looked most saddened of all by this. "That kind of mellow happiness might as well be death to her. She thrives on passion. You children filled her world with colour for years, especially you. I think she clung to you most of all, as the last vestige of Juliette. But when you grew up and drifted away, as well you should," he said emphatically, "it left your mother with only a devoted friend, and to Maggie that would always be lacking. Besides, she should never have been mine. But for Tiff's trickery she would have been with Juliette."

"And then?"

"I realised I'd lost her. When she and Juliette would meet, and they would, it would be folly and grossly unfair to stand in their way." He looked embarrassed. "I went home and drank myself silly at a bar." Then he chuckled. "Very mature I know. But, it happened that Caroline Argent was there, doing exactly the same, drinking away her sorrows after putting her husband in the care home. We became friends. And after Maggie and I decided to live apart, we became more."

A few weeks ago Richard with this new woman would have seemed ludicrous, now it seemed the least remarkable change.

"Does she make you happy?" Jude asked.

"Yes," Richard replied. That this was a surprise for him was evident. "She's very good company. I'm, again, a very lucky man."

"Bollocks, Dad," Jude replied. "You deserve happiness."

"Again, my dear first born, you sound just like your mother."

Jude was tempted to nudge him with her foot before realising that's what Maggie would have done too.

Then she surprised herself. "Yes, sometimes I am like her." And she thought perhaps that wasn't such a bad thing after all.

43

After a trip home to change and shower, it was late when Jude returned to the hospital and the lights were low. Maggie slept on, but in the shadows beside the bed sat the stricken figure of Maggie's former lover.

"I'm sorry." Juliette rose from the seat and smoothed her dress, all her usual poise and confidence gone. "Celia let me in. I accompanied her. I can go."

"There's no need," Jude said, stepping forward quickly. "You must stay as long as you like. Please don't leave on my account."

Juliette gave the slightest of nods, her gaze averted. "I talked to your father also. He doesn't mind me visiting."

"I'm sure he's more than happy."

"I can't stay long in any case – an unavoidable meeting – but I hate to leave. Please, would you keep me informed?" She peeped towards Jude. "A message or two to reassure me everything is well?"

"Of course," Jude smiled.

"I would ask Eli or Richard, but I trust your judgement more. I think you would tell me if things took a turn for the worse."

"I'm happy to."

They fell into an awkward silence.

"Dad told me what happened." Jude hesitated. "He said you were very much in love but split apart."

Juliette's features pinched with grief. She reached out for Maggie's hand and clasped it with a tenacious anguish. She gulped in an obvious struggle to contain her feelings, but a tear trailed down her cheek.

"Please forgive her." Juliette whispered. "I hurt her so badly." She stroked Maggie's hand with a firmness that betrayed deep regret. "I know you must find her opinions frustrating and they surprised me when I arrived. How could the biggest lesbian activist be unsupportive of gay relationships? But when you have been burned like that, it's difficult not to keep away from the fire, and of course you protect your children doubly so. And I did hurt her very much."

She looked towards Jude. "She thought I'd deserted her at her most vulnerable when we should have been enjoying the tender anticipation of a new family. That kind of pain and betrayal destroys your faith in people, and I understand why she became fixated on her misguided beliefs."

"But why?" Jude said, her curiosity getting the better of her. "Why didn't you fix it? How could you leave her then?"

Juliette winced at the question.

"I'm sorry. It's just Dad said a friend forced you apart. It's none of my business–"

"Of course it's your business." Juliette gave her a shattered look. "I would have been your mother."

Jude twitched back with the force of Juliette's grief. If nothing else had convinced Jude of Maggie and Juliette's affection and the power of their relationship then this certainly did. She could see it in the older woman's eyes and the way she cradled Maggie's hand to her heart.

"I had everything to lose and no assurance I could keep it," Juliette said. "I had a woman I adored as much as any husband loved a wife. A child I was ready to give my life for but with whom I had no familial rights. I was already terrified I would lose you both. I imagined you and Maggie steadily bonding with the other biological parent, and I would be the odd one out – the one the child never resembled, the one whose parents wouldn't be called Grandmother and Grandfather, the mother who couldn't sign forms as a parent. Always on the outside."

Juliette gazed at her. "Despite every fear, I still wanted you and Maggie with all my heart. But that came crashing down when I saw Richard together with Maggie, his hands stroking Maggie's tummy, protective of their baby. My friend confirmed the worst, and it felt like I was dying. "

"Didn't you want to fight for her?"

Juliette let out a tired laugh. "I thought I'd walk to the ends of the earth for Maggie. And I was sure it was the same for her. But when she was expecting suddenly all the stakes seemed higher. Maggie would no longer be my whole world. That world was about to get bigger and more magical. A longed-for daughter was soon to arrive and Maggie would no longer simply be my lover but the mother of my child.

"Already she was in love with you. You were growing inside her and she could feel your little feet pushing out her belly. It was almost as miraculous for me, but I couldn't touch you like she did. I was waiting, impatient, to hold you in my arms and finally have you next to me. Then I saw it all being taken away."

She looked at Jude with unwavering despair. "Did you ever love someone so much, found the thought of losing them so unbearable, that you almost wished you'd never met them? Have you needed someone so acutely it seemed less painful to leave rather than live with the fear of losing them?"

Jude didn't respond.

"That's how I felt about you and Maggie as the birth approached. And when I saw Richard and Maggie together I had a choice – to meet you and fall in love irrevocably with my small family then have that love denied for the rest of my life. Thank God we all have more rights now. The already privileged underestimate the improvement of quality of life they bring. But back then, with nothing, I chose to run."

Juliette stood straighter. "It was self-preservation that made me leave. I had every reason to believe I would lose you both right there in front of my eyes; Tiff made sure of that. But like many acts of self-preservation it ended up hurting me more."

Jude didn't know what to say. She'd had such devoted and complete parents in Maggie and Richard it was hard to fathom another losing out.

Juliette pursed her lips in a resigned smile. "Of course, later I had Selene, and from that moment I could no longer regret anything in my life. But I thought of you many times over the years." Her eyes sparkled. "When I arrived in Ludbury, it made me so happy to see how you had turned out. I can understand why Maggie is so proud."

Jude couldn't help a dismissive laugh. "Oh believe me, Maggie's far from proud."

Juliette's frown gave away her confusion.

"She's had some choice things to say about me recently."

"About your relationship with Abby?"

"Yes."

Juliette shook her head. "She was coming round to it. Please be patient."

"They were harsh words."

"Of course. I wouldn't expect anything else from Maggie Goodman. But anything she complained of, compared with the depth of her love and esteem for her beautiful daughter, would have been as inconsequential as raindrops on a flower. And sometimes those imperfections are as stunning as jewels if viewed in the right light."

Jude smiled. Not at Juliette's reassurance that Maggie was proud, but at show well suited Juliette and her mother were. Maggie's fire and energy were balanced by Juliette's cool serenity. They fitted.

"It sometimes breaks her heart that you no longer need her," Juliette continued. "It is always the way – one of life's harshest acts. It is such a remarkable force, a child's love and the mother's returned. It's so brutal that the child's love must change while the mother carries on devoted. It's a debt only collected a generation later when it is repaid in cruel kind."

44

Maggie had woken in the night in unexpected pain, and after some quick ministrations and a hefty dose of morphine was now drifting in and out under a drug-fuelled haze.

She'd gazed at Jude, drunk on her medication, and said something about bananas or bandanas. Jude suspected neither were of consequence, and in the early hours it was Jude who was wide awake and Maggie asleep.

Eli wandered in at breakfast time, looking grey with insomnia, and Maggie was still no more coherent. Eli mocked Maggie's confusion mercilessly all day. She would get her revenge though, and Jude knew him well enough to understand he was only distracting himself from anxiety, and they sat either side of the bed into the evening when Maggie slumbered again.

"The meeting," Jude said, suddenly. "About the church? It's today isn't it."

Eli nodded. "I tried putting something together last night, but my head's a mess. It was Mum who knew the details and it's Mum who everyone respects."

"Is anyone going?" Jude said, concerned.

"Caroline's presenting plans for the church and said she'd try to muddle through the courtyard proposal."

"Shit. I'm sorry Eli."

Jude looked at Maggie and her brother knowing how much this development meant to both. The timing was rotten.

"Mum put so much work into this," Eli said, then he looked at Jude with a sparkle in his eye. "Until this project, I didn't realise quite how charming people found Mum."

"Charming?" Jude laughed. It wasn't a word she associated with her mother.

Eli smiled. "Yes, she's brusque, and outspoken, and she rants and she rages. But it's honest. You know she means every word and you never have to watch your back with Maggie Goodman, because she'll say everything to your face."

"And this makes her charming?"

"Yes, because when she gives you a compliment, and she will, she never holds back on anything, you know she means it."

Jude still didn't quite believe him.

"Have you seen people when Mum gives them praise?" The sad sparkle in his eyes was heart-breaking. "It's like they grow. She's generous with encouragement. We benefitted from it as children, don't you remember? And you won't find a bigger heart or anyone who cares like she does. Yes, there are those in Ludbury who show their local pride with nice pansies on the roundabout. But if you want someone who really gives a shit about its people then that's Mum. "

Eli stood up and walked around to Jude. "I know you and Mum have your moments, sis, but she has a big heart and I think it's in the right place."

They both looked towards the dozing and babbling Maggie, with her large and slightly broken heart.

"Come on," Jude said. "Maggie's stable. Let's go to the meeting. We can at least be supportive. And maybe we can heckle Mrs Petty's presentation on her behalf."

Eli sniggered.

The church, for the first time since Christmas, was full. The vicar, two other members of the clergy and a sombre man in a suit tapping at a tablet sat at the front. Every single

340

pew was occupied. It surprised Jude how many faces she recognised. Mrs Malady, a permanent fixture in Ludbury, sat at the front with what Jude guessed were several little grand Maladys and their parents. The Patels. Dean, the builder for the project, and his Dad were there too. A large bunch of teenagers still in their school uniform took up two pews and were rapt with attention. The girl from the square, Amelia, waved from between her parents. Staff from behind supermarket tills who Jude had simply greeted but whom her mother engaged every time she shopped.

The meeting was well underway and Jude assumed most of the presentations complete. They squeezed onto a back bench while Caroline stood before the panel explaining the finances for purchase of the church building itself.

"My husband was a long-standing member of the congregation until two years ago," Caroline explained, "and a large part of the funding will be from the sale of my husband's assets. He would have found it fitting that he could save this cherished building for the use of the community. Plans include shelving for the east end of the nave to house books from the old library. The two sizable aisles will be sympathetically separated to provide rooms for multiple purposes. We have interest from groups as diverse as DJ Youth and Tea Dance Pensioners. I find it heartening that the people of Ludbury will have a shared space and hope over time those groups will explore each other's interests. And with funds to be raised in the future, we propose a small annexe to house a multi-faith centre."

Caroline took her seat to thoughtful nods from the panel, but a single strident voice echoed across the nave. "This is a Christian site. These plans are sacrilegious and offensive. I must voice my objections– "

"Mrs Petty," the vicar said calmly. "Please keep your objections to the proposal for the end of the presentation. They will be heard."

341

The irate neighbour and Maggie's arch enemy took her seat again with a clatter.

"Please continue with your proposal for the courtyard development," the vicar said.

Jude could feel Eli sag despondent next to her, but they both lifted higher in their seats when they saw who stood for the presentation. It was Abby.

The audience seemed far from shocked though. Recognition and smiles of regard spread across their faces from the front to the back of the church. It had struck Jude before how highly people regarded Maggie, but it was with a sense of pride, and not a little shame, she realised they also held Abby in the same highest esteem. Jude had underestimated both.

"I am Dr Hart," Abby introduced herself. "I am a GP in the town surgery. I treat everyone from landed gentry to the homeless. I've worked in Ludbury for several years and the decline in health of the town has been marked over that period. There are many reasons, but when people either have nowhere to live or pay so much they can no longer afford to eat, their health suffers. And while that suffering in itself is intolerable, it also puts pressure on a health service which we all need.

"Mrs Goodman cannot be here today, but together with a local builder she has proposed what they hope will be the first in several co-operative developments, where groups buy unused buildings and make them habitable for local residents, with a high proportion of affordable and social housing and micro-homes to house the most urgent of cases.

"Property, more and more, has been turned into a business, but its most important function is as a home. Social housing has been sold off and private sector rent is no longer capped. It's no surprise this leaves people without a roof over their heads. When it comes to housing it can't be left simply to market forces. Markets don't care about people, but we should.

"Everyone should have food and a roof over their head. That they don't in twenty-first century Ludbury and England is barbaric. I hope the panel will consider Mrs Goodman's plans."

"Well this is insufferable." Mrs Petty had jumped to her feet. "This is personal greed wrapped in a philanthropic sweetener."

The audience grumbled.

Mrs Petty turned vicious, with almost a snarl twitching at her lips. "Mrs Goodman is trying to get her son a flat in the courtyard," she snapped. "There's no difference between this proposal and mine. But my son is a God-fearing member of society. It's disgusting that these hallowed grounds be overrun with the likes of the immoral Goodmans. And you know what I'm talking about Caroline Argent."

Jude wanted to leap to her feet to defend Abby, but Eli held her back.

Unruffled, Abby considered the protest. "It is no secret that Eli Goodman is part of the co-operative. But that wasn't Mrs Goodman's initial motivation." Abby took stock again before carrying on. "Maggie Goodman saw a need in this town and wants to keep it for the majority rather than the few. She's done this all her life. She looks out for the children at school and everyone she meets." Abby turned back to nods rippling across the audience from Mrs Malady to the intrigued teenagers.

"And I can vouch for Mrs Goodman's generosity personally," Abby continued. "When I came here, I'd lost all of my small family, and without someone like Maggie," Jude could hear the emotion in Abby's voice, "I'm not sure I'd be standing here today able to serve you as a doctor.

"I think that's the difference between the proposals. Yes, Mrs Goodman may be doing this for her son, but she also realises he's not the only son in the village, or the only daughter, or grandmother who needs a home."

You could hear a pin drop.

"Maggie may not be a perfect woman," Abby said, her voice wavering. "But she is a good one and I do not doubt her motivation."

The audience shuffled, nodding and quietly applauding Abby's words. Jude stared at Abby, full of so many thoughts and feelings. She wanted to rush to her and tell her every single one.

"This is ridiculous," Mrs Petty said. "These are not God-fearing people. These lands are Christian and should be kept as such. And that the proposal is financed by the Argents is tantamount to desecration. Don't think I haven't noticed your sinful visits with Mr Goodman, before your husband is even in his grave."

Caroline stood with enviable poise, steadied by a kind touch from Abby.

"Mrs Petty," Caroline said firmly. "If you insist on making this personal then here it is: my husband no longer recognises me. He hasn't for over a year. He thinks I'm a random old woman who visits and he makes inappropriate comments to our daughter who resembles me in my youth. It's the most degrading, humiliating and cruellest kind of death – a vicious disease for the entire family. And, mark my words, yes, when I meet my maker I will be having a word about it. But my husband never had any doubts. The church will be financed in his name, not mine. I am not my husband. And he is not me."

Jude smiled at Caroline's forthrightness and wondered whether she and Maggie had more in common than Jude had initially thought. Eli clearly had the same inspiration because he whispered, "Do you think, by any chance, that Dad has a type?"

And speaking of the devil, it was Richard who cleared his throat and offered, "It might be of interest that archaeological finds suggest this site was a place of druid worship long before it was a Christian church. So we already have a precedent for a multi-use and multi-faith site."

The panel, audience and presenters all broke to discuss matters, the whole church buzzing with excitement and not a little gossip.

Jude pushed through the crowd, peering across the tops of people's heads trying to find Abby.

"Do you think this has a chance?" Eli said, following her.

"I don't know," Jude said. "But I think we have Abby to thank if it does."

They broke out at the front where the panel and presenters were energetically discussing proposals. Jude gently took Abby's arm to let her know she was there.

"Hey." Abby beamed when she saw her. "I didn't think you'd be able to come."

Jude could barely speak. "Maggie's stable," she stuttered. "We only popped in."

"How are you?" Abby said softly, coming close and cradling Jude's face in her hands.

Jude's eyes flooded warm with tears. "Grateful," she sniffed. "So very grateful."

Abby looked confused.

"Thank you, thank you, thank you," Jude said, and she hugged Abby tight.

Abby laughed quietly beside Jude's ear before pulling back a little to see her face.

"Of course," Abby said. "I knew you and Eli would be in no state to present at the meeting, and Maggie never stops rabbiting on about the plans to me, so I knew enough."

"It's not just that," Jude replied. "It's for everything. For being there for Maggie. For making this your home with my family. For appreciating Maggie for who she is, when I didn't."

Abby smiled at her with sympathy in her eyes.

"You're always there for her," Jude continued, "always have been." And not for the first time Jude chilled inside when she imagined what might have happened if not for

Abby at the hotel. "You always loved her without question and always forgave her when she was wrong."

Abby gave a timid shrug. "You and your family were there for me. I will always be there for you."

Jude gazed at this unassuming woman. How lucky Jude was to know her. A cherished friend for years, a lover beyond her imagination. How calmly Abby had taken a stand in the meeting, a quiet tower of strength. Jude was in awe through to her bones and her esteem for Abby colossal. Abby was a long way from the young woman traumatised by her mother's loss, now with the loving strength to have saved Jude's.

"I love you," Jude said. "I can't even count the ways that I do."

It was beyond due that Jude truly recognised the strength of Abby and her support, but she would never overlook it again.

Maggie was sleeping when Jude arrived back at the hospital. The lights were on low but Jude could see colour had returned to Maggie's cheeks.

Jude sat beside the bed, overwhelmed by the day and turmoil of the last weeks. She lay her head on the mattress and closed her eyes. She reached out and held Maggie's hand and let the full force of her anxieties wash over her while she held tight to her mother.

She breathed fast as images of Bill, the force of Abby's love, her mother's heart attack, her father's grief and her new family of Juliette and Selene swirled through her head in chaos. She screwed her eyes tight and all the while held Maggie's hand.

She must have slept awhile, because she had the heaviness of slumber when her eyes eased open. The hospital was quiet and Maggie slept on although she must have stirred in the night because it was now Maggie who held Jude's hand.

Jude stared at her mother, her impossibly complicated mother, who dozed on.

"You're right," Jude whispered. "I didn't need you beyond a teenager." She stroked Maggie's hair. "You raised an independent woman to stand on her own feet, and I would survive without you. But that doesn't mean I don't want you."

She played with Maggie's hair, sorting the tufts and tangles from her stay in hospital.

"I love you, Mum, and I'm sorry I didn't always show it. But believe me, I regard you so highly. I think the world of you. You," Jude sighed, "the most infuriating, inspirational, cantankerous, loyal, ferocious," Jude smiled as the tears ran, "irritating, nurturing, encouraging, unfathomable mother in the world.

"And I owe you everything because you saved Abby."

45

Maggie opened an eye and groaned. She'd been asleep, again. When was she going to stop dozing off at the drop of a… What was it? Bugger it. And when was this foggy brain going to clear? She'd been semi-coherent for a couple of days and was hoping to get her sorry arse back home.

She opened the other eye and tried to focus on the room. It was as expected except for a blurred black shape beside the bed. She blinked. Then blinked again. And after several seconds the form sharpened into a short female figure, and after stretching her eyes wide and mouth low the clear vision of the vicar came into view.

"Oh dear," Maggie said. "Is it that bad? They've sent in the priest?"

The vicar chuckled. "It is true then. You're recovering well."

"Yes," Maggie muttered, "although frankly, it's humiliating to be here."

"Jude said you'd be annoyed."

"Jude?"

The vicar nodded. "She's rarely left your side, although she very kindly messaged to keep me informed about your health. Me and many other people. I imagine she's been tapping out messages constantly."

Maggie was humbled at the complimentary connotation. "People have been very kind," she said. And it hadn't gone unnoticed that whenever Maggie woke it was Jude's face she saw first. It was with a pleasure which could have filled her heart that Maggie noticed her daughter had softened towards her. Not that she did let it fill her heart, because she was terrified it would break again, the blasted ticker.

Maggie munched her mouth fully awake then frowned. "What day is it?"

"Saturday."

"Then?"

"Yes, they've made a decision, which is why I'm here." The vicar beamed.

"And? Did they go for it?" Maggie said, leaning forward.

"Well, I imagine they discussed the proposals at length."

"Yes?"

"I don't think you appreciate how colourful the meeting was. Some of the accusations about character concerned the bishop."

"But?"

"Indeed, I too raised an eyebrow at one point."

"For the love of Christ!" Maggie said through gritted teeth.

The vicar chuckled with satisfaction. "They chose your proposal."

"Oh thank God for that."

"We may have to thank many. The bishop was especially pleased with the proposal for a multi-faith centre."

Maggie sniggered. "But," she started to get out of bed, "there must be so much to do."

"And not by you," the vicar said, and she hastily restrained Maggie.

"Oh come on," Maggie shot out. "Is this what life's going to be like – every bugger under the sun telling me to take it easy as if I'm one hundred and five?"

"It's not even a week since you had a heart attack. So yes. This is what it'll be like."

"Great."

"Please take it easy, Mrs Goodman." The vicar smiled. "I would like to visit you at home if I may."

"Of course."

"I'm very excited about this project. If people can work together across political boundaries and faiths it gives me hope. Now," the vicar said, standing up, "I believe someone has come to take you home."

Maggie swung her legs over the side of the bed and readied herself to leave. Eli and Jude had both promised to pick her up, as had Richard and Caroline. Maggie had gone from feeling isolated to every bugger wanting to be there for her. She readied herself for whoever arrived and blinked in surprise when an immaculate and always beautiful Juliette entered the room.

"Hi," Maggie said. "I didn't think you'd be able to get away."

"I called in a few favours," Juliette said, that bewitching smile curling at her lips. She wandered nearer, and Maggie's body awakened in ways that were medically unwise. Just that fluid step was enough for Maggie to desire her.

Maggie groaned at being dressed in grey yoga trousers. Why, when Juliette sauntered into the room, did Maggie have to be wearing an elasticated waist. And heart attacks. They weren't sexy.

Juliette stopped in front of her. She even smelled good.

"I was worried about you," Juliette said, concern and affection in her features.

"I'm fine," Maggie snapped. "I'll be up and running in no time."

"Actually." Juliette grinned. "It sounds like you will from what the doctors say." Her features pinched with concern again. "You really scared me. I stayed in Ludbury until after the operation, but had to return to Paris for the start of term. I think I've used up all of Jude's goodwill, calling her every few hours."

"It's nothing. Nothing to worry about," Maggie said.

"Good," Juliette said. "Because I plan on enjoying you for many years to come."

Those medically unwise feelings. They were definitely surfacing again.

"Do you mean that?" Maggie whispered.

"Yes," Juliette murmured. "If you want me."

"I do, very much."

"Times like this provide a lot of clarity I think," Juliette said. "And I don't want to waste another moment apart from you."

"How long can you stay?"

"The weekend this time. But I will be back for the next too and I'm discussing shifting my classes to allow me to lecture part-time and spend more days in England."

Maggie pursed her lips, trying to keep her feelings inside. "I love you," she said. "I never stopped."

Juliette came closer and stroked her cheek. "Hush now," she said gently. "Let's keep you calm." And she wiped away a tear that escaped Maggie's eye.

"Oh when the hell have I ever kept calm," Maggie tutted.

Juliette laughed, her eyes glistening. "I love you too. And it sounds such a weak and pathetic declaration for everything I've felt for you over the years."

Juliette leant forward and delicately kissed her. Maggie could taste the saltiness of their tears that tickled down her cheeks to her lips. Sensations rose up her body. Not just arousal but that longing to get as close to Juliette as possible. It had always overpowered her.

She held Juliette's face when their lips had parted. "I did understand you know," Maggie said, quietly. "That desire to have a child with the one you craved."

Juliette blinked back her emotions.

"I thought you the most incredible person I'd ever met," Maggie said. "And I thought it so unfair that I couldn't make a child with you. I'm sorry I wasn't patient. I should have showed you more understanding."

351

"No matter now," Juliette said. "We have so many incredible things to share."

The sun was shining when they arrived home in Ludbury. Juliette held Maggie's arm as they climbed the steps to the front door.

"Everyone's here," Juliette said. "They wanted to surprise you, but I've warned them to be on their best behaviour."

Maggie shot her a look. "Really, handling me with kid gloves is going to make me very grumpy, very quickly."

"However will I tell?" Juliette shot back.

Damn it. If this wasn't motivation to get better then nothing was. She wasn't going to have Juliette out-sparring her this easily.

She stared at her, straining to come up with a riposte. "You win this time. But I will get better, and I will be back."

"Yes, you will," Juliette said. "Because you are going to put these yoga pants to use. We will be speed walking around the hills of Ludbury and I'll force feed you lettuce."

"This is not how I envisaged the rest of our lives together," Maggie grumbled.

"Well if you do those, we can indulge in more pleasurable activities too," Juliette insinuated.

Shit. Heart palpitations. "OK," Maggie conceded. "Deal."

They opened the door and shuffled into the lounge before a small crowd leapt up from behind the sofa and theatrically whispered, "Surprise!"

Maggie laughed. It was all her favourite people in the world. Celia limped to meet her and held her tighter than a nutcracker. Jude hugged them both from her great height, and Abby piled in too. From beneath the cosy pile of family she noticed Richard smiling and Caroline at his side. And it filled Maggie with no little happiness that Caroline felt she could be there. Only Eli and Selene hung back a little.

Maggie blew out a lungful of air to keep her composure as the family released her from their huddle. Juliette took her hand and gave her a concerned look.

"I'm surviving," Maggie said.

"Ladies and gentlemen," Eli declared to the room.

Maggie rolled her eyes. Bloody Eli. Would he ever stop stealing the limelight?

"Now you are all gathered," he said, raising a mug of tea, "and we welcome our dearest mater back into the home, there is something I would like to say."

He let the shuffling die down and everyone turned to face him. He grinned from ear to ear, thriving in the attention.

"We have known for a little while, but I think it's about time we were all honest and open. So it gives me great pleasure to announce that my wife-to-be and I are also parents-to-be."

Everyone stared.

"We are expecting our first baby," he shouted with his teacup aloft.

"What?" Maggie gasped.

"Yes, my dear mother. And yes, dear Juliette. You are to be grandmothers."

Juliette's sharp intake of breath was the first reaction. And now that Maggie regarded Selene, she did have that soft glow of pregnancy about her. Eli's attentive behaviour made sense now. How silly that she'd overlooked it.

"This is wonderful news," Juliette cried out. "I am so happy for you both. And of course for all of us."

Then, at the exact same moment as Maggie, she must have realised. Trembling fingers sought Maggie's and Juliette slowly turned towards her. Their faces must have been a picture.

"We're going to have a grandchild," Juliette said.

Maggie covered her mouth. She needn't have bothered. Her ecstatic smile must have been obvious to the whole world.

"A child together," Maggie said, beaming. "A little child together."

And as the pile of bodies embraced Eli and Selene, unreserved joy and congratulations pouring in from every member of the family, Maggie clung to Juliette's hand and didn't let go.

Epilogue

It was some months later, with the summer sun high in the sky, that Jude Goodman found herself on a train, returning to Ludbury across the Shropshire plains, then walking once again through the town square. It was Friday and she had finished for the day at a clinic in a town not far away. She was due at a party at her parents' home, to celebrate the recent election of town councillor Maggie Goodman. How life had changed, and so much for the better.

She knocked on the front door and was greeted by her father, whose cheerful face seemed to be defying time and reversing the ageing process.

"Come in, love," he said, beckoning her in. "Everyone's here."

She left her bag by the front door and followed him in.

"Such a beautiful day. We're all out in the garden, except your mother and Juliette who are getting more drinks."

They poked their heads around the kitchen doorway. The two women were setting out glasses and bottles.

"Prosecco?" Juliette said, holding a bottle toward Maggie in accusation. "You celebrate your election with Prosecco?"

Maggie put her hands on her hips and glared.

"Clearly," Juliette pronounced, not without a smirk, "the position means nothing to you if you celebrate it with this 'pop' and not a Champagne."

"It gets better," Maggie said with a challenge in her narrowed eyes. She drew out another bottle from the fridge. "We also have English sparkling wine."

"*Mon dieu*. I suppose you have slices of hot dog for your canapes?"

Jude shook her head at their bickering then noticed a smile on her father's lips as he watched them.

"Look at them," he sighed. "They're happy."

Jude laughed. He was right. The newly invigorated Maggie with enviable biceps and iron thighs, and a flush of rose gracing her cheeks, could never be content without something to irk her. And Jude couldn't help grow fonder of Juliette, the woman who could have once been her mother and had been a constant source of support during her voyage into Sapphic waters.

"I'll help them bring the drinks out. Abby's outside," he said, nodding towards the garden.

The garden was in full bloom and alive with the sound of everything from children to Desmond's deep chuckle. He and Celia reclined on a rattan sofa and Eli, Selene and six-month-old Alicia lay on a blanket, the baby lying on her father's chest picking at his face, fascinated by his nostrils.

Caroline sat by the river chatting with Maggie's sister, and Maggie's two nephews, Liam and Mathew, scampered around so fast they seemed to occupy the whole garden simultaneously. The vicar, Dean, several of Maggie's new colleagues and several of old were happily scattered around the garden enjoying the summer sun and an earlier round of sparkling wine, apparently none the wiser as to whether it was Champagne or otherwise.

And sitting on the grass at the back, her eyes closed to the sun and her beautiful face basking in its glow, was Abby. Jude crept up and, careful not to let her shadow fall across her face, leant down to kiss Abby. A fraction away, her warm breath on Abby's lips betrayed her. Her lover's eyes shot open and Abby's face burst into a satisfied smile.

"Hello," Abby said, putting her arms around Jude's neck. "I've missed you." And she closed the gap between them.

The sensation of Abby's lips on hers had an instant effect on Jude. She melted inside and without thinking knelt down and stroked her hands around Abby.

"Mmm," Abby moaned, and the sound only seduced Jude further, her kiss beginning to deepen.

She felt Abby's fingertips gently push at her chest. "Don't." Abby grinned up at Jude. "I will not be held responsible for my actions if you keep kissing me like that."

Jude laughed and sat down beside her, having to content herself with an arm around her lover and a breast nestled against her warmth.

"Later," Jude whispered, and it was almost torture when Abby's face flushed and her eyes darkened at the suggestion.

"You know," Abby said quietly. "I never imagined you'd be like this."

"How?"

"So keen and hungry."

"And do you have a complaint about that?"

"No, no, no," Abby gasped. "I just sometimes have to pinch myself to make sure I'm not dreaming."

Jude kissed her cheek, luxuriating in the sensation of Abby's tender skin. Definitely torture.

"When did you know?" Abby asked.

"What's that?"

"When did you know that you wanted to go to bed with me?"

"Oh."

Jude knew exactly when. She would never forget that vivid moment. In fact, it was still most affecting to this day, as the rush of blood proved. Jude had tried not to dwell on it over the months, feeling ever more guilty for having witnessed it, but it wasn't something she could easily wipe from her mind.

"Jude?"

"Yes?"

"You're blushing."

"Am I?" She was. Her cheeks were burning. Between the erotic memory and her embarrassment her face was on fire.

"You never blush." Abby's lips twitched, amused and incredulous. "When was it? What happened?"

"Oh, nothing." It was so not nothing. That wasn't fooling anyone.

"OK," Abby said, a naughty smile on her lips. "You're allowed some secrets. But I'm intrigued."

"It's... But... Oh God." Jude was still aflame. "It was the night of the engagement party," she blurted out.

"I did wonder. You were rotten." Abby laughed. "Have you any idea how much that dancing turned me on?"

"Um. Yes," Jude said, still a shade of scarlet.

"I mean, it drove me insane."

"Hmm," Jude mumbled. "Me too." So not convincing.

"What's up?" Abby said, wrinkling her nose.

Jude could never resist that confused look of hers. She melted inside again. Hadn't there been enough secrets, although Jude had planned on taking this one to the grave. Perhaps after everything that had happened, honesty was best. She took a deep breath.

"It was after the dance."

"What's that?"

"I wanted to tell you that I was attracted to you, even if it wasn't already obvious from that dance."

"In retrospect it was." Abby grinned.

"So I..."

"So you?"

"I thought you'd gone home."

"I did." Then Abby seemed to stall, perhaps beginning to recall.

"So I followed. When I caught up, your lights were on and I knocked on the door."

"Yes?"

"But you couldn't hear because you had music playing."

"Uhuh." Deep red consumed Abby's cheeks, almost as glowing as Jude's. "Yes, I remember something like that."

"So...."

"So?"

"I tried the door and called up to you."

Abby gulped.

"And I could hear you upstairs." Jude's heart was beating like thunder. And that blush on Abby's cheeks had stopped in its track and was blanching to white.

"I saw you," Jude hesitated, "touch yourself."

Abby was frozen and stared at the grass. Jude wasn't sure if she'd entered a catatonic state.

"Oh God," Abby choked. She lifted her legs and embraced them, burying her face beneath her arms. "Oh fucking God," she said muffled into her knees.

OK. That had been the wrong decision.

"I'm sorry," Jude chattered. "I'm so sorry. I had no idea you were doing that when I came in."

"This is the most embarrassing moment of my life."

"Please don't be embarrassed," Jude said, holding her arm. "Please."

"I want to die."

"You mustn't."

"Seriously, if the ground could just open up that would be great."

"I'm sorry." Jude couldn't help giggling. "I've wondered whether I should tell you ever since."

"Oh God oh God oh God. It's not getting any better."

"Please don't feel like this."

"Did you by any chance turn off the radio?" Abby groaned.

"Yes."

"And lock the door?"

"I did."

"Oh God."

Jude leant in and pulled Abby to her. "Please stop, because I have another confession to make."

"You're bloody kidding," Abby moaned.

"This one's about me."

Abby's sheepish face peeped at her.

"Please don't feel embarrassed because," Jude gulped and whispered beside Abby's ear. "Because it was, without a doubt, the sexiest thing I've ever seen."

Abby was silent. The babbling had stopped. She continued to peep from beneath her arm. "Really?"

"Absolutely." Jude nodded. "It made me so wet."

"Oh." That brought a healthy colour back. "Hmmhmm?"

"I couldn't stop picturing it all the way home," Jude said. "You coming was all I could think about."

Abby was wide-eyed.

"And I when I got home."

"Uhuh?"

"I jumped straight into bed."

"And?"

"Touched myself."

Abby's mouth had dropped open with an, "uhuh," a pitch higher.

"Beyond a doubt, seeing you like that was the most erotic moment of my life."

Abby suddenly deflated. "And the most embarrassing of mine. Oh God." She buried her head in her knees again. "I can't bear it."

Jude gazed at her, filled with adoration, and arousal at the vivid memory that kept popping into her head.

"How about I make it up to you," she said naughtily.

"I don't think anything can make this better."

"Well," Jude smiled, "how about we even things up?"

Abby looked round. "In what way?"

"Perhaps," and Jude leaned in so close to Abby's ear that she knew it would tantalise her, "you should watch me?"

Abby's gulp was possibly audible to the whole garden.

"Do you mean....?"

"To make it up to you, I'll undress, lie on your bed and touch myself. And you can watch or join in as much as you desire."

Abby was motionless, except for her chest, which rose and fell with rapidity. Jude wondered for a moment if the idea appealed. Then a grin began to spread on Abby's face. It widened and widened, and she beamed and beamed, until it was impossible to look more pleased.

"Let's go home," Abby rasped. And before Jude could respond Abby had grabbed her arm and was hauling her to her feet.

Maggie and Juliette sauntered into the garden, a glass of Champagne for Maggie and English sparkling wine for Juliette, at Maggie's insistence.

"Sorry, Mum." Jude and Abby came thundering past. "Forgot. Erm. Something. At home. Back in a bit." And the two blushing woman sped past.

The front door slammed shut and Maggie and Juliette looked at each other.

"They're going home to have sex, aren't they?" Juliette deadpanned.

"Yup." Maggie rolled her eyes. "Do they ever stop?"

"Do we ever?" Juliette smiled, suggestively. "Which reminds me." She sidled closer. "I brought you a present."

"Oh yes?" Maggie's whole being perked up at Juliette's tone.

"A very fetching pair of cuffs are lying on your bed, next to a slender double dildo in black."

Maggie's grin couldn't have been wider.

"Are you free later?" Juliette asked.

"I don't know," Maggie purred. "I think I might be tied up."

Juliette laughed. "Good. We'd better do the rounds before we disappear."

The two women strode into the garden towards their growing family. Maggie sank onto the blanket to steal her granddaughter from Eli's nostrils. She cradled Alicia in the crook of her arm, marvelling again at the delicate perfection of a young baby. Juliette nuzzled next to them both and they gazed at the baby who seemed wide-eyed with marvel at them.

"She has your eyes," Maggie said. "Beautiful dark irises like yours and Selene's."

The baby smiled and stuck out her tongue. "Hmm," Juliette said. "Maybe some attitude from a different lineage too."

Maggie chuckled. "That's my girl."

And as she looked up, Maggie Goodman marvelled at her fortune, so different to what she'd envisaged all those months ago. And in her mid-fifties, with a new political career, the love of her life, a best friend, children and a first grandchild, she had to confess she was the luckiest woman in the world. No matter what life threw at her now, she vowed to never regret another moment.

"Auntie Maggie?" Liam cried. "Can we play with the police costume?"

"What's that?"

"The truncheon and cuffs from your room?"

Well, maybe apart from that one.

###

Acknowledgements

Thank you beta readers for feedback and almost infinite patience. As you have gathered, I haven't mastered the art of taking criticism gracefully, but I do always appreciate your feedback, eventually.

Thank you Diana Simmonds, for having the force of personality to make me rewrite the first quarter and most of all for simply being Diana.

Chris Paynter for your encouragement from the very first. Authors give up in the absence of people like you and I am always grateful.

Cindy Rizzo with your enviable knowledge of lesfic and always insightful comments as well as finally persuading me that epilogues aren't pure evil.

Gabby Benson for fabulous and giggle-worthy commentary and you also have a mean eye for plot holes and wonky character motivation. Although, I still haven't forgiven you for spotting every turn of the plot!

The above are all authors I admire and I feel very lucky to have had their input.

Thanks to my wife for so many things beyond the cover, editing and general agony of having to live with an author, too many things to mention here (besides being either embarrassing to me or my wife).

Please note, beta readers and editors can only go far with a bloody minded author, and all remaining errors are my own.

Finally, thank you to my kids – just-a-fart Ellie and killer-fart-bats Joe – inspiration and delight always.

About the Author

Clare Ashton's first novel, Pennance, was long-listed for the Polari Prize and After Mrs Hamilton is a Golden Crown Literary Society (Goldie) award winner. Her first foray into romantic comedy, That Certain Something, was a Goldie and Lambda Literary Award finalist and Poppy Jenkins won the Rainbow Award for contemporary romance.

Clare Ashton grew up in Mid-Wales and having a brain stuck somewhere not particularly useful between the arts and science ended up studying History and Philosophy of Science at Cambridge University. After college, and still at a loss as to what to do with such a brain, she bimbled around the UK from London to Sheffield being everything from Little Chef waitress to software engineer. On the way she met a wife, had two children and recently came to a rest in the Midlands with the vocation of lesbian romance writer – nothing like the career they suggested back at school.

Also by Clare Ashton:
Pennance
After Mrs Hamilton
That Certain Something
Poppy Jenkins

Find out more about Clare:
http://rclareashton.wordpress.com
https://www.facebook.com/pages/Clare-Ashton/327713437267566

Poppy Jenkins

CLARE ASHTON

THE BEST-SELLING AUTHOR OF 'THAT CERTAIN SOMETHING'

Love or money? Follow the head or heart?

That certain something

clare ashton

The bestselling author of *Pennance* and *After Mrs Hamilton*

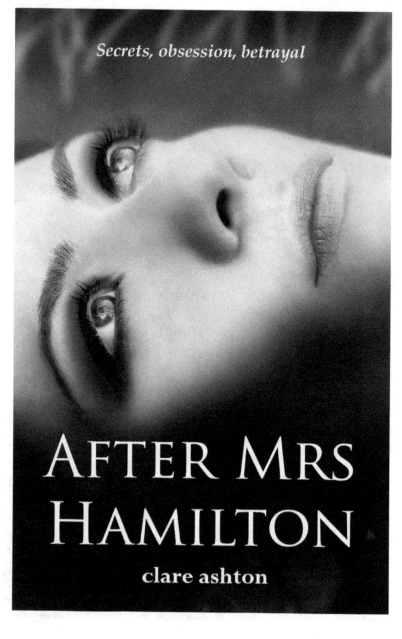

Secrets, obsession, betrayal

AFTER MRS
HAMILTON

clare ashton

be careful who you love

PENNANCE

clare
ashton

'a brilliant love story / mystery, beautifully written'
T.T. Thomas